SURRENDER

She wanted to kiss his mouth. He was so close. His chest felt rock hard beneath her hand, as he held his breath. She swayed toward him, her eyes drifting shut. It was as if she was under a magical spell, entranced by the depth of his green eyes and the sensual shape of his lips. She didn't like O'Brian much, but there was no denial of this sexual attraction to him.

He whispered her name, "Ah, Liz . . ." He kissed the tip of her nose, the dimple at her chin. His warm mouth pressed against the pulse of her throat, sending tremors of excitement through her trembling body.

"I can't do this," she whispered. But even as she spoke, she was running her hand up the corded muscles of his arm, to his broad shoulder, around his neck. She pulled herself closer to him, molding her soft body against his rock solid frame.

"Kiss me," she whispered. "Kiss me, O'Brian."

When he brought his mouth down on hers, there was nothing gentle about his kiss. His mouth met hers, hard and unyielding, steadying her with his hand securely in the small of her back.

Elizabeth had never been kissed like this before. O'Brian's kiss was full of power, demanding her response. But she couldn't think. She couldn't reason.

She was losing herself to O'Brian and his passion . . .

O'Brian's Bride

COLLEEN FAULKNER

ZEBRA BOOKS
KENSINGTON PUBLISHING CORP.

ZEBRA BOOKS are published by

Kensington Publishing Corp.
850 Third Avenue
New York, NY 10022

First Printing: April, 1995

Printed in the United States of America

Prologue

The Brandywine River
Delaware Colony
July, 1773

The blast of the explosion and the sound of the splintering window glass tore Elizabeth from a deep slumber. For a heart-stopping moment, she was completely disoriented. Chunks of plaster and fine dust from the ceiling fell onto the bed. The bedchamber walls shook with another, smaller explosion, and a portrait flew off the wall and clattered across the plank floor.

Elizabeth bolted upright in the bed, bringing her hand to her pounding heart. The entire room was illuminated by the orange light of a blaze outside her window.

With a cry of fright, she threw back the counterpane and leaped out of bed. Her bare feet hit the glass and plaster that littered the floor. "Dear God," she murmured as she searched frantically for her silk mules pushed beneath the high bedstead.

Her feet protected, she ran to the window, the broken glass making a sickening crunch beneath her. Carefully, she lifted the heavy wood frame of the shattered window and stuck her head out. The heat of the blaze down the hill from the manor house hit her full in the face, and she instinctively pulled back, striking her head on the window frame.

"Ouch," she muttered, running her hand across the crown of her head. The ground below was alive with activity, as workmen raced down the dirt lane toward the burning wooden building perched on the edge of the river. A bell clanged and a woman wailed. Somewhere a child was crying. A wagon filled with men with buckets rolled by beneath her. The sounds of shouting men, pounding feet, and the roar of the enormous fire assaulted her ears. The air was filled with the stench of sulfur and smoke, and the glowing red cinders of the burning building.

Elizabeth could do nothing but stand there, paralyzed with fear, and stare at the fiery blaze below. Paul had once mentioned the possibility of explosions in the powder mills, but he'd said it was nothing to worry her pretty head over. He said the explosions were rare at his mills. He said he and his men were careful.

Paul . . . Oh, God, where was Paul?

Elizabeth spun around to stare at their empty bed. Suddenly she couldn't breathe. It had to be well after midnight. Where was her new husband?

One

One Year Later

"I'll not have it!" Elizabeth Lawrence struck her fist on the polished hardwood desk. "How will we ever improve our reputation, if we're known as thieves by our own neighbors?"

Jessop leaned against the doorjamb, crossing his arms over his chest. "We're not thieves. The price for the coal was agreed upon by both parties. It's business, dear, plain and simple."

"Robbery, plain and simple." She thrust her quill into the inkwell and added another figure to a column of numbers on the paper. She rubbed her temple absently. She had a headache. Discussing the black powder mill she'd inherited from her deceased husband always gave her a headache. She and Jessop, her fiancé, disagreed on basic ethics concerning how business should be conducted. "Give him twenty-five percent more, Jessop."

"Twenty-five percent!" Jessop let his long arms fall to his sides. "Liz, you haven't got much of my brother's money left to throw around. You should see this as an opportunity. Take the money you save, and use it to pay one of your creditors in Philadelphia."

She didn't look up. "Do it, Jessop. Twenty-five percent. I still get a good deal, and so do they."

"Liz—"

"It's mine to do as I please, isn't it? *My money,* what little there is of it," she went on, trying not to sound accusatory. Her late husband had led her father to believe that he and his brother were both far better off financially than they actually were. *"My stamp mill and magazine,* which are only half reconstructed after more than six months of building. *My waterwheel* on the river, that won't turn the blessed grinding stone!" Elizabeth hadn't meant her last words to come so forcefully. She was a lady, and ladies didn't shout at the gentlemen they intended to marry. But, by the king's cod, she'd do what she thought right, and neither Jessop nor any other man was going to change her mind. She intended to get this black powder mill up and running at a profit, something neither of the Lawrence men had been able to accomplish.

Jessop smoothed one prematurely graying temple. He was a handsome man, taller than Paul had been, but with the same clear blue eyes, the same pleasant face. "Liz, you're making a mistake," he said quietly. "I'm not trying to tell you what to do. I—"

"The hell you're not!" Elizabeth dropped her quill into the inkwell and rose from her chair. "Every decision I make, every step I take, you have an opinion!"

"Elizabeth." He was speaking like he was her father now. God, how Elizabeth hated that condescending tone, that *you're a woman and therefore too stupid to know what you're doing* sound in his voice. "I'm just trying to keep you from making any serious mistakes. You lost a great deal in the explosion; supplies, two men killed with twelve injured—"

"I lost my husband," she intoned softly.

"I lost my brother." His gaze met hers and his face softened. "And, as your brother-in-law, as the man who loves you, it's my duty to guide you. I've been in the shipping business many years."

She held up a palm. "I know, I know. And I'm the little

lady come from Yorkshire with nothing but dancing, teas, and music lessons for experience." She indicated him, then herself with a wave of her hand. "And, of course, there's the fact that you're a man and I'm a woman."

"Yes, you are, aren't you?" He leaned to kiss her mouth, trying to make light of her words, but Elizabeth pulled out of his reach. She was in no mood for pleasures, his or her own.

"I'm serious, Jessop. I don't appreciate your criticizing every decision I make. You agreed that I would run the powder mills, at least until we're wed." She made a tight fist. "I know more about chemistry than anyone on this river. I know that if I can get the right ingredients, the right equipment up and operating, the right foreman to run the whole damned thing, I can make it work. I could make the best black powder these colonies have ever seen. We go to war, there'll be no more imports. Either we make our own gunpowder, or we won't have a chance."

"We?" He lifted an eyebrow. *"We?* A good English-woman like yourself would dare sell black powder to rebels?"

"I'm not going to discuss politics with you, Jessop. I haven't the time nor the energy. Just increase the payment for the coal, and see to the delivery, will you?"

The door to the front office opened and slammed shut, and from her private office in the rear, Elizabeth could hear the nervous scrape of a man's boots. A worker . . . a worker who had not washed his hands at the washbasin in the front reception area, there for that purpose. Something was wrong.

Elizabeth let out a sigh as she strode to the door leading to the front office. What now? It wasn't yet noon and she already had an earful of problems. Her house-keeper was complaining of shiftless housemaids, her shipment of potassium nitrate couldn't be located in the Philadelphia harbor, and she hadn't made a single plan for the engagement dinner party she and Jessop were having in less than a month.

"Yes. What is it?" Elizabeth looked at the clerk perched on a high stool behind the front desk, and then to the worker standing awkwardly near the door, his entire body covered in a fine layer of coal dust. "Can I help you, Johnny?"

Johnny Bennett swept off his battered felt hat anxiously. "Ye . . . ye gotta come quick, mistress. I . . . I'm afraid he's gonna kill 'em!"

"What? Who are you talking about?" Elizabeth followed Johnny out of the office and down the granite steps that would lead them past the manor house to the mills that lay along the riverbed.

"Bad fight, Mistress. Him and Samson. I'm afraid he's gonna kill 'im!"

"Who?" Elizabeth quickened her pace. She could hear the sounds of a brawl on the dirt lane below the manor house. Men's shouts mingled with the thuds of fists meeting flesh, one after the other. "You're afraid Samson's going to kill who?"

"Ye got it turned around, ma'am." Johnny stepped out of his mistress's way so that she could see the fight at the bottom of the hill. "It's yer new foreman, ma'am. Look, he's beatin' the tar outta Samson."

"God save us from men," Elizabeth muttered, taking the next set of stone steps down the hill two at a time.

"Elizabeth! Elizabeth!" Jessop hollered from the office door. "Let me handle this. You shouldn't be—"

Her fiancé's words were lost to her as she set her attention on the altercation below. Samson, one of her workers, a free black man, and a blond-haired stranger were struggling on the dusty ground. He couldn't possibly be the new foreman she'd been waiting for all these months, could he?

The stranger had managed to climb on top of Samson

and was now hammering her worker's face with sturdy fists.

"Enough! Enough!" Elizabeth shouted.

The crowd of mill workers separated, allowing her to walk through the middle of the crowd that had gathered around the fight.

"Samson!" Elizabeth shouted. "You know we do not permit fighting at Lawrence Mills." She was looking down on Samson, who was pinned on his back by the brawny blond. "Mister . . . Mister—" She snapped her thumb and forefinger. *God's teeth, what was the name of the man she'd hired? O'Brian?* "Mr. O'Brian, that will be quite enough!"

Somehow Samson managed to flip the new foreman over and roll out of his reach. Her worker stumbled to his feet.

"Now step back," Elizabeth shouted, waving her hand at Samson. "Just step away."

The crowd of dirty-faced men that had gathered had quieted. Everyone was staring at Elizabeth and the men in the center of the road.

Samson's nose was bloody, and one eye was already swelling shut. His dirty muslin shirt was torn, and he was missing one shoe. The blond got to his feet. Elizabeth still hadn't caught a good look at his face.

"Now tell me what this is all—"

The blond swung his fist, cracking Samson square in the jaw, and the shouting rose again. Samson swung in response, and suddenly the men were fighting again as if they'd never heard her or seen her to begin with.

Elizabeth swore beneath her breath. She'd never cursed in her life before she'd come to the Lawrence Mills. But this new land, the harsh realities of being alone in the world, had hardened her in the last year. Hardened her too much she feared.

Elizabeth heard Jessop shout to her from behind, but

she ignored him. Men brawling on her property! She
wouldn't have it. The both of them could take their wages
and go if they liked, but she'd not have fighting among
her employed!

"Gentlemen!" Elizabeth shouted above the hoots and
jeers of the mill workers, now crowded around her and
the fighting men again. "I will not stand for this!" She
grasped Samson's sleeve, sweaty and splattered with
blood. "That will be—"

Elizabeth didn't know exactly what happened next.
Did she step in front of Samson, or did he step back?
All she knew was that suddenly a fist made contact with
her cheekbone.

"Ouch! Son of a—" The impact of the punch knocked
her backward onto the dusty ground.

The mill workers were stunned into silence. The brawl
came to an abrupt halt.

"Good God!" Jessop shouted from somewhere behind
her beyond the throng of men. "Let me through! Liz,
are you all right? Are you hurt? Let me through!"

Elizabeth scrambled to her feet, resisting the urge to
touch her smarting cheekbone.

"God sake, Mistress Law'ence." Samson reached out
with one meaty black hand, but Elizabeth was already
standing again.

"What in God's name has vexed the two of you?" she
demanded furiously.

"He said somethin' I didn't like"—Samson pointed at
the stranger—"and don't no one talk to Samson that away.
This man be a free man. I don't take nothin' from no one!"

Elizabeth turned to the stranger. "Well, what have you
got to say for yourself?" she panted.

The blond, a tall man with shoulders as broad as a
blacksmith's, ground the ball of his boot into the dirt
and slowly lifted his head to look at her for the first
time.

Elizabeth was immediately taken back by the rugged good looks of the stranger. He didn't look like a mill worker. His face lacked the pinched cheeks, the empty eyes—results of generations of poor living conditions and lack of proper nutrition. It wasn't that he was handsome in the way Jessop was, but there was animal-like magnetism that made him frighteningly attractive. He had a broad face covered with short blond whiskers, and green eyes, eyes as green as a summer meadow. His shoulder-length hair hung straight and clean down his back. His mouth, a sensuous mouth, was drawn in an odd smirk.

He was staring at her with more male interest than Elizabeth thought appropriate. Still, she knew she flushed. There was something about the way he looked at her that made her feel overly warm.

"With all respect, ma'am,"—the virile stranger picked his hat up off the ground and beat it against his knee— "he was the one that started it first, not I."

Proper speech—an educated man? And what accent was that? Elizabeth wondered. O'Brian was an Irish name, but there was a hint of the sound of France in his rich tenor voice. This was not the man she had expected at all . . . in more ways than one.

Elizabeth cleared her throat. "Is that so?" she questioned sharply, hiding her discomfort. "And whom might I ask, am I addressing?"

"Patrick O'Brian, ma'am."

"Patrick?" She frowned. "I thought I hired a Michael O'Brian."

"Michael Patrick O'Brian," he answered smoothly. "A Mr. E. Lawrence is expecting me."

Jessop appeared at Elizabeth's side. "I told you this wasn't a good idea, bringing him here like this," he said softly in her ear. "He's not been here five minutes, and already he's a troublemaker. Dismiss him at once."

Elizabeth ignored Jessop. "E. Lawrence?" she questioned. "You're speaking to him."

O'Brian shifted his gaze to Jessop. "Pleased to meet you, sir. I only apologize for the circumstances. I didn't mean to clip the lady. She but—"

Elizabeth shook her head, crossing her arms over her chest. "No. You misunderstand. *I* am E. Lawrence. I'm the one who hired you, Mr. O'Brian."

O'Brian glanced at her suspiciously. "You?"

"Yes. I own these mills. I hired a foreman experienced in the black powder industry, apprenticed in the finest mill in France. Has there been a mistake?"

He was staring at her as if she'd grown a horn in the center of her forehead. Elizabeth would have laughed, except that she'd grown tired of this reaction among men when they discovered that E. Lawrence was a woman. Men didn't want to do business with her simply because she was a woman, and it made her furious.

O'Brian was looking at Jessop as if for confirmation.

"I'm speaking to you, sir. I said, has there been a mistake? Are you or are you not the Mr. O'Brian my solicitor hired to run my mill?" She turned away, giving him a moment to think about his answer. "That will be all," she told the mill workers still crowded around and listening intently. "Samson, I'll see you after supper in my office."

"Yes, ma'am."

The workers began to shuffle off, disappointed that they were being excluded from the conversation between their mistress and the new foreman.

Elizabeth turned her attention back to O'Brian, who had returned his hat to his head and was now standing at an easy stance. He didn't look like a man who feared he was about to be released from the job he hadn't yet started. "Well?" she asked. "Are you the man I hired? Do you have the experience you claimed to, or was this all a ploy to get to the colonies on my hard-earned coin?"

"Just dismiss him," Jessop repeated. "Haven't you got enough trouble without hiring the likes of this *Irish*man?"

O'Brian shot Jessop a look that could have carved him into neat equal parts.

"I can handle this, Jessop." She forced herself to smile sweetly. "If you'll just see to the coal shipment, I can deal with Mr. O'Brian."

Jessop opened his mouth to say something, but then gave a wave of his hand. "Fine. Be stubborn, Liz. I'm going home to look in on Sister. I'll see you this evening before dinner."

Elizabeth didn't speak again until Jessop was out of earshot. He'd be angry with her for a few hours, but he'd get over it. Slowly she turned her attention back to the disturbing man before her. "You were about to say?"

He glanced up the hill at the retreating Jessop, then back at Elizabeth. "I'll be honest with you, because it's my way. I didn't agree to work for a female. Had I known, I'd not have taken the position."

Elizabeth touched her cheekbone lightly. "Who says you've got the position? You struck me."

"It was an accident. I apologize, but you stepped in my way. Women have no place in the midst of men fighting."

"Look, the fact of the matter is that I paid good money to get you here. I'm desperate for a decent foreman. If you've got the experience you claim you do, I'll just forget this ever happened, and we'll start from a clean slate." She glanced at his face. What was it about this man that was so unsettling? "The truth is I need you. I have the knowledge to make this powder mill run, I just need someone who can see to the implementation."

He crossed his arms over his chest. "What do you mean, you've got the knowledge?"

She glanced at her dusty boots, uncomfortable with the way he continued to appraise her. The other workers didn't dare stare at her like this, like a man looked at a woman. It was as if the others saw her without a gender at all. They didn't treat her like a man, but they certainly didn't treat her like they did their wives and girlfriends either. Not even Jessop looked at her in the way this stranger was looking at her now, as though . . . she felt a heat rise in her cheeks . . . as though he were mentally unclothing her.

"I . . . I studied chemistry in England before I came to the Brandywine." She lifted her shoulders in a graceful shrug. "It always interested me. Odd for a woman I know, some say inappropriate, but a fact nonetheless."

O'Brian gave a sigh, looking away. "I need the job, but I've never worked for a woman."

"My gender should be of no interest to you, Mr. O'Brian. This will be a simple business arrangement. You will do the job I lay out for you, and in return I will pay you. Get my mill up and running, show me a profit, and I'll pay you handsomely."

Patrick tugged thoughtfully on his whiskers. This wasn't what he'd expected. Maybe he'd made a mistake. Michael hadn't told him his employer was to be a woman. Patrick almost smiled. So the joke was on him. Michael O'Brian had died on board the ship that would have taken him to the Colonies and to his new position as yard foreman in a black powder mill. After Michael's death, Patrick had taken his identity, and now it was Patrick stuck working for an uppity Englishwoman. He hadn't thought there would be any harm in him taking a dead man's job, but the idea was already backlashing.

Patrick knew he could just walk away, but that really wasn't an option. He needed a decent job. He'd made a vow to change his life, and here on the Brandywine River seemed as good a place as any to begin.

Patrick looked up at the Englishwoman with the silky dark hair and tongue that cut to the quick. A feisty little chit, she was. And clever. He had to give her that much.

"Perhaps I could give it a try." He heard an audible sigh from her.

"Perhaps you could, Mr. O'Brian."

"Then you and I have a bargain, Mistress E. Lawrence." He offered her his hand to seal the agreement. "Might I ask what the *E.* stands for?"

"Elizabeth."

Her warm hand trembled slightly as they made physical contact.

O'Brian couldn't resist a grin. So she wasn't as cold as she let on, after all. He'd always had a way with women. It was interesting to see that the rich ones were no different than the tarts. He let his hand linger over hers for just a second too long before he pulled it away.

Elizabeth cleared her throat, dropping her hand to the folds of her sturdy petticoat. "Let me take you to the house you'll be occupying." She started down the road, obviously expecting him to follow.

Patrick noted with interest that she walked without an entourage. Only a few barking hounds that had come down the hill accompanied her. So she was going to be a hands-on boss. That could be good or bad, depending on whether or not she was as knowledgeable with black powder as she claimed.

"I understand that once you're settled, you'll be sending for your wife and children. Isn't that correct?"

He only hesitated for a moment. "Yes. Yes, that's right." He walked beside her. "Once I'm sure I want to stay, that is."

She looked at him with a sideways glance. They were walking along the road that wound with the river. Granite stone buildings lined the bank. Workmen dotted the landscape.

"I see you've had an explosion recently."

"A year ago." She had lost the aggressive edge to her voice. "Almost to the day."

"How did it happen?"

She shook head. "I don't know. I'd only been here a few months, so I didn't know much, but I've talked to men up in the Jerseys with their own mills, and it doesn't make any sense. The explosion took place at night. None of the mills were running. Had we been in full operation, I understand we could have lost everything."

Patrick nodded thoughtfully as he scanned the hilly forest that surrounded them. "You've plenty of granite for construction, that's good. I noticed you're rebuilding the magazine. How thick are the walls?"

"Three feet, and I've doubled that in the buildings where there's loose particles in the air."

He chuckled. "So you do know something of the business."

"Powder pressed in the kegs is not the real danger," she said, as if she were a student reciting to her master. "It's when the ingredients are airborne that they're the most volatile."

They had turned and were climbing a hill. Ahead lay workers' housing. He could hear the laughter of children and the hum of women talking as they went about their daily chores. "I'm impressed."

She looked at him again. "I told you I knew what I was doing."

He winked at her. "I know what you said, Mistress. I'm still impressed."

She scowled. "A business arrangement, sir. That's what we've agreed upon. You can keep your antics to yourself."

Patrick gave a nod, a smile playing on his lips. "The gentleman, he your husband?"

"My husband is dead."

"The explosion?" He stopped.

She kept walking. "Yes. Look, O'Brian, I have a lot of work to attend to. Let me show you to the yard foreman's residence. Settle yourself in, and then come up to the office next to the big house." She came to a halt outside the door of a small, two-story stone and frame house. "We'll discuss your duties there."

He caught up to her. "I know my duties. I've been a yard foreman before."

She pushed open the front door and stepped aside. "Good. Then it won't take us long, will it?"

Before Patrick could respond, Elizabeth had started down the hill again, her stride as long and determined as any man's.

He gave a low whistle. Sweet Mary, mother of Jesus. He'd put his life on the line for the *Cause* when he'd lit the fuse to the powder keg at Dublin Bridge, but something told him this fine-bred, English beauty was going to be more dangerous than a hundred kegs of loose black powder in a summer thunderstorm.

Two

Patrick O'Shay closed the plank door behind him and leaned back to bang his head in a deliberate rhythm. *Michael O'Brian. Michael O'Brian. Michael O'Brian.* He was O'Brian now, and he had to remember that. How could he have been so stupid as to have told the woman his name was Patrick? From this moment on, he had to become Michael O'Brian. From this moment on, Patrick O'Shay no longer existed.

O'Brian massaged his temple, perturbed with himself. He'd gotten himself into many a tight corner since his young days in Ireland, but this might be the tightest spot yet. Perhaps he ought not to have taken his dead friend's identity the way he did. But who could it hurt? Surely not poor dead Michael at the bottom of the Atlantic, God rest his soul. He crossed himself.

And it would surely not hurt Mistress E. Lawrence either. The fact of the matter was, that she was getting a better yard foreman than she'd have gotten with Michael.

O'Brian stepped away from the door to survey his new surroundings. The house was small, two rooms downstairs, probably another two upstairs, but it was like a mansion compared to the tiny cottage he and his brothers and sisters had grown up in. Eleven of them living in that hovel, working the land, trying to carve a living out of bad soil and potato blights. Of course, that had all changed the day Tarrington had taken the land for his new country estate.

O'Brian wiped his mouth with the back of his hand. Just the name Tarrington put a bad taste in his mouth. But that was all long in the past, and he wasn't a melancholy person to dwell on his ill fates. Today was the day he became a new man. He could chart his own course this fine day. He'd made some foolish choices in the past, chosen the wrong path more than once, but he'd not make that mistake again.

Here was an opportunity that would not come a second time. He would work the Englishwoman's mill. He would get it up and running at a profit, and he'd save his pay. One day he'd have enough money to buy his own land on the river, and then his mill would be the best powder producer in these colonies. It was just a poor man's dream now, but O'Brian knew he could do it. He knew it in his bones.

A knock came at the door.

"Yeah?" O'Brian called.

The door swung open, and a sooty-faced worker appeared. He tugged off his hat, offering a small leather pouch. "Six months' wages, the mistress said. She tole me to bring it to ye. It's what she said she owed you, you coming here from Ireland like you done."

O'Brian took the money pouch. The heavy coins jingled. Mistress Lizzy Lawrence was paying top wages for his expertise. She was a smart woman. The best coin provided the best workers. "Thank ye."

The worker eyed the interior of the house. "Name's Johnny, Johnny Les Bennett. Handsome cottage ye got here, Mr. O'Brian."

O'Brian glanced at the great room he stood in. The walls were plastered and whitewashed, the furniture—cast-offs from the big house no doubt—sparse, but sturdy. It was probably meager compared to trappings in the manor house, but it must have looked like a palace to the mill worker. It was certainly better than anyplace O'Brian had ever occupied for more than a night or two. "It is, isn't it, Johnny?"

"Guess ye be bringing your family like the mistress said?"

"Not if I can help it." O'Brian gave a wink. "Might get in the way of me recreation, if you know what I mean. You boys do have recreation about this place, don't you?"

Johnny sniggered. "Got us the Sow's Ear. A little ole tavern cross the river and down a piece. Old Maddie, she's the one that runs the place. She got decent drink, gaming tables, and lady companionship, if that's what a man be lookin' for." He tipped his hat, still chuckling. "Good day to ye, sir. After the way ye tucked Samson's ears, we're all lookin' forward to meetin' ye down in the yard."

O'Brian watched the man go out the door, then he turned back to the sunlit room. There was a tall desk on the far wall. Paper, quill, and ink had been left for his convenience.

O'Brian walked slowly to the desk. He perched himself on the corner of a three-legged stool and took a single coin from the bag. That would be enough for a nip of whiskey and an ante in a game of dice. With a little luck he could keep himself in stiff drink and women for the next six months on his gambling. He weighed the coin in his hand to be certain the mistress hadn't cheated him. Satisfied, he tucked it into the top of one knit stocking.

Flexing his fingers, O'Brian added a bit of ink powder to the inkwell and stirred the fresh ink with the quill. He took his time, watching the cloudy water grow thick and black as he stirred. Finally he pulled out a square of paper and dated the top.

He glanced out the small-paned window, trying to

come up with something profound to say. What did a man say when another man was dead? How could he possibly console the widow with words on a bit of paper, words she'd not even be able to read herself, but would have to find someone from the nearest manor house to read to her.

Dear Sally, O'Brian eventually began. With a sad smile, he remembered her in her younger days, when she and Michael had first wed. She'd had a head full of orange red hair, silky, freckled skin, and a laugh that made a man forget his troubles.

Sorry to be the one to tell you, but your Michael is dead.

He went on to tell her that Michael had passed on in his sleep, stone dead of blood poisoning, and that he hadn't been ill long. Sad truth was that a piddling wood splinter was what sent him to his Maker.

O'Brian told the widow how he had appreciated Michael's friendship back in their younger days in France, when they had both been apprenticing in the DuBois black powder mill. He finished the letter by explaining that the money enclosed was for her, sent by her dear, departed husband. He wished Sally good luck, and a future husband as kind as Michael had been. He did not sign his name to the bottom. Patrick Xavier O'Shay was dead and gone, and he couldn't very well sign the dead man's name. Instead, he simply signed off with the words *God bless ye and yours . . .* Sally would know who had sent it.

O'Brian sprinkled the damp ink with a little sand. It would cost him a bit of the coin to get the money safely to Ireland, but at least the widow would have something to start a new life with. A dowry as substantial as this would make her the wealthiest widow of her social class in the county. She'd have no trouble finding a new husband.

The ink dry, O'Brian folded the letter neatly and pushed off the stool. He'd send the note to Philadelphia and have it go out on the next ship bound for the green grass of Ireland. Home, but home no longer.

He glanced out the window thoughtfully. This place, this Delaware Colony was beautiful . . . different than the jagged, wet hills of his birthplace, but beautiful in its own right. He would make it his home. He would make his fortune here. He had to. It was his last chance.

Elizabeth crossed out a numeral and made a correction. Then the ink pooled at the tip of the quill and blotted out the entire number. She dropped the quill onto the desk in exasperation, and rose to stretch her legs. She had to step over two sleeping hounds to make her way to the window.

She smiled to herself as she looked out on the granite hills. After the explosion last summer, she had insisted that this office be built, despite Jessop's objection to the cost. She didn't want workmen in and out of her private home. Besides, from here she could easily watch the goings on of the struggling business she'd inherited from her deceased husband. From here she could look down the slope to the fast running river she fell in love with the day Paul had brought her to Lawrence Mills.

Paul. A lump rose in her throat, and she was filled with the familiar ache of loneliness. They hadn't been together long, married just a few weeks, but she missed him even a year after his death. She missed the laughter they had shared, laughter that didn't come as often between her and Jessop. A silly smile played on her lips. She missed the physical relationship, too, and she wasn't afraid to admit it either. She missed Paul's gentle lovemaking and the comfortable warmth of his embrace afterward.

Elizabeth shook her head to clear her wanton thoughts. Jessop was right. She was a woman who needed to be married. An acceptable amount of time had passed since Paul's death. There was no need to wait any longer for her and Jessop to make the official announcement of their betrothal. There was no need to wait to be married.

She dropped her hands to her hips thoughtfully. So why was she stalling? Why wasn't she as excited about marrying Jessop as she had been with Paul? Was it because for her first wedding she had crossed the ocean to join her husband? Had it been the excitement of the adventure rather than the actual marriage that had thrilled her? Or was it something that ran deeper? Had the last year of struggling with the mill stolen her naivete? She'd entered her marriage to Paul in innocence, innocence of the marriage bed, innocence of the way it really was between men and women? Now Elizabeth knew what it was to be a wife, to always stand behind her husband, to always be ushered from the room with the ladies when talk of politics began.

Paul had wanted to coddle her, to keep her protected. He treated her as if she were so fragile, she might break like a porcelain tea saucer at any moment. He had never once taken her down to the mills to show her the company he was building. When Elizabeth had questioned her new husband on the compounds he was using, he had explained to his new bride that the dirty business was better left to the Lawrence men. It was her duty, he explained gently, to keep his house in order and keep him happy.

It wasn't until after the explosion . . . until after Elizabeth had sifted though the rubble, and dead and maimed bodies, beside the workmen, that she'd begun to learn the process of black powder production. And once she had become intrigued and decided that she would not go home to her father's house in England as everyone expected, but take on her husband's duties, Jessop had not tried to stand in her way. He was not particularly supportive, he complained, but at least he'd not tried to forcibly deter her. For Elizabeth, used to men controlling her life, that was enough.

Elizabeth wiped the windowpane with her sleeve ruffle. It seemed that every object was covered with the fine coal dust used to make the black gun powder. She had hated the dirt when she'd first come to Lawrence Mills, but these days it was just the nature of the work. The washbowl of dirty water she left behind each night was proof of her accomplishments. It had become a visible sign of her toil. She could only hope and pray that this new yard foreman would be the answer to her troubles with the mill.

Heavens, there he was. Elizabeth leaned closer to the window, watching O'Brian as he took the granite steps up the side of the hill two at a time.

Was she asking for trouble, keeping this man on? she wondered. Jessop had been insistent about not hiring him, even before he'd arrived. Irishmen didn't know their place, Jessop had declared more than once. She'd be asking for trouble, putting an Irishman in charge of her powder yard.

But Elizabeth liked him, this O'Brian. No . . . that wasn't true. She didn't *like* him. He was apparently a troublemaker, his self-worth obviously lofty. There was nothing likeable about the man. It was just that she had this instinctive feeling that he could accomplish what needed to be done here at Lawrence Mills. He could do what she couldn't. He could pull the workers together. He could get the refinery, the wheel mill, the composition house, and the stamp mill to work integrally.

So was intuition enough to go on? The man had struck

her. She should be having him arrested, rather than hiring him. Why should she trust him? Was she being stubborn as Jessop accused? Was she just set on keeping O'Brian to show Jessop she could? Was that a way to begin her marriage with Jessop?

O'Brian passed the window, taking no notice that Elizabeth watched him. He walked around the corner, and she heard him enter the front office. Lacy, one of Elizabeth's hounds, lifted her head to look with droopy eyes through the doorway at the stranger.

Elizabeth could hear O'Brian's voice as he chatted with her clerk, Noah, seated at the high desk out front. She couldn't make out what the foreman was saying, only that he was amused by his own words. Now Noah was laughing. Noah never laughed.

She walked to the doorway. "Mr. O'Brian, I've been waiting for you."

O'Brian nodded to Noah and pushed through the swinging half door that led past the clerk's desk to her private office in the rear.

Lacy growled deep in her throat, and her mate lifted his head.

"It's all right," Elizabeth told the dogs. "You needn't worry. I'll let you know should I want you to attack him."

"Funny." O'Brian came to stand in front of her in the doorway. He had left his waistcoat behind and was bareheaded. He wore nothing but a pair of sturdy broadcloth breeches and a muslin shirt with the sleeves rolled up to bare, corded muscular forearms. His yellow blond hair was pulled back sleekly in a neat queue.

"Lost your trunk on board ship, Mr. O'Brian?" she asked, indicating his casual dress with a nod of her head.

O'Brian struck his chest with his palm. "Ye didn't ask me to dinner and dancing in the big house. Ye asked me to get that mess of a powder yard operating. Besides,"—

he tugged at the neckline of his stockless shirt—"it's hotter than a day in hell here."

Elizabeth had to turn away to keep him from seeing her smile. She, too, had had a difficult time adjusting to the heat of the Colonies last summer when she'd arrived. "I'll grant you, it is warm. I'll give you a little leeway, but I would ask you to dress properly, should you be called to any business outside Lawrence Mills."

"I need no lessons in manners from you, Mistress."

"Good." She turned back to him. "Now, let us get to the business at hand." She pointed in the direction of the mills. "You called my yard a mess."

He walked to the window. "Good view from here," he said, plucking his whiskers. He turned back to her. "It is a mess. No semblance of order. You know you've got men fishing off your refinery dock?"

"Fishing? You jest." Elizabeth knew the men were lax with their duties, but she hadn't realized they were that blatant about it.

"They've caught three nice perch already. Also, you've got two men asleep in the loft above the stamp mill, and a jug of whiskey cooling in a barrel in the composition house. I won't tell ye where I found the young man and his betrothed half-naked."

Elizabeth gasped. "Ye needn't be so crude, Mr. O'Brian."

He grimaced. "See, that's why I don't think I can work with a woman. Ye highborn ladies, you're too delicate for this type of work. I can't be thinking on every word I say before I say it, else I'll never get anything said."

Her eyes widened. Though there were some women who would have liked the idea of being referred to as delicate, Elizabeth knew he meant it as an insult. "Delicate. I'm not delicate. I might have been once, but no longer." Suddenly, all she could think of was Paul, and the way they had found him. Pieces . . . just pieces. Seeing his body like that, seeing the others, it had taken away any delicacy she ever had.

One moment of silence stretched into two. Elizabeth didn't trust herself to speak yet.

"Ye got to give me full run of the place, if ye want me to succeed," O'Brian finally said.

"I want you to succeed. I don't want you to take over."

He grinned at her. He had one of those smiles a woman could lose herself in. *Heavens, where was her mind, thinking such silliness?*

"Yer the one with coin, the one with the big house and the servants. This is no ship I could lead a mutiny on."

"There's not as much coin as you might think," she responded dryly. "My debts are far greater than my assets."

"A gift from your dearly departed?"

She ignored his sarcastic remark, proceeding. "Which means we must keep costs at a minimum until we actually have some decent sales. A contract or two would be perfect."

O'Brian leaned against the windowsill in thought. "Who's running the yard now?"

"No single man. I give the orders, Johnny Bennett carries them to the yard, and then I have a man in charge at each step of the operation."

"Too many fingers in the sweets jar."

"I know that." She threw up her hand. "That's why I hired you."

"Ye needn't take every word I say as criticism." He looked directly at her with those green eyes of his. "I'd say you've done a blessed fine job, considering the circumstances. You've done well with the changes since the explosion."

Elizabeth couldn't resist a smile. Jessop had never

complimented her on how she'd been running the mills. Not once. "Thank you."

"Ye got a decent setup here. Perfect spot in the river to run your wheel. Ye got a hell of a lot of power rushin' out there in that white water."

"But the wheel isn't turning the grinding stone right. I can't get the charcoal and sulphur pulverized the way it should be."

"Give me time. First things first. I want to watch how things are done now. A man can't come in and change everything in a single day. Workers don't like it. Make them a part of the changes,"—he wove his fingers together—"and you'll get more work, better work out of them with less sick time, less accidents, and a hell of a lot less complaining."

"So you want me to tell the men to just go on with their daily work?" Elizabeth glanced out the window to see her sister-in-law coming toward the office from the house. That was all she needed right now—a visit from Claire. "Anything else I can do, Mr. O'Brian?" She walked toward the door to excuse him.

"I'll need to see your compositions. Exact numbers."

Elizabeth heard Claire come in the front door with a swish of her starched ruffled petticoats. She was hoping she could get O'Brian out of the office without encountering Claire, but that was apparently not going to work. "I . . . we'll see about that, Mr. O'Brian. I've been working very hard on a new mixture. I'm toying with the thought of trying to use sodium nitrate rather than potassium nitrate."

O'Brian gave a low whistle. "Remind me not to be near ye when you try lighting that."

"Well, it's just on paper now, so I'd ask you to keep the idea to yourself."

Claire came through the swinging door, her hand outstretched to Elizabeth.

Claire was a woman Elizabeth's own age, with ringlets of honey hair and slanted blue eyes. She was comely by male standards, with a minute waist and petite stature. "Liz! I couldn't find you in the house, so I came looking for you here." She made no acknowledgment of O'Brian's presence. "Brother let me come early, because I was bored at home. You'll never guess what I've found." Despite the July heat, Claire was dressed properly in a gown with gloves and a wide-brimmed straw hat.

"What is it?" Elizabeth inquired. It was so awkward when strangers met Claire for the first time. She never knew if she should come right out and mention Claire's mental condition, or pretend it didn't exist.

Claire held out her cupped hand. "A mousey," she whispered.

Out of the corner of her eye, Elizabeth could see O'Brian studying Claire, a look of bemusement on his face.

"A mouse?"

Claire held her hand to her ear and made a squeaking sound. "Do you hear him? Squeak! Squeak!"

Elizabeth glanced at O'Brian, then back at Claire. "I do hear him." She forced a smile. She didn't want to upset her. Not here. Not now. She just didn't have time to deal with the consequences.

Claire offered her hand again. "Want to hold him?" She lifted one pale eyebrow. "I'll let you hold him, if you like."

"No. No, that's all right, Claire." Elizabeth played along as best she could. "You hold him for me."

"Oh." Claire sounded genuinely hurt. "Why don't you want to hold my mousey?"

Elizabeth was beginning to feel silly now. This was not how she had intended her first meeting with her new foreman to go. If she didn't know better, she'd have thought Jessop had sent Claire on purpose. "All right. Let me hold him, but just for a moment. This is my new foreman Mr. O'Brian, Claire. He and I have business to attend to."

O'Brian nodded politely at Claire, who turned to look at him. She smiled a pretty smile and turned back to Elizabeth.

"All right. Here's my mouse, but you must be careful not to let him go," she warned.

Left no choice, Elizabeth held out one hand to receive her sister-in-law's invisible mouse. But when Elizabeth touched Claire's fingers, Claire threw open her hand with a squeal. "Ah! He was too fast for you." She stared at the ceiling above. "Mousey flew away." She giggled. "You never catch my mouse, Liz. Why don't you ever catch the mouse?"

Elizabeth glanced at O'Brian, who was staring at the ceiling with Claire. It was so absurd she almost laughed. Of course, it wasn't funny. Claire was ill. Since the explosion last summer, she just hadn't been herself. The surgeons said she had a simple nervous ailment, but her condition ran deeper than that. No one dared suggest that Claire Lawrence might be mad. There were times when she behaved perfectly normally, but there were other times . . . Elizabeth shook her head with a sigh.

"I suppose you got me again," Elizabeth conceded to Claire. "Now, why not go in and see to tea? I'll come in and we'll share a cup."

"Will you?" Claire clapped her hands. "I do love to have tea with you, Liz. You're much better company than Brother." She wrinkled her nose. "All he wants to talk of is taxes and tobacco crops." Claire gave a cordial nod. "Liz . . . Mr. O'Brian. Good day."

Elizabeth kept her back to O'Brian, until Claire had left the office and passed the outside window on her way back to the house. Finally Elizabeth had no choice but to turn back. What was she going to say? How was she going to explain to O'Brian what physicians couldn't understand?

"Mr. O'Brian, my sister-in-law—"

He held up one hand. "Truth be known, we've all got them in our family, haven't we, Mistress?" He grinned lazily. "She's harmless—charming."

"Sometimes . . . on both counts." She smiled back. "I appreciate your understanding. Everyone knows Claire here at Lawrence Mills, and we all try to look out for her. There are times when she . . ." She let her sentence dangle. She didn't want to go into the details.

"I understand."

"No. You probably don't." She sighed. "Should you see Claire down along the river, could you direct her up to the house? She gets lost sometimes and can't find her way home to her brother's, where she lives."

O'Brian moved toward the doorway, stepping over one of Elizabeth's sleeping hounds. "I think I'll go on down to the yard and have a look around. I'd like to meet with you here tomorrow afternoon to discuss what conclusions I've come to."

Elizabeth followed him out to the front office past the clerk. "I'm here most every afternoon. I want you to feel like you can come to me at anytime, Mr. O'Brian. I'm not opposed to coming down to the yard, should you need me."

O'Brian turned to her at the outside door. "You stick to the numbers, Mistress. I won't be needing ye in the yard. It is what you hired me to do, isn't it?"

His words were full of politeness, but there was something in his tone that irritated her. He sounded like Paul, telling her not to worry her pretty head. "Yes, it is, Mr. O'Brian. So see that you tend to your job and tend it well." She swept away toward her private office, before he could get another word in.

Elizabeth did not go to the window to watch him return to the yard.

Three

The following afternoon Elizabeth found herself in her office sitting idly. It wasn't like her not to keep busy, but all day she'd had a difficult time concentrating on the pile of bills that littered her desk. She just couldn't focus on the paperwork. Her mind kept wandering. Her eyes kept straying to the window.

She turned on her stool. It was a beautiful July day, hot and humid. Through the open windows she could hear the rushing water of the Brandywine, and smell the last blooms of the late lilac bushes.

Elizabeth rose and walked to the open window. A hot breeze blew the tendrils of damp hair at her temples. Absently, she tucked the stray wisps behind her ears. She wondered how O'Brian was making out. She'd done as he asked; she'd stayed out of his way all morning, but her curiosity was beginning to get the best of her.

She ran her finger along the windowsill. He'd told her to stay out of his way and out of the yard, but what right did he have to be making demands of her? This was her land, her mill, her hired men.

She dropped her hand to her hip. She had a right to inspect her workers whenever she wished. The water wheel had been started up this morning. Why was she in this hot office wondering if the charcoal was being ground properly, when she could be outside inspecting the process?

Elizabeth turned sharply and started for the front office. As she went through the doorway, she snatched her straw hat off a wooden peg. "Lacy, Freckles, come." She slapped her thigh, and both dogs leaped up to run after her.

Elizabeth sailed past her clerk's desk. "I'm going down to the yard, Noah. Come for me if you need me."

Noah hopped down off his high stool, bobbing his head. "Yes, Mistress. I won't be needing you, Mistress. Have a fine walk."

As Elizabeth pushed open the door, her hounds bounded out ahead of her. She hesitated on the granite steps to drop her hat on her head, to shade her face from the hot sun. She'd never had a freckle in life prior to coming to the Colonies, but a year here and she already had a patch across her nose. Cora Tarrington was most likely rolling over in her grave at the thought of her youngest daughter with freckles, and skin as dark as a red man's.

Elizabeth tugged on the straw brim as she started down the steps, trying not to let the dogs trip her. "Let's go," she called, laughing as the hounds jockeyed for a position at her swaying chintz petticoats. "Let's go down to the river for a cold drink."

Jessop grumbled that it wasn't proper for her to walk through the powder yard unaccompanied, but Elizabeth had refused to give into him. Just who was she supposed to be afraid of on her own property? Her workers wouldn't dare lay a finger on her, and strangers rarely came to Lawrence Mills. And if safety wasn't his true concern, but rather propriety, who was it that she was attempting to please? She was a widow with no husband to be concerned with. Her own family was thousands of miles away across the Atlantic, and as for friends, she had none. It was Jessop's acquaintances they entertained, and the fact of the matter was that they were all so petty and dull that she really didn't care what any of them thought of her.

Still, to keep peace with Jessop, she took the dogs with her whenever she walked along the river. They would protect her from anyone who dared get too close to her. In the back of her mind, Elizabeth worried that once she and Jessop were wed, he would put an end to her daily walks.

Once they were married, she feared much of her life would change. This sense of freedom she had gained with the death of her husband could easily be lost. Once she married Jessop, the powder mill would be his. He would have the legal right by English law to prevent her from participating in the running of the business. Damned English law; it wasn't right.

She slowed her pace. Perhaps it was her freedom Elizabeth feared for. Perhaps that was why she was stalling on the marriage. She sighed. Why did life have to be so difficult?

Elizabeth reached the bottom of the hill and turned onto the hard-packed dirt road. The dogs ran ahead, barking at a wagon that rolled toward them loaded with empty half kegs.

"Afternoon, Mistress." Joe Tuck touched the brim of his sagging straw hat. "Hot one today, ain't it, ma'am?"

Elizabeth gave a nod. "That it is, Joe. How's that new son of yours?"

Only last week Elizabeth had attended the birth of the Tuck's fourth child. As mistress of the mills, she felt it was her duty to look after the men, women, and children who lived on her land. The workers rented small houses from her up on the hill. They slept, ate, gave birth, and died on her property. In a way, that made them all her family, didn't it?

"The boy's fit as a cypress fiddle. Thank ye for

askin'.'' Joe tipped his hat again as the wagon rolled by on creaky wheels.

Elizabeth gave a wave. Common people, that was what Jessop called the workers. More than once he'd warned her not to allow them to be so familiar with her. He cautioned her about being so friendly with them. She was the landowner; she was the employer. It was imperative that the workers and their families respect her, that was what Jessop said.

Elizabeth felt that she did have their respect. Though not always in a timely manner, the men did as she asked. It was their hands that were rebuilding the destroyed powder magazine. It was their hands that were rebuilding the mill, after the devastation of last year's explosion. She didn't care what Jessop thought or said. These were free men and women. Poor or not, they had the right to be treated as equal human beings. Elizabeth felt that she could be friendly, be concerned, while still remaining the employer. She chuckled to herself. More politics. Jessop said ladies had no business in politics. Jessop said a lot of things she didn't agree with.

You're being too hard on him. He's a good man, she chided herself silently. *And he cares for you. He's been a godsend since Paul's death.* He was only trying to protect her. Her best interest was always at heart when he made suggestions.

The sound of a woman's wail tore Elizabeth from her thoughts. Her dogs turned immediately toward the river. Someone else shouted, and Elizabeth broke into a run. She raced past the powder-drying racks down the bank, along the side wall of the composition house. The dogs followed at her heels, barking wildly.

"Help me! Help me!" the woman's voice begged shrilly.

Elizabeth still couldn't see her, but her voice was coming from the direction of the river.

One of the workers came out of the composition house. "What is it, Mistress?"

Elizabeth shook her head, passing him, her petticoats bunched in her fists. "I don't know, Eli." She turned the corner and spotted a black woman on the far side of the river, waist deep in the rushing water.

"My baby! My baby!" she wailed, pulling at her damp hair.

"Where?" Elizabeth shouted above the sound of the roar of the rushing river.

All the woman could do was point.

Elizabeth followed her line of vision. "Oh God," she breathed, stopping abruptly at the edge of the bank. Water seeped over her calfskin slippers and dampened the hem of her striped under-petticoat.

A small, dark-haired child clung to a rock jutting from the center of the river. Elizabeth couldn't tell if the child was a boy or a girl, but he or she couldn't have been more than a year and a half old.

Elizabeth's dogs ran in circles, barking at the child, sounding an alarm.

"What is it?" O'Brian suddenly appeared at Elizabeth's side, from the composition house she guessed. She hadn't seen him approach. He was just there.

"Down stream, Mr. O'Brian." Eli pointed. "It's Ngozi's little'n."

Elizabeth heard O'Brian swear a foul French oath beneath his breath.

She glanced sideways to see him hopping on one foot as he tugged off a boot. "What are you doing?"

He dropped one boot to the rocky ground and reached for the other. "Going in after the wee thing. What do you think?"

The mother, a woman Elizabeth didn't recognize, was still standing in the water across the far side of the river, wailing and wringing her hands.

"The water is faster even than it looks," Elizabeth warned her foreman. "The rainfall from last night has swollen the river. Take care. We lost a man last year just a little upstream. He was a good swimmer, but the current took him anyway."

His boots and stockings discarded, O'Brian reached over his back and jerked on the hem of his muslin shirt, pulling it over his head. He cast it carelessly onto the bank and waded into the rushing water.

Elizabeth felt her heart trip as she watched his bare back sink into the chilly water. If she lost her foreman to a drowning, the mill was gone. This Irishman was her last chance. She clenched her hands, half-considering going into river with him. Most of her workers couldn't paddle a stroke, and she was a strong swimmer. She could let the current carry her most of the way downstream to the child, then swim to the center of the river to save him.

But, of course, that didn't make sense. O'Brian had gone in. There was no need for the both of them to risk their lives. If O'Brian needed help, she'd go then.

Elizabeth walked downstream, picking her way over the rocks, not caring that the water would ruin the new dyed leather slippers Jessop had brought her from Philadelphia only last week. All that mattered was the safety of the child and her new foreman.

Elizabeth clenched her fists. "Please God," she murmured. "Bring him back to the shore safely."

O'Brian had waded out as far as he could, and now he was swimming along with the current with controlled, even strokes. The mother was still wailing, and now Elizabeth could hear the faint sobs of the child who still clung to the rock.

"What's his name?" Elizabeth shouted to the mother.

The mother made no response.

"Ngozi. Her name's Ngozi. She's Samson's woman. Lives in the woods."

"The woods?" Elizabeth turned back to the woman. "Ngozi!" She cupped her hands around her mouth and shouted again. "His name, Ngozi! What's the child's name?"

"Dorcas!" The woman hollered back. "My girl-child, she's Dorcas."

Elizabeth ran along the bank until she was even with O'Brian. He was nearly parallel with the rock the little girl was stranded on, but he was struggling against the current to reach the center of the river. If he was dragged past the rock, he would have to swim ashore and start upstream again. "Her name is Dorcas!" Elizabeth called.

O'Brian turned, fighting to keep his head above the rushing white foam as he attempted to tread water. "What?"

She watched as the bare muscles of his shoulders and back flexed at the strain of the swift current. "The baby!" She pointed. "Her name is Dorcas!"

O'Brian nodded.

The little girl had spotted O'Brian now, and she was screaming. Even above the sound of the rushing water, Elizabeth could hear Dorcas' frightened cries. The little girl was still hanging onto the rock, but the current had caught her chubby legs, and they were now dangling in the swirling water. Elizabeth didn't know how the girl had made it safely to the rock, but if she was swept further downstream, she would surely drown.

A crowd was growing along the riverbank. Men had appeared from the mills. Woman and children had gotten word of the accident and come down the hill from their homes.

Elizabeth grabbed the shoulder of the nearest man. It was Johnny Bennett. "Take one of the wagons and go upstream to the bridge. Bring the woman across. Her

name is Ngozi. And find Samson. If O'Brian does get
the child, he'll try to bring her in downriver."

"Yes, Mistress."

She watched Johnny scramble up the bank. He met Joe
Tuck with the wagonload of kegs up on the road. Elizabeth
saw him speak to Joe, and then Joe climbed down out of
the wagon. A moment later Johnny was up on the seat,
turning the horse around and heading upstream to the only
bridge that crossed the river for several miles.

Elizabeth turned back to see O'Brian still making pro-
gress toward the stranded child.

Just a little further, Elizabeth thought, grimacing as
he struggled against the current to swim the last few
feet. O'Brian was holding his hand out to the little girl
now. He'd almost reached her.

Suddenly, Elizabeth spotted a large branch coming fast
down the waterway. "Look out, O'Brian!" she screamed,
pointing behind him. The main limb of the branch was
as big as a man's calf. If it struck O'Brian, it might
knock him unconscious.

O'Brian battled the current to turn to see what Elizabeth was pointing to.

Elizabeth couldn't stifle a cry as the branch swept over
O'Brian. She couldn't bear to watch, yet she couldn't
look away. Then, at the last instant, he ducked under
water. The limb went by, brushing against the rock, but
the little girl held on for dear life.

When O'Brian's head popped up out of the water,
Elizabeth knew she gave an audible sigh of relief. He
had almost reached Dorcas now.

A moment later, O'Brian passed the rock and swept
the child off as he went by. A shout rose up out of the
crowd of onlookers on the bank. Across the river, Elizabeth spotted Johnny Bennett in the wagon with the
child's mother climbing aboard.

Elizabeth laid her hand on her breast. Her heart was

pounding. She ran along the riverbank as O'Brian let himself be carried on the current. "It gets rockier further downstream," she warned, picking her way over the jagged granite rocks. "You'd best start for the shore!"

O'Brian lifted a hand, acknowledging her. Slowly, carefully, he was making his way to the bank with young Dorcas clinging to his shoulder.

Elizabeth met O'Brian at the bend in the river. "Oh, thank God," she cried, offering her hand to help him out. "You're all right? The child's all right?"

He waded the rest of the way in, panting heavily. "F . . . fine. Just a little wet." He jiggled the girl. "Aren't you, darlin'?"

The keg wagon came to a halt on the road above the bank, and the woman called Ngozi came half-running, half-sliding down the bank. "My baby! My girl baby chil'."

At the sight of her mother, little Dorcas burst into tears. O'Brian handed the wet baby to her mother. "There you go. Now no more swimming, until you get a lesson or two." He ran his hand over the little girl's plaited head as her mother carried her off.

Elizabeth spotted Samson up on the road and made a mental note to speak to him later. If this woman and child were his, he was going to have to take responsibility for them.

She turned back to O'Brian. The crowd was parting. Men walked by O'Brian, slapping him on his back.

"Fine job, Mr. O'Brian," said one man.

"Wouldn't have believed it, if I hadn't seen it," said another.

O'Brian nodded, thanking them awkwardly. It was obvious he was uncomfortable with the attention.

When he started to make his way back upstream to where he'd left his clothing, Elizabeth fell into step beside him. She didn't speak until they were alone. "That was a brave thing you did, O'Brian," she said. "That woman's child was no one to you. You could have let her drown."

He shrugged his broad, bare shoulders. " 'Twas nothing. Any man would have done the same."

Fascinated, Elizabeth watched how the water ran from his dripping hair down his muscular back in rivulets. She was certainly no stranger to a man's body. She was a widow, for heaven's sake! But this man, this common Irishman, had a torso that appeared to have been carved from the very granite of the hills that surrounded them. Every muscle, every tendon, was visible on his suntanned frame. Elizabeth turned her head, embarrassed by her scrutiny of her foreman's body, but not before she caught sight of the line of dark hair that parted the wide expanse of his chest, disappearing below his navel into the waistband of his breeches.

Elizabeth felt her cheeks grow warm. There was no denying this man's virility. His soaking wet breeches left nothing to a woman's imagination.

She brushed back a tendril of damp hair off her forehead, wondering what ailed her. She'd never been one before to gawk at a man. Even one as handsome as this foreman. She glanced at him walking beside her, their strides matched. "No, not any man would have done the same. You could have let her drown, and no one would have batted an eye. It would have simply been an unfortunate accident."

He turned his head, his green-eyed gaze settling on her face. "Would you have let her drown?"

She felt unnerved by his scrutiny and looked away. "No. I'm a good swimmer. If you hadn't been there, I'd have gone after her."

He lifted a hand. "So you and I have more in common than we thought, don't we, Mistress?" He was smiling at her now. It was as if there was a joke between them, only she wasn't privy to the joke.

Elizabeth kept her eyes focused on the rocky footing of the riverbank. Damn, but this new foreman was unsettling. What was it about him that made her feel queasy and light headed at the same time? God in heaven, if she didn't know better, she'd think she was attracted to him. Imagine that, Elizabeth Tarrington Lawrence attracted to a worker! She nearly chuckled out loud. Jessop was right. It was time he wedded and bedded her.

Elizabeth spotted her hounds wading into the shallow water in front of the composition house, and called out to the bitch, Lacy. Both dogs came bounding toward her and the foreman. Reaching them, the dogs shook their coats, splattering both Elizabeth and O'Brian with water.

"Damned dogs," O'Brian muttered. Elizabeth laughed. The cold water felt good on her skin. "I don't know what you're complaining about, Mr. O'Brian. You're already wet."

He scowled. "Do you take the beasts everywhere you go?"

"Everywhere. They're here to protect me from the rabble, or so says Jessop."

He glanced at the dogs circling them. "I can see how ferocious they are."

She laughed with him.

"Tell me, the gentleman—"

"Jessop Lawrence," she offered.

He gave a nod. "Who is he?"

Elizabeth wondered why he wanted to know. "It's really not your concern, Mr. O'Brian, but to satisfy your curiosity, he was my deceased husband's brother. He lives on the adjoining property. Claire is his sister." She didn't know why she didn't tell him she was engaged to be married to Jessop.

They had reached the composition house by now. He tugged his muslin shirt over his damp chest. This time Elizabeth made no effort to look away. What harm was there in a widow casting an occasional glance at one of her hired men anyway?

"So he really owns the place, does he?"

"No." Elizabeth crossed her arms over her chest. "I own Lawrence Mills, Mr. O'Brian. I told you that yesterday."

"You needn't get short with me." He stood on one foot, tugging a wet stocking over his thick calf. "I just wanted to make sure I wouldn't straighten things out, only to have a gentleman in a coat change it all back."

Suddenly it seemed that they were adversaries again. Elizabeth didn't know what she'd said to set him off. She didn't care. The man didn't have to like her. He just had to do his job.

She turned to climb up the bank, taking the granite slab steps embedded in the soft earth. "I've given you a day, Mr. O'Brian. We can't waste any more time. I want a full report in my office in the morning."

"You said you'd give me a few days."

"I changed my mind. I have a shipment of potassium nitrate due in tomorrow. I want the mills back on line by the end of the week, Mr. O'Brian."

Elizabeth heard him mutter something. It sounded like *bitch* to her. She turned around sharply, her wet skirts sticking to her damp stockings. "Did you say something, Mr. O'Brian?"

He smiled sweetly. "Nary a word, Mistress." He tipped an imaginary hat. " 'Til morning. Good day to you, madame."

Four

O'Brian set one heel of his boot on the dirt floor of the public room of the Sow's Ear Tavern, preventing the red-haired barmaid from passing.

She was a petite thing with wild, tangled, red ringlets, eyes as green as his own, and flushed rosy cheeks. She was dressed like any barmaid in any public room in any country he'd ever sat in for an ale and a game of dice. Her striped petticoat was too short, her stockings baggy. The muslin of her low-cut bodice was stained yellow at the armpits and worn from wear. But she had a full set of pearly teeth, and a pert smile that welcomed a man. "Evenin' to you, sweet."

She bobbed her head, shifting the heavy tray of sloshing ale horns to her opposite arm. "You must be the new yard foreman to Lawrence Mills everyone's been flappin' their jaws about."

"Name's O'Brian, lass."

She swayed her hips seductively. "I heard you saved a babe from drowning this afternoon, but no one said you was so comely."

O'Brian smiled broadly. He had a way with women. It wasn't that he was boastful. It was just a fact. Since that afternoon in the neighbor's dairy when he was just short of fifteen years, he'd known it to be a fact. Patience McNaught, a dairy maid near twice his age, had given him his first tumble after pursuing him for weeks.

O'Brian still remembered it like it was yesterday. He could still taste her mouth on his, when he closed his eyes. She'd really been something that Patience, but then they'd all been something, every woman he'd ever laid. He could still recall each one, the color of her hair, the taste of her skin.

Some wenches said they were attracted by his charm, others his cod. O'Brian realistically owed it more to the simple fact that he liked women: skinny women, fat women, handsome women, homely women, smart women, stone-stupid women, and they could sense it. He liked the smell of their hair, the pitch of their throaty laughter, the depth of their passion for life.

Truth was, just about any woman could brighten his day, except maybe one Elizabeth Lawrence. Thinking of his new employer, he frowned. She was attractive enough, what with that mane of dark hair, those flashing eyes, and pursed lips, but the woman had a tongue like a wasp stinger. Nope, this little piece of fluff here was much more to his liking.

O'Brian gave the tavern wench a lazy smirk. "Got a name, lover?"

Her laughter was light. "My Christian name be Mildred, but my friends, they call me Red."

"Sit a while with me then, Red." He pulled up his foot and tapped his knee. "And tell me if you've always been so fair."

She glanced at the heavy tray of ale. O'Brian watched the exposed flesh of her full breasts as they rose and fell beneath the cotton drawstring of her soiled bodice. He wondered absently if her nipples would be long and red, or tiny brown buds. He was a man who liked full breasts and small nipples.

"I got to serve the ale, else Miss Mattie will be after me. That's what she says she pays me for." She appeared disappointed.

O'Brian grabbed one wax ale horn off her tray, spraying foam with a swing of his hand. "So serve your drinks and come back to me." He winked before taking a swallow. "I vow I could make it worth your while."

She chuckled deep in her throat, her pink tongue darting out to moisten her upper lip. "I just bet you could, couldn't you?"

He gave her a swat on her tight, round bottom as she sashayed by him. It looked like the night would go a hell of a sight better than his day had. He took another long pull on the ale, wiping the foam from his mouth with the back of his hand.

Over in the corner of the public room near the cold fireplace, was a group of men gathering with a pair of wooden dice. O'Brian figured he'd play awhile, win a handful of their coin, put back a couple of horns of ale, then he'd take the barmaid home to try out that new rope bed of his.

He chuckled. Wouldn't Miss High And Mighty Englishwoman be appalled—her foreman and a whore under her cottage roof. He didn't know why he cared, but for some reason the thought of shocking Elizabeth Lawrence appealed to him.

He frowned. The woman just rubbed him the wrong way, she and those damned dogs of hers. She was too masculine for his tastes, ordering men about, talking of chemical compounds and efficiency rates.

So how the blast could she appear so entirely feminine at the same time? Against his will, O'Brian recalled the way the tendrils of her dark hair had brushed her flushed cheeks when she stood on the riverbank this afternoon. Her straw bonnet had blown off her head to hang by a ribbon down her back. The hem of her petticoats had been wet and soiled from the riverbank. Her disheveled appearance seemed to soften the rough edges of her personality. She had looked so relieved when he'd climbed out of the rushing water with the child under his arm, almost glad to see him. He had liked the way her mouth had turned up in the corners in a smile when their gazes had met. He always liked a pretty smile, when it was genuine.

O'Brian drained his horn with a groan. Sweet Mary, Mother of God, what ailed him? Elizabeth Lawrence was his employer. She was a highborn English wench with a sour attitude.

He got up and crossed the noisy, smoke-filled public room of the tavern. He couldn't fathom why he kept thinking about Mistress Lawrence. She was too rich and too snotty for his tastes. Barmaids were far more to his liking.

The redhead caught his eye from across the room and blew him a kiss.

O'Brian grinned. Now there was a woman who could appreciate a man . . .

Elizabeth lit the oil lamp on her desk with the stub of a tallow candle, replaced the glass globe, and turned down the wick a little. She blew out the candle and tossed it onto her desk. The steady flame from the lamp cast a circle of soft yellow light across the floor and up onto the whitewashed walls of her office.

She stared at her own reflection in the wavy, dark glass of the window. It was twilight. Jessop would be perturbed with her. By now their guests had arrived, and he would be serving them wine in the front parlor. He would be apologizing for her tardiness and assuring them she would be with them directly.

Most likely Mary Hart would be playing the pianoforte and laughing senselessly, as she often did. The men would be huddled together talking of dogs, horses, and taxes. The women would be standing near the piano gossiping about their hostess and her lack of manners.

Elizabeth didn't care. In the last few months she had grown to despise these late dinner parties. She had too much work to do. She had to get up too early in the morning to be drinking and eating heavily so late in the day. It just took too much energy to play the charming hostess.

But Jessop enjoyed entertaining. He said it was good for his shipping business. He said it would be good for the powder mill, if it got up and running again. So Elizabeth played the hostess to his weekly parties, she said the right things, she laughed at the jokes, and tried not to yawn when it got late.

Elizabeth walked to the window and cupped her hands around her eyes to see outside. It was dark now. Where the blast was Samsom? She'd sent Johnny for him nearly an hour ago.

She came away from the window, smoothing the watered silk of her floral-stitched petticoat. Thank goodness she'd had the sense to dress before returning to the office. She tucked a wisp of hair into the back of her simple coiffure. Jessop surely would be angry if she joined their guests in the parlor with her hair ratted and wearing the water-stained morning dress she'd waded into the river in.

Impatient, Elizabeth began to pace the sand-polished pine floor. Her new foreman had impressed her today. He might be insolent, but the man had a conscience. She considered that an admirable trait. That little black child meant nothing to him, and yet he had risked his life to save her. That said something about his heart. Perhaps she had judged him a little harshly. After all, he was new to the colonies. He was here far from his homeland without his wife, his children. He had to be lonely. Loneliness did strange things to people.

Elizabeth wondered what her foreman was doing right now. He was probably seated before a cold fireplace, eating a bit of bread and cheese. She guessed he would turn into bed early and lie there thinking about his wife so far across the ocean.

How many nights had Elizabeth lain in her own bed unable to sleep, after Paul had died? How big the bed had seemed. How small she had felt in it. So many nights she would have given anything for the sound of someone's light breathing, for the touch of someone's hand.

Elizabeth caught a glimpse of the small wooden trunk pushed beneath her desk, and a lump rose in her throat. She hadn't thought about that trunk in weeks. She'd been too busy with the mill, too caught up in the day-to-day worries of the business. Slowly she walked to her desk and stooped, pulling the trunk out, wood scraping against wood.

If Jessop knew she had kept what was inside, he'd make her destroy it. He wouldn't understand. How could he, when she didn't understand herself?

Those first days after the explosion Elizabeth had been numb, so numb that she'd barely been able to function. Then she'd become angry. How could this terrible tragedy have happened? How could Paul's life have been lost so quickly, so senselessly? Nothing made any sense. Why was Paul in the stamp mill in the middle of the night? How had the explosion been ignited, when none of the equipment had been in operation?

When Elizabeth started sifting through the cinders, Jessop had grown impatient with her. He hadn't understood her need to make sense of the explosion, to understand why it had happened. He had told her to accept the accident and stop dwelling on it, else she'd make herself crazy. He had reminded her again and again that she had lost a husband of a few weeks, but he had lost a brother of more than thirty years.

She lifted the latch and hesitantly opened the lid of the wooden trunk. Jessop wouldn't understand this either . . .

The acrid smell of smoke immediately filled her nostrils, and she wondered if the trunk truly still smelled of smoke, or if it was her memory of that horrible night and the days that had followed her husband's death that still haunted her.

Elizabeth stared at the boot in the bottom of the trunk, fighting the tears that clouded her eyes. It was odd how black powder explosions worked. A body could be blown to shreds, nothing but bone fragments and charred skin, but an article of clothing—blown free of the explosion— could remain completely intact, unharmed. She ran her fingers across the smooth leather. Paul's boot had still been soft and supple when she'd hidden it in the trunk, but a year later, it was beginning to harden. The leather was growing brittle and firm. She bit down on her lower lip. She knew it was silly to hold onto this bit of her dead husband, but somehow she found comfort in it.

The door to the front office clicked open, and Lacy, her spotted hound lying in the doorway, immediately lifted her head and growled deep in her throat.

Elizabeth let the lid of the trunk fall with a bang. "Samson?" She pushed the trunk back under her desk, out of view, with the toe of her dyed green slipper.

"Aye, Mistress."

"Come back here, Samson."

She heard the swing of the half door and the scrape of Samson's feet as he approached the back office. He halted in the doorway, eyeing the two hounds stretched out on the floor at his feet.

Like many of the workers, Samson was just a little frightened by the dogs. "Lacy, Freckles!" Elizabeth called. "Come."

The dogs leaped to their feet, panting excitedly.

Elizabeth pointed to the cold hearth behind her. "Go. Stay."

The dogs obeyed without hesitation, walking to the fireplace and settling onto the floor.

"Good dogs. Good boy, good girl." Elizabeth turned back to her worker. "Come in, Samson. I want to talk to you about a serious matter."

Samson pulled off his battered cocked hat as he stepped through the doorway, still remaining outside the circle of lamplight. "Yes, Mistress?"

She studied Samson there in the shadows. He was a big man, immense, but without an ounce of fat on his frame. His skin was chocolate black, his hair shorn. He was not a handsome man; his nose too broad, his eyes set too closely together. But he had an honest face, the face of man who worked hard, the face of a loyal man.

"Samson, I understand that little girl Mr. O'Brian rescued from the river today was sired by you. I want you to be honest with me. Is that true?"

He lowered his gaze, fidgeting with the hat knotted in his fingers.

Elizabeth took a step closer. He was more than a head taller than she was. "Is it true?" she repeated without condemnation in her voice.

"Might be," he answered beneath his breath.

She raised a dark eyebrow. "Might be? Samson, it's a simple question. Did you lie with the woman called Ngozi, or didn't you?"

"I did, Mistress."

"Could the child be yours then?"

He nodded, still not raising his gaze from the floor.

"I'm told the woman and child live in some sort of bark hut in the woods. I'm told they forage for their food. Is that true, also?"

He nodded.

Elizabeth shook her head with a sigh. "Samson, how

could you sleep at night in the bunkhouse with a roof over your head and food in your stomach, knowing your child eats berries and sleeps on a bed of leaves in the forest?"

"I take 'em food," Samson defended. "When Ngozi laid in with the girl chil', I got Johnny's wife to he'p her out. I takes good care of 'em, Mistress." He raised his gaze to meet hers. "Best I know how."

"Samson, this is not acceptable. You can't leave the woman and child in the forest. You have to take responsibility for what's yours. You took the woman into your bed, and you got her with child. Do you understand what I'm saying? Both of them are your responsibility now."

He nodded. "Yes, ma'am."

"Now I want you to bring them here. The Craigs left last month. You can take their side of the cottage. It's tiny, but I think you can make do."

"Yes, ma'am." He twisted his mouth. "Thank you, ma'am."

"And, Samson, I want you to marry her."

"Ma'am?"

"Neither of you is already wed, are you?"

"No, ma'am. Not as I know."

"Then marry her. The child has a right to have her father's name. Marry her, and I'll increase your wages."

He broke into a toothy grin. "Yes, ma'am."

"Elizabeth?"

Elizabeth heard Jessop's voice as the outer door opened and closed behind him in the front office.

"In the back office, Jessop. Here."

Jessop came through the swinging door, from the darkness into the lamplight of the rear office. He was dressed in a handsome burgundy waistcoat with matching breeches. He wore silk, clocked stockings and a pair of fashionable, high-heeled shoes, the cloth dyed to match his coat. His dark hair, peppered with gray, was pulled back in a smooth queue with the front locks curled tightly around his face. His dress would have been acceptable in any drawing room in London.

"Jessop, I'm sorry I'm late. I'm coming now."

He twisted his face in a scowl as he took one look at Samson, then at her. "What do you think you're doing, Elizabeth?"

Elizabeth could tell he was angry. He always enunciated each word when he was angry. "I had some business to attend to with Samson, but we're done now." She gave her worker a quick smile. "You can go now, Samson. I—"

"You've been alone here with him at this time of night?" Jessop spat. "You and this nigger? Where the hell is your head, woman? What will people think?"

Elizabeth was shocked into silence for a moment. Jessop had never spoken to her like this before, and certainly not in front of someone else. What was wrong with him, calling Samson that name? He knew how she felt about her African workers, slave or free. "Jessop—"

"Get out of here," Jessop bellowed at Samson, striking him in the chest with the back of his hand. "Get the hell out of here right now, and if I ever, *ever* catch you alone with Mistress Lawrence again, I'll have your black hide. Do you understand me?"

Samson was backing out of the office, nodding his head, his eyes wide and startled.

"Get out!" Jessop shouted again, and Samson turned around and ran out of the office, slamming the outside door behind him.

Elizabeth stood there for a moment trying to gather her wits. Never had she been so angry, so embarrassed. What in God's name had gotten into Jessop?

She turned to him, narrowing her eyes. "How dare

you," she said, her voice barely a whisper. "How dare you talk to my worker like that!"

"He needs to be taught a lesson. I ought to have gotten my riding crop out and done so here and now. I see how he looks at you. I see how he wants you."

"Jessop!" She stared at him, thinking to herself that this couldn't possibly be the kind, thoughtful man she was engaged to be married to. "I've never seen you like this. What's gotten into you?"

He tugged on his shirtwaist, casting his eyes downward. When he spoke, it was with controlled effort. "Elizabeth, if you haven't the sense to protect yourself, then I must do it for you. I've given into you up to this point. I have tolerated your peculiarities, but it's time I reined you in before something happens. You and your virtue are my responsibility. You and Sister are both my responsibility, and I won't have you molested by the likes of that animal."

"Molested?" She stared at him, utterly confused. "What in sweet God's name are you talking about? I called Samson here because I had a matter to discuss with him. He's never laid a hand on me. He's never spoken an improper word. This is all in your head, Jessop."

He flicked an imaginary bit of dust from his coat sleeve. "I believe we'd be better to finish this conversation later, Elizabeth. If you'll recall, we have guests. Sister is famished. I promised we would eat immediately, so if you don't mind . . ." He indicated the doorway with a sweep of his hand.

Elizabeth stood there for a moment in indecision. She couldn't let him get away with this. But the others were waiting, and it was obvious that she wouldn't be able to reason with Jessop in his present state of mind.

She sighed beneath her breath. All right, so she would yield this time. She would smile prettily and play the hostess to his friends like an obedient lap dog, but she'd be damned if Jessop Lawrence wouldn't get an earful later.

With a swish of her layered petticoats, Elizabeth sailed by Jessop and out of the office without a word to him.

Five

"I don't understand why you're so mad, Brother." Claire walked into the front hallway ahead of Jessop, and handed her gloves and calash bonnet to a waiting servant. "Liz was just doing her work. You do your work and sometimes you don't come to dinner at all. I hate to eat by myself in that big room, Brother."

"It's not the same thing at all, Claire." Jessop handed his cocked hat to the housekeeper, addressing her. "We'll be having brandy wine in my library. We won't be needing you again tonight, Martha. You're dismissed until morning."

Many thought it odd that Jessop didn't allow his servants to sleep in his home, but he liked his privacy. Some of his servants lived in small cottages on the edge of the property along the river, while others lived in their own houses nearby and walked to work each day.

The middle-aged woman bobbed a curtsy. "Yes, sir. Clean glasses on the lowboy, just like you like 'em. And Miss Claire's bed things is already laid out. I'll light the lamps upstairs then be goin' home, but I'll be back by dawn, sir. Same as always."

With a nod, Jessop dismissed the servant. "A glass of rhenish to settle you, Sister?"

Claire followed Jessop down the dark hallway to his library. She wrinkled her nose. "I don't like it. It tastes like dishwater."

He walked into the library. Martha had left several candlesticks burning. She knew her master's habits well. He poured himself a glass of French brandy and reached for the rhenish bottle. "Have a drink anyway, Sister. It's good for your nerves. You and Elizabeth would both be well-served to just do as I say. There are many matters where a man knows best."

Claire accepted the glass he pushed into her hand. "I don't know why you're picking on Liz tonight. You weren't very nice to her. I thought you wanted to marry her."

He dropped into a brocade-covered, wing-backed chair and propped one heeled shoe on the footstool. "I do want to marry her," he answered tersely. "I will marry her. I'll marry her, give her a child, and she'll soon forget this silly nonsense of hers—trying to run Paul's powder mill. I thought it a whimsy from the first day. Paul couldn't pull it off. She certainly can't either." He looked up to see Claire's lower lip trembling.

He sat up in the chair. "Oh, dear, I'm sorry, sweet. I've upset you. I know better than to mention his name."

She took a sip of the wine and swallowed it with a grimace. "You're going to make me cry. Don't make me cry, Brother."

He extended his hand toward her, wanting to comfort her. "I'm sorry. I truly am. I was thinking of myself and not you, Sister. Come here."

She shook her head like a stubborn child. "I don't want to come over there. I want to stand right here and drink my wine."

Dropping his hand, Jessop stared into the golden brandy in his glass. "Sometimes I think you spend too much time with her. You were better-behaved before she came."

"Who?"

"Liz. She puts ideas in your head. Ideas women have no business with."

Claire stuck out her lower lip defiantly. "I like her. She doesn't let people hurt her." She lifted her gaze, breaking into a smile that lit up her face. "And I like her new man, too. Mr. O'Brian. He has nice arms."

"He is not *her man,* Claire," Jessop stated, enunciating each word. "And I would appreciate it if you would not repeat such nonsense. O'Brian's just another blasted worker like the others."

She took another sip of her wine and swayed her hips a little. "He's mighty handsome, that Mr. O'Brian. He has a nice mouth, too."

Jessop looked up quickly. "That will be enough, Sister. Continue this conversation, and you'll be locked in your room the remainder of the week. I'll do it." He shook his finger at her. "You know I will. I want none of your waggery. Do you understand me?"

She laughed a deep, sultry laugh as she drained the wineglass. "You hate it when I'm naughty, don't you, Brother? You hate it when others know I'm naughty."

Jessop rose. "I said that will be quite enough, young lady."

She giggled. "I think I want another glass of wine."

"No more wine. It's gone to your head. It would be best if you went to bed now." He reached for the brandy bottle, intent on pouring himself another.

"I . . ." There was the slightest quiver in Claire's voice. "I don't want to go to bed yet."

"It's been a long day. I'm certain that's why you're speaking such nonsense. Now go up to your bedchamber, undress, put on your sleeping gown, and get into bed. Martha is probably still upstairs. I'm sure she'll unhook your stays, if you ask nicely."

Claire set her wineglass on the lowboy and pushed it toward the center of the table with a delicate finger. When Jessop reached to touch her hand, she drew back. "I don't like you very much sometimes, Brother," she said, her eyes downcast. "I liked Paul better. He was nicer to me."

Jessop's head snapped up. He'd had just about enough of Liz and Claire's mouth tonight. "And why wouldn't Paul have been nice to you, hmmm? You didn't become a lunatic until after he died, did you?"

Claire's delicate chin dropped. She looked as if she was going to burst into tears. The sight of her face washed away any anger Jessop felt for her in an instant. "Oh, Sister, I'm sorry." He set down his glass and went to her, taking her into his arms. "I'm sorry, sweetheart." He smoothed her silky hair with his hand, as she made little mewing sounds. "I'm so sorry. I've been overwrought. It was wrong of me to lash out like that at you."

"They say I'm crazy, don't they?" She sniffled. "But I'm not. I'm not crazy, Brother." She looked up into his eyes, her own blue ones clouded with tears. "I'm not, am I?"

He pulled her against her chest, feeling her pain as if it was his own. "Oh, no, of course, you aren't," Jessop soothed. "It's just a little nervous disorder. That's what the physicians say. That's why you get confused sometimes, love. That's why you do those naughty things. It's nothing more than just a little nervous tic."

She smiled up at him and gave a sniff. "I'm sorry I upset you. I didn't mean to make you angry. I want to do the right thing. I don't want you to be cross with me."

"Shhh," he soothed, still stroking her silky blond hair. "It's all right, little sister. All's forgotten already. Just try to be a better girl, try to do as I ask, that's all." He smiled down at her.

"I think I'll go to bed now." She withdrew from his embrace. "Is that all right?"

"Yes." He reached for his brandy again. "You go to bed, and I'll come and say goodnight shortly."

Claire disappeared into the darkness of the hallway, and Jessop finished his drink alone.

Elizabeth stood on the dirt road, her hands on her hips. She tipped her straw hat to look up at O'Brian. "I can't believe you did it!" She looked back at the wood panels laid out in the sun, covered in a fine layer of damp gunpowder. "You did it, O'Brian!" She touched his muscular arm lightly. She couldn't stop smiling. "Two weeks, and we've got our first shipment!"

O'Brian grinned, squinting in the bright noon sun. "You're the one who found the buyer, Mistress. I just got the product out."

She ran her finger through the damp gunpowder, feeling like a child on Christmas morn. "It's good, isn't it? It's good powder." She stared at the black on her finger.

"Will be, once we get her dry and into kegs."

Elizabeth was so happy she could have kissed the man. Two weeks and he had their first shipment nearly ready! She hadn't made a mistake in hiring O'Brian. She'd known what she was doing. She'd been right, and Jessop wrong. She clasped her hands. "I just can't believe it." Her gaze met his. His green eyes were laughing. They were happy eyes. He was as proud of his work as she was. "I've waited a long time for this. People said it couldn't be done. People said I couldn't do it."

O'Brian reached out, caught a wisp of her hair on his finger, and tucked it behind her ear, startling Elizabeth. It was a casual gesture. His hand was gone before she had time to think about it. Yet she couldn't stop thinking about it. For some reason his innocent gesture seemed intensely intimate to her. Suddenly, she couldn't tear her gaze from his.

"I told you that you had a good setup here," he went

on, as if he touched her every day like that. "You just needed a man like myself to give it a push."

Elizabeth felt strangely uneasy. She tried to concentrate on the conversation and not the fluttering in the pit of her stomach. She'd certainly been touched casually by a man before. Why was she in such a dither?

"I . . . I've more charcoal coming in tomorrow. It'll be delivered directly to the grinding mill. I want you to be there to receive the goods. Be certain it's top quality."

"No problem."

"I want you to keep this up, O'Brian. I want to see just how much powder we can produce in a week, if we set our minds to it."

He scratched his blond head.

His hair's always clean, she thought. So clean . . .

"You have another buyer?" he continued. "It doesn't do a mill any good to produce powder, if you haven't got a buyer for it. You've got to be able to pay for your materials within a reasonable amount of time."

She started down the dirt road, her hounds at her feet. She was headed to the completed powder magazine to inspect the new slate roof. O'Brian fell into step beside her. "I've a mind we may have several new buyers shortly," she said. "I don't know what the talk is at the Sow's Ear, but I hear a great deal of grumbling these days. They say *taxation without representation.*" She cut her eyes at him. "I think we're going to go to war, that's what I think. Men who fight need black powder."

O'Brian gave a low whistle. "Peculiar words coming straight from an Englishwoman's mouth, Lizzy."

Lizzy . . . First he'd touched her like no worker had ever dared touch her before, and now he was calling her Lizzy. No one had ever called her Lizzy, not even Paul.

In the back of her mind, Elizabeth recalled Jessop's warning. He said she was too familiar with her men. He had warned her to keep her distance from this new foreman of hers. But Jessop was paranoid. The episode in the office with Samson had been proof of that.

Elizabeth gave O'Brian a sassy smile. "It's not the women of these colonies who will make the decisions about war, or anything else for that matter. It'll be men who decide to fight or not to fight, same as it's always been. Besides,"—she narrowed her eyes—"I didn't say which side I'd be selling my powder to, did I?"

He shook his head. "Digging your heels in the dirt, telling Mother England you won't play her games any longer, it would get ugly, fast. King Georgie would take the rebels' weapons, he'd take everything they owned. Rape and murder their women, take their children from them." The tone of O'Brian's voice was changing, growing harsher, more bitter with each word. "They've done it before, you know that, don't you? It's what Mother England does best." He looked away. "I saw it myself with me own Ireland."

Elizabeth looked at the man walking beside her, speaking to her as if she were his equal. Jessop never talked politics with her. He never spoke with the emotion in his voice that O'Brian had just spoken with.

"Futtering Englishmen," he muttered angrily beneath his breath. "Take, take, take, with no thought for the poor man, the hungry man, the man just trying to survive. That's all they know—bastards."

Elizabeth knew she'd struck a raw nerve in O'Brian. What had she said that made him so angry? She didn't know what she'd said wrong, but he was suddenly angry not just with England's steel grip, but with her. The devilish grin on his face was gone, as if it had never been there. Once again they were mistress and servant. The comradery was gone. Now she really was confused.

"Mr. O'Brian." Elizabeth didn't know why she cared what he thought or why he was angry, but she did. "O'Brian, I—"

"You take a look at the slate roof. I haven't the time. Just let me know if it's to your liking, *Mistress*." He walked away from her. "I've got work to do."

Elizabeth stood there for a moment in the center of the road, watching him go. When he disappeared down the bank, she started walking again. The dogs ran ahead.

That was the moodiest man she'd ever met. Where were his manners? Touching her like that, speaking to her in such a familiar way. He'd called her Lizzy, for heaven's sake! Lizzy!

The angrier Elizabeth got, the faster she walked. The faster she walked, the angrier she became. She was a lady, and she was the one who put the coin in that man's pocket. She deserved a little more respect than he'd given her. Maybe Jessop was right, maybe it was important to remind servants of their place. Maybe Mr. O'Brian needed to be reminded of his position here.

Elizabeth had half a notion to call him back. But after second thought, she decided to just let him go. He was doing a excellent job as yard foreman. So he made a breach of etiquette. He shouldn't have addressed her in such a familiar way; he shouldn't have touched her hair like that, but for God's sake, it was just hair. She wasn't like Jessop. She didn't jump to unwarranted conclusions. O'Brian certainly wasn't attracted to her, and she by no means attracted him. The thought was ludicrous. Ridiculous. Unfathomable . . .

Late that night O'Brian lay in his new rope bed in the loft bedchamber of his yard foreman's cottage. The single window beneath the eaves was open; a warm breeze blew through the room, cooling his damp skin.

The bar wench, Red, lay asleep on her side beside him, her arm flung over his bare chest. The moonlight poured in through the window, casting patterned shadows across her face. Her breasts rose and fell as she slept, making a little whistling sound through her teeth.

O'Brian stretched his arms out and tucked them beneath his head, taking care not to disturb the girl. He couldn't sleep, not even after a good screw and half a bottle of whiskey. There was too much on his mind to let him sleep.

He reached for the bottle on the floor beside the bed and took a long pull. The whiskey burned a path down his throat to his stomach, the satisfying way good liquor did.

He just couldn't stop thinking about the Englishwoman—about Liz. He knew it was ridiculous, but the truth was, he was attracted to the bitch. Today, when he'd stood there talking to her, he hadn't been thinking about the gunpowder, he'd been thinking about her. He hadn't been looking at the drying racks, he'd been looking at her, at her breasts.

O'Brian groaned aloud. He'd touched her. Before he realized what he was doing, he'd found himself catching a wisp of her magical hair. He just tucked the stray lock behind her ear like he'd seen her do a hundred times, but there had been something lustful in his gesture. The funny thing was, she didn't react, she just went on talking like he always touched her . . . like she wanted him to do it.

"Christ almighty," O'Brian muttered beneath his breath, as he took another pull on the whiskey bottle. "I got to stop drinkin' this colonial shit. It's killing me brain. I'm losin' what little sense I ever had."

The redhead in his arms turned in her sleep, rolling off his chest to curl on her side, her tight, little buttocks pressed against his hip. He ran his hand across her ribcage and down over the dip in her waist, following the line up over her hips.

He had a fine piece right here in his bed, willing and

talented in the ways a man liked to be pleased. Why couldn't he stop thinking about his mistress? Why couldn't he stop thinking about the idea of kissing her, just once, just one kiss. Sometimes she ordered him about until he wanted to slap her mouth—that or kiss it—and the thought of kissing those rosy lips was growing more appealing to him with each passing day.

Kiss his mistress? He was out of his skull! She'd terminate his position; she'd have him beaten. Christ, that man of hers would have him hung, if he could manage it!

Samson had told O'Brian about how Lawrence had gone off half-cocked in the office one night, insinuating that Samson had desires for his mistress. Jessop Lawrence had spooked Samson with his ranting and raving like a mad man. Poor Samson was petrified he was going to lose his job.

Still, the thought of kissing Miss Lizzy was tempting. And she might be more willing than either of them thought. He often found women were like that; they didn't realize the depth of their own sexuality, until someone led them to it.

O'Brian took another drink of the whiskey and set the bottle on the floor beside him. Of course, this wasn't just any woman he was thinking about here. This woman was rich; she owned her own black powder mill. That was pretty remarkable in itself. Where he came from back in Ireland, most people never owned anything their entire lives, but a few battered pots and the clothes on their backs. Here was this Englishwoman who had inherited a business that had the potential to become very profitable.

That thought brought O'Brian to another matter that was keeping him awake. He'd been doing a little investigating on the side, nothing obvious, just some questions, a little clever observation. The explosion that had taken place last year leaving Mistress Lawrence a widow was suspicious. And the longer O'Brian looked, the more convinced he became that someone was not giving him the full story. Black powder didn't just explode, at least not at night it didn't, not when there was no equipment running, no workmen at their stations.

And the thing was, the series of explosions that followed the initial blast in the composition house didn't happen the way it should have happened. O'Brian's gut instinct was that someone had something to do with the blast that killed the owner of the mill and wounded many others.

The question was, who? What person or persons gained from the explosion. A competitor? There was no one producing black powder within a hundred miles of Lawrence Mills. An enemy? So far, O'Brian had heard nothing but good of the previous master. That left him with Mistress Lawrence. With her husband's death, she gained the land, whatever money there was, and apparently another husband rather quickly.

O'Brian tugged on his short whiskers. The thought that Liz might have been involved in her husband's death was intriguing . . .

Six

O'Brian lifted a shovelful of coal and fed it into the hopper that funnelled to the grinding wheel. Liz's shipment had arrived from Penn's Colony on time, and a fine shipment it was.

He reached for another shovelful in a comfortable rhythm. Sweat ran in rivulets at his temples, stinging his eyes. His muscles quivered from the weight of the coal and the length of time he'd been working, but he kept shoveling beside Samson. O'Brian was a foreman who prided himself in the fact that he could work beside his men; he couldn't ask them to do what he wouldn't. That was how he earned the respect due a yard foreman, that and his fairness.

O'Brian tossed another shovel of coal into the hopper, listening to the sound of the mineral being ground by the turning grindstone. He wiped the sooty sweat from his forehead with the back of his hand, never breaking stride.

Hard work was good for a man, when he couldn't keep his mind off a woman. The pain made him forget. He shoveled faster.

"How's that woman of yours?" O'Brian asked Samson, making conversation. "Babe well?"

Samson grinned. "Tickled with the house, both are. I shore 'ppreciate what the mistress done for me. What ya both done."

"A man's got to own up to his responsibilities, Samson, else he's not a man. You did the right thing marrying Ngozi."

Samson frowned, continuing to shovel. " 'Scuse me for sayin' so, sir, but you don't look to me like a man who got a right to talk 'bout things bein' right or not right."

O'Brian let the flat blade of his shovel hit the grinding mill's wooden floor. "What do you mean by that?"

Samson shrugged his massive, black shoulders, covered in a thin sheen of perspiration. "They say you got a wife and little 'uns in Ireland. But I seen you with the whore. We all seen you."

O'Brian went back to shoveling without responding to Samson's accusation. He was right, of course. A man whose own morals were questionable certainly didn't have the right to tell another man what to do.

O'Brian groaned under the strain of a heavy shovel of coal. It had all seemed harmless at the time, him taking his friend's place after the poor soul died, but it wasn't as easy as O'Brian had anticipated. He realized now that when you took a man's identity, you took the whole identity, not just the pieces you chose. Everyone kept asking him when he was sending for his wife and children. Even Liz had mentioned his family.

A part of O'Brian wanted to tell the truth, or at least some form of it. Part of a yard foreman's job was to monitor the morals of his men. It just made good business sense. A hell of an example he was setting, them all thinking he was cheating on his wife and a cottage full of red-haired babes.

But O'Brian knew he couldn't tell the truth. He had to stick with his story. He'd just have to figure out a way to get out of the wife and children situation. Maybe after a few months he'd let on like he had sent for them. Later he could receive a letter saying they had all died at sea, poor wee things.

O'Brian dug into the heap of coal that seemed to grow no smaller. It was as hot as any day in hell in the grinding mill, even with the window thrown wide open, but he kept working. He ignored the burning in his biceps and the tremble in the muscles of his thighs. He kept up with Samson's pace.

Only a few moments later the sound of a commotion outside the mill window caught O'Brian's attention. He fed a shovelful of coal into the hopper, glancing outside. He couldn't see what was going on, but there was a crowd of workers gathering down near the river.

O'Brian leaned his shovel against the wall.

Samson kept shoveling. "What is it?"

"I don't know. I'll find out. You keep feeding the grinding wheel. I want this entire pile of coal moved by tonight. We'll get another man in here, if we have to."

O'Brian ducked out the door and a breeze struck his bare chest. It was a full ten degrees cooler outside beneath the trees. He could hear the men laughing, making catcalls and coarse remarks. He turned the corner of the building.

"What the hell?" O'Brian swore, coming to an abrupt halt. He scarcely trusted his own eyesight.

More than a dozen workers had gathered in a circle. Claire Lawrence was standing in the center of the circle, laughing gaily and swaying her rounded hips—wearing nothing but her summer silk parasol.

"Sweet Mary, Mother of God," O'Brian swore beneath his breath. It took him a moment to react. The workers were laughing and jeering. They were shouting crude remarks. They were closing in on Claire like hounds on their prey. Claire didn't seem to care—that or she didn't understand.

"Lay one hand on her, and I'll cut it off, I swear by

all that's holy, I will!" O'Brian boomed above the clamor of the men.

Everyone turned to look at him. Their laughter subsided; the smiles fell from their dirty faces. They all looked like little boys caught peeking in a maid's window.

"You ought to be ashamed of yourselves," O'Brian shouted furiously as he strode toward the circle of men and Claire. "All of you with wives, daughters, for god's sake!"

O'Brian reached Claire, but he didn't have a thing to wrap around her slender, naked body. His own shirt was thrown on the grinding mill floor. He put his hand out to the closest man wearing a shirt. "Gimme your shirt, Petey."

"My shirt? My wife she'll have my hair if—"

"Now, you jackanape!"

Petey peeled off his tattered, muslin shirt and tossed it to his foreman. Trying not to stare at any one part of Claire's feminine form, O'Brian took her parasol from her hand and tossed it to the ground. Gently, he pulled the shirt over her head, slipping her hands through the sleeves. "Put this on. Good girl," he murmured softly. "That's it."

Claire smiled prettily. "What's the matter?" She pouted as the muslin slipped down over her hips. "You don't like what you see, Mister Foreman?"

One of the men laughed.

O'Brian had only to glance at the worker, and he lowered his head. "Nah, it's not that at all," he told Claire. "You're as pretty a lady as I think I've ever seen, but you don't belong out here. Not with these men." He picked up her parasol and handed it to her. "They might hurt you, love. Do you understand what I'm saying?"

"Ain't the first time she's done it, you know," one of

the workers in the crowd offered. "She gives us a peek 'bout once a month."

Several of the other men agreed with raw laughter.

O'Brian gave them an icy stare that silenced the lot of them. "What the hell are you talking about?" He stood between Claire and the men, as if he couldn't somehow protect her from herself and her own confused mind.

"What Josh says is true," Petey offered. " 'Bout once a month Miss Claire pays us a visit. Usually Master Lawrence comes down after a while and carries her off shoutin' and screamin'. Guess he ain't tracked her down yet."

"This has happened before, and he hasn't stopped her?"

" 'Pparently he can't." Petey shrugged.

O'Brian glanced at Claire, who was standing beside him looking at him with a flirtatious innocence.

O'Brian eyed his men. "Let me tell you something right now." He pointed an accusing finger. "I won't have this, not in my powder yard. You understand me?"

"We didn't do nothin' wrong. We didn't touch 'er, or nothin' like that. We was jest lookin'."

"Yea, that's all we was doin'," said another.

"Well, I don't want you looking anymore, you understand me? Turn around!" O'Brian shouted. "All you bastards, turn around this minute!"

Slowly the workers turned their backs on O'Brian and Claire. "That's what you do if you see Miss Claire unclothed again, you understand me?"

"All we did was look," someone protested.

"Well, there'll be no more looking!" O'Brian ordered fiercely. "I don't care if she comes down here every day but Sunday, bare as a babe, you turn around and you keep your eyes to yourself! You go on with your work like you never saw a thing. You understand me? And anyone I catch gawking again will take his pay and go.

Now, I'm serious about this!" O'Brian wiped his mouth with the back of his hand, disgusted by his men's behavior. "Now get the hell out of here, before I really get pissed!"

One by one the workers walked off in silence, their heads hung like ill-behaved schoolboys. O'Brian just stood there until they were all gone. He'd been in many a situation in his days in the powder mills in France, but this was new to him. What the blast was a man supposed to do with a naked woman in his gunpowder yard? Finally he turned to Claire.

Petey's shirt was so old that the sunlight came through the weave, revealing more of her lithe form than it covered. But it would have to do until O'Brian could get her up to the office. Liz could take over from there.

He glanced at her, trying to figure the best way to get her to the office without another exhibition. It was odd, but he felt no stir of arousal. To him, Claire was a child, a child in her mind at least.

Gingerly he touched her arm. "Let's go now, Miss Claire. Let's go up to the office and see what Liz is doing."

Claire giggled. "I like Liz, don't you?"

"Aye, well enough, I guess."

She cut her eyes at him, throwing her head back so that her blond curls bounced on her shoulders. "No, you really like her. She doesn't see you looking at her titties, but I see you."

O'Brian knew he blushed. A man full-grown in his mid-thirties, and a woman had made him blush. "Let . . . let's go, Miss Claire. It's not much further to the house. We'll find you something to put on there."

Claire spun her parasol. "I don't want to put anything on. It's hot. I think I'd like a cool syllabub. Would you care to join me?"

O'Brian guided her along the bank, trying to take the

shortest path to the office with as few people seeing them as possible. "I'm afraid I can't, Miss Claire. Not today, at least. I've a lot of work to do."

"Pity." She smiled coyly. She behaved as if she always walked down the road in broad daylight wearing naught but a man's dirty shirt.

O'Brian led Claire up the granite steps to Liz's office window. He stuck his head through the open window. The room was empty save for one of the mistress's hounds; Freckles lifted his head and growled.

"Blast!" O'Brian struck the heel of his hand on the sill as he pulled his head out of the window. "Damned dog," he muttered. He turned back to Claire, forcing a smile. "Liz isn't in her office. Let's go around to the house, shall we?"

She walked along beside him, wiggling her toes in the grass as they crossed the lawn. O'Brian had never been to the big house. He always met Liz in her office.

Claire walked up to the front door, skipping across the granite stepping stones. When she reached the front door and lowered her parasol, O'Brian stopped on the walkway. He looked at himself. He was nearly as naked as Claire was. He was wearing just his boots, stockings, and a pair of broadcloth breeches. His hair, having escaped from his queue, hung sweaty on his shoulders. He knew his face had to be as black as his workers' with all the coal he'd shoveled today.

"You . . . you'll be all right, Miss Claire?" he asked awkwardly. Why was it that he, a man who was always comfortable with women, had such a difficult time with the Lawrence women? "Can you find Liz on your own?"

She glanced over her shoulder. "Maybe." She gave him that coy smile again. "But then maybe I'll go right out the kitchen door and back down to the mill. I like the workers. They wait for me, you know."

"I just bet they do," O'Brian muttered beneath his

breath. He gave a groan as he looked up at Claire. He supposed he'd have to go into the house. Maybe he could find one of the serving women to take her. At least he'd know she was safe then.

After a moment of dreaded hesitation, O'Brian knocked on the front door.

No answer.

Claire stood beside him on the giant grinding wheel that served as the step, singing a ditty more appropriate for a tavern wench, and spinning her parasol. O'Brian groaned and reached over Claire, knocking again. He didn't want to have to go in the house and dress the woman himself, but he would if he had to. People like Claire had to be protected from the likes of those in the powder yard.

Just when O'Brian thought he would open the door himself, it swung on its hinges.

"Christ Almighty," O'Brian muttered beneath his breath. This was just what he needed.

It was Jessop Lawrence.

"What the hell!" Lawrence shouted.

"Afternoon, Brother. Warm day." Claire slipped under her brother's arm and disappeared into the front hallway of the house, leaving O'Brian to make any explanations.

"What have you done to my sister?" Jessop demanded, so angry that his face had gone beet red. He swung his fist. "What have you done!"

"It's not as it appears, sir." O'Brian held up one hand. He didn't want to get in a brawl with Mr. Lawrence, but he'd not let the man strike him. "If you'll calm down, I'll explain to you what's happened."

"Calm down!" Lawrence gripped the doorway with white knuckles. "Calm down! You've just delivered my sister to me nearly nude and you, you—" He pointed at O'Brian's state of undress.

"I was shoveling coal in the grinding mill when I

found Miss Claire like that, actually in less than that. She was down in the yard, Mr. Lawrence, giving the workmen quite a show."

"How dare you lie about my sister like that! How dare you try to blame my innocent sister—"

"Jessop!" Liz appeared in the hallway behind Lawrence. She looked startled to see O'Brian. "Mr. O'Brian, the entire yard can hear your shouting. Could you please bring your discussion inside?"

O'Brian hadn't seen Liz today. She was as pretty as a summer tiger lily, dressed in a yellow gown with her hair pulled back in a frill of yellow ribbons. She swept her arm in invitation. "Mr. O'Brian, please come inside."

O'Brian didn't want to go into her house. Not dressed like this, not under these circumstances, but what choice was he left with? He entered the cool hallway with its vaulted ceiling and Italian tile floor. She closed the door behind him, blocking out the blinding sunlight.

It took a moment for O'Brian's eyes to adjust to the dimmer light. "Good day to you, Mistress. I apologize for my appearance. We were grinding the charcoal when—"

"Don't address Mistress Lawrence, address me," Jessop demanded.

O'Brian tore his gaze from Liz's rosy cheeks. God help him, he had it bad for this woman . . . "As I was saying, Mr. Lawrence, I was shoveling coal in the grinding mill when I heard a disturbance down by the river. I went out to see what the workers were making such a fuss over, and it was Miss Claire. She was, um, she was nude, sir."

"Oh, no, not again," Liz said with a groan.

Jessop glanced quickly at Liz, then back to O'Brian. "You must be mistaken."

O'Brian lifted one eyebrow. Lawrence was a jackass. He'd been fighting that conclusion for two weeks, but the better he got to know him, the truer it stuck. "No offense to your sister, sir, but I know a naked woman when I see one. Of course, she did have her parasol, if that counts for something."

"I'm sorry. I should have warned you." Elizabeth pushed back a lock of dark hair off her forehead. "Unfortunately this isn't the first time Claire—"

Jessop turned around angrily. "Elizabeth!"

She dropped her hand to her curved hip. "What? You're going to pretend it hasn't happened before? Every man for a mile has seen her, Jessop. It's not as if you can hide it. I'm surprised that wasn't the first thing Mr. O'Brian heard at the Sow's Ear."

Lawrence turned back to O'Brian. "You shouldn't have walked her here! You shouldn't have looked at her like I know you did! You . . . you should have come for one of us!"

"And leave her to the wolves!" O'Brian laughed, but without humor. "Now there's a clever idea, Mr. Lawrence."

"Mr. O'Brian, that will be enough of the sarcasm." Liz suddenly sounded tired.

O'Brian couldn't help wondering what Liz saw in Lawrence. He wasn't her type. He didn't appear to be any woman's type. O'Brian looked away. "I apologize. I just wanted to be certain Miss Claire reached the house safely. She didn't seem to understand the danger the men posed, if you know what I mean."

"Just leave, O'Brian," Jessop spat. "Leave now before you get yourself into deeper trouble, will you?"

O'Brian didn't like the idea of leaving Liz and Claire with this raving maniac. Hell, he was as crazed as his sister. But then, that wasn't his problem, was it?

Elizabeth nodded, dismissing him. "Go on back to the yard, O'Brian. We'll see to Claire."

He hesitated for a moment. Liz was obviously upset by Claire's latest display of herself. O'Brian wanted to say something that would make her feel better. But what was there to say? It wasn't his place.

O'Brian walked out the front door and into the bright August sunlight. He'd have to hurry if he and Samson were going to get all that charcoal ground today.

Elizabeth sat on the edge of her bed, the bed she and Paul had shared. She ran her hand over the light counterpane. It was getting more difficult each day to remember Paul. When she closed her eyes, the image of his face was dimmer. She couldn't remember what he smelled like anymore. She no longer smelled his scent on the sheets or in the library. She could still remember his touch, but not the way she had right after his death. After Paul died, she had lain in his bed at night and conjured him up in her mind until she swore he was actually in the bed beside her, touching her, whispering to her.

Elizabeth let her eyes drift shut as she fingered the cotton threads of the counterpane. What scared her the most about losing Paul in her mind, was that it wasn't Jessop who was replacing him. No, the person who crept into her thoughts was O'Brian. Her foreman, for heaven's sake.

Elizabeth found herself watching him from her office window. She found herself actually looking forward to his daily appointments with her. She found herself daydreaming about what it would be like to kiss him. Kiss him!

Elizabeth's eye flew open. O'Brian was a married man. He was little more than a hired servant. She had agreed to marry Jessop. It was Jessop she should be fantasizing about!

But Jessop had been preoccupied lately, and they quarreled often. Suddenly there were so many aspects of his personality that she hadn't recalled him possessing. She didn't like his petty jealousy, nor the way he had been trying to control her. He was attempting to take her household over, and they'd not even officially announced their engagement yet.

Then there was the matter of how he treated the men and women who worked for her. He seemed to have no respect for them, simply because of their station in life. He didn't like O'Brian, and he swore she would live to regret hiring him.

O'Brian . . . her mind came back to O'Brian again. He had done a good thing today, rescuing Claire from the workers. He had handled the entire situation well, from the flirtatious Claire to the shouting Jessop. He had kept his cool in both situations. Jessop shouldn't have lashed out at O'Brian the way he did. Elizabeth understood that he was just upset that the incident had occurred again, that he felt responsible for Claire. But Jessop should have been grateful to the yard foreman. He should have been grateful to know that if it happened again, there would be someone else out there to protect her.

And Jessop hadn't even thanked O'Brian. Come to think of it, Elizabeth hadn't either.

She glanced at the case clock on her mantel. It was ten thirty, too late to see O'Brian tonight, too late to thank him. She got up off the bed. One of the house-maids had already loosened her stays. Her gown would never close across the front, and she couldn't tighten her own stays enough to get back into her clothing without help.

But it was important to her to thank O'Brian. She wanted him to know she appreciated what he had done for Claire today.

Her gaze strayed to her clothes press. She didn't want to wake one of the maids; she didn't really want the household to know she had gone to the foreman's home

at this time of night. Gossiping was too popular a pas-
time at Lawrence Mills. It wouldn't seem appropriate,
even though it would be perfectly proper. She went to
her clothes press and swung open one polished cherry
wood door. Surely there was something inside she could
wear to cover herself decently.

Elizabeth tugged at her bodice that fastened by hook
and eye down the front. With her stays loosened, the
blasted pieces just wouldn't come together. She mentally
went over the contents of her press. The hooded caraco
jacket wouldn't close either. She'd not be seen in a dressing gown on the road. There was nothing there! It was
too hot to wear a cloak. Anyone who spotted her would
immediately be suspicious of where the mistress was going so late at night so strangely attired.

Elizabeth grabbed a large, square linen and lace kerchief, and tossed it over her shoulders. It would work.
She hooked the bottom hook and eyes she could manage,
then crossed the linen material over her breasts. As long
as she held it securely with her hand, she'd be fine. She'd
go down to O'Brian's house. She'd thank him for what
he'd done for Claire, and then she'd come back to bed.

Elizabeth walked to her bedchamber door. Besides,
she'd been having a difficult time sleeping lately. The
night air would do her good.

One of her hounds rose to follow her out the door.
"No," Elizabeth ordered. "Stay, boy. I don't want you
barking from here to O'Brian's and back." She put out
her palm to the dog. "Stay."

Freckles whined, but slumped to the floor in obedi-
ence. Elizabeth closed the door softly behind her and
slipped out of the house.

Out on the road she stuck to the shadows, walking
quickly. It felt good to be out in the night air. It felt good
to sneak out of the house like she had done when she
was a little girl. Only then she had slipped out of the

house to play with kittens forbidden by her father. This was far different. She ran her fingers through her unbound hair, feeling the same sense of excitement she had felt as a child. It was the freedom that excited her.

Elizabeth walked up the hill toward the workers' cottages. She passed no one in the darkness, although she could hear the faints sound of a fiddle and the raucous laughter of men and women. The smell of roasting pork filtered through the night air. Someone was celebrating something.

Elizabeth reached the yard foreman's cottage and rapped on the door with her knuckles without hesitating. Light shone through the loft window, so she knew O'Brian was still awake. When he didn't appear, she knocked again, harder this time.

After a moment she heard O'Brian's voice. "Yeah? What is it?"

Elizabeth looked both ways and crept around the side of the house to the open upstairs window. O'Brian was hanging his head out. His hair was unbound, his chest bare.

"I . . . I'm sorry for disturbing you." Elizabeth felt silly now. She didn't belong on Workers' Hill after dark. "It's all right." Holding her kerchief in place, she waved with the other hand. "It can wait until morning." The sight of his bare chest and his long, honey-colored hair was a little unnerving. "Really."

"I'll be right down," O'Brian called. Before Elizabeth could protest, he had disappeared from the window.

She walked back around to the front door, peering into the darkness. This was definitely inappropriate, talking back and forth to her foreman through his bedchamber window. But she was here now, and he was coming down. She would say her thank yous, and she'd be off. No one but she and O'Brian would ever know she'd come.

The door swung open, and O'Brian appeared in nothing but a pair of breeches. He had been in bed. He stepped out onto the dirt road in his bare feet. The moonlight shone off his golden hair.

"What can I do for you, Mistress?" He was so close that she could smell the faint scent of mint on his breath.

"I . . ." She looked down at his bare feet, then up again. "I wanted to thank you for what you did for Claire today." She fiddled with the kerchief she held with her hand. "I . . . Jessop . . . we should have thanked you when you brought her back. I don't know what we were thinking."

He looked at her with those green eyes of his, eyes that seemed to see through to her very soul. "I didn't do it for thanks," he said, his voice oddly gentle.

"I know you didn't." She couldn't keep her eyes off him. The way he looked at her made her palms grow damp and her heart flutter. She glanced down at the ground. "But I wanted to thank you anyway. And I wanted to apologize for Jessop's behavior. He—"

Elizabeth felt O'Brian's hand touch her chin, and suddenly she was looking at him. He had taken a step closer to her. Her petticoat brushed his bare feet. She could smell his clean hair, the pungent aroma of shaving soap, and a masculine scent that was his alone.

Suddenly she was dizzy. Her breath was short. She knew she had to be trembling. She knew she shouldn't be letting him touch her like this. Now he was caressing her cheek. But it was as if she were powerless to resist him. She couldn't tear her gaze from his lips, lips she had fantasized kissing.

Seven

His kiss; it was even better than she'd imagined it would be.

At first, as his mouth brushed hers, it was a gentle caress. But then the pressure of his lips against hers increased with a mounting passion they shared equally. Still holding her kerchief in place, she raised her other hand to rest it on his bare shoulder. It was like granite.

Elizabeth heard herself sigh, or was it a groan? She parted her lips to the urgency of his kiss. *Madness, this was madness.* She pulled her hand from her kerchief to snake it around his neck, to pull him closer.

The taste of him, it hadn't satisfied her curiosity at all, it had only intensified it.

He tasted of whiskey, raw masculinity, and of the forbidden. Their tongues met . . . intertwined. He made a sound in his throat she felt in his chest, pressed against her breasts.

Elizabeth didn't realize O'Brian had moved his hand until she felt the callused skin of his fingertips brush the swell of her breasts.

Heavens, her bodice. It was unhooked, her stays loosened. She wanted to pull away. This was wrong, only a husband should touch his wife this way. But his hand, touching her, stroking her, it felt so good, too good. It had been so long . . .

Elizabeth moaned as their tongues joined together, her

hips pressing against his. She could feel the bulge of his manhood stiffening against her thigh. She could feel her nipple puckering in his cupped hand. She knew what he wanted. She knew what she herself wanted.

But Elizabeth knew she couldn't do this. She was engaged to be married to Jessop. O'Brian was a married man, for heaven's sake! She had to stop him, stop herself before it got out of control.

It took every bit of inner strength Elizabeth had to pull away from him. Her breasts heaved as she brought her fingertips to her lips. "You . . . you kissed me," she whispered.

He was breathing as hard as she was. She didn't look up at him. She couldn't.

"You kissed me back," he accused with an air of amusement in his voice.

Elizabeth lifted her gaze, forcing herself to look into those haunting green eyes of his. "I . . . I don't know what to say. I don't know how this happened. I've never . . ." She looked down again, fumbling with the ends of her kerchief, trying desperately to cover her nearly exposed breasts.

Oh, god. She hadn't just let him kiss her, she'd let him touch her. She'd never allowed Jessop to touch her like that. She'd never wanted him to.

O'Brian gently pushed aside her trembling hands and gathered the two corners of her linen kerchief, covering her open bodice. "I'll not kiss and tell, if you won't," he teased softly in his rich tenor voice.

She almost smiled. But there was nothing to smile about. What she'd just done was a sin. She'd kissed a married man.

She was so confused. She could still taste his mouth on hers. She could still feel his hands on her breasts. And even now that she had her head about her, that she realized how foolish she had been to let him kiss her, she wanted him to do it again.

Elizabeth took a step back, trying to look at him without really looking at him. He was so startlingly masculine standing there bare-chested, barefooted, with his blond hair brushing his, broad shoulders. "You have to promise me you won't speak a word of this, O'Brian."

He was smiling a lazy smile. He was being so damned cocky about the whole thing.

He crossed his arms over his chest. "I said I'll not tell. You have my word."

"I've been overwrought." She gestured weakly with her hand, searching for an acceptable excuse. "There's been a great deal on my mind. I—" Elizabeth's head snapped up at the sound of the front door behind him opening. God, there was someone in his house! Someone who could have seen them through the window!

A young woman with a head full of tangled red curls appeared in the doorway. She was wearing nothing but a thin cotton counterpane wrapped around her slim, obviously naked form. She couldn't have been more than nineteen or twenty. And she was pretty, very pretty.

"What are you doing chitchatting, Paddy?" the woman asked in a sultry voice. She stroked his muscular arm, the same arm Elizabeth had touched only a moment before. "I thought you said you'd only be a minute." Spotting Elizabeth, the young girl bobbed her head respectfully. "Evenin', Mistress." She turned back to O'Brian. "You comin', luv? I told ye I can't stay long. I got milkin' in the mornin'."

Elizabeth was mortified. Beyond mortified. She had practically thrown herself at this man, a yard foreman, and he . . . he had been upstairs with this little slut. Elizabeth had kissed his mouth, the same mouth that had just kissed the lightskirt's.

Elizabeth took a step back, almost tripping. O'Brian's

hand shot out to catch her, but she jerked from his reach. She'd never been so embarrassed in her life. "I . . . we . . . we'll finish this discussion in the morning, Mr. O'Brian," she managed woodenly.

"Wait. Liz!"

Elizabeth heard him call her name, but she had already turned around. She had already started down the lane at as quick a pace as possible without actually running.

Elizabeth crept back into her house and slipped upstairs into her bedchamber without being seen. Once inside her room, she threw the door shut and leaned back against it, her entire body trembling.

She could still taste O'Brian's mouth on hers. Her breasts still tingled from the touch of his rough-skinned hands. She could still feel the heat of his passionate kiss.

God in heaven, what had possessed her to go down to his cottage in the middle of the night? Elizabeth tore off her clothes, stepped over two sleeping hounds, and crawled into bed without bothering to find a sleeping gown. She was too hot for clothes anyway.

Elizabeth just couldn't imagine why she had let O'Brian kiss her, why she'd kissed him back like some wanton slut, like the chippy had done only moments before, no doubt. Damned redhead. She'd never liked redheads.

Elizabeth had come to her marriage bed chaste. She had never been a woman free with her affections. How could she have lost her head like that? What was it about O'Brian that rendered her so senseless?

She rolled over in her bed, pounding her pillow with her fist, trying to make herself more comfortable. The strain of the last year was suddenly hitting her. That was it; that was why she had behaved so irrationally tonight. She'd never really had time to grieve. Paul's death, rebuilding the powder mill, her engagement to Jessop, hiring O'Brian, suddenly it was all crashing down on her. It was making her crazy.

So O'Brian wasn't really the problem, she rationalized. He was just a symptom of her problem. She was working too hard, that was all. She wasn't getting enough sleep.

Elizabeth tried to close her eyes, but when she did, she saw the red-haired whore. She saw O'Brian's grinning face. "Son of a bitch," she murmured, staring at the ceiling above her. The man was married. He had a wife and children, and here he was lying with a young woman barely past her first bleeding. He was cheating on his wife!

. . . And Elizabeth had helped him. She had gone to his house knowing it was inappropriate. She had known he was going to kiss her. It had been coming for days. Hell, she'd gone there knowing somewhere in the back of her mind that she was going to kiss him.

Elizabeth closed her eyes again. What was done, was done. She'd sweep up the spilt powder, and she'd go on with her life. She would tell Jessop it was time they set a definite date for their wedding. She'd been single too long. Women had natural sexual desires, just like men. She'd just been too long without a husband. That was all.

As for Mr. O'Brian, Elizabeth decided she'd keep him on as her yard foreman. She was smart enough to know she needed him, if her business was to prosper. This week, though, she'd speak to him about bringing his family. That would certainly end his visits with the tart.

As for her own little indiscretion, Elizabeth decided she'd forget about it, and so would O'Brian, if he wished to remain yard foreman of Lawrence Mills or any other powder mill in the colonies.

Several evenings later, just as Elizabeth was closing her ledger, she heard the sound of O'Brian's voice in the front office. She glanced at the case clock on the shelf over her desk. It was nearly eight. Jessop was expecting her at nine for a late dinner.

She glanced at the doorway. She could hear O'Brian and her clerk laughing about something. Then she heard the sound of footsteps coming down the hallway toward her private office.

Lacy and Freckles both lifted their heads and growled deep in their throats.

O'Brian stuck his head through the doorway. "Got a minute?"

Elizabeth looked at the case clock again. "Just a minute."

"I can come back tomorrow."

"No." Elizabeth felt awkward. This was the first time they'd spoken privately since they'd kissed. "No, it's all right. Just come in."

"Want me to tell Noah he can go, or do you still need him?"

Elizabeth hated O'Brian for being so comfortable with her, with what he had done. Of course, he was probably used to this, considering his popularity among women. Elizabeth had just heard through Johnny Bennett that two nights ago there had nearly been a brawl between O'Brian and a man from Tanner's flour mill. Apparently the man had accused O'Brian of sleeping with his wife. Mr. O'Brian was a busy man.

Elizabeth dropped her quill onto the desk. She was hesitant to let Noah go. She didn't know that she trusted herself to be alone with O'Brian. She feared she might kiss him again, that or shoot the bastard. Maybe she'd kiss him and then shoot him . . .

"You're dismissed, Noah," Elizabeth leaned back and called through the dim hallway. "I'll see you in the morning."

"Aye."

Elizabeth heard Noah slide off his stool, take his hat from the pegboard, and go out the office door. Now she was alone with O'Brian. Now she'd have to talk to him. She crossed her arms over her chest. "You needed to see me, Mr. O'Brian?"

He stepped into the light of the room. She noticed for the first time that he was freshly shaven. His blond whiskers were gone.

Realizing she had noticed, he stroked his bare chin. "Too hot for this tropical climate of yours. Makes me look more respectable anyway, don't you think?"

She refused to be drawn in by his charms. "I really only have a minute, O'Brian. Jessop's expecting me."

He frowned at the mention of Jessop's name. "I had some drawings for you to take a look at. Some ideas as to how we could speed up the process between the refinery and the magazine." He shrugged his shoulders, draped by a clean muslin shirt, minus the stock. At least he'd had the decency to wear a shirt. "But I can come back tomorrow, if you'd like. This can wait."

"No. Bring them here." She held up her hand, turning her back to him to face her desk.

He slipped the papers into her hand. She unrolled the drawings, flattening them on the desk. O'Brian remained directly behind her stool. He wasn't touching her, but she could feel the heat of his body so close to hers. He was so close that she could smell his shaving soap. His hair was still damp. He'd apparently bathed before calling on her.

He leaned over her, pointing to the first drawing. "You see, deliver the sulfur and the saltpeter here, instead of here. It'll take fewer men to move it into the refinery. They can do it by cart rather than wagon. Use the wagons here to move the barrels from the cooper's shop down to the packing house."

Elizabeth glanced over her shoulder at him, her face stoic. "What cooper?"

"That was one of the other things I wanted to talk to you about."

Elizabeth turned on the stool to face him. "I can't afford to pay a cooper on the premises."

"You can't afford not to, Liz." O'Brian bumped into one of her dogs with the heel of his boot, and the dog gave a yelp. He glared at the hound, moving away. "You see, the way I figure it, we're spending too much money buying the barrels from Wilmington and then having to transport them here. We need to find a cooper, put him up in a cottage, and build a shop for him."

"I don't have any empty cottages."

"We'll build one."

"O'Brian—"

He lifted his hand. "Think about it, Liz. The more self-sufficient you are, the better off you'll be if this war of yours comes along."

"I don't know." She turned back to the sketches. They were very good. Better than Elizabeth could ever have drawn. And they were well-thought through. She hated to admit it, but O'Brian was more than fulfilling his contract with her. He wasn't just doing his job, directing the day-to-day tasks; he was trying to improve the business. She began to roll up the drawings. "I really need to go now. I'll look at these tomorrow."

"Wait. There's one more thing." He came across the room to lean over her. "This," he went on, pulling a sheet of paper from the bottom of the stack, "this is a picture of what the yard looked like before the explosion. These dark lines represent the fire damage." He turned his head so that his face was only inches from hers. "Liz, you notice anything wrong here?"

She stared at the drawing. "The explosions shouldn't have blown like this," she said softly.

"Aye."

With the sheet of paper in her hand and O'Brian so close, Elizabeth suddenly felt very vulnerable. It wasn't a comfortable feeling. She had grown used to being in control. She liked being in control. But she wasn't in control of whatever this electricity was between her and her foreman. And she hadn't been in control the night her husband had died.

"How . . . how could this have happened?" she questioned, unable to tear her gaze from the charcoal smudges that represented the fiery explosions.

"You tell me . . ."

There was almost a hint of accusation in his voice.

She looked at him. "You don't think I—"

"I don't know what happened down there, Liz, but I'm going to figure it out."

Her gaze went back to the sketch. She kept her tone matter-of-fact, for fear she might do something stupid, like begin to cry. "Jessop said dwelling on the explosion would do me no good. He said it didn't matter how it happened. Sometimes there is no explanation . . ." She let her voice fade.

"There's always an explanation. It just depends how deep a man's willing to dig. I once saw four wagons of powder drawn by a dozen horses blow on a Paris street. They said there was no explanation," he lifted a finger, winking at her, "but I figured it out. One of the horse's hooves in the front wagon struck a stone on the street, the metal from his shoe threw a spark, lit some powder that had been leaking from a keg, sprinkling the ground as the horses went down the street."

"Blew them all up?" Elizabeth asked in morbid fascination.

"Straight to heaven or hell, depending on the man or horse."

Elizabeth smiled at his analogy. The man might be a

womanizer, but he had a wit. She began to roll up the drawings again. "I'd appreciate it if you'd pass on any information you find concerning my husband's death, O'Brian."

Her back was to him. She knew he was looking at her. The room suddenly seemed too small, too dimly lit. The night sounds of the summer drifted through the window with the warm, humid breeze. She heard the croak of the peepers, the steady chirp of the crickets.

"Look, Liz, about the other night."

The sound of his voice startled her. She didn't want to talk about it. Not to him. Not with herself.

"Forget it, O'Brian." She rose to face him. She was no coward. "Just forget it ever happened."

"I would if I could, Lizzy, but I can't. I can't shut my eyes without seeing your face. I keep touching my lips to feel yours on mine."

What a sweet talker. He'd even touched his lips when he'd spoken. The little redhead might have fallen for it, but Elizabeth wouldn't.

"It was a mistake, O'Brian," she said sternly. She made herself look him in the, eye. He had to understand that she was serious about this. "I didn't mean for it to happen." She looked away. "Jessop and I will be announcing our engagement at a party here the last Saturday of the month."

"You going to marry that jackass? He'll never make you happy, Lizzy. He hasn't got it in him."

"And who are you to speak of making women happy?" she flared, turning on him. Lacy lifted her head at the sound of her owner's voice. "You, sir, have a wife and children, and there you are spending your coin on whores!"

O'Brian looked like he wanted to say something. He opened his mouth, then closed it. She supposed he realized there was nothing to say.

"I want you to send for your family, O'Brian," she went on in her best mistress's voice. "I want a family man for my yard foreman. If you haven't the necessary coin, see Noah. I'll advance you the money." She reached for her bonnet. "Now, if you wouldn't mind, I need to lock up. I'm going to be late for supper."

O'Brian stared at Elizabeth for a moment, wondering if this could possibly be the same woman who kissed him there on his doorstep the other night. That woman, Lizzy, had had more warmth, more passion in her kiss than he'd experienced in a lifetime of whores and other men's wives.

But this woman standing here, this woman who'd barely reacted when he'd told her he suspected her husband had been murdered, was as icy and as unfeeling as a February wind.

Face it, O'Brian, he told himself as he passed her and her damned dogs in the dark hallway, *Mistress Elizabeth Lawrence is a cold, uncaring English bitch.*

And what the hell was that crap all about? I see your face when I close my eyes? he chastised himself silently as he went down the steps. *What's the basic rule?* his mind shouted. *Never tell a woman what you feel, about her, about anything. She'll only laugh in your face. She'll make you regret the day you were born.*

O'Brian turned onto the dirt road. He'd intended, after completing his business at the office, to go by the Sow's Ear and bring Red home with him, but the mistress had left a sour taste for women in his mouth. He walked off into the darkness toward the workers' cottages, whistling an old Irish tune. All he wanted now was a nip of whiskey and a blessed empty bed.

Eight

Elizabeth smiled, accepting words of congratulations from a thin, middle-aged woman with a pinched face like a rabbit and a tower of unnaturally straw-colored hair.

"What a perfect match," she squeaked. "I know you two will have many sons together."

"Cora Maybell, Martin's wife," Jessop whispered in Elizabeth's ear.

"Thank you so much, Cora," Elizabeth said, feeling like her face was frozen in a gracious smile.

The rabbit moved on.

Elizabeth shifted her weight impatiently. She hated parties. She hated attending parties. She hated giving them. All these pointless conversations. All the gossip. All she could think of was how high the pile of paperwork on her desk was.

Besides, she was uncomfortable. Her new heeled slippers had rubbed raw blisters on both her feet the first hour of the engagement party. The bodice of her rose-colored, floral silk robe *à l'anglaise* was so tight it was cutting off her breath.

Elizabeth hadn't particularly liked the gown to begin with. She preferred greens and blues to pinks and reds, but Jessop had commissioned the gown for their betrothal party. He'd ordered the material from France and hired a French mantuamaker from Philadelphia to sew the gown. After the amount of money he'd spent on it,

Elizabeth couldn't very well have told him that she didn't like it. She'd tried to get the mantuamaker back to make a few alterations, but she hadn't been able to return in time, she was in such demand. So Elizabeth was now the one sewn inside the ill-fitting gown, and Jessop was the one enjoying how tiny-waisted his betrothed was.

Another couple Elizabeth didn't know passed through the receiving line. She nodded, she smiled, she laughed at the husband's jest just like a proper hostess should. She even held onto Jessop's arm and proudly displayed the band of gold and rubies she wore on her middle finger.

Jessop was dressed in the height of fashion in breeches, a shirtwaist, and a waistcoat in the same rose-colored silk as her gown. His clocked stockings were pale pink, and his heeled shoes dyed rose. His outfit had been as costly as her gown. Frankly, Elizabeth didn't care for it. Jessop looked like a rose-colored peacock to her.

A lull in the line of guests came and Jessop leaned to brush his lips across her cheek. "You look lovely tonight, my dearest. As lovely as I believe I've ever seen you. I much prefer this to those cotton sacks and work boots you've taken to wearing."

She lifted her lashes to look at him. "Was that a compliment? I couldn't tell."

He laughed. She didn't.

He kissed her again. "I was only saying that you're so beautiful, I don't understand why you want to cover yourself in those drab, shapeless garments."

"It's hot this time of year, Jessop. It's hot in the office." She lifted her petticoats. "All this material is stifling."

"Sister always manages to look lovely, despite the heat." He was smiling. Another well-wisher was approaching.

"The mill is dirty, Jessop," she whispered, nodding to the advancing couple. "I wouldn't want to spoil a good gown with coal dust."

"John, dear Agnes, how good to see you again." Jes-

sop extended his arm past Elizabeth to take dear Agnes's
chubby hand. "How is your gout? I understand you were
down again with it only last week."

Elizabeth exhaled softly, only half-listening to the conversation that commenced. She had no interest in Agnes's
gout, or in John's latest shipment of exorbitantly priced
goods from England.

What's wrong with me? Elizabeth wondered. Why was
she quarreling with Jessop tonight of all nights? She
liked him, she truly did. He was a perfect match for her.
They were equally educated, both business-minded. They
would get along well in the years to come. What more
could a woman ask for in a marriage?

The word *love* crept into her mind. She didn't know
where it came from. She couldn't recall ever having
thought about it before. Love was such an unrealistic
word. It came out of books, out of fairy tales. It wasn't
present in the marriages she knew of, nor was it necessary for a husband and wife to make a good marriage.
Her own parents had certainly never loved each other,
and they'd gotten along just fine all those years before
her mother's death. They'd produced a houseful of
healthy children and increased their wealth two-fold in
twenty-five years. Both had been content.

The question was, just because her parents had believed in marriages of comfortable convenience, did that
mean that *all* marriages had to be that way? Was contentment all Elizabeth wanted out of life? She thought
about Samson and Ngozi, and how much they appeared
to be in love with each other. She thought about how
happy they were together; how Ngozi's face lit up when
Samson approached her. Elizabeth couldn't honestly say
that either of her parents had ever made the other happy.

Elizabeth glanced at Jessop. Would he make her happy?

She groaned. What was wrong with her? Why did she
suddenly feel the need to reevaluate her thoughts on mar-

riage? Was it just a bride-to-be's nervous jitters? She'd certainly had them before wedding Paul.

Jessop offered Elizabeth a glass of wine, and she accepted it. It was so hot in the parlor. Even this late in the evening, even with all the windows open, the entire house was too warm. Between her stays and the heat, she could barely breathe.

Elizabeth accepted the congratulations of several more guests and drank the bubbly French wine Jessop had ordered especially for the occasion. By the time she had reached the bottom of the glass, she wondered if she'd made an error in judgment. She hadn't eaten all day. She'd been too busy with the party preparations, and now she was feeling light-headed.

Jessop leaned to speak in her ear, pointing to a table weighted down with sumptuous foods. "The breads haven't been replenished, and the ham is nearly gone. What are those women in your kitchen doing? I haven't seen a maid out here in ten minutes."

"I'll go see what the trouble is."

"I can do it, dear," he offered.

"No. No, that's all right, Jessop." She pushed her empty glass into his hand. "I could use a breath of air, anyway."

He smiled a genuine smile. "Let me know if you need my help. I'm not above carrying a tray from the kitchen to the house myself. I want everything to be right for you this evening, Liz."

Elizabeth lifted her petticoats, excusing herself as she made her way through the crowded parlor, smiling and nodding to her guests. Jessop was such a kind man. He really did care for her. She was just being silly with this thought of love. She couldn't say she had ever loved Paul and yet look how good their marriage had been. Look how much she'd missed him when he'd died. Paul Lawrence had been a good husband, she told herself firmly. Jessop Lawrence would be, too.

Elizabeth went down the hall and out the door through the breezeway to the summer kitchen. The night air, cooler than the air inside the house, was refreshing. The breeze was so invigorating that she would have liked to have lingered outside for a moment or two, but, of course, she couldn't. She had guests to attend to, and tonight she belonged at Jessop's side as the hostess he wanted her to be.

Elizabeth heard the sound of feminine laughter even before she reached the kitchen. Inside the door, Cook had her back to her, rolling a pastry. The laughter was coming from the rear of the kitchen, but she couldn't see the source from where she stood. "Margaret, we've need of more bread for our guests. Ham, too."

The cook glanced over her shoulder, up to her elbows of puffs of flour. "It's those girls, Mistress. I can't do a thing with 'em. I tell 'em to get off their bottoms, and all they do is flutter they's lashes and twitter between themselves like a pile of crickets." She punched the dough out with a tin cutter as she spoke. "I cook, but I don't serve." She turned back to her pastry. "I'm sorry, I am, but a Cook don't serve, Mistress. She just don't."

Elizabeth massaged her temples. It was even hotter in the kitchen than it had been in the house. The pungent smell of roasting duck mixed with the sweet smell of oranges and baking butter cakes was making her nauseous. *I shouldn't have had the wine,* she thought as she walked around the double pie safe blocking her view of the giggling servants.

Elizabeth came to a halt at the sight of what was keeping the girls from their work. It was O'Brian!

Why did that surprise her?

There her yard foreman was, perched on a stool pulled up to a work table eating half an apple plum pie straight from the pie pan and washing it down with a jug of her sweet cider.

At the sight of their mistress, the girls went quiet. Two of them scooped up loaded trays of food and hustled past Elizabeth with a guilty nod. The other two began to peel fresh peaches furiously.

O'Brian stuffed a piece of pie into his mouth. "Evenin', Liz. Good pie."

"What are you doing here?"

He gave her one of those smiles of his and went right on eating. "Meg invited me in for a piece of pie." He pointed in the direction the servants had just gone. "You know Meg. The redhead."

Meg was a redhead. She was also engaged to be married to the young man in charge of the Lawrence Mills stable.

"O'Brian, this is my betrothal party. I need those girls to be in the house serving my guests, not in here serving you."

He picked up a piece of flaky crust and popped it into his mouth. "I apologize. I didn't mean to be a distraction. The pie just sounded good."

Elizabeth felt light-headed. She didn't have the time or the energy to deal with O'Brian right now. Not here. She turned away.

"Where are you going?" he called after her.

"Outside."

Elizabeth pushed out the back door into the kitchen's small herb and vegetable garden. The garden was dark except for the light that poured out the kitchen windows. She tried to take a deep breath, hoping the cooler air would clear her head.

"Liz?"

At the sound of O'Brian's voice, she turned, swaying a little.

"You all right?"

She brushed her palm over the flat bodice of her gown. "I'm fine," she said weakly.

He came down the brick walk toward her. He was dressed in a pair of simple broadcloth breeches and a muslin shirt that hugged his muscular upper body. After spending an evening in a room full of peacocks, his dress was as refreshing to her as the night air.

"Liz?"

She looked up. "I'm fine. Really. Just too much wine, my damned dress is too tight," her voice quivered as if she were going to cry, "and my heels have blisters on them from these blessed shoes."

"Christ, damned women's fashions." He grabbed her hand, leading her to a small gardener's bench. "Sit down before you fall over. Did you eat today?"

She shook her head as she sat. It felt so good to be off her feet. "No." She touched her forehead trying to recall. "I don't know. A pastry this morning. I had a taste of the ham at noonday."

He crouched in front of her and reached under her petticoats, grasping her ankle.

"O'Brian!"

"Hell, it's just a foot, it's not your virtue, Liz. Let me see how bad the blisters are."

She wanted to protest, but he was already slipping the shoes off her feet. The release of the pressure felt so good that she sighed aloud.

"Better?" He rubbed her foot, kneading the ball with steady pressure.

"Better," she sighed. It felt glorious.

He massaged each toe between his thumb and forefinger. "You're bleeding through your stocking, but just a little. Want me to take it off?"

"No," she managed.

What he was doing to her, the steady pressure of his hands on her aching foot was extraordinary. She sighed again as he removed the other high-heeled slipper and began to work her foot between his large, steady hands.

"You should have worn your boots. Boots always fit right."

"Oh, certainly." She leaned back a little, letting the waves of pleasure wash over her. "That would certainly be appropriate with watered silk and French ruffles."

He looked at her, raising an eyebrow in obvious response to the gown.

"Don't like it, huh?"

He shook his head.

"Ugly, isn't it?"

"Not your color. You look like a fading rose instead of a blooming one."

She laughed. It felt good to release the tension of the day. O'Brian irritated her to no end, but she was comfortable with him. Perhaps it was because of the long days they spent together in the powder yard, in the office. There was always something about familiarity that put Elizabeth at ease. The sad truth of the matter was that she was more comfortable with her workers than men and women of her own station. The longer she worked in the powder mill, the truer the fact became.

O'Brian lowered her foot. "Feel better?"

"Much."

"Want me to get you something to eat? I know where I can snitch a great piece of pie."

She laughed. "Not this minute. I'll have something when I go back into the house."

He sat down beside her. "So, where are your companions?"

She looked at him inquisitively.

"The dogs."

"Oh." She laughed. "Upstairs, locked in my bedchamber. They like to nip from the dinner table. I thought it inappropriate to invite them."

"Ah, hell, I don't know why, Liz. Their manners are probably as good, maybe better than some of your guests'."

She didn't know why she chuckled. He was insulting Jessop's friends, but it was funny, and it was sadly true. She put her face in her hands, still laughing. "I don't know what I'm doing here with my shoes off. I have to get back to my guests."

"No, you don't."

She reached for her shoes. "Yes, I do. My guests— Jessop will be looking for me."

"Having a good time, then?"

She glanced at him. He knew her so well. Why? How had this relationship of theirs developed so quickly, so easily to this point?

He was looking at her, his brow lifted. He was waiting for an answer.

She frowned, conceding. "No."

"Why not?"

"None of your damned concern," she snapped, thrusting her foot into her shoe.

"Seems to me, a woman ought to be enjoying her betrothal party."

She reached for her other shoe with her foot, just out of reach. "Well, it seems to me that a married man ought not to be sitting in my kitchen flirting with my serving girls, who are supposed to be working for their pay."

"I wasn't flirting. I was eating pie." He kicked her other shoe toward her with the toe of his boot.

"You were flirting. You flirt with every woman you meet. I saw you yesterday with Mrs. Morris. She was laughing like a girl on her first May Day. By the king's cod, O'Brian, the woman is old enough to be your great grandmother. Admit it." She stood carefully in her heeled slippers. "You flirt with every woman you encounter. Old, young, handsome, ugly."

He stood up, facing her. "I don't flirt with you," he said.

Elizabeth couldn't tell by the tone of his voice what he meant. Was he teasing her? She swayed a little on her too tight shoes, and instinctively put her hand out to his chest to catch herself.

Their gazes met and all she could think of was, *Hell, I've done it again. I've made myself vulnerable again when I swore I wouldn't.*

She wanted to kiss his mouth. He was so close. His chest felt rock hard beneath her hand as he held his breath. She swayed toward him, her eyes drifting shut. It was as if she was under a magical spell, entranced by the depth of his green eyes and the sensual shape of his lips. She didn't like O'Brian much, but there was no denial of this sexual attraction to him. Even before his mouth touched hers, she was taking his hand and lifting it to her breast.

But his lips didn't touch hers. He whispered her name, "Ah, Liz . . ." He kissed the tip of her nose, the dimple at her chin. His warm mouth pressed against the pulse of her throat, sending tremors of excitement through her trembling body.

O'Brian cupped his hand beneath her breast, brushing his thumb against her hardening nipple. All the material of her gown and shift seemed not to be a deterrent, but instead heightened the pleasure of his touch.

"I can't do this," she whispered. But even as she spoke she was running her hand up the corded muscles of arm, to his broad shoulder, around his neck. She pulled herself closer to him, molding her soft body against his rock solid frame.

"Kiss me," she whispered. "Kiss me, O'Brian."

When he brought his mouth down on hers, there was nothing gentle about his kiss. His mouth met hers, hard and unyielding as he thrust his tongue between her lips, steadying her with his hand securely in the small of her back.

Elizabeth had never been kissed like this before. Not by Jessop, not by Paul, not by the few beaus she'd had back in England. O'Brian's kiss was full of power, demanding her response.

Elizabeth could feel she was losing herself to O'Brian and his passion. She couldn't think. She couldn't reason. He held such control over her with the stroke of his hand, with his brutal lips, that this almost made sense, the two of them here in the garden groping like desperate lovers.

"Elizabeth! Elizabeth!"

The sound of Jessop's voice hit Elizabeth like a bucket of icy river water. When she took a step back from O'Brian, he released her so suddenly that she almost fell in her too tight slippers.

"Elizabeth, where the hell are you?"

Elizabeth brushed her mouth with the back of her hand as if she couldn't wipe away her foreman's touch. "H . . . here, Jessop," she called, her voice surprisingly strong.

O'Brian just stood there, facing her, staring at her, his chest heaving. Elizabeth struggled to catch her breath as she caught sight of Jessop coming through the back kitchen door.

"What are you doing out here?"

She pressed her hand to her stomacher, hoping to calm her pounding heart. This was foolishness. Madness. She'd almost been caught! "I . . . I came out for a breath of air, because I felt faint."

Jessop brushed past O'Brian, taking Elizabeth's arm and jerking her. He didn't pull her arm that hard, but it was enough to make O'Brian flinch.

"Where the hell did he come from?" Jessop demanded.

O'Brian looked like he was going to pounce on Jessop at any second.

"This doesn't appear right, Elizabeth," Jessop went on.

"Not right at all. I've spoken to you on the matter several times now. What will our guests think with you out here alone with this Irishman?" He said the word as if it were distasteful.

"They'll think I came out for a breath of air, and my foreman was kind enough to check on me," she snapped back, irritated by Jessop's entire attitude. He hadn't said that he cared what she was doing. All that seemed to matter to him was what his guests thought, and that made Elizabeth angry. Would he be jealous if he'd known she'd kissed O'Brian, or would he simply be concerned with who knew about it? The thought alarmed her.

"You'd best come inside," Jessop said tersely, pulling her arm roughly again. "And you," he glanced at O'Brian, "had best get back to Worker's Hill. You don't belong creeping about the house at this time of night."

Elizabeth didn't like the expression on O'Brian's face. He suddenly appeared to be a man looking for a fight.

Good god, not here, was all Elizabeth could think of. "J . . . Jessop's right, O'Brian. You'd best be returning to your cottage. I thank you for your assistance."

"You shouldn't let him talk to you that way," O'Brian said, his voice agitated. "Men shouldn't talk to women like that."

"I'll be fine. Just go." She knew O'Brian was a hothead. All she could think of was that he would hit Jessop, and Jessop would call the High Sheriff. Elizabeth didn't want her yard foreman in jail. She needed him here. "Just go now," she repeated.

O'Brian hesitated for a moment, then stalked out through the rear of the garden into the darkness.

"Let's go," Jessop demanded. "Before the others miss us."

Elizabeth yanked her arm from Jessop's grasp. "I don't know what's gotten into you lately, but there are times when I don't like you much." She looked him eye to eye. "I just hope this wasn't a mistake."

His face suddenly softened. "Oh, Liz, don't say that. You mean the world to me."

"I don't want you touching me like that."

"Like what?"

"You pulled on my arm hard, Jessop. Too hard."

"I didn't mean to. I swear I didn't. I was worried about you. I was afraid you were ill, and here you were outside with *him*. You need to be more careful about O'Brian, dear. I've heard some nasty, disturbing rumors."

Probably all true, she thought. "Well, I'm sorry I upset you. But I'm telling you, Jessop. I'll not be physically abused. Not by any man."

He leaned to kiss her, but she turned her face just in time so that he missed her lips and kissed her cheek instead. "I'm sorry," he whispered. "I'll make it up to you. I swear it. Now, no more talk of calling off our wedding," he whispered in her ear. "I can't live without you, Liz. I won't."

"Let's go inside and see to our guests." Elizabeth walked ahead of Jessop, and he hurried to catch up.

Elizabeth's head was clear now. The dizziness was gone. Now she was left only with the weight of her guilt and the tremble deep in the pit of her stomach of unfulfilled desire.

Nine

Elizabeth leaned over the wooden rail to watch the huge waterwheel turn. The river water roared as it poured down from the overshot waterwheel, producing up to sixty percent more power than the flour mill downriver. The power of the rushing water was turning the millstone inside the wheelmill's granite-walled building, which, in turn, pulverized the charcoal and sulfur needed to make the black powder.

"It's not as if he struck me," Elizabeth said to O'Brian, really not wanting to be drawn into this conversation. The spray from the water pouring off the waterwheel was dampening the brocaded corset she wore over her new blue chemise, but she didn't care. There was no one at the mills to see her. Jessop had gone to Wilmington and wouldn't be home until tomorrow. Claire, who was staying with Elizabeth while he was gone, was taking a nap, as she often did in the heat of midday.

"I don't care whether he hit you or not." O'Brian leaned over the wooden fence, his elbow brushing hers. "A man who will jerk a woman like I saw him jerk you the other night would strike you just as easily."

"That's ridiculous." She turned away from the waterwheel and started up the hill, her chintz cotton petticoat in a blue print bunched in her hands. Elizabeth's hounds ran in circles around her and her foreman, as they made their way up the road. "He was simply concerned for my welfare. He apologized profusely and swore it wouldn't happen again."

"I'm sure he did." O'Brian shook his head. "I've seen this before, Liz, home in Ireland. The first few times it's just an isolated incident—he gets a little heavy-handed. Next thing you know, ye've got a black eye and broken bones."

She cut her eyes at him, her view shaded by the flat brim of her woven horsehair hat. The keys she wore at her waist jingled as she walked, her own stride matching his. "This discussion is pointless. Jessop would never hurt me. Besides, this is my personal business, and we agreed you would stay out of my personal business, *as I would try and stay out of yours,*" she added tartly.

"I just don't want to see you get hurt, Liz. He lays a hand on you, and I swear by the Virgin, I'll make him wish he hadn't."

She looked around, fearing one of the workers passing them on the dirt road might have overheard them. O'Brian was speaking too personally with her. After what happened the other night at her betrothal party, she realized their entire relationship was getting too personal. They were getting to know each other too well. That was what was leading them both astray.

"Tell me about what you've learned concerning the explosion last year," she said, changing the subject. "Anything new?"

"With the new buildings you've put up, the rebuilding, and the time that's passed, it hasn't been easy. I have to rely on what the workers can tell me. The trouble is, everyone remembers an incident differently. One remembers two distinctly separate explosions, another remembers only one big bang. Some say the first explosion started in the grain mill, others, the packhouse. And everyone has their own personal opinion on what started it, and why they're right and the man beside them is wrong." He shrugged. "It's just human nature."

"I told you what I knew. Not that I was much help. There was so much confusion. I never even heard Paul leave our bedchamber that night." She chewed on her bottom lip. "Actually, I never figured out what he was doing in the packhouse. Jessop guessed he'd been screening some powder to be packed and sent to the magazine the following morning. He had a shipment due to go out, and they were behind on production."

"Did you happen to salvage anything from the explosion in the packhouse?" They went up the granite steps toward her office, while the hounds raced through the greenbriars in the woods beside them.

"Nothing. I had the packhouse leveled and rebuilt with a slate roof this time. There was nothing left to salvage."

"Damn. I wish I could have seen the buildings after the explosion. Gunpowder, she always leaves a telltale pattern." He tugged at his neat queue. "I wish I knew how many separate explosions there were." He narrowed his eyes in thought. "You certain there's nothing left from the packhouse?"

"Nope. Not a thing." Then Elizabeth remembered the boot. *What a gruesome thing to save,* she thought. O'Brian wouldn't understand. But if it would help in the investigation . . . She glanced up at him. "Wait. There was one thing."

He opened the office door for her. "What?"

"Afternoon, Noah." She nodded to her clerk perched on his stool.

Noah nodded. "Afternoon, Mistress. Miss Claire says she has a drink ready for you on the front porch. She's been waiting a good piece, ma'am."

Elizabeth sighed. Her sister-in-law was supposed to be napping. She didn't have time for Claire today, but she knew she'd have to make the time. It seemed that when Claire felt the most isolated, that was when her illness became the most pronounced. "Come into my office, and I'll show you what I have," she told O'Brian quietly. "Then I have to go up to the house."

Inside her office, she pointed to the door. "Close it."

He did as she bid, leaving the two dogs in the front with the clerk. One of the hounds began to whine and scratch at the door, but he ignored it.

Elizabeth tugged her hat off, stalling for time by adjusting the small lace cap she wore on the back of her head. She'd not shared what was in the trunk with anyone. She wasn't certain she was ready to. Especially with O'Brian. But she wanted to know what had happened to Paul. If there was something that could have been done to prevent the explosion, she had to know. It was the only way she could protect the mills from another disaster, one that could be far worse, with more lives lost.

"It's in the trunk." She pointed beneath her desk. "I didn't tell Jessop I saved it. He wouldn't have understood."

O'Brian appeared confused, but he didn't say anything as he walked across the office and reached beneath the desk. That was something she liked about his character; the man was patient. He knew when to speak and when not to.

Elizabeth watched from the far side of the room as he lifted the lid. The smell of the acrid gunpowder and bitter smoke filled her nostrils, and for a moment she heard the sounds of the explosions in her head. For an instant she was gripped with the same fear she had felt that night.

"A boot?" He held Paul's boot in his hand, facing her, still down on one knee.

She nodded, barely trusting herself to speak. "It . . . it was my husband's."

He stood slowly, turning the leather boot in his hands. "I don't mean to make this any worse for you than it has to be, but . . ." he sighed. "But, Liz, the men told me his body—"

"There wasn't anything left of him," she finished for him, trying to remain detached from that horrible night. "Just pieces. I understand that's often what happens in an explosion of that magnitude. We only knew it was Paul because he was missing, that and we found a few bits of clothing. I found the boot up in the woods days later, a good hundred yards from the packhouse."

O'Brian was studying the sole of the boot intently. He swore.

"What is it?" she asked. "Did you find something?"

He turned the boot to show her the sole. "Notice anything odd?" His voice was strangely terse.

She came to him, staring at the boot. "No. It was new at the time. Paul had had the boots sewn for him in Philadelphia, just to wear down at the mills."

"Precisely."

She glanced at O'Brian's handsome face. "I don't understand."

He tapped the sole of the boot halfway between the toe and the heel. "See that?"

She squinted. At first she saw nothing, but then, a glimmer of light bounced off the sole. "A nail?" she whispered. "It couldn't be a nail. Shoes with nails aren't permitted in the yards. It's too easy to strike a spark."

"Why didn't you notice it before?"

"Why didn't I notice that tiny nail?" she asked indignantly. "Do you hear yourself! My husband was dead. Blown to bloody bits. And you ask me why I didn't notice a damned nail in the only thing I had left of him!"

"A person with any black powder experience would have noticed it in a second."

She dropped her hands to her hips. "Well, I didn't have any damned experience at the time," she shouted angrily. "I'd only been here a few weeks!"

He came toward her. "Where did it come from, Liz?"

"How would I know? Maybe Paul put it there."

"A man who has boots sewn for him in Philadelphia so that he's certain there's no metal in the construction doesn't add a nail to the sole, Liz."

"I can't believe Paul could have caused the explosion himself," she murmured. "One lousy, stinking nail."

"This boot may well have done it, the question is, was your husband responsible, or was it someone else?"

She looked up. He was standing only a few feet from her. The question was directed toward her. He expected an answer.

"You sound like you're inferring *I* could have had something to do with this."

"See, that's the difference between men and women. Women infer, they interpret every word they hear. Men just say what they mean." He tossed the boot back into the open trunk. "I don't know who did this, but I can tell you, I'm going to find out."

Elizabeth walked to the desk to close the trunk, trying to think of someone who would have done this to Paul. He had no enemies. Everyone liked him down at the mills. She pushed the small trunk back under her desk. "Could Paul have stepped on the nail accidentally somewhere, and carried it on his boot?"

"Not that nail. Did you see the way it was driven in? It was put there on purpose, all right."

Elizabeth leaned against her mahogany desk, sitting on the corner. She could hear Lacy whining at the door to get in. "I don't know what to say, O'Brian. I'm shocked. I never really thought anyone was responsible for the explosion. I just wanted to know so it wouldn't happen again." She looked at him. "You really think someone killed Paul?"

"I don't know."

She followed him with her gaze as he walked to the window. "I didn't do it," she said after a long moment of silence.

"I didn't say you did." He leaned on the sill with his elbows.

"But you thought it. I was the one who gained something by his death. I inherited the mills, the land, what little money there was."

"You also got yourself a new husband-to-be in a rather short period of time."

"I know you're not suggesting there was anything between Jessop and me before Paul's death," she flared, coming away from the desk.

He glanced over his shoulder at her. "You can't blame a man for thinking through the possibilities. Stranger things have happened, Liz."

"Son of a bitch!" She walked over to him, giving him a push in the center of his broad chest. "I'd never have cheated on my husband. I'm not that kind of person! You know, not all of us are like you, O'Brian. Some of us have some sort of moral fabric."

"Fine. So you became fond of each other after Paul's death. But tell me something, did you love him?"

"Who?"

"Your husband, of course. Did you love the man?"

He was looking out the window now. It would have been easy for Elizabeth to lie. "No," she said softly. She was angry that he would ask such a question. He had no right to ask. She was angry with herself for feeling compelled to tell O'Brian the truth. "But I could have, in time," she added defensively. "We'd only been together a short time."

He came away from the window. "I apologize. I didn't mean to pry. It's not my business who you love and who you don't. But as the yard foreman of these mills, I need to know what happened that night. If it was an accident, then I want to be able to prevent another one. If I've got some madman out there, I need to know that, too."

"So you're just doing your job?" she asked, her anger barely in check. "Talking to all the suspects."

"Why must you turn every conversation we have into an argument?" He walked up to her, bringing his face inches from hers. "I didn't accuse you of anything. I was just thinking out loud. I wouldn't be as good at my job as I am, if I didn't think through all the possibilities. You make too much of nothing, Liz."

She turned to the door, uncomfortable by how close he was to her. The masculine smell of his clean hair, his skin, was distracting.

He threw up his hand. "Why do you keep running from me like I'm going to bite you?"

She pressed her back to the door. She could hear her dogs outside, pacing.

He took another step toward her. "Look, Liz, what happened the other night—"

"Was a mistake."

His green-eyed gaze met hers. "Aye."

"Let's understand something here, Mr. O'Brian. I'm the mistress of these mills. You work for me. There can't be any fraternization between us. It would be bad for business."

"You got no argument from me." He lifted his hands. "I kissed you again because you expected me to."

She laughed, but without humor. "Are you saying that was my fault in the garden the other night?"

"I'm not saying—"

"Shh! Do you want Noah to hear you!"

"I'm not saying," he said a little quieter, "that anyone

was to blame. The fact of the matter is that I find ye attractive, Liz. You make me mad as hell, but you're a hell of a kisser. You can't blame a man for taking what's offered."

He was practically calling her a whore. Trouble was, what he said was true, and Elizabeth knew it. She'd behaved shamelessly the other night in the garden. She was an adult woman; she should have been able to control her urges better. She stepped out of the way of the door. "Let's just end this conversation here," she hissed. "Before one of us says something that can't be taken back."

O'Brian shrugged. "Fine with me. You keep your distance. I'll keep mine. I'm going back down to the mill." He opened the door and the dogs came barreling in. "Damned dogs!" He sidestepped the last hound and went out the door, slamming it behind him.

Elizabeth gave O'Brian a moment to get out of the front office, and then went down the short hallway, yanking her hat on her head as she went. "I'm going up to the house to see Claire. I'll be back shortly."

Noah just nodded as she brushed by, taking care not to look up from his ledgers.

A short time later Elizabeth sat on the second-story porch built over a ravine that ran between the house and the road that led to the mills. From here, through the thick foliage of elm, maple, and oak trees, she could see the river and the slate rooftop of the composition house. The sweet smell of wild, red honeysuckle filled the hot afternoon air.

Elizabeth took the glass of icy fruit syllabub Claire offered her. She smiled at her sister-in-law. "You're looking pretty today. I like your gown."

Claire sat down, arranging the skirt of her yellow and

green sac gown. "Brother doesn't like this dress. He says I look like a canary in it." She giggled. "But I wear it when he goes away." She pointed at the serving platter on the small tea table between their chairs. "Have a cinnamon cookie. Cook made them this morning. She let me cut them out."

Elizabeth didn't really care for a sweet, but Claire was so anxious for her to try the cookie, that she didn't have the heart to turn her down. Elizabeth took a bite. "Mmmm."

"Told you it was good." Claire took one herself and turned the cookie in her delicate hand. She bit it and then peered up anxiously. "Brother says you're going to marry him. You had a party and you told everyone. That means you have to get married."

Elizabeth took another bite. "Yes, we are going to marry. Next spring. But we don't *have* to get married. We're getting married because we want to. Is that a problem for you, Claire?"

She chewed thoughtfully. "Will you get angry if I tell you what I think?"

Elizabeth noticed that she was holding the cookie so tightly in her hand that it was beginning to crumble. "No, I won't be angry."

"It makes Brother angry when I tell him what I think, if it's different than what he thinks."

Elizabeth popped the last crumb of cookie into her mouth and leaned forward. "You know I would never be angry with you, Claire. You were the first friend I made when I came to the colonies. Even before Paul."

Claire began to break her cookie into tiny pieces, letting the pieces fall onto her lap. "You shouldn't marry him." She shook her head. "You shouldn't."

"Why do you say that? You and Jessop will move into the house here with me. It'll be great fun, Claire. We'll be just like sisters then."

Claire was breaking the cookie into tinier pieces, her small fingers moving rapidly. "I hate him!" she cried vehemently.

"Oh, no, you don't, Claire. You love Jessop." She reached out to try to take Claire's hand, but Claire pulled away. "You couldn't hate him, sweetheart. Jessop is your brother. Jessop is the one who takes such good care of you."

She shook her head compulsively, again and again, beginning to rock in her chair. "He doesn't like it when I'm naughty. He won't like it if you're naughty. He might hurt you."

"Jessop would never hurt me." Elizabeth slid forward in her chair. "I don't understand what you're saying, Claire."

"I think you should marry Mr. O'Brian," she said, the tone of her voice changing suddenly. She looked up with a smile, ceasing to rock, the darkness gone from her lovely face.

"Mr. O'Brian!" Elizabeth laughed.

Claire nodded enthusiastically. "He thinks you're pretty. He likes your voice." She wrinkled her nose. "But he hates your dogs. He says he going to roast Lacy on a spit and eat her."

Elizabeth took a sip of her drink. Claire was normally prone to making things up. "Where did you get such nonsense?"

"He told me."

Elizabeth looked up, almost choking on the last sip of syllabub. "Claire! You know you shouldn't be down by the mills with the men. We've talked about that before."

"I didn't take off my clothes. And I didn't see him at the mills. So I wasn't naughty." She folded her hands neatly in the crumbs in her lap. "I saw him at the tavern. You know, the Sow's Ear."

"The tavern!" She set down her glass with a bang. "You shouldn't be there, either! My god, Claire, that's worse. You don't know what kind of people frequent places like that!"

"That's what Mr. O'Brian said, too. He walked me back to the house. That's when he told me he thought you were pretty—when we were walking."

Elizabeth didn't know that she liked the thought of Claire and O'Brian walking alone at night, considering his reputation. "You and Mr. O'Brian were alone?"

"Oh, no." She smiled. "He and the nice lady with the red hair. She brings you ale at the tavern, if you ask. I like ale. Mr. O'Brian gave me a sip before he said I had to go home."

Great, Elizabeth thought. *O'Brian and his whore walking Claire home. If Jessop knew, he'd have a cow.* "Listen, Claire. You shouldn't be walking around at night with men. It's not fitting for a lady like yourself. And you shouldn't be discussing me with my foreman."

"Oh, he wasn't discussing you." She smiled, her blond curls bobbing as she spoke. "He has good manners. I was the one who started it. I asked him if he thought you were pretty. He said yes. As pretty as me."

Elizabeth groaned. She'd have to have a talk with O'Brian about Claire. It just wasn't proper. He shouldn't be carrying on conversations like that with her and he certainly shouldn't be walking her home in the middle of the night.

Elizabeth rose. "I will speak to Mr. O'Brian, and you, missy, stay away from the tavern. You understand me?"

Claire was now picking the crumbs up from her lap, one tiny piece at a time. "I'll try not to be naughty again." She looked up. "But you really should marry Mr. O'Brian. He has a fine cock."

Elizabeth went ashen, halting where she was. This wasn't the first time Claire had used such foul language.

Elizabeth didn't know where it came from, where she'd heard such words, but she was using them more frequently. "Claire!"

Claire bobbed her head, covering her mouth to stifle a giggle. "Oops. A naughty word?"

"Did Mr. O'Brian say that to you?"

"Certainly not," she answered indignantly. "I told you, Mr. O'Brian has manners. Men with manners don't say words like that in front of ladies."

"No, they do not," Elizabeth said sternly. "And ladies don't repeat them, wherever they got them to begin with."

Claire went back to cleaning up her crumbs and Elizabeth stood there in the doorway for a moment, watching her. Claire seemed to be getting worse. She was becoming compulsive about cleanliness, bathing and changing her clothing sometimes several times in a day. Now she was wandering off. Elizabeth couldn't imagine how she could have gotten to the tavern after dark without Jessop knowing it, but she would speak to him. For Claire's sake, he was going to have to be more careful.

"Well, thank you for the drink, Claire. I have to get back to work now, but I'll see you later. You stay here on the porch where it's cool, all right?"

Claire nodded, still picking up crumbs.

With a sigh, Elizabeth stepped inside the upstairs hallway and started down the staircase. There was plenty of paperwork waiting for her in her office. She had to place an order for sulphur from Italy and hope it would arrive before she ran out. She also had bills to pay. But her head was so full of other thoughts, that she doubted she'd be able to concentrate. She was worried about Claire. And it was time she and Jessop began discussing plans for their wedding. Then there was Mr. O'Brian. He and his backhanded accusations. He made her so mad she could spit!

So why was it that when she closed her eyes at night, all she saw was that wry smirk of his?

Ten

After a light dinner with Claire, Elizabeth returned to her office around eight o'clock, to finish a letter to a cooper near Philadelphia. The more she had thought about it, the more she had realized that O'Brian was right, damn him. Lawrence Mills needed to be as self-sufficient as possible. Each time Jessop returned from Philadelphia he had news of conflict that was quickly escalating between England and her American colonies. The first Continental Congress would meet in Philadelphia in September. The purpose of the congress (with representatives from each colony but Georgia) was to try to adopt measures to secure the colonists' rights, and to restore peace and mutual confidence between the colonies and their mother country.

Jessop was still insisting that it would all blow over. No one would dare challenge the most powerful country in the world, he said. But Elizabeth wasn't certain she agreed. The closing of the Boston Harbor, the Intolerable Acts taxes that had been imposed and then rescinded, even the Boston Massacre some years before, were pointing to a frightening conclusion—the colonies at some point might feel forced to declare their independence.

Elizabeth knew that if there was even the possibility of war, Lawrence Mills would have to become self-sufficient if it was to survive. The new taxes being imposed monthly and the possibility of the Philadelphia harbor being closed even temporarily could harm her fledgling business. Having a cooper would be a good step in the right direction. A cooper on the property to make the gunpowder barrels would save her time and money in the long run. Next week she'd have Johnny Bennett break ground on a new cottage. Hopefully they would have a cooper by mid-September.

Reaching the office door, Elizabeth turned the lock with one of the keys she wore at her waist. Lifting her lamp high, she went inside, letting Lacy run ahead, and locked the door behind her.

Jessop didn't approve of her working late at night alone in the office. He said it wasn't safe. How was she not safe? The door was locked, and Lacy was here to protect her. Besides, who was it she wasn't safe from?

Elizabeth's leather boots tapped hollowly on the hardwood floor, as she made her way to her private office in the rear. She set the lamp on her desk and took a seat in her chair. Lacy sprawled herself on the floor at her mistress's feet and rested her head between her paws.

Elizabeth patted the hound on her head, scratching behind her ear. "Good, Lacy, good dog."

The dog whined contentedly.

"I'm not going to let that bad foreman cook you and eat you, no, I'm not." Elizabeth gave the hound one last pat and then turned in her chair, chuckling to herself. She couldn't believe O'Brian would have said such a thing to Claire. Eat her dog! But it was just like him—full of sweet talk and nonsense.

Elizabeth reached for her quill to finish the letter to the cooper she'd left on her desk. She penned the last details and then sprinkled sand on the ink to dry it. Once she had sealed the letter and placed it in the box to be posted, she began to sort through a pile of correspondence she hadn't had time to look over all week.

The case clock on the shelf over her head struck the half hour, then nine, then nine-thirty. Elizabeth was growing sleepy. She knew she should return to the house, check on Claire, and turn in for the night, but the office was so cozy. Here was where she felt most at home. Paul had built the house, but she'd built the separate office after the explosion, so it was all hers.

Elizabeth rested her head atop her crossed arms on the desk. She let her eyes drift shut. She'd just rest for a moment, and then she'd go up to the big house.

The blast of the explosion and the sound of splintering glass tore Elizabeth from a deep slumber. For a heart-stopping moment, she was completely disoriented. Chunks of plaster and fine dust from the ceiling fell onto the bed. The bedchamber walls shook with another, smaller explosion, and a portrait flew off the wall and clattered across the plank floor.

Not another explosion, Elizabeth screamed in her mind as she bolted upright in her bed. The room was illuminated by the orange light of the blaze outside her window. It was happening again, sweet god in heaven, it was happening again. Instinctively she reached out to the place beside her in the bed. Paul was dead, of course. She knew that. Who was it she was looking for?

The roar of the fire outside the window was deafening. She heard screams of fear and the moan of collapsing walls.

She had never felt so alone in her life . . .

Elizabeth brought her hands to her ears and squeezed her eyes shut, trying desperately to block out the sights and sounds that left her paralyzed with fear.

Her mouth opened and she heard herself scream. "O'Brian," she cried. "O'Brian, where are you?"

Elizabeth woke with a start, her heart pounding. She jerked her head off her desk to see her dog standing beside her, staring with round, brown eyes. Lacy barked and pushed her cold nose into her mistress's shaking hand.

"It's all right, it's all right," she soothed, trying to catch her breath. "Just a dream," she said, feeling foolish. "Nothing but a nightmare."

But it was so real . . . and so similar to what had actually happened. Only the end of the dream had altered fact. Last year when the packhouse exploded, she'd jumped out of bed and run to the window. Only in her dream had she been too frightened to move. Only in her dream had she cried out for help . . .

. . . To O'Brian?

Why O'Brian? It didn't make any sense. The idea rattled her. Why hadn't she cried for Paul, or even Jessop? *O'Brian* . . . That scared her. She knew enough about the unconscious mind to know it meant something, she just didn't want to think about it now.

Elizabeth rose, a little shaky on her feet. It was time she went to bed. She wiped the dots of perspiration above her lips with her finger. "Come on, Lacy, let's go." She picked up the lamp and was halfway to the door when she stopped suddenly.

The dream had been so real, so accurate . . .

Suddenly O'Brian's words from earlier in the day came back to her. He had said no one could even remember how many initial explosions there had been. She remembered. She remembered now quite distinctly. There had been only two. One big explosion, followed by a second, smaller one seconds later. It wasn't until minutes later that the magazine had gone up, as a result of the sparks and flying cinders, no doubt.

She had to tell O'Brian. Maybe it would help him figure out what had happened. Maybe then he would have a better idea of where the explosion began.

Elizabeth slapped her thigh. "Come on, Lacy, let's go, girl." She'd find O'Brian now, while the memory was still fresh in her mind. She didn't care if she did have to pull him out of the bed he shared with his little red-haired whore. Paul's death was certainly more important than her foreman's pleasure.

Elizabeth blew out the lamp and left it on Noah's desk. With her dog at her side, she strode out of the office, locking the door behind her, and went down the hill in the darkness.

The light from the bright three-quarters moon illuminated the dirt road Elizabeth followed to Worker's Hill. When she reached the yard foreman's cottage, she saw no light coming from the upstairs window. She knocked on the door. Lacy perched herself on the brick stoop, watching the door.

There was no answer.

Elizabeth knocked again, louder this time. She didn't care if O'Brian was asleep. She could still hear the roar of the fire from the explosion in the back of her mind. She wanted to tell her foreman what she remembered before it grew dim.

"Mistress?"

The voice from behind Elizabeth made her start. "Y . . . yes?" She turned around. It was Samson and Ngozi.

Ngozi curtsied, nodding her head. "Evenin', Mistress," she said in a liquidy voice.

"Evening, Ngozi." Elizabeth nodded in return.

"You lookin' for Mr. O'Brian?" Samson asked. He seemed even more massive than usual, standing next to his petite wife.

"I am. I've something important to speak with him about. He doesn't seem to be home. Do you know where he is, Samson?"

"Down to the Sow's Ear, I'd 'spect. Want me to fetch him for you, Mistress?"

"No, no, it looks like you two were going for a walk. It's a beautiful night for it. I'll find him myself."

"Let me go, Miss 'Lizabeth." Samson released his wife's hand. "That ain't no place for a lady like yourself."

"Nonsense. Go on your romantic walk with your wife, Samson. I've got Lacy with me. I'll be fine."

"Well, all right," Samson gave in reluctantly. "But you have Mr. O'Brian walk you home from that place. It gettin' to be too late for you to be walkin' the road. They's soldiers and all kinds of bad men out there, ma'am."

Elizabeth tapped her thigh, and her dog immediately rose and came to her side. She waved. "Good night, Samson. Good night, Ngozi."

" 'Night, Mistress," the couple chimed.

Elizabeth smiled to herself as she walked down the hill and turned right, headed for the Sow's Ear downriver another mile. Samson and Ngozi were like young lovers the way they smiled at each other, the way they held hands. Somewhere deep inside Elizabeth, she longed for that type of relationship, that type of mutual admiration. She was jealous of the love they shared, a love she knew she would never experience.

Fifteen minutes later, Elizabeth reached the Sow's Ear. The tavern, which served the working men of the flour, grist, cotton, and fulling mills up and down the river, was little more than a two-story frame shack built on the Brandywine riverbank, where two roads met. Light poured from the unshuttered windows, and the sound of laughter, dancing feet, and fiddle music filled the night air.

Elizabeth had never been inside the Sow's Ear. She'd spent a few nights in taverns when traveling, but they'd always been establishments for a higher social class than the one that frequented this place.

The unmistakable sound of bawdy laughter rose above

the other voices, and Elizabeth glanced up to the second-story. She saw the silhouette of a feminine form move through the darkness of the upstairs room. She heard the rumble of a man's voice.

Elizabeth frowned. She hadn't realized *that* was going on at the Sow's Ear as well.

She walked up to the open door and gestured to her hound. "Sit, Lacy. Good dog. Stay." She couldn't very well take the dog inside.

The dog gave one bark, but sank into the dry grass.

Just then, a man in a red, cocked hat stumbled through the door. He gave a loud belch. "Even', sweet," he said, wiping his mouth with the back of his hand.

Elizabeth stepped out of his way. Lacy growled deep in her throat. "Good evening," Elizabeth said curtly, hoping the tone in her voice indicated she wasn't interested in furthering the conversation.

Apparently, he got the message. He gave another loud belch, attempted to straighten the cockeyed hat on his head, and wandered out onto the road.

"Sit, Lacy. Stay," Elizabeth repeated. Then she stepped through the low, open doorway into tavern.

The public room smelled of stale ale, smoke, and urine. The light was dim, the smoke thick in the room. There were not even any floorboards to the building, she realized, as she stepped onto the hard-packed dirt floor. A fiddle played wildly from somewhere in the rear, and Elizabeth heard the distinct sound of men brawling coming from a room directly behind the public room.

She hung back, turning the ball of her boot in the dirt in indecision. Maybe Samson was right, maybe this wasn't a good idea. She was out of her element here.

Two redcoat soldiers were playing dice at the nearest table. Both turned to stare at her. One dared to wink at her. It was no wonder, the way she was dressed. In dusty cotton petticoats and a mobcap, she looked like a mill

worker's wife. Only the expensive German boots, her
pearl earbobs, and the keys that hung on her waist, gave
any indication of her station in life.

Elizabeth looked away. Directly in front of her was a
group of mill workers, some her own, leaning over the
table, laughing and poking their fingers at something in
the center of the table. Elizabeth craned her neck.

"Disgusting," she murmured to herself with a shudder.
The men had captured a rat and had pinned its tail to
the scarred wooden table with a knife. The rat was
squealing as it tried desperately to escape.

The brawl in the back room was gaining momentum.
Elizabeth couldn't see the participants, but a crowd was
beginning to gather near a cold, stone fireplace.

She spotted a tavern maid passing with a tray of sloshing ale horns. To her dismay, she recognized the young
woman as the same woman that had been with O'Brian
that night. It was the redhead.

"Excuse me," Elizabeth called, deciding that if she'd
come this far, she was not going to give up now. "Excuse
me . . ."

The redhead turned. She must have recognized Elizabeth, because she came directly across the room, stepping over a man unconscious on the floor. "Good even',
Mistress." She was all smiles. Elizabeth couldn't help
notice that the girl's breasts were pushed so high above
the ruffle of her stained bodice, that she could see the
pale areolas. "What can I do for ye?"

Elizabeth could hear someone retching behind her.
"I—" She took another step toward the redhead, doubt-
ing the girl would hear her above the din of the public
room. "I was wondering if you might know where Mr.
O'Brian is."

"Paddy?"

Elizabeth didn't know where the girl had gotten Paddy
from, but she'd heard her call him by that name that

night. Some sort of vulgar, little pet name, she guessed. "Mr. O'Brian, yes."

She hooked her thumb over her shoulder. "Paddy's that a way. In the back. Last I saw 'im, he and Peg was gettin' into a tussle."

Elizabeth looked over the girl's shoulder. "That's O'Brian fighting back there?" She gave her a nudge. "Excuse me, but I pay that man too much to have him laid up with broken bones."

Elizabeth pushed past the girl, past the rat table, over the drunk on the floor, toward the back room. Men and women blocked the doorway, but Elizabeth pushed through with an air of authority no one dared question.

Once she made her way through the crowd, she spotted O'Brian. He and the man he was fighting with were rolling on the dirt floor, pounding each other's bloody faces. To her horror, she realized that the man her foreman had attacked was missing one leg below the knee.

"O'Brian!" she shouted as she crossed the room.

Laughter bubbled up behind her.

"Mr. O'Brian, what the blessed hell do you think you're doing?"

O'Brian rolled on top of his victim, trying to pin down his arms. "Liz? That you?" He looked a second time. "What are you doing here?"

"Get up, O'Brian! Get up and let that man go!" She grabbed the nearest piece of furniture she could lay her hands on. She raised the three-legged stool above her head. "Get off that man, or I swear to God, I'll cold conk you."

There was more laughter from the tavern patrons, a guffaw or two.

The man missing the leg managed to free one of his arms and caught O'Brian square in the jaw.

"Ouch, damnation!" O'Brian cursed. "Just trying to teach this jackanapes a little lesson." He slammed the man in the cheek. Both men were covered in dirt and bleeding from their noses and the corners of their mouths. O'Brian had a gaping wound above his brow, that was bleeding down the side of his face.

"I don't care what you're doing, I don't want you fighting!" She raised the stool directly over O'Brian's blond head. "Get up, I said!"

O'Brian looked down at the man he had pinned to the ground. "Had enough, Peg? You going to keep your mouth shut about Miss Claire?"

The man called Peg grimaced. "I guess so, O'Brian. Now get the hell off me!"

O'Brian jumped up and offered the man his hand to help him up. Someone in the crowd offered Peg's detached wooden leg, and O'Brian handed it to the man. "Need any help with that?" he asked graciously.

"Nah," Peg answered, leaning over to refit the peg into the leg of his breeches. "See ye next week, Paddy."

Elizabeth stood in disbelief, the stool still in her hands, as Peg hobbled off. One minute the two were in a bloody brawl, the next they were the best of friends. She would never understand men, never.

O'Brian turned back to her. "What the Christ are you doing here?" He snatched the stool from her hand and tossed it onto the dirt floor. "You don't belong in a place like this!" He dropped a hand possessively on her shoulder and directed her through the parting crowd of patrons.

"What are you doing fighting that poor, crippled man? God sakes, O'Brian! What kind of man are you that you knocked him off his peg?"

"Knocked him off his peg, hell!" O'Brian waved to someone across the room, as they cut across the public room headed for the outside door. "He's the one that pulled it off his leg and struck me in the face with it." He touched the gash over his eyebrow with his fingertips. "Caught me good, too."

He still had his hand on her shoulder, as they stepped outside into the fresh night air.

Elizabeth stopped to have a look at his eye. "You need a stitch or two," she said, touching the cut gingerly. This close she could smell the whiskey on his breath.

He pushed her hand away. "Aw, hell, I do not."

She crossed her arms around her waist. "What were you fighting about?" she asked.

"Doesn't matter." He started walking in the direction of Lawrence Mills. "You need to get home. You don't belong out on this road this late at night. It's not safe, and you know it."

She fell into step beside him. "I heard you mention Claire's name. Why were you fighting over Claire?"

"Old Peg had too much to drink. He was running his mouth, so I shut it for him. Peg'll stay away from her." He shrugged. "Nothing to be concerned with, Liz."

"Nothing to be concerned with?" She walked backwards in front of him so she could face him. "Claire told me she'd come down here. She isn't in any kind of trouble, is she? With one of the men, I mean."

He shook his head. "Naw. I took her home, and I told her to stay away." He gave her that smile of his. "She and I have an understanding, now. She'll do as I ask."

Elizabeth frowned, walking beside him again. "I can't believe you walked her home with that slattern."

"Slattern? Such language from a lady like yourself! I'm appalled, Mistress. See, the ladies and I just happened to be going in the same direction. I merely escorted them home."

"Yes, right. I believe you. And I'm the next queen of bloody England," she snapped.

He laughed, his rich tenor voice rising above the leafy tree limbs overhead. "That's what I like about you, Liz. You say what you think. That kind of honestly is rare in a man, rarer in a woman."

His compliment made her uncomfortable, not because it wasn't true, but because she liked it when he complimented her. She looked at his face, trying to get a better look at his wound in the moonlight, trying to change the subject. "Well, I can tell you what I think. I think that definitely needs a couple of stitches. You're bleeding again." She brushed a lock of his golden hair back off his forehead. "Have you thread and a decent needle at your cottage?"

He lifted his injured eyebrow and then cringed. "I don't know that I want you near my face with a sharp object. You certain you know what you're doing? I wouldn't want a scar to mar me comely face."

She raised her gaze heavenward in frustration. "I can sew a bit a skin on your thick skull, O'Brian, I assure you. I was quite good at my crewel work at one time."

He laughed. "Well, just so you don't sew the Lord's Prayer across my forehead, I guess I'll let you stitch me up."

They reached his cottage a few minutes later. Elizabeth followed him inside, bidding Lacy to remain just inside the door.

"Have you a tinder box?" Elizabeth asked, walking to the fireplace, reaching for the mantel.

"Right there, to your left," he answered. "I'll get the needle and thread upstairs."

"And some water, a clean cloth, and a bottle of spirits, if you have it," she called after him.

"It just so happens that I do."

"Why am I not surprised?"

O'Brian disappeared up the narrow staircase in the rear of the room, his laughter echoing in the stairwell.

At least he's a jolly drunk, Elizabeth thought as she lit a tallow candle and then several more. She'd need good light to stitch him properly.

By the time O'Brian had come down the stairs, she

had dragged the stool from his desk over near the cold hearth, where the candlelight was brightest. She took the bowl of water and rag and the half-empty flask of whiskey from his hands, and pointed to the stool. "Sit."

He obliged her, holding out the thread and needle. Elizabeth drew the thread between her lips and tried to concentrate on threading the needle, knowing he watched her closely.

"Stop," she finally said, the third time she missed the eye of the needle.

"Stop what?" He was teasing her with that lazy sensual voice of his.

"Looking at me like that. It's inappropriate."

"I can't help myself." She was standing directly in front of him, where he perched on the stool. It was too easy for him to reach out to rest his hand on her hip. "You're so beautiful tonight with your dusty skirts, cockeyed mobcap, and rosy lips."

She reached up and jerked her mobcap on her head, straightening it. "I've had a long day," she answered tartly. But she didn't move away from him. She couldn't bring herself to do it.

Just as she slipped the silk thread through the needle's eye, he lowered his other hand to her hip. His pressure was light, but steady. "I've a mind to kiss you, Lizzy."

She looked down at him as she drew the thread through the needle and knotted it. Still, she didn't move, even knowing she played with fire. "That's not why I came."

Eleven

"Aye, I don't doubt that, lass," he answered, a sincerity in his rich-timbered voice. "But now that you're here . . ."

He was pulling her closer to him, drawing her between his open knees. She must have dropped the needle and thread, because she found her hands resting on his shoulders. She found herself staring into those green eyes of his, eyes a woman could lose herself to. Elizabeth couldn't help herself. She was out of control, and she knew it. All she could think of was the taste of his lips on hers.

Without hesitation, Elizabeth lowered her mouth to O'Brian's. It was madness, but she didn't care. This man with his crude ways and aggressive manner made her feel like no man had ever made her feel, or ever would again, she feared. Their tongues twisted in frenzied desire, as she rested her hand on his and slowly drew it up beneath the curve of her breast.

Trapped between O'Brian's knees, she sank down on his lap, reaching her arms around him, giving him access to the drawstring of her gathered bodice. He tugged the white linen and lace modesty piece from her neckline and let it float to the floor.

"Liz, Liz," he murmured. "I can't get ye out of my head. I know it's crazy, but I can't help myself." He reached behind her head and tugged at the tortoise comb that held up her hair. With one pull, her dark hair came tumbling down over her shoulders. He buried his face in her tresses. "The smell of you," he whispered. "The sound of your voice," he turned her hand in his, "your touch. I can't stop thinking about you. I can't stop wanting you, wanting this . . ."

His words made her tremble inside. She knew it was all pretty lies, but she didn't care. All her life she had wanted a man to say those things to her.

Their lips met again; Elizabeth molded her body to his. Somehow he had managed to work his hand inside her clothing. She could feel his warm touch on her breast, his thumb caressing her budding nipple. He kissed her again and again, until she was lost to the sensations of her desire.

All reason was gone. At this instant, this seemed the most natural act to Elizabeth. She was breathless, dizzy, her heart pounding. This was what she wanted. Who was she fooling? It was what she had wanted since the first day O'Brian had walked into her life, all mouth and brawn.

The feel of his broad, muscular shoulders beneath her fingertips made her shiver. There was something about his strength that gave her strength. There was something about his virile masculinity that made her feel so feminine. Their lips met again and again in a frenzied passion Elizabeth had never known she was capable of. O'Brian tasted of whiskey and tobacco, but mostly of himself.

When he lowered his head, she leaned back, relaxing in his arm. She wanted to feel his mouth on her breast. She wanted him to take her nipple between his teeth and suckle. It was all she had thought about for days.

"Yes," she whispered in his ear, running her fingers through his silky blond hair. "Kiss me there," she dared.

His lips brushed her breast in a teasing fashion. "Here?"

"Ah, yes," she breathed, guiding his head with her hands.

"Like this?" He closed his mouth over her nipple and sucked gently, sending waves of pleasure through her.

She arched her back, looping her arms around his neck. "Oh, yes," she moaned. "Yes . . ."

Minutes later Elizabeth found herself on her knees facing O'Brian, locked in a fevered kiss. Her bodice was pushed down around her waist to expose her pale breasts. His shirt was on the floor. As they kissed again and again, she marveled at the feel of his hard, muscular flesh beneath her fingertips. The blond hair sprinkled across his chest brushed against her sensitive breasts. Her entire body trembled; she throbbed with the heat of her desire for him.

It would be so easy, Elizabeth thought as he stroked her breast, kissing the pulse of her throat. It would be so easy to give myself to him here, now. *I've not wed Jessop yet. O'Brian is offering me something here at this moment that I know in my heart I'll never experience again.*

But it wasn't that simple. Elizabeth knew it wasn't that simple.

No matter how she tried to justify making love with O'Brian, the cold fact of the matter was that he was a married man. Just because he had already committed adultery with others, didn't make it all right. This wasn't something she wanted to contribute to; it wasn't something she wanted to be a part of. She would never want her husband to dupe her, how could she do it to another woman?

Elizabeth dropped her head to O'Brian's bare shoulder for a moment, trying to catch her breath, trying to slow her pounding heart. The heat between her thighs throbbed.

"What? What is it, Lizzy?" he asked, his voice as gentle as his lover's caress.

"Don't call me that," she murmured. "Don't you know I hate it when you call me that?"

He kissed her earlobe. "Tell me what's wrong."

She forced herself to let go of him and sit back on her heels. She made no attempt to cover her naked breasts. What was the point? "I can't do this," she said softly, wanting desperately not to turn this into a fight.

"You don't like my touch? Tell me what you like, Liz." He brushed her forearm with his fingertips. "Tell me how you want to be stroked, how you want to be kissed. I want to please you."

"No, no, it's not that." She gave a little laugh. She knew it was wrong to compare her deceased husband to this man, but could she help it? Paul's lovemaking was a schoolboy's fumbling compared to this man's experienced touch. "Not that at all. It's just that—" She hung her head, unable to bear looking at him. "I can't do this with a married man. I'd almost give my own soul to the flames of hell to have you right now, but I can't do this to another woman. I can't."

O'Brian sat back on his heels, exhaling. He ran his fingers through his thick hair, pushing it back over the crown of his head. He, too, was breathing heavily. "What . . . what if I was to tell you I wasn't married, Liz?"

She got to her feet, ignoring the hand he offered her. How had she known he would say that? Because he was a rogue, and she knew it. "I'd say you were a liar," she answered, suddenly so tired she didn't have the energy to be angry with him. "I would say that you were a liar who wanted desperately to get into your mistress's drawers."

Pushing on his thighs, O'Brian rose. He didn't say anything for a full minute.

Her words had actually rattled him. *Good god,* she thought. *The man actually has a conscience.*

She pulled at the bodice of her wrinkled gown, trying to cover herself as best she could. "Let me sew up the wound and, then I'll go."

"No." He pushed her hands aside and smoothed the material of her bodice, tucking the modesty piece back in place. "I'll sew it myself. You best go on home before someone realizes you're missing." His voice was husky. "I know you wouldn't want that."

She nodded. She was staring at the rough-hewn plank floor, at his boots. She wanted to say something. Obviously she could no longer deny her desire for this man. The question was, how were they going to deal with it? She didn't want to fire him. She couldn't. But this couldn't happen again, either. It just couldn't.

"Look, O'Brian . . ." She exhaled, not knowing where to begin, still trembling from his touch.

He dropped his hand to her shoulder, leading her to the door. It was a comfortable gesture, unintimidating. "Let's not talk about it tonight. You and I, we've got something here between us. We can't go on pretending these incidences are accidents."

"But we can't keep doing this," she whispered desperately. "I can't."

He stopped at the door and reached out to touch her cheek with his fingertips. "I know, I know. You being my English mistress, me a poor Irish—"

"It's not just that," she argued. "I have certain plans for my life, the mill—"

His tone sharpened. "Jessop Lawrence."

She nodded. "Jessop." She touched his arm, marveling at the strength of his corded muscles. "This just can't be. It's inappropriate. It's a sin, O'Brian!" She withdrew her hand. "I want you to bring your wife here. Just as soon as possible. If . . . if I can't control my rutting, maybe someone needs to control it for me."

She turned away before he could answer and tapped her leg. "Come on, Lacy. Let's go home, girl."

Elizabeth walked out of O'Brian's cottage, her dog at her side, and started down Worker's Hill, refusing to turn around, knowing he watched her go.

"You gave him permission to *what?*" Jessop shouted across the open garden, making no attempt to remain in control of his temper.

Elizabeth leaned over the bed of cultivated wildflowers and cut another stem. They were relaxing in the front garden, or had been relaxing until she had told him about O'Brian's suspicions concerning the explosion.

"I gave him permission to talk to the workers. I said he could look around. That's all."

"I thought we agreed, Elizabeth, that we would put Paul's death behind us. We decided to let him rest in peace."

"No." She cut another flower, concentrating on not raising her voice. She'd not play his game. She'd not get into a shouting match with him. "No," she repeated firmly. "You decided. You decided, Jessop. I was the one from the beginning that said there was something not quite right about the explosion, about how it started."

He sat back on the garden bench, stretching his long legs and crossing his arms over his chest. "You know nothing about black powder except what I taught you."

That was too much. Elizabeth spun around, throwing down the cut flowers and the garden shears. "You taught me? You?" She stepped over the cluster of tiger lilies. "Jessop, you were against me taking over the mill from the first day! Once you realized I was determined, you went along with it because you had no choice in the matter, but don't you tell me that you taught me anything. You've never been any real help to me!" She came toward him, down the narrow brick walk, pointing an accusing finger. "I learned on my own. I learned by working beside those men. I learned by sitting up all night reading every word ever printed about black powder production. I learned by using my mind to come up with solutions. I've learned by making mistakes—some of them pretty stupid—but I learned." She came to a halt directly in front of Jessop.

Elizabeth had tried to please Jessop. She'd tried to be the woman he wanted her to be. She'd yielded, she'd conceded for the good of their relationship. She'd worn ugly dresses and tight shoes for him; she'd sat through long, boring dinner parties; she'd entertained his friends. But no longer . . . she'd come to that conclusion in the last sixty seconds. Suddenly she realized that what she and O'Brian had between them was honesty, an honesty she didn't have with Jessop. So, if he was going to wed her, that would have to change. Today. And if Jessop didn't like the person she was, then to hell with him! She didn't know why she thought she needed a damned husband to begin with.

Jessop stared at Elizabeth, his face perfectly expressionless except for the twitch in his upper lip. He was angry with her, as angry as she'd ever seen him, angrier even than he'd been that night in the kitchen garden with O'Brian. For a moment Elizabeth thought he might strike her.

She dropped her hands to rest them on her hips. She'd not back down. Not this time. And if he hit her, she'd hit him back.

"I don't know what's come over you, Elizabeth." He rose stiffly from the bench. He was dressed casually this afternoon in yellow breeches and a turquoise waistcoat. He looked like a blessed parrot in the ridiculous costume. "This is not the woman I fell in love with. You are not the same woman I fell in love with."

The tone in his voice told her this wasn't just another argument. This was serious.

"Just come out and say what you're thinking, Jessop. Say it! What? You don't want to marry me now that my mill is actually operating? You don't want to marry me now that I might become successful, is that it?"

He looked down at her like a father looks at an unruly child. "I'm saying that it's time you and I seriously considered our relationship. I feel I've been more than patient. I've been here for you since my brother's death. I stayed at your side when the creditors came banging at your door. I remained at your side when your father demanded you return home to England to be married off again. I have stayed at your side whilst you traipsed about these mills, acting more like the master than the mistress." Now he was pointing at her. "I think it's time you took a hard look at yourself and what you're doing, Elizabeth. What decent man is going to marry you, if I don't?"

"Oh, I see." She let her hands fall to her side, her sarcasm thick. "You're marrying me because no one else will. You're just doing your duty by your dead brother, is that it?"

He stared at her coldly. "I'm not certain I'm marrying you at all, Elizabeth. Now, I have business to attend to in Philadelphia. I'll be taking Sister along with me. I have to be honest in saying I'm not certain that, in your state of mind, you could be considered an appropriate guardian for her. We should only be gone a week. In that time, I ask that you seriously consider your recent actions and their consequences." He lifted his turquoise-feathered cocked hat off the bench and set it on his head. Presenting his leg, he nodded cordially. "Good day, madame."

Elizabeth only let him go a few feet before she caught up with him. She tugged off her garden glove. "Here, take this back," she said, sliding the ruby ring off her middle finger.

"I don't think that's necessary as of yet," Jessop replied.

"Well, I do. *Just whilst I'm considering my actions.*" She opened his hand and slapped the ring into his palm. She'd never liked the ring to begin with. Emeralds, she'd asked for an emerald ring.

Elizabeth watched Jessop walk the remainder of the way down the brick path toward his horse tied at the office. Despite the hot, humid day, she felt herself shiver, and she wrapped her arms around herself for warmth. She didn't know quite what to make of their conversation. It was obvious what he was saying. He was saying he wasn't certain he wanted to marry her.

The scary thing was, she didn't know if she cared.

The late afternoon shadows lengthened into early evening. Noah said good night, leaving Elizabeth in her rear office to continue working. The dogs had grown restless, scratching at fleas and whining until she'd finally pushed them out the door. Through the window she could see the spotted hounds racing up and down the hill that ran along the office building.

Elizabeth smiled to herself and went to dip her quill into the inkwell.

The sound of the explosion rocked the office. Elizabeth jumped, knocking over the inkwell of fresh ink. She knew she must have made some sort of sound, because the dogs were beneath her window in an instant.

Elizabeth leaped out of her chair and raced down the hallway. She flung open the office door, not taking the time to close it.

Oh, my God, not another explosion, her mind screamed. She'd been through this a hundred times, a thousand times in her dreams, but she'd prayed she'd never have to actually relive another explosion.

Down the hill she could see thick, black smoke, but she couldn't see where it was coming from. *One explosion,* she kept telling herself as she raced down the granite steps leading to the road. *Just one explosion. It can't be that bad. It must be contained.*

By the time Elizabeth reached the bottom of the hill, she spotted men running. But instead of running downstream in the direction of most of the mills, they were running upstream, where the new magazine lay.

"Oh, no, no," she murmured. But the nagging logic in the back of her mind told her this was nothing like the explosion last year. Not even the glass windows in her office had broken. It was a small explosion. And there was only one . . . one.

"Where is it?" Elizabeth shouted to one of the men running by.

"I don't know, ma'am! This way!" he hollered as he raced past her.

Elizabeth turned onto the road, running in the direction of the thick column of smoke. In the winter she could have seen the magazine through the bare tree limbs, but with the dense, tangled foliage of the Delaware summer, she could see nothing.

She managed to keep up with the men, and as she rounded the bend in the river, she saw a smoldering pile in the center of the road.

A wagon. It had been a wagon! She stopped in the center of the road, trying to catch her breath. Her heart was pounding, her lungs burning. Even from here she could see two dead horses burned almost beyond recognition. Someone had been transporting packed barrels of gunpowder to the magazine.

Sweet Jesus . . . O'Brian had said he was going to move barrels. It could have been O'Brian . . .

Elizabeth pushed herself through the men trying to put out the small fires along the roadway. The smoke was so thick that it choked her, stinging her eyes. She grabbed the first man carrying a bucket she came to. "Who was driving?" she demanded.

He shrugged. "Don't know, Mistress. Ain't no one said."

She walked closer to the black cinders that had been the wagon. Wagon pieces were strewn on both sides of the road and up into the trees. A stake of unharmed barrel wood hung precariously from a tree branch overhead. "O'Brian?" she asked the next worker she bumped into. "Have you seen O'Brian?"

The man, his face so sooty that she couldn't recognize him, shook his head grimly. "Ain't see 'im, Mistress."

Elizabeth circumnavigated the smoldering pile in the center of the road and the dead horses. On the far side, near the magazine, she spotted a group of half a dozen men crowded together. They were all covered in black soot.

"What happened here?" she shouted. "Someone tell me what the hell happened here! Where is my foreman?"

The men parted the way for her, and just ahead on the grassy bank she spotted O'Brian. She instantly heaved a breath of relief.

He wasn't killed. He wasn't hurt. He was safe, thank God, he was safe.

Beside O'Brian lay a man barely conscious.

She walked up to O'Brian. His shirt had been torn and singed, and there were several holes in his breeches where cinders had burned through. "What the hell is going on here?" she demanded, covering her concern for him with anger. "Did you blow up my damned wagon and my horses, O'Brian?"

He grinned at her, wiping a black smudge from his cheek with the back of his hand. "Hell, no, Mistress. I didn't burn up your wagon! It was Tom here. Smoking a friggin' pipe."

Elizabeth's eyes widened. A pipe? He was smoking a pipe while he moved gunpowder? She stared at the man who was trying to sit up. "Who's Tom?"

O'Brian got to his feet slowly. "We just hired him this week. Remember?"

"You hire him this week, and the first job you give him is to transport gunpowder?" she flared. "Tell me you're not that stupid."

O'Brian ran his sooty fingers through his hair. "I didn't, do it. I was in the magazine shifting barrels. Marble was supposed to be driving the wagon. I don't know what happened, but I can promise you I'm going to find out."

She glanced over his shoulder at Tom. The man's clothing had obviously been on fire, and there were several burn marks on his shoulders, but they didn't appear too serious. "He's not hurt too badly, is he?"

"Nope, thanks to Mr. O'Brian, he ain't." Johnny Bennett stepped forward, dragging his hat off his head as he addressed her. "I saw it all from down the lane. See, the blast threw old Tom off his seat, pipe and all, but his clothes was on fire. He was running down the road like he had no sense, but Mr. O'Brian, here, he tackled him and put out the fire with his hands."

Elizabeth glanced sideways at O'Brian. He could have been killed performing such wild heroics. "Get this cleaned up, O'Brian. See to the man's burns, pay him, and send him on his way. Any man without enough common sense to know not to smoke a pipe around live powder won't work for me."

She turned away, starting back down the road again. She didn't want her men to see her trembling. She didn't want them to know how badly this had frightened her.

"Liz! Liz, wait."

She heard O'Brian call her name. But she didn't turn back, and she didn't answer him.

She didn't want him to see the tears in her eyes.

Twelve

The dogs circled Elizabeth as she climbed the granite steps up the hill to her office, rubbing her eyes in frustration. Why was she crying, damn it? One wagon, two horses, and a dozen kegs of powder—that was all she'd lost.

She reached the office door she'd left wide open in her haste. "Stay out," she ordered her hounds. "Make yourselves useful for once. Catch a rat or something!"

She slammed the door shut and, in the fading light of early evening, walked back to her private office. She couldn't stop crying, and she was angry with herself for being such a ninny.

Outside she heard one of her dogs bark. Someone was coming. She heard the front door open.

"Liz? Liz, are you here?"

It was O'Brian. She dashed at her tears, embarrassed for him to see her like this.

"Here. Back here," she said, trying not to sound meek.

He came through the office door.

She couldn't take her eyes off him. She'd lost Paul. She'd probably lost Jessop. Now here, today, she'd almost lost O'Brian. He could have been killed by the explosion or by his foolhardy rescue.

"Liz. It's not that bad. The losses are minor. Accidents are going to happen."

"You stupid ass!" she heard herself shout at him. "You

could have been killed. Tackling a burning man and slapping the fire out with your hands! A few weeks ago it was throwing yourself into the river! Do you want to die? Is that it?" She wiped her eyes again, tears slipping down her cheeks.

"Ah, Liz. Liz."

He started towards her, but she met him halfway. He put his arms out to her, and she grabbed the sooty, rumpled muslin of his shirt, twisting it in her fingers. "You could have been killed," she said again and again. "You could have been killed, you fool."

He was laughing as he pushed back the hair that had escaped her Irish lace mobcap. "Ah, Liz. I'm too fast and too ugly for the devil to catch me just yet."

His arms tightened around her shoulders, and she found herself pressing her cheek to his chest. The sound of his heartbeat pounded in her ear. She was trembling all over.

O'Brian had scared her. He'd scared her badly. Worse, she'd scared herself. She cared about this man. It didn't have to make sense. Suddenly she knew how she felt about him deep in the pit of her stomach.

O'Brian was smoothing her tangled hair, whispering soothing nonsense in her ear. He smelled of cinders and pipe tobacco; he smelled like a man.

Elizabeth lifted her head from his shoulder to look into the sea of green. His gaze held her captive, spellbound. She knew what was happening. He moved his stroke from her hair to the line of jaw. When he leaned to kiss her mouth, she lifted up on her toes, needing him, needing to feel his lips on hers.

She ran her fingers through his silky blond hair, pulling it free from his queue. She couldn't stop touching him as he touched her. Fully clothed they stood there in the center of her office, in the shadows of twilight, touching, kissing. They took their time, and yet there was an urgency about their lovemaking that was pushing them both past the point of turning back.

Elizabeth explored the crown of his forehead, the bridge of his Irishman's nose. She brushed his lips with her fingertip, the same lips that had touched her own only a moment before.

He traced the line of her collarbone through her bodice and ruffled shift. He kissed the pulse of her throat. He turned her hand in his own larger one, his touch like the brush of a feather.

Elizabeth could feel her breath quickening, as she began to anticipate each stroke of his rough-skinned fingertips. She held her breath, as he slipped his hand beneath the drawstring of her bodice to cup her bare breast.

"O'Brian," she whispered, placing a hand on each beard-stubbled cheek, forcing him to look her in the eye. "Make love to me," she whispered.

"Aye, Liz, do you know what you say?" he asked, his voice husky.

She ran her hand boldly down his thigh, over his tight, soiled breeches. "I know what I say," she answered softly. "I say that I can't live another moment without your touch."

"Liz . . ." O'Brian brought his mouth down hard against hers, forcing her lips apart, thrusting his tongue. Elizabeth hung on to his broad shoulders, molding her soft curves against the hard flesh of his body.

Running her thumbs along the waistband of his breeches, Elizabeth pulled out the tail of his shirt and tugged it over his head.

His laughter was deep and sensual, as she let the material float from her hand. Then she watched as O'Brian pushed her gown down over her shoulders, amazed by how excited she became at the sight of his broad hands touching her own pale skin. He followed with her shift, baring her breasts to the warmth of the evening air.

Elizabeth leaned for another kiss, entranced by the feel of the crisp, blond hair on his chest brushing against the sensitive skin of her breasts.

"So beautiful," O'Brian whispered, lowering his head to press a kiss in the valley between her breasts. "Forbidden . . ."

"Not forbidden," she murmured. "Not tonight." Elizabeth knew it didn't make sense—making love to this man in such a public place. She knew how dangerous it was. She knew she'd regret it tomorrow. But she didn't care. She was tired of propriety. She was tired of always doing the right thing. She was tired of always giving, never receiving. So tonight she would take—she would take the pleasure O'Brian offered, and tomorrow she'd pay the consequences.

He nudged her back a step or two, until she felt the hard edge of her desk and leaned against it for support. Her breath came ragged as he pushed her gown down over her sprigged-cotton petticoat to the floor. A moment later he tossed her boned stays aside, followed by a puddle of petticoats. O'Brian went down on one knee, his gaze locked in hers as he lifted her shift to bare her stockinged calves above the smooth black leather of her work boots.

"That's not necessary," she heard herself say in a voice she barely recognized. "Someone might come, just—"

"I'll have all of you," he breathed, "or none of you, Liz."

She held her breath; their gazes locked. She could feel the heat of his hands through the clocked silk of her stocking. She could feel the throb in her woman's place as shivers of pleasure rose on her leg. "Hurry," she whispered. "Hurry, then . . ."

But O'Brian took his time, removing one boot, then

the other. Then slowly he untied her garter ribbons and rolled her stockings down her calves. Elizabeth had never thought of her legs as being a particularly sensitive area, but the way he touched her, the way he stroked her, was maddeningly erotic.

By the time O'Brian stood, he still in his breeches, she in naught but her shift, she was trembling from head to toe. Her mind was heady with the scent of his masculinity and the magic of his touch.

"Tell me what you want," he whispered. "I want to make you happy, Liz. You deserve to be happy."

She lifted his hand to her cheek. She knew his words were lies. She knew he said the same to everyone he slept with, to his wife . . . But the words, the words that made him sound like he truly cared for her were enough. "Make love to me," she whispered.

"I am."

"No." She closed her eyes, embarrassed by her own words. "No." She took his hand in hers. "Touch me here." He pressed his fingertips to the damp apex between her thighs. Only the thin linen of her shift separated his hand from that private place she had shared with no other but her husband. "Take off your breeches," she went on, "and love me."

Elizabeth heard O'Brian groan. She didn't know if what she had said was wrong, but he swept her into his arms and lowered her to the plank floor of the office.

She took no notice of the hardwood beneath her. All she could think of was his body touching hers, his body inside hers . . . He pushed her shift down over her hips, and then she lay there naked beneath him.

O'Brian covered her entire body with light, fleeting kisses, kisses that were making her mad with want of him. Why had she never felt like this before? Why had her husband never given her what this man was giving her now?

O'Brian slipped out of his breeches, stockings, and boots. Finally there was nothing between them but the humid night air and the heat of their passion.

It was nearly dark in the office now. The sound of night peepers blew in through the open window, on the tail of the summer breeze. A thin sheen of perspiration covered them both as they lay touching, being touched.

O'Brian took her nipple between his teeth and tugged gently. Elizabeth moaned. He was touching her with his fingertips, the tip of his tongue. Soon she was so lost in sensation that she no longer knew the difference.

It was not until Elizabeth felt the heat of his breath on the dark bed of curls between her thighs that she half sat up in protest.

"Ah, Lizzy," he cajoled, resting his cheek on her thigh. "You smell of honey and fire. I swear by all that's holy, I must taste you, or else I'll go mad."

His words were ridiculous, and yet as they left his lips, she lay back, relaxing . . .

"Liz, my sweet Lizzy," he whispered, brushing the curls with his fingertips.

After that moment, Elizabeth was powerless to resist. She lay back on the hardwood floor of her own office and let the sensations of pleasure take over her thoughts. Never had any man touched her like this, made her feel like this. After only moments she found herself writhing on the floor, calling O'Brian's name, dragging her blunt fingernails over his shoulders, as he lifted her higher and higher in a sea of delight.

The sudden wave of ecstasy that hit her took her completely by surprise. One moment she was arching her hips, lifting her body to meet his fingers, his tongue, and the next moment, her world exploded in overwhelming pleasure.

Elizabeth gasped, struggling for her breath. Her husband's touch had always felt good, it had always been pleasant, but never, never had she experienced the feeling she had just experienced, now fading in waves.

"What . . . what did you do to me?" she whispered in the darkness when she finally trusted herself to speak.

O'Brian's face appeared above hers. He was laughing, but not mocking her. "Don't tell me that husband of yours never took proper care of his wife? Hell, Liz, you've been mistreated worse than I thought." He pressed a kiss to her breast, her mouth. The taste on his lips was odd, but not at all unpleasant.

Elizabeth's breath was coming more evenly now. She waited in the darkness for him to mount her. But he made no move to take her. He only touched her with that light torturous touch of his.

After a few moments she got up the nerve to speak. "Are . . . are you done?"

Again, there was his husky laughter. "I would think you had quite enough for the evening, Mistress."

He was teasing her. He knew what she meant. He was trying to embarrass her again and make her say it. "No," she said, running her hand along his muscular forearm. "You . . ." She knew her cheeks were coloring, "You didn't take your pleasure."

He laid his head on her breast. "That isn't always necessary, you know." He spoke to her as if she were a child being taught from her first horn book.

"It isn't?"

He rolled off her and sat on the floor, drawing up his knees. "No, it isn't. Sometimes a man takes his pleasure. Sometimes he simply gives it. It only seems fair to me."

Elizabeth sat up beside him. Their clothes were strewn all over the tiny office floor. If anyone had walked by the open window and peered inside, they'd have seen their mistress and her foreman stark naked.

She pushed back a thick lock of dark hair, forcing herself to look him in the eyes.

"Don't say anything, Lizzy," he said softly. "Not tonight. Let me help you get dressed and leave me with the thought of your cries of pleasure, and not the berating I know you're about to give me."

Elizabeth covered her mouth with her hand, horrified. "You mean I made noises?" *Like an animal,* she thought.

He smiled, leaned to kiss her pursed mouth. "Barely a sound, love."

She dropped her forehead to her knees, drawn-up beneath her.

"Come on," he urged gently. "Let's get you dressed. I should get back down to the magazine and check up on the cleanup."

The explosion . . . Jessop . . . Her dead husband . . . O'Brian's wife . . . It was all coming back to her too quickly, weighing down on her like a ton of black powder. *Not tonight,* she thought determinedly. *I won't think about any of it tonight.*

So Elizabeth rose and let O'Brian help her dress. Few words passed between them, but he was as gentle a lover as he dressed her, as he had been when he had undressed her.

Finally, when she was respectably clothed and her hair in some fashion of neatness, O'Brian put on his dirty, rumpled clothes and made himself presentable.

She watched from near the doorway as he covered his naked body. From here in the shadows, here at a safe distance, she could look at him.

O'Brian's body was much larger than Paul's had been. Paul had been tall, but slender. O'Brian was all muscle and brawn. A huge man. His chest was very wide at the shoulders, narrowing to the hips. His thighs were thick and corded with muscle.

She smiled in the darkness. The man was well endowed. She was surprised by the urge she felt to touch him there. To touch *it.* Her mind got away from her, and suddenly she was imagining his rod in her hand, soft at first, but then hardening as men did . . .

"Ah, no, no more tonight," she heard him say.

Elizabeth looked up to see him looking at her. How had he known what she was thinking? She was embarrassed, shocked by her own wanton thoughts. A sliver of pleasure rippled through her body, as he tucked his member into his breeches. He had grown hard again. Just her eyes on him, her thoughts had excited him.

The idea was intriguing.

"Want me to walk you to the house?" O'Brian asked, as he picked his cocked hat up off the floor and dusted it on his knee. His hand fell comfortably to her shoulder as they approached the front office.

"No. No, you go out, and I'll go in another minute or two." She looked down at the floor, unable to meet his gaze."

O'Brian hesitated for a minute. She knew he was looking at her. What did he want her to say? What was there to say?

Finally he just leaned over and brushed his lips against her cheek. As he pulled away, she reached up to let her fingertips draw through his blond hair. "Good night," she whispered.

"Good night, Lizzy."

O'Brian slipped out the door. She heard a noise, then heard him curse—something about damned dogs.

Then O'Brian was gone, and Elizabeth stood in the darkness. Alone again.

Thirteen

O'Brian reached under his balls and gave a tug, trying to shift his cod in his breeches. "Saints in heaven, what have I gotten myself into?" he wondered aloud. He took the granite steps down the hill past the office, hoping that in the confusion of the wagon explosion, no one noticed him coming or going.

He wiped the perspiration from his forehead. It had taken every bit of control he possessed to keep from taking Elizabeth there on the office floor. When she'd asked him to make love to her, he'd fully intended to honor her request. *Sweet Mary, he'd thought of nothing else for days.* But then something changed his mind. Somewhere between the passionate kisses and the caress of her inexperienced hand, he'd realized the seriousness of his actions. Liz was no barmaid, she was no libidinous wife of an elderly gentleman. Liz, had probably never slept with any man but her husband.

O'Brian groaned. Why did he have to be a thinking man? Why couldn't he have simply ignored the nagging guilt he felt, and taken what she'd offered? From the way she'd responded to him, he knew she'd be a hell of a ride.

The trouble was, he also knew that in Liz's mind, she would be an adulteress if she slept with him. He hadn't wanted to hurt her like that. He hadn't wanted her to feel the pain of remorse he'd experienced so many times in his life. He'd just wanted to make her happy, to give her pleasure.

Hell, it was his own fault he hadn't had her tonight. He'd lied to her. He lied to her from the beginning, when he'd called himself O'Brian. O'Brian had a wife and children, and now to the eyes of the world, he, too, was wed. He couldn't have his pudding and eat it, too. He knew that. When he'd made the decision to take on Michael's identity, he'd made that bargain with himself.

But sweet Mary, Mother of God, how he wanted to make love to Liz. He balled his fists at his side as he stepped down onto the dirt road and turned toward the magazine upriver. He wanted her more than he'd ever wanted a woman in his life. The barmaid, she was a clever little fox in his bed, but her bawdy antics dimmed in comparison to Liz's innocent, but passionate touch.

O'Brian shifted the front cloth of his breeches again. Just thinking about her made his blood boil. He knew he could go down to the tavern, pick the tart up, and carry her home with him. He knew he could ease his need between her sweet thighs, but the thought just didn't interest him—not tonight, not when he could still taste Liz on the tip of his tongue.

He closed his eyes for just a second, allowing himself to remember the curve of Liz's bare breasts, the scent of her silky clean hair. It wasn't just her body that attracted him, it was the way she thought, it was the way she did business. He heard the men in the mills whisper, he heard their jokes about the fact that she was the one who would wear the breeches in her marriage to Lawrence. But the truth was, her intelligence was what attracted him to her. He liked a woman who could stand up for herself; he liked a woman who would stand up to him.

O'Brian opened his eyes, groaning aloud. Now what was he going to do? He'd saved Liz once from her sinning, imagined or otherwise, but he didn't know that he could do it again. Day and night the woman haunted him. He heard her laughter in every breeze, he smelled the scent of her skin in every empty room.

O'Brian stopped suddenly in the center of the road, the hair bristling on the back of his neck. *Sweet Mary* . . . he'd been so careful all these years. How had this happened?

This was as close as he'd ever come to loving a woman.

For two days Elizabeth avoided O'Brian. She sent messages concerning the powder mill to him by way of Johnny Bennett. She kept herself so occupied in her office, that she didn't find the time to go down to the mills. And O'Brian made no attempt to see her.

Actually, she wasn't that busy; she had plenty of work to do, but she couldn't concentrate. If anyone had paid attention, they'd have known that for two days Elizabeth sat at her desk staring out the window, twirling her quill. All she'd done was try to look busy, while she contemplated what she'd done with her foreman.

Just thinking about him made her warm. Everytime she closed her eyes, she could still feel his hands on her body, stroking, kissing . . . and she ached for him.

Elizabeth knew she had sinned, but she didn't care. The truth was that she wanted O'Brian at this moment even more than she had that night. She could think of nothing else. Jessop didn't matter. Even O'Brian's wife didn't matter. All that she could think about was her overwhelming desire for him. She just didn't know what she was going to do about it.

Elizabeth glanced out the window. It was growing dark. She wondered if O'Brian would go to the tavern tonight to meet the redhead, or if he would stay in his little cottage, lie on his feather tick, and think of the Mistress of Lawrence Mills.

Elizabeth didn't want the tart to have him. She wanted him for herself. And she didn't just want to be touched by his magical hands, her lust was worse than that. She wanted to touch him. She wanted to give him pleasure the way he had given her pleasure—without asking for anything in return.

She knew there was no future in such an illicit affair. She knew that she'd pay penance for the rest of her life, if she allowed herself to be tempted into such evil doings. But something deep inside her told her that if she missed this opportunity, she would regret it always. Something told her that this overwhelming attraction only came once in a lifetime.

Elizabeth knew an affair with O'Brian would be dangerous. Jessop's response was unpredictable. He might not care; he'd pretty much said their relationship was over. But he might take it upon himself to attempt to *save* his brother's property. He might take her to the English courts and challenge her inheritance. Paul had left a will giving the entire property to her, but women lost such inheritances in courts every day. Even if she didn't actually lose the powder mill, she could lose her orders. A powder mill that had no customers was quickly out of business.

A woman also had to consider the possibility of pregnancy. Luckily Elizabeth knew she didn't have to worry about that. The women in her mother's family had all been cursed with the late onset of childbearing. Not a woman in her mother's family had given birth before being wed at least five years.

Elizabeth dropped her goose quill pen into the empty inkwell, and rose, stepping over Lacy in the doorway. "Noah?"

"Ma'am?" her clerk called from his stool.

She hesitated for a moment, realizing what she was about to do. The nagging common sense of her dead

mother told her to pack her bag and have Johnny take
her to Philadelphia tonight. If she went to Jessop and
apologized for her behavior, for her words, he would take
her back. She knew he would. He would return the ugly
ruby ring to her finger, and she would marry him. The
arrangement would be convenient; it would become comfortable.

The trouble was, Elizabeth didn't want comfortable.
Her parents had been *comfortable*. Every married couple
she'd ever known had been *comfortable*. No, she wanted
what only O'Brian could give her. Passion. He had such
a passion for life, a passion she stifled inside her own
self to suit those around her.

So the hell with comfort . . .

"Noah, I'd like you to take a message to Mr. O'Brian
on your way home."

"Yes, ma'am?"

She walked to his desk, picking up a small scrap of
foolscap. Taking her clerk's quill from his hand, she
printed a brief message. She noticed that her hand shook
ever so slightly as she scrawled the words across the
page.

O'Brian,
   *Business to discuss. Supper, my home, eight on
the clock.*

                E.

Elizabeth folded the note and handed it to Noah, before she could give herself a chance to change her mind.
"That will be all for tonight. Deliver my message and
go home with you."

"But it's not yet even six." Noah twisted his thin fingers as he climbed off his stool. "I've not nearly completed the day's work."

"It will still be here in the morning," she told him

with a chuckle. "You work hard. Go home and enjoy your family, Noah."

Her clerk looked at her oddly. "Very well, if . . . if that's what you wish . . ."

She opened the office's front door, handing him his felt, wide-brimmed hat. "It's what I wish. Good night."

Once Noah was gone, Elizabeth went back to her office to retrieve her straw bonnet. "Let's go, hounds," she called, feeling lighter at heart than she believed she'd felt in years. "Let's go. I've a supper engagement I don't want to miss."

Elizabeth dressed carefully that evening. She wanted to appear provocative, but not whorish. If she was going to seduce O'Brian, she wanted to do it right.

She stood in front of the oval, floor-length mirror in her bedchamber, scrutinizing the gown she'd chosen. Sewn of Italian hunter green silk, her corset matched the bodice, joining at the center front with concealed hooks. Her elbow-length sleeves, worn turned back, were ruffled, ecru lace. The silk outer skirting of her petticoats opened in the center to reveal the same ecru lace.

Elizabeth had done up her freshly washed hair three times before she'd been satisfied. First she had worn it up . . . too matronly. Then down . . . too childish. Finally she'd compromised by pulling a thick handful of dark hair over the crown of her head and tying it with a bit of green ribbon, so that the mass of curls hung down her bare back. On the top of her head she wore a small cap sewn of filmy ecru lawn.

Elizabeth smiled as she turned in the mirror, first facing one way, then the other. She was pleased with what she saw. She may not have been as young as the redhead, but her nose was straighter, her lips fuller, and she was blessed with a face unmarked by pocks.

She heard the sounds of the dogs barking down below, and knew that O'Brian had arrived. She checked the case clock on the bedchamber mantel. He was early, it was barely half past seven. She bit down on her lower lip. He knew why she'd called for him. She knew he knew.

A moment later there was a knock on her chamber door.

"Yes?"

"Mr. O'Brian here to see you," one of the housemaids called. "What should I do with him, Mistress?"

"Send him into the parlor. Let Cook know we'll be ready to dine. I'll be there directly."

Elizabeth heard the girl's footsteps as she made her retreat back down the hall toward the center staircase.

She glanced at the mirror one last time. "You certain this is what you want?" she whispered. "Will you sell yourself to the devil for want of fleshly desires?"

Yes. She turned away. Yes, she was certain. As certain as she'd been of anything in her life. Her plan was simple. If she and O'Brian could come to some sort of verbal agreement with boundaries for their relationship, then she'd sleep with him. She didn't know where. She wasn't even certain when. She would have to be very careful. If word got out, her reputation would be ruined. Not only would no decent man in the colonies wed her, but she'd lose every customer she'd worked so hard to obtain.

Elizabeth went downstairs before she lost her nerve. Stepping over Lacy, who lay in the parlor doorway, she walked into the airy room smiling. "Mr. O'Brian, I'm pleased you could make it." She kept her tone polite and reserved, for the sake of the housemaid she knew was lurking around the corner trying to get a peek at the yard foreman come to dine with the mistress.

O'Brian had his back to her, looking up at the portrait of her Paul had had commissioned in England prior to their wedding.

"Good evening." He turned to face her. He had come dressed in indigo homespun breeches, a white lawn shirt with a stock, and a homespun waistcoat with cherry wood buttons. Rather than detracting from his appearance, the somber material seemed only to enhance his rugged good looks.

O'Brian indicated the portrait of Elizabeth above the fireplace with a nod of his head. Coals glowed on the hearth to chase away the chill of the September breeze. "It doesn't look much like you. Pretty, but not you."

"I think the artist drew the same simpering look on every woman's face he painted." She glided into the room, trying to pretend she always invited men to supper for the sole purpose of getting them into her bed. "Would you like a refreshment? I thought we'd let the business go until after we've dined."

He put up his hand. "No. Thank you. Nothing for me. I fear I need to keep a clear head when you're about, Mistress."

She glanced at him from across the room. He had that cocky grin on his face . . . that grin she despised . . . that grin that made her feel giddy inside.

"Let's have something to eat," she suggested, pointing to the small table that had been set up under the draped windows that ran along the garden in the front of the house.

O'Brian came to pull her chair out for her. As she took her seat, he brushed his fingertips over hers.

Elizabeth lifted her lashes.

"Pray, tell me one thing," he said softly, "before I take my seat. Have I come to be seduced, or fired?"

A smile played at the corners of her mouth. The sound of his rich tenor voice made her certain she was doing the right thing. "That depends," she whispered.

He slid into his armchair and lifted his napkin from the Chinese supper plate. "Upon what?"

She picked up her napkin and shook it so that the square of pristine white linen covered her lap. "Upon whether or not you can comply with my wishes."

The sound of a servant's footsteps halted their conversation. She smiled sweetly and made some remark in reference to the new cooper coming in two weeks. Supper was served; cold ham and roast pork, sweet peas, pumpkin biscuits, an egg-squash pie, followed by dried fruits and a creamy lemon syllabub.

Elizabeth and O'Brian chatted through the meal as a mistress and hired man would chat. They talked of the mill, of the competitor in New Jersey, of the families who lived at Lawrence Mills.

Elizabeth could barely eat as she tried not to appear nervous. She didn't want to take the chance of having any of her servants suspect anything. O'Brian ate with zealous enthusiasm, taking several helping of each course and commenting repeatedly of the talent of her cook.

Finally the meal was over, the plates cleared, and Elizabeth dismissed the servants for the night, saying she and her foreman would be discussing business now. The last servant to leave the room closed the door behind him as he went.

Elizabeth rose from her chair. The meal had been relaxing; she'd actually enjoyed O'Brian's company. She much preferred talking about the mill and the people who made it run, to talking the exorbitant price of Indian silk. But suddenly she was nervous again. *What if he really wasn't interested in her? What if what had happened the other night had happened because he wasn't attracted to her? What if he'd just been a servant trying to please his mistress—trying to keep his job?*

Elizabeth glanced at O'Brian, who had pushed back from the small dining table and was now watching her. He was attracted to her. It was just something any woman, past her first bleeding knew. She could see it in his eyes. She could tell by the expression on his face, by the way he watched her move.

"I'll make this easy on you, Liz." He folded his hands behind his head. "Tell me why you called me here."

She knew her cheeks were coloring. "You know why," she said softly.

He lowered his hands, watching her. "Do I?"

She hated this, the way he was dragging her along, trying to make her say things she didn't want to say. She walked slowly toward him, aware of the sound her stiff petticoats made as she walked across the hardwood floor. "Why do you enjoy taunting me? Why do you want me to hate myself?"

He came out of the chair. "You're wrong about that. I don't want you to hate yourself. And I don't want you to have any regrets. I want to be sure you know what you're doing, Liz."

He was standing so close that her petticoats brushed his knees. "Is that why you did that the other night?" she asked. This was so hard for her to say, but she had to know. "Was that why you touched me without taking your own pleasure? Because you didn't want to take advantage of me?" She looked down. "I thought . . . I thought maybe you didn't find me very inviting . . ."

"Ah, hell, it's not that I didn't want you, Liz, because I did. I ached for you. I ache for you now." He paused. "It's just that I want you to be sure you understand how dangerous this could be for you." He lifted a curl off her bare shoulder with his finger. "Me, I've got nothing to lose but a job, but you—"

She pressed her finger to his lips, wishing it was her mouth. "I'm an adult woman. I know what I'm about."

"Aye . . ." He brought his hand to each side of her breasts, pressing gently. "You're an adult woman, I'll give you that."

"I'm serious, O'Brian. You have to listen to me." She touched his jaw with her fingertips, forcing him to look her in the eye. "No one can know about this. No one. You know what would happen if anyone found out."

"Jessop?"

"I'd not just lose Jessop. This isn't about him. He doesn't even want to marry me anymore. I'm talking about the powder mill. I could lose it. Jessop could contest the will. People could just stop buying from me. They could stop selling me the ingredients I need to produce my powder."

He smoothed her hair. "I understand, Liz."

She took a deep breath, trying to concentrate on what she had to say. "Now I'm the one who will be in control here. We meet when I say we meet. And I'll not pay you, not half a crown."

He looked hurt. "I'm no leman, Liz. I expect no payment."

"And it's over if I say it's over. There'll be no questions, no discussion. And if you breathe a word of this to anyone, *anyone,* I swear by all that's holy you'll regret the day you ever left Ireland."

"Phwew." He gave a low whistle, his hands still resting on either side of her breasts. "I agree to all this, and what do I get?"

She lifted her lashes to stare into his eyes, that were as green as a spring meadow. "You get me, O'Brian."

He thought for a moment, his gaze locked with hers, and then he smiled, nodding. When he spoke, it was in a husky whisper. "A fair agreement, I think. More than fair for a woman like you, Liz."

She let her eyes drift shut as he closed his arms around her. She thought surely he was going to kiss her, but instead, he brought her head to his chest and stroked her hair. He touched her like a lover, like a man touched a woman he cared for.

He was very good with women. So good that she had to remind herself that this was a business arrangement of sorts. It would be an equal exchange of fleshly pleasures. Nothing more.

She lifted her head from his shoulder, where it seemed to fit so naturally. "Not in my home, you understand. Never here."

He kissed her forehead, then her cheek, brushing his lips against her skin so that he barely made contact. "Tell me where."

He was running his hands down her sides, and even through the layers of clothing, she could feel the heat of his touch. Even through the thickness of the gown and undergarments, he excited her. "I don't know. The office?" she whispered.

He kissed the pulse of her throat. "Not terribly romantic, sweet. Fun perhaps, but not romantic. Certainly not comfortable."

Elizabeth was beside herself. Here she'd made this decision to practically prostitute herself to her foreman, and she couldn't even think of a place to actually do it!

He threaded his fingers through hers and kissed the swell of one breast before looking up at her. "My cottage. Come to my cottage. It's nothing fancy, not what you're used to, but at least we'll have a bed, Liz. You'll be safe there. No one ever comes to the foreman's home without a personal invitation—unless, of course, the mistress sends for him," he added lightly.

She lowered her head to his shoulder again, enjoying his leisurely caresses. "I can't believe I'm doing this. I can't believe I'm actually telling you I'll come to your bed."

"Your rules. You say no at any time, and I'll abide," he whispered. "Let no lassie ever say I forced her to do what she didn't want to do." He tugged on the lobe of her ear with his teeth. "Take your time. Think about it."

"I don't want to take my time." She could already hear a change in the rhythm of her own breathing. She could already feel her body growing warm with desire for him. "I made up my mind. I want to come. Tonight."

He lowered his mouth to hers, his kiss filled with the promise of things to come.

When Elizabeth withdrew, breathless, she made herself take a step back from him. "Go home," she said softly, her voice breathy. "I'll come after everyone is abed. It'll have to be late."

He took her hand and bowed, brushing his lips across her knuckles. "I'll wait for you, Lizzy. I'll wait all night."

Elizabeth watched O'Brian as he crossed the room toward the door. As he walked away, his broad shoulders swaggering ever so slightly, a smile played on her lips. When he reached the door and went to turn the polished knob, he looked back over his shoulder and winked at her.

I'd best take care, she thought, suddenly uneasy, the smile fading from her face. *Else, I could fall in love with this man.*

Fourteen

It was well after the midnight hour by the time Elizabeth reached O'Brian's cottage on Worker's Hill. For close to ten minutes she stood in the shadows of the stone and frame building, trying to get up her nerve. It wasn't that she didn't want to go in, because she did. She was just apprehensive, even more apprehensive than she'd been on her wedding night.

That first night with Paul, she'd expected nothing. Her knowledge of the actual act of intercourse had been hazy. When she'd found the sexual act pleasing, she'd been pleasantly surprised. But now she knew there was more, she knew it could be better, and that's why she was hesitant. What if she didn't please O'Brian? What if she didn't find the actual act with him enjoyable? What if it had been the flirting she was looking for all along, and not the intimacy?

Elizabeth turned the knob on the outside door before she changed her mind. She stepped inside and closed the door behind her, fearful she might be seen by some worker returning late from the Sow's Ear.

Inside, she pressed her back to the rough-hewn door. A dim light came from the far side of the room near the stone fireplace. O'Brian sat in a battered chair that had once been in the big house. He sat comfortably with his bare feet crossed, a book cradled in his hands. An open bottle of Virginia whiskey rested on the table at his side, but very little had been taken from it.

He looked over the edge of his book. "Liz . . ."

She didn't know what to do. Did she go to him? Did she wait for him to come to her? She felt so awkward, so inexperienced.

O'Brian rose, seeming to sense her discomfort. He set the book aside.

"Bacon's Works?" she mused, reading the cloth binding.

"Aye." He walked toward her, his bare feet noiseless on the wide-planked floor.

"Where did you get it?"

"Your study."

He laughed when she frowned. "I'm no thief. It's me own, sweetheart. Bought and paid for." He studied her face. "Why do you look so surprised? I *can* read, you know."

She crossed her arms over her chest, giving a shrug. "I know. You just don't seem like a man who enjoys Bacon, except perhaps with his hotcakes and eggs."

He placed one hand on each side of the door, trapping her between his massive arms. A smile tugged at the corners of his sensual mouth. "And what sort of man likes Bacon, might I ask?"

"I don't know," she whispered honestly. "I don't know what I think about anything anymore. It seems that you've changed many of my opinions, since you've come."

He leaned forward to brush his lips against hers. "I'm glad you came. I feared you'd change your mind."

She looked up at him. She felt so vulnerable right now, a feeling she didn't welcome.

"I'd offer you a drink, but I've no lady's wine," he said, gazing into her eyes.

"I . . . I think I'd like a taste of the whiskey." She pointed.

He grinned. "Whiskey, is it? Don't tell me you plan on getting so sotted you can't appreciate my talents."

She laughed, ducking under his arm to escape his embrace. She walked to the table and poured herself a small portion of the amber libation. "Would you be shocked if I told you I actually liked the taste?" She took a small sip, letting the heat of the homemade liquor burn a path to her stomach.

He stood near the door, watching her. "Nothing would surprise me about you, Liz. Not a thing."

She took another sip. He was watching her.

"I like the petticoats." He indicated the homespun clothing she wore.

She took another sip of the whiskey from his mug, dropping a low curtsy. "Rather close to a tavern doxy, no? I thought I'd be less conspicuous."

He came to her. One hand swept the muslin mobcap off her head, and her loose hair fell over her shoulders. "You're so beautiful, ye take a man's breath away, Liz."

She laughed nervously. "You needn't think you must ply me with your shameless lies. I'm here, O'Brian, because I want to be. You've already charmed the petticoats off me."

He took the mug from her hand and set it on the table behind her. Then he wrapped his arms around her waist and pulled her to him. "You needn't be so hard on yourself, Liz." He caressed her cheek with the knuckles of one hand. "This is what God Almighty put man and woman on this earth for. Ye can't help your desires any more than you can help your thirst or hunger."

She leaned back in his arms. The whiskey had fortified her. It gave her confidence. She ran her hand along his broad shoulder. *That or it gave her an excuse for her boldness.* "Let's go upstairs," she said huskily. "I wouldn't want anyone to see us through the window."

She reached for his mug with the whiskey, but he took

it from her hand. "You don't need it, sweet." He brushed his lips across her cheek and took her hand in his. "Come with me."

Side by side, hand in hand, Elizabeth and O'Brian climbed the narrow, twisting staircase to his bedchamber loft. She had never been in one of the worker's bedchambers before, and was shocked by its sparsity. No lamp burned in the tiny, warm room, but moonbeams streamed through the open window, casting light on the only piece of furniture, a rope bed in the center of the rough, planked floor. The roof was slanted over their heads, so that in places O'Brian couldn't walk without stooping.

Elizabeth stood in the moonlight, knowing her hands trembled. "Do you . . . you want to take off my clothes?"

He laughed. "Christ, sweetheart. You act as if you're bound for the gallows." He took her hand in his to cease its shaking. "Are you certain this is what you want?"

She stepped up to him, placing both hands on his muscular shoulders. "Yes," she whispered desperately. "I want to feel like you made me feel that night in the office. I want you to touch me." She brushed her palm over the rough weave of his shirt, over his chest, down his hard, flat belly. "I want to touch you."

He took her hand and raised it to his lips. He kissed each pad of her fingertips. He stroked her back.

Elizabeth watched the expression on his face, fascinated by the strong jut of his jaw, by the dark shadow of his beard stubble, by the curve of his lips, and spun gold hair. Finally she lifted up on her toes and pressed her mouth to his. That first kiss was a gentle kiss, a kiss that seemed to seal their bargain.

But gentle kisses were not what she'd come for. Gentle kisses were not what she risked her business for. She'd had that with Paul. What she wanted now was passion, O'Brian's passion.

She wove her fingers through his unbound hair, deepening the kiss. He moaned when she brushed her hand over his chest, grazing the nub of his male nipple. She smiled in the moonlight.

"What?" he whispered.

She touched his nipple again. "I . . . I didn't know it felt . . . *you* felt the same as I."

He reached both hands over his head and grabbed the muslin shirt, tugging it over his head and dropping it to the floor. "I don't know that it feels the same, because I've never been a lassie." He took her hand, laying it on his bare chest. "But it feels damned good, I can tell you that."

Elizabeth brushed her fingertips over his nipples, fascinated by the idea that she could give him pleasure, that she could have the same control over him that he could hold over her. They kissed, and then she lowered her head, crouching a little so that she could touch his nipple with the tip of her tongue.

He groaned again.

This time she sucked gently.

"Sweet Mary," he swore. "Ye've a knack for learning, haven't you, sweet?"

She laughed. His teasing put her at ease.

"Come," he took her hand and led her to the rope bed, "let's stretch out. We've got 'til dawn—all the time in the world."

The bed ropes creaked and moaned as O'Brian rolled on his side and reached out to draw her in beside him. Had there been a headboard and footboard, he'd have been too tall to stretch out. As she curled against him, her fingers on the curly hair of his chest, she wondered absently if he would fit in her own four-poster bed up at the big house.

O'Brian brushed his palm across her cheek, pushing the heavy, dark hair that obscured her face. "I want to see you," he whispered. "I want to savor every moment."

He leaned and kissed her full on the mouth. "I want to remember every kiss, every touch, every cry of pleasure that passes your lips."

Paul had never spoken a word to her once they were beneath the sheets, so it was strange to hear O'Brian's voice. But she liked it, she decided. She liked it very much. Somehow the sound of his voice added to the excitement of the caress of his hands.

Taking his leisure, O'Brian kissed her again, this time tracing her collarbone with his finger.

Shivers of anticipation rippled through her body, as she thought of him touching her breasts . . . as she waited.

When he loosened the drawstring of her bodice, Elizabeth sighed. That was another reason why she'd worn the garb usually reserved for annual cleaning days. It was easily accessible.

O'Brian slipped his warm hand over her breast, and she tugged on the muslin bodice, opening it for him.

"So beautiful," he murmured. "So perfect. Look . . ." He cupped her breast in her hand. "They fit perfectly," he teased. "They must be mine."

Elizabeth threw back her head and laughed. His humor was crude, but she liked it. If she would allow herself to admit it, she liked him.

She lifted her leg and threw it over his, showing off a bare calf and thigh.

"No stockings, Mistress? I'm shocked."

"You are not." She kicked off her leather slippers, hearing only one hit the floor. "Those tarts of yours probably wear no stockings, no shift either, would be my guess."

He covered her mouth with his. "Hush," he muttered against her lips. "I'll not hear talk of other women, nor other men, in my bed. That's *my* rule." He ran his hand along her side, down the dip in her waist, and over her hips. "Didn't anyone ever tell you it's rude?"

She ran her finger along the line of his breeches, watching how his muscles contracted at her touch. "Sorry. No one did. I've not nearly the experience with debauchery that you have."

"Saints preserve me, you've a wicked tongue." His fingers had found the hook and eyes of her petticoat's waistband, and he was already sliding the burgundy homespun down over her hips. A moment later he tossed her day corset to the floor with the petticoat. Now only her shift and his breeches stood between flesh and flesh.

"Liz, Liz," O'Brian murmured, kissing the arched fullness of her breast. "Tell me what you want. Tell me how you want to be touched."

"I . . . I don't know," she answered. "I told you, I've little experience."

"So you did." He kissed the tip of her nose. "So, just tell if you don't care for something." He broke into a grin. "Better yet, tell me if you like something I do."

He was running his hand over her hip now, down her thigh, under her shift. His warm hand on her skin made her flush. She could feel the heat diffusing through her cheeks.

As they lay side by side, he continued his gentle assault, while Elizabeth took her time exploring his body. It was funny. She had seen Paul nude. She'd even touched him a couple of times, but she'd not really known him. He'd never encouraged her to touch him, only to lie there and let him have his way.

Elizabeth pressed a kiss to the blond curls that were sprinkled across O'Brian's chest. She liked this much better, for it seemed that with every stroke of her hand, her own desire mounted. She liked the feel of his corded muscles at her fingertips. She liked the taste of his salty skin.

When O'Brian sat her up to remove her shift, she surrendered it gladly. The warm attic chamber had grown even warmer. As he tossed the bleached muslin to the floor, she tugged at his waistband playfully. "Your turn, too, I think."

He grimaced. "But I was saving the best for last, sweet."

She laughed, knowing that he was teasing again. "I think it's my right to see the goods." Daringly, she brushed her hand over the bulge in his tight homespun breeches.

O'Brian groaned.

Elizabeth lay back, tucking her hands beneath her head to support it. "Go ahead," she urged. "Here I lie in my birthday suit. 'Tis only fair."

Giving her a look of feigned irritation, he slid off the far side of the bed and dropped his hand to the tie of his indigo breeches.

She smiled as she watched him in the moonlight, knowing she was wicked, but not caring. The sight of him standing there with his broad, bare chest, sinewy forearms, and burgeoning breeches, made her damp between her thighs. She lifted a hand, waving with her fingers. "Come, come, I'll not tolerate shyness."

His green-eyed gaze locked with hers, he slowly began to unlace the flap of his breeches. Elizabeth licked her dry lower lip with the tip of her tongue. He was teasing her, undressing so slowly. She knew he was teasing her. She knew he knew she liked it, too.

Finally the laces were undone, and he caught the homespun at the waistband and tugged his breeches down over his hips.

Elizabeth felt her cheeks grow hot as his manhood sprang from its confinement, tumescent and glistening. He was large, larger than Paul had been . . .

O'Brian added his breeches to the growing pile of garments on the floor, and climbed over the bed toward her. Elizabeth put out her arms. The sight of him, the heavy-limbed aching in her body, made her open her thighs. He covered her body with his own, taking care to rest his weight on his forearms. When he lowered his mouth to hers, she arched against him, a moan parting her lips as he pressed his hips to hers.

"Damn woman, but you make a man hot for you," he whispered. "I meant to take it slow, but—"

She shook her head, raising her body up, pressing her groin to his. "No," she whispered. "Not this time. I need you now. I need to feel you inside me."

He kissed her again, shifting his weight to run his hand over her woman's mound. Elizabeth moaned again and again, not caring that she was making enough noise to wake the dead. It felt so good . . . *he* felt so good.

His fingers probed, and she lifted her hips to the rhythm of his hand. But this wasn't what she wanted tonight. She wanted consummation. "No," she whispered. "Not again. Not this time." With her own hand she reached with shameless abandon and grasped his rod.

O'Brian made a sound deep in his throat. "Liz . . . Liz . . ." he muttered.

Trying to ease her own need, she fumbled with her hand, so mad with want of him that she could no longer think clearly.

Laughing, kissing the damp tendrils of hair that clung to her temples, he brushed aside her hand and grasped his member.

Elizabeth lifted her hips in reception to his first thrust, crying out in what seemed like relief. It had been so long . . . too long.

O'Brian buried his face in her hair. They were both damp with perspiration, the dark attic filled with the scent of their heady passion.

Finally, after what seemed an eternity to Elizabeth, he

began to move inside her. At first his strokes were short and shallow. She clung to him, knowing she left marks on his back with her fingernails. She felt like her entire body was consumed in flames. The heat was unbearable; the need for fulfillment was unbearable.

She called his name. He drove deeper.

Elizabeth twisted her fingers in his golden hair, pulling his head down so that she could look into his stormy green eyes.

He thrust his hot tongue between her lips, as he increased the rhythm of his movement. The throbbing, incandescent heat of her groin spread quickly, as she felt herself rising higher and higher, reaching, aching for that single solitary moment of ultimate pleasure.

Just when Elizabeth thought she couldn't stand the sweet frustration another instant, her world burst in a thousand pinpricks of white light. Her muscles contracted and relaxed again and again. She heard herself cry out. O'Brian groaned and gave a final thrust, spilling into her.

They lay still like that for a long time, their bodies still joined, their breath still rapid. Eventually O'Brian rolled off her and onto his side. He rested one hand on her flat belly, snuggling close to her.

Elizabeth didn't think she had ever felt so good in her life. She wanted to laugh; she wanted to cry.

O'Brian stroked her temple, brushing the damp hair off her face.

As he pulled back his hand, she raised her head and kissed it. "That was really something, wasn't it?" she said tentatively.

He rolled onto his back, exhaling. "Sure as hell was, Liz. I don't say this to brag, but I've been with many women and no one . . . no one has ever—"

"I told you. You don't have to lie to me." She pushed

on her elbow to look at his face. "That's not what I'm looking for."

He rolled onto his side so that he faced her. "I'm no liar. I never say anything but what I mean, what I truly think. And I'm telling you, Elizabeth Lawrence, that I've never made love to a woman I've enjoyed more."

More wooing. She flopped back to stare up at the slanted ceiling. "I should go."

"No." He rolled over, trapping her with one long arm. "Not yet. You can't take advantage of me like this, *Mistress,* and then cast me aside so quickly."

His calling her mistress made her uncomfortable. But then, what had she expected? Nothing had really changed between them. He was still her foreman, and she still paid his wages. This, what they had here, was just a business arrangement of a different sort.

O'Brian was quiet for a moment, and Elizabeth just lay there beside him, enjoying the feel of his body touching hers. He traced over her bare chest and stomach with his fingertips, drawing an imaginary line.

"Liz," he said after a few moments. "I suppose this is late to bring up the subject, but . . . but what if you were to become pregnant?"

She waved her hand over her head. "Can't happen." She looked at him. She saw no reason to give him the details of the female curse her mother's family had passed onto her. "You needn't worry."

"What do you mean, it *can't* happen?"

"I really don't want to discuss my female ailments with you, O'Brian, all right? I'm just telling you, there's no need for you to be concerned. There'll be no child."

O'Brian nodded, seeming to want to respect her privacy. "I just . . . you said you hadn't had much experience. I didn't want you to think I didn't care. I should have asked before, but the truth is, I wanted you so badly, Liz, that I guess I didn't care."

"Don't worry about it." She rolled out of the rope bed. "I'm one woman who can take care of herself. I'm not the kind to try and trap a man like that." She knelt on the floor to retrieve her shift. "Why don't you get some sleep now. I want you to oversee that load of powder being shipped to Philadelphia in the morning." She dropped her shift over her head, her entire body still tingling from their lovemaking. "I can let myself out."

He watched her from the center of his bed, as she redressed and searched for her lost slipper. When she was acceptably clothed, she leaned over and kissed him. " 'Night, O'Brian."

" 'Night, Liz." He seemed amused. "When?"

She knew what he meant; she didn't have to ask. "Tomorrow night. I'll come here." Then she left the attic chamber and went down the winding steps. *Less than twenty-four hours and I'll be back,* she thought, smiling in the darkness. *Heavens, the man's worse than an opiate . . .*

Fifteen

O'Brian dragged the small-toothed rake through the damp, black gunpowder spread over the rack to dry. He moved onto the next rack beside Samson. The September breeze blew gently down the hill out of the trees above. O'Brian stopped for a moment and closed his eyes, enjoying the feel of the wind on his face.

"What you doin'?" Samson asked.

O'Brian opened his eyes, feeling a little foolish at having been caught by his friend. Since their exchange of obscenities and fists the first day he'd come to Lawrence Mills, the two had gotten along just fine. Samson and Ngozi had even had O'Brian to supper once. "I'm just glad to see the days of Hades pass. The breeze feels good."

Samson chuckled. "Ya cain't fool me. Yer a man pinin' for a woman. Tell ole' Samson what her name is."

O'Brian dropped the rake to the sloped ground and leaned on the handle. "What *whose* name is?"

"Yer lady." Samson leaned on his own rake and thrust a wooden toothpick between his lips.

"I don't know what you're talking about."

Samson slapped his patched breeches. "God hulp the foreman! He got it bad."

O'Brian frowned. Was it so obvious that even Samson could see it in his face?

These last weeks with Liz had O'Brian worried. He'd

expected he'd have tired of her by now, just like he'd
tired of the redhead down at the Sow's Ear, just like he'd
tired of that captain's wife, just like he tired of them all.
But Liz was different. He'd known it before he'd been
with her.

He cursed himself for not having followed his own
gut instinct and kept his cod in his breeches.

They'd met every night for the past two weeks. She
made the choice to come each night, but he craved her
like a man in prison craves the sunlight. All day as he
worked, he thought of nothing but her. And when he saw
her about the mills, it was all he could do to keep up
the game of mistress and servant. Instead of listening to
her orders, he found himself studying the color of her
hair, remembering the feel of her touch.

O'Brian felt like a besotted schoolboy. In his bed
Elizabeth was as exciting, as tender a lover as he'd ever
had. But the moment she swept out of his cottage, she
was the mistress again. The woman was as cool, as demanding, as focused on the work at hand as any slave
driver. O'Brian found himself staring into her dark eyes,
searching for some recognition, whilst she looked clear
through him, demanding to know why the waterwheel
wasn't turning again.

O'Brian looked at his friend's broad, dark-skinned
face. He needed so badly to talk to someone, anyone.
What harm would it do? The way Liz acted in public
with him, no one could possibly ever suspect the truth.
Besides, Samson, like most of the other workers, thought
he was married. Everyone just assumed he was a philanderer.

O'Brian looked up at Samson, who waited patiently.
"She's driving me mad, Samson. No woman's ever set
me in such a spin."

Samson's laughter came out in a deep rumble. "I know
what you mean. I'm not sayin' it's right, you already

havin' a wife and all." He gave a low whistle. "But my Ngozi, she done the same to me. What Miss 'Lizbeth done, makin' me marry Ngozi, it was the best thing that coulda happened to me." He looked down at the ground, studying his dusty boots. "Best thing ya could do to cure that love sickness is get yer wife and little ones here."

O'Brian spun his rake in the grass. "Women just get in the way. You know what I mean, Samson. I'm a loner. I've got plans. There's no room in my life for a woman, any women. A few years here, and I'll be on my way upstream. I want my own powder mill. I want to be my own man."

"Phew! You let Miss 'Lizbeth hear that talk, and you'll be out on your ear, foreman!"

O'Brian grinned. It was funny, but he liked to hear men talk about her that way. He liked the idea that such a strong woman would have chosen him to—

What was she doing with him?

Using him for sex, of course. Nothing more. That was what he didn't like. She seemed to take it so easily. Their relationship seemed to mean nothing to her but a quick tumble.

The same that all his relationships in the past had meant to him . . .

O'Brian guessed that that was why he was having a hard time dealing with Liz in his mind. Because in her, he saw himself. All these years he'd taken pride in his pleasant emotional detachment from the women he was involved with. It wasn't that he hadn't cared for them when he was with them, he'd just never stayed around long enough to let them get under his skin.

Liz was different. She'd been under his skin since the first day he'd come to Lawrence Mills.

O'Brian picked up his rake and began to push the damp black powder around one of the large drying racks. He didn't like feeling like this, so off balance, his thoughts so overrun with emotions. A man with plans had no time for emotion. It would do nothing but get in the way of his ambition.

He wondered if maybe it would be better just to break it off with Liz now, before he got himself or her into trouble.

No, not yet, he told himself. *I can't. . . . I'd not want to insult her like that,* he rationalized. But soon, soon he'd find himself another woman to warm his bed. That, or maybe he'd get lucky and Liz would just tire of him. That way there'd be no hard feelings between them. She'd just stop coming to his bed at night, and he'd stop dreaming she was there with him even after she'd gone. The relationship would run its course and be over. That would be clean; it would be easy . . . he prayed to sweet Mary.

Elizabeth knelt in the grass in the front garden, pulling the brush over Lacy's short, glossy coat. As Elizabeth ran her hand over the wiry-framed hound, she tried to decide if the bitch was going to have pups this fall or not.

Claire sat on a bench, a picture of loveliness in a gown of fall colors. She was busy arranging a handful of the last of the orange and yellow marigolds she'd picked from the garden.

Elizabeth had seen little of Jessop since his trip three weeks ago, but she'd barely noticed. She was too wrapped up in O'Brian and her own awakened sexuality. It was all Elizabeth could do to concentrate on her work during the day, for thinking of the night to come.

"I don't like when you and Brother fight," Claire said out of the blue. "He's not very nice to me when you fight."

Elizabeth lifted her head in surprise. A moment before, they'd been discussing a neighbor's ague. "What makes you think Jessop and I are arguing?"

She plucked a marigold from the flowers laid out on the bench. "I'm not stupid."

"I didn't say you were," Elizabeth answered gently. "I only wondered how you knew we'd had a disagreement. Did your brother discuss our disagreement?"

"He said he didn't know if he was going to marry you. He said you must be suffering from a woman's ailment, because you've not been yourself lately."

Elizabeth threw down the comb. "I am no such thing!" She looked down at her dog, dropping a hand to her hip. "Damnation, but that makes me mad when he says things like that!"

"See." Claire plucked a perfect petal from the marigold and let the wind take it. "I knew you were fighting. Brother curses when he talks about you, too. He says he doesn't know what he's going to do with two women with nervous disorders."

Elizabeth gritted her teeth. She didn't know what she was going to do about her relationship with Jessop. They had barely seen each other in weeks, and yet he spoke to others about her as if he still had a claim to her. He hadn't informed any of his friends or business acquaintances that their marriage was quite possibly off. He still walked about her property as if he owned it. And now he was comparing her to Claire!

Elizabeth glanced up at Claire. "Claire dear, would you happen to know where your brother is right now? I think I need to have a word with him."

She went on plucking petals. "Last I saw, he was meeting with one of his gentlemen friends. Talking business. Mr. Mullen was a nice piece, but their talk was boring, so I left and came to visit you."

Elizabeth frowned. "Claire, you shouldn't speak of your brother's business friends that way. It's not proper for a lady." She shook her head, speaking more to herself than her sister-in-law. "I wish I knew where you got these colorful references."

Claire tossed her hair back. "It's chilly. I think I'd best go inside. Might I play your spinet?"

Elizabeth was looking up at Claire, when she suddenly noticed a mark on her neck. "Claire, what is that?" Startled, Elizabeth got up from the ground.

"What's what?" Claire asked innocently.

"That, there." Elizabeth brushed aside Claire's hair to reveal a blue pulpy mark on the side of her neck. It appeared to be a bruise of some sort.

Claire touched her neck. "I don't know. Is it a skin irritation? I always use my lotion before I go to bed."

Elizabeth dropped down on the bench beside Claire to get a closer look. Had someone tried to choke Claire? Were those finger marks? Had some man done this? One of the workers, perhaps?

No . . . Elizabeth swore softly. It was a man all right, but he'd not made that mark with his hands.

"Claire." Elizabeth spoke sharply. "Have you been with someone?"

Claire got a strange look on her face. *"Someone?"*

Elizabeth exhaled. It was so hard to deal with Claire sometimes. She was an adult woman in most ways, yet there seemed to be some subjects that were beyond her understanding. "Yes," Elizabeth went on gently. "With a man. You know. Did . . . did you let a man kiss you?" Elizabeth brushed her own neck, remembering the feel of O'Brian's lips. "There maybe."

"Brother says men are evil. He says they will take advantage of an innocent like myself. Futtering devils!" She peered into Elizabeth's face. "Brother says he will protect me always from the frigging bastards."

Elizabeth ignored her sister-in-law's foul language. She didn't care what Claire said. That mark on her neck had definitely come from a man's mouth. The girl might not have known what he was leading her into, but she'd obviously been with *someone*.

Elizabeth laid her hand gently on Claire's arm. "Claire, dear. Let me tell you something. Your brother is right. Men can be devils. They will take advantage of you. Claire, you mustn't let men kiss you or touch you. Do you understand what I'm saying? Those men, they don't love you like I do . . . like your brother does. They'll hurt you, sweetheart. They'll make a baby in your belly, and make you very sick."

Claire looked into Elizabeth's face, but her eyes were unseeing. For a moment she just stared. Then she offered her hand, turning her pretty face. "Would you like to see my mousey?" She broke into a mischievous grin. "I'll let you hold my mousey, if you want to." She offered her closed fist. "I dare you."

Elizabeth got up from the garden bench. "Didn't you say you wanted to play the spinet?"

Clair bounced up. "Oh, yes!" She hurried down the stone path that led to the house, her petticoats rustling. "Can mousey play, too?" she called over her shoulder. "He plays the spinet well, you know."

Elizabeth smiled sadly. Claire acted so normal at times, that she almost forget how severe her illness was. But it was moments like this when she realized Claire might not ever recover from Paul's death.

A week later Elizabeth found herself picking her way through the forest along the Brandywine River. It was late afternoon, and a crisp breeze rustled the tree limbs overhead. Dead golden leaves drifted through the air, lighting on her shoulders and in her hair.

O'Brian had said there was an abandoned stone shed somewhere close by, but if she didn't find it soon, she'd turn back. She didn't like the idea of meeting in the light of day. Somehow that seemed more wicked than meeting one's lover in the cover of darkness.

So why had she come?

Because she couldn't get enough of him. Because she'd make love with him this afternoon and still want to go to his cottage tonight. She knew she was barely getting enough sleep to function. She was dozing off at her desk in the office in broad daylight, and at the evening supper table. But she was happy. Happier than she'd ever been in her life.

Elizabeth tightened her light wool kerchief over her shoulders and ducked beneath a low-hanging branch. A dilapidated stone structure came into view through the pine boughs.

"O'Brian?" she called tentatively. "O'Brian, are you there?"

She waited a moment, listening to the sounds of the forest. A squirrel scampered by with an acorn in his mouth. "O'Brian!"

She heard the crunch of footsteps in dry leaves, and O'Brian appeared from behind the building. His spun gold hair was unbound, his coat slightly rumpled, his eyes sleepy.

"Did I catch you napping by chance?"

"Sweet Mary, Mother of God, Liz! You keep me up all night with your needs, and then you expect me to put in a full day at the mills. You're breaking me, woman!"

She laughed. "I can go, if you like. Then you could finish your nap."

He caught her by her shoulders. "I think not."

She pressed her mouth to his warm lips. "You certain?"

"Mmm hmm," he answered against her lips, the desire plain in his voice. "Quite."

She kissed the patch of chest hair that showed through

the cut V in his muslin shirt. "Do you own a proper stock, Mr. O'Brian?" she asked. "Because you never wear it."

"I own one—meant for weddings and funerals, nothing more." He nibbled on the lobe of her ear. "I'm a common man. Ye forget that sometimes, Lizzy. Common men have no use for lace stocks and fancy breeches. Work, that's what makes men like me tick like a Swiss case clock."

Elizabeth lifted her chin, letting him kiss the base of her throat. O'Brian was right. She did forget who he was. She did try to compare him to Paul, to Jessop, even to her father, and it wasn't fair. She had no right to try to make him anyone but himself, even in her own mind.

"I like it when you kiss me like that," she whispered. He brushed aside the hem of her kerchief, kissing the exposed skin above her apple green chintz bodice.

"Like this?"

"Yes."

"How could I improve it?"

"Lower," she responded with throaty laughter.

He threw back his head and laughed with her, their voices joining as one to echo in the pin oaks overhead.

"You're always full of surprises, lassie, that's what I like about you." He dropped his hand over her shoulder to lead her around to the leeward side of the abandoned outbuilding. "You're about as predictable as the eye of a storm. Similar disposition, too."

She jabbed her elbow into his side. "Keep it up, *lad,* and you'll be shoveling horse manure from my barns tomorrow."

He grimaced. "You keep a tight rein on me, that you do."

The far side of the stone building had crumbled so, that most of one wall was missing. Inside on the leafy dirt floor, O'Brian had spread out a wool barn blanket. A basket rested in the corner, with a quarter wheel of cheese and a loaf of bread sticking out. Upon closer inspection she spotted two shiny red apples and a jug of sweet cider beneath a linen napkin.

She turned back to him. "A picnic?"

"What can I say? Ye and your wild ways give me an appetite."

She glanced at the rafters overhead, then the crumbled wall. "We're certainly out in the open, aren't we?"

Coming up behind her, he wrapped his arms around her waist. "Nothing like making love beneath the blue sky, Liz."

She closed her eyes, leaning back, letting his strength support her. "But someone might see us," she said, already feeling herself relax in his embrace.

He turned her around so that she faced him. "There's not a house or a mill for a mile. Only the squirrels will take notice, and they'll not tell."

"Only the squirrels . . ." Her laughter bubbled up as she leaned into him, offering him her lips, wanting to feel his mouth on hers.

Time stood still as they kissed there in the open air of the abandoned shack. Leaves drifted through the air, and bird song filled their secret hideaway.

O'Brian pushed the shoulders of her green, flowered-cotton chintz gown down, so that he could kiss the mounds of her peaked breasts. Her nipples puckered in the cool autumn breeze, and she sighed. The heat of his mouth, the flicker of his velvet tongue made gooseflesh rise on her bare chest.

Elizabeth laughed deeply in her throat, as she slid her hands down over his broad back to the waistband of his homespun breeches. "I want them off," she whispered, even as her fingers found the laces and pulled on them. In the last weeks she'd become rather deft at removing a man's clothing.

O'Brian moaned, his hot breath in her ear as she

pushed the rough cloth over his muscular buttocks. His mouth on hers, his hands on her breasts, made her burn with desire for him.

She lowered herself to her knees in front of him.

"What are you doing?" he asked huskily.

She wrapped her fingers around his hardened shaft and touched the tip with her tongue. "Must I explain? And I thought *you* were the one giving *me* the lessons," she teased.

He had already pulled the horn hairpins from her hair, and now ran his fingers through the thick, curly mass. "Making me mad," he answered thickly. "That's what you're doing, making me mad as May butter."

Her laughter bubbled up as she took him into her mouth, reveling in the pleasure it gave her to please him.

"Liz, Liz . . ." He called her name again and again, as she stroked with her tongue, with her lips, experimenting, testing him.

As Elizabeth waged her wicked assault, she found herself as amazed by O'Brian's reactions as she'd been of her own. She had never fathomed a man and woman could give each other such pleasure. Why had no one ever told her the truth? Why had she never experienced this with Paul?

O'Brian tightened his grip on her shoulders. "Enough," he growled. And then he lifted her in his arms, bringing her completely off her feet. "Come here so that I can taste you, witch."

She felt the leafy ground under her back, as he threw her petticoats up over her waist. She tangled her fingers through his hair, as he lowered his head to touch her the way only he could touch her.

Elizabeth's senses soared. She knew she cried out. She couldn't help herself. She knew now why women were so attracted to him. She knew why the red-haired whore still fawned after him. It was his magic.

Wish You Were Here?

You can be, every month, with Zebra Historical Romance Novels.

AND TO GET YOU STARTED, ALLOW US TO SEND YOU

4 Historical Romances Free

A $19.96 VALUE!

With absolutely no obligation to buy anything.

YOU ARE CORDIALLY INVITED TO GET SWEPT AWAY INTO NEW WORLDS OF PASSION AND ADVENTURE.

AND IT WON'T COST YOU A PENNY!

Receive 4 Zebra Historical Romances, Absolutely <u>Free</u>!
(A $19.96 value)

Now you can have your pick of handsome, noble adventurers with romance in their hearts and you on their minds. Zebra publishes Historical Romances That Burn With The Fire Of History by the world's finest romance authors.

This very special FREE offer entitles you to 4 Zebra novels at absolutely no cost, with no obligation to buy anything, ever. It's an offer designed to excite your most vivid dreams and desires...and save you almost $20!

And that's not all you get...

Your Home Subscription Saves You Money Every Month.

After you've enjoyed your initial FREE package of 4 books, you'll begin to receive monthly shipments of new Zebra titles. These novels are delivered direct to your home as soon as they are published...sometimes even before the bookstores get them! Each monthly shipment of 4 books will be yours to examine for 10 days. Then if you decide to keep the books, you'll pay the preferred subscriber's price of just $4.00 per title. That's $16 for all 4 books...a savings of almost $4 off the publisher's price! (A nominal shipping and handling charge of $1.50 per shipment will be added.)

There Is No Minimum Purchase. And Your Continued Satisfaction Is Guaranteed.

We're so sure that you'll appreciate the money-saving convenience of home delivery that we guarantee your complete satisfaction. You may return any shipment...for any reason...within 10 days and pay nothing that month. And if you want us to stop sending books, just say the word. There is no minimum number of books you must buy.

It's a no-lose proposition, so send for your 4 FREE books today!

YOU'RE GOING TO LOVE GETTING
4 FREE BOOKS

These books worth almost $20, are yours without cost or obligation when you fill out and mail this certificate.
(If the certificate is missing below, write to: Zebra Home Subscription Service, Inc., 120 Brighton Road, P.O. Box 5214, Clifton, New Jersey 07015-5214

Complete and mail this card to receive 4 Free books!

Yes! Please send me 4 Zebra Historical Romances without cost or obligation. I understand that each month thereafter I will be able to preview 4 new Zebra Historical Romances FREE for 10 days. Then, if I should decide to keep them, I will pay the money-saving preferred publisher's price of just $4.00 each...a total of $16. That's almost $4 less than the publisher's price. (A nominal shipping and handling charge of $1.50 per shipment will be added.) I may return any shipment within 10 days and owe nothing, and I may cancel this subscription at any time. The 4 FREE books will be mine to keep in any case.

Name _____

Address _____ Apt. _____

City _____ State _____ Zip _____

Telephone ( ) _____

Signature _____
(If under 18, parent or guardian must sign.)

LP0495

O'Brian lifted his head, but it was a full second before she realized he'd ceased his exquisite torture.

She tried to sit up, her mind blurred by the surges of warm pleasure that still rippled through her body. "What is it?"

He brought his finger to his lips as he rose, looking rather foolish in naught but his boots and shirt. From his crumpled coat, he retrieved a flintlock pistol.

Elizabeth covered her mouth with her hand to keep the sound of her strangled cry from escaping. Someone was out there! Someone could have seen them! She looked down at herself. She was bare to the waist, with her petticoats and shift bunched around her so that a passerby could see the patch of hair between her legs.

She shoved down her skirts and tried to pull the shoulders of her bodice up.

O'Brian crept out of the building and disappeared around the corner.

Elizabeth heard the sudden sound of rustling leaves, and then O'Brian's voice reverberated through the tree tops.

"Stop!" he barked. "Else I shoot you down . . ."

Sixteen

Elizabeth heard a woman shriek. Pulling up her bodice and tossing her wool kerchief over her bare shoulders, she stumbled out of the lean-to. O'Brian had removed her boots and stockings, so her bare feet sank down in the dry leaves and soft humus of the woods. "O'Brian?" she called.

"Stay there," he ordered from the other side of the wall.

But Elizabeth had no intention of heeding his words. She came around the corner of the building to see O'Brian holding his pistol on someone. She followed his line of vision. It was a woman. She was hiding behind a tree whose bark had been pulled away by some animal. The woman's ivory petticoats embroidered with green vines billowed from behind the tree, where she hid her face.

Elizabeth knew those petticoats. Her heart skipped a full beat. "Claire?"

O'Brian glanced at Elizabeth, and then slowly lowered the pistol.

"Claire, it's Elizabeth." She picked her way through the trees, wincing as she stepped into a patch of green-briars. "Claire?"

Claire peeked from behind the tree, still holding on with white-gloved hands. "E—Elizabeth?"

"Claire. Come here. No one's going to shoot you.

Come here for heaven's sake, and stop hiding behind that tree!"

Timidly, Claire came from behind the tree in clear view of Elizabeth and O'Brian. She looked like she was dressed for afternoon tea, but her blond hair was disheveled, the sleeve of her gown torn at the shoulder.

"Claire! What are you doing out here?" Elizabeth threw a glimpse over her shoulder. "Will you put your breeches on, man?" she hissed at O'Brian. As she turned back to Claire, she heard O'Brian make his retreat to the lean-to.

Claire took the hand Elizabeth offered her. She was trembling.

"What happened?" Elizabeth asked, leading her back toward the stone building. "Did you get lost?"

Claire chewed on her lower lip. "Not . . . not exactly. Well, yes."

Elizabeth could feel her own heart pounding in her chest. What had Claire seen? If she *had* seen anything, would she understand? Would it matter? If she repeated the tale, others would easily come to the obvious conclusion.

"What do you mean you got lost?"

"I . . . I don't know what happened," Claire murmured. "I don't know how I got here, honest, Elizabeth. Please don't be mad at me."

"You decent?" Elizabeth called to O'Brian.

"As decent as a man of my fabric can be," he answered drolly from behind the stone wall.

Elizabeth led Claire around the side of the lean-to to where O'Brian stood. He had slipped on his breeches, but left his long shirttail hanging. The pistol was tucked into the front waistband of his breeches.

"Get her a drink of the cider," Elizabeth ordered O'Brian. She still held onto Claire's hand.

Claire glanced around uneasily. Her gaze came to rest

on the rumpled blanket spread out on the shed's floor. Elizabeth's boots and stockings were tossed carelessly on the edge of the blanket.

She looked up into Elizabeth's eyes, obviously trying to be brave. "Did . . . did Mr. O'Brian hurt you?" Her voice trembled.

Elizabeth shuddered. *So* she *had* seen them . . . "No. No," she said gently. If she was caught, she was caught. She'd not blame O'Brian for her own failing. "He didn't hurt me, Claire. I was as much a part of this business as Mr. O'Brian."

O'Brian handed Claire a pewter cup of the sweet cider and took a step back.

Claire took a sip, watching O'Brian over the rim of the battered cup. "He didn't hurt you? But . . . but I heard you making noises."

Elizabeth knew her cheeks colored. She didn't dare look at O'Brian. "He didn't hurt me," she repeated firmly.

Claire nodded, taking a little sip. "Just as long as he didn't hurt you, because if he did, I'd have to blow his head off." She looked at Elizabeth with such innocence in her eyes. "I wouldn't want a man to hurt you. I wouldn't want Mr. O'Brian or Brother to hurt you."

Elizabeth looked to O'Brian for assistance. She didn't know what to say.

O'Brian leaned over, scooped up Elizabeth's worsted stockings, and tossed them to her. "Get dressed," he said. He began to stuff his shirt into his breeches. "Look, Claire, you know I'm fond of Mistress Lawrence, right? I mean, you and I talked about that before."

Claire nodded solemnly.

"And you know I wouldn't hurt her. I would not hurt either of you for all the fortunes of the Indies."

Claire nodded again.

"But see, the thing is, if you tell anyone about what you saw—"

"You kissed her," Claire accused.

Elizabeth had her back to them, trying to balance on one foot as she rolled up her stocking. She held her breath, waiting for O'Brian's response.

"Aye, I did. I did kiss her. But what I'm saying here, Claire, is that you mustn't repeat what you've seen today. You mustn't tell your brother, or your maid or anyone. You understand?"

Elizabeth turned around to see Claire twisting her mouth. She was trying to understand, God help her.

"Because Brother would think you were hurting her?" Claire questioned.

"Exactly," he agreed. "Brother wouldn't understand. No one would understand, Claire."

She studied him. "Because Elizabeth likes it when you kiss her down there?"

He broke into a grin. "Right." He touched her arm gently. "You understand. You understand perfectly. I knew you would."

Elizabeth slipped one foot into her boot and tugged it on, hopping on the other foot to keep her balance. Sweet Jesus, what were they going to do? She knew she should never have come here. She knew it!

O'Brian walked over to the picnic basket and broke off a piece of bread. "Ladies?" He offered the bread.

Elizabeth made a face of disgust.

Claire shook her head daintily.

O'Brian bit off a chunk and chewed with enthusiasm.

Elizabeth couldn't believe he was taking this so calmly. They'd been caught! He would lose his job. She might lose the mills, if word of her indiscretion got out! How could he eat?

Yanking on the other boot, she went to him, lowering

her voice so that Claire couldn't hear her. "What are we going to do?" she whispered harshly.

"Do? We're not going to do anything. Piece of cheese?"

Elizabeth groaned. There were still places in the world where women were stoned to death for adultery. "O'Brian, she saw us. She knows what we were doing—or at least has some idea."

He broke off a piece of the curded yellow cheese and added it to the bread in his mouth. "So what, you want me to kill her and bury her here?"

Elizabeth was horrified. "O'Brian—"

He laughed. "I was teasing. Don't be so serious, sweetheart. She won't tell."

Elizabeth felt like she was talking to a five-year-old. "O'Brian, this is a woman with an invisible pet mouse in her pocket. How can you be certain of anything?"

He brushed a wisp of hair off her cheek. "You just have to understand her illness."

"Meaning you do?"

"Not exactly, but I'm telling you, Claire won't tell a soul. Not if you ask her not to. Not if I ask her not to."

"How is it that you seem to know her so well? Why does she trust you? You haven't—"

The handsome lines of his face hardened. "No. I haven't. I admit to you I'm a philanderer of sorts, but I tell you, Liz, I never ever laid a hand on Claire or anyone like her. I'm not that kind of man, and if you think I am—"

Elizabeth grasped the hand he raised to her. It was wrong of her to even suggest O'Brian might have taken advantage of her sister-in-law. She knew him better than that. He was too honorable a man. "I'm sorry," she whispered, looking up into his stormy green eyes. "I know you wouldn't do that."

"Let me take her home."

"And set Jessop off again?"

He went to gather the blanket they'd been making love on only a short time before. "I'll lead her in along the river. I'll just tell the man I found her wandering whilst I was fishing."

"Fishing midday." Elizabeth laughed, a little calmer now. "He'll be insisting I fire you again, for laziness this time."

The blanket folded neatly in his broad hands, he came up to Elizabeth, lowering his voice. "I'm sorry this turned out this way. I meant to make it an enjoyable outing for you."

Elizabeth hung on his words. She wanted him, even now, even with the fear of being caught. "I'll try to come tonight," she intoned.

"You know I keep me light burnin' for ye. Always, Lizzy."

Then he kissed her. It was a tender kiss, a kiss that made her sigh and wonder how their relationship had changed. She told herself time and time again that it was just sex that drew them together, but deep inside she wondered. Was that truly all it was, or had it become something more?

"Come on, Claire darlin'," O'Brian called cheerfully, pushing the blanket into Elizabeth's hand. "Save it for next time," he whispered as he walked away.

Elizabeth watched as O'Brian slipped on his home-spun coat and offered Claire his hand.

"Go with Mr. O'Brian, Claire. He'll see you get home safely."

She lifted her petticoats with dainty hands. "You're not coming?"

"Not yet." She smiled. "But soon."

Claire turned to go, but then stopped and turned back. "I won't tell," she said in a voice as lucid as anyone's. "I won't, Liz. I promise."

Elizabeth gave a wave, and then the two were gone.

Alone in the silence of the forest, she sat down in the leaves beside the picnic basket and reached for the left-over bread and cheese. It had suddenly grown darker and cool. Thunder rumbled in the distance, and she could smell the scent of rain in the air. As Elizabeth nibbled on the brown edge of a chunk of bread, she thought about what had just transpired.

They'd been caught. Claire said she wouldn't tell, but she might. Elizabeth knew the most sensible thing to do would be to end the affair with O'Brian here and now. But even as she thought of the logic of her conclusion, she remembered the two of them together beneath the canopy of trees.

She knew she'd have to give him up . . . just as surely as she knew she couldn't. Not yet . . .

The moment Elizabeth set foot on the dirt road that ran the length of her property, she knew something was wrong. There was something in the air that smelled of danger . . . of fear.

She'd barely passed the new stone powder magazine when she spotted Johnny Bennett racing down the dusty road toward her. "Miss Lizbeth, Miss Lizbeth," he shouted, waving his battered straw hat. "Thank God I found ye!"

A light mist of rain had begun to fall. Elizabeth tugged on the round brim of the black wool hat she wore, seating it further down over her face. The hat wasn't particularly feminine-looking, but it kept the rain from her eyes. "What is it, Johnny? Calm down!"

He wrung his hands. "You've got to come fast, ma'am. They're trying to take Ngozi off! They already done knocked Samson out cold."

Elizabeth felt an involuntary tremble of fear. Few men

had-the nerve to take on Samson. "Who, Johnny? Who's trying to take Ngozi?"

His eyes widened. "Slavers, Mistress. Slavers come to take her!"

Slavers? That was unusual for this far north. Elizabeth lifted her skirts, angry at the thought that men such as those who retrieved runaway slaves would be here on her property, laying a hand on her workers. The sons of bitches had no right! "Where are they?"

"Up on Worker's Hill, right in front of Samson and Ngozi's cottage. God sakes, Mistress. They say they got a right to the child, too!"

Elizabeth quickened her pace down the dirt road that was beginning to puddle in the ruts. The rain was falling harder. "Johnny, I want you to run up to the office and get the pistol from the center drawer of my desk. Cut across the woods and meet me at the foot of the hill. I don't know who these men are, but they'll take no one from my land that doesn't go freely." She looked at Johnny, who was standing in a puddle in front of her, staring. "Well go on," she ordered. "And hurry!"

Johnny turned and ran, cutting across the road and climbing up the hill to take the shortcut to the office through the woods.

A few minutes later Elizabeth made her way up Worker's Hill through the blinding rain, her stride long and determined. The weight of the pistol Johnny had brought her, tucked into the waistband of her mud-splattered petticoat, strengthened her confidence. Something had to be done about these slavers. Most were men beyond English law, men that tracked humans like prey, returning them to their masters for a steep price.

Johnny Bennett had to run to keep up with Elizabeth. "Want me to fetch Mr. O'Brian or Mr. Lawrence, ma'am?"

Elizabeth's first instinct was that she could handle this

matter alone. But she didn't want to be a fool for pride's sake. That was a masculine tendency she never wanted to lose herself to. "Yes, see if you can find Mr. O'Brian."

He peered up the hill ahead of them. They could make out a crowd of men and women standing in front of Samson and Ngozi's stone cottage. "You sure you want me to leave ye?"

"I'll be all right." She stared straight ahead, steeling her nerves. "Just hurry."

The crowd of soggy workers, their wives, and their children, parted to let their mistress through. Through the sheets of driving rain, Elizabeth could make out the forms of three men and a woman and her child. Samson's huge body lay motionless on the ground that was fast turning to mud.

Above the sound of the wind, Elizabeth heard Ngozi shriek. One of the men reached for her child, but she held the toddler to her bosom, cursing in the Ibo tongue. Elizabeth knew it was the tongue of the southern Nigerian people, because it was the same language the slaves in her household spoke.

One of the men, dressed in tan breeches and a torn coat, raised a riding crop to strike Ngozi.

"That will be enough," Elizabeth shouted in her deepest voice. She reached out, and caught the sting of the leather crop in her hand before it struck Ngozi or the child. She jerked the crop from the slaver's hand, ignoring the searing flesh of her own palm. "How *dare* you strike one of my women!"

The slaver pushed his hat up off his forehead to stare at her with gray eyes. The man's teeth were black and jagged. She could smell the stench of the rot from where she stood. "Your woman? This niggard is a runaway slave. I got the papers on her." He patted the inside of his sailcloth coat.

Elizabeth took his crop and tapped her palm rhythmically. "You are obviously mistaken, sir. Ngozi is wife to my freeman Samson here." She was careful to give no more information than necessary.

"Who the hell is *she?*" one of the other slavers called from behind the man who seemed to be the leader. "Let's grab the niggard whore and her whelp and be gone. We've spent long enough in this godforsaken colony." He spat a stream of chewing tobacco close to the toe of Elizabeth's muddy boot.

She gave him a look that forced him back a step in the pooling rainwater. She turned her gaze back to the leader, shading her forehead with her open palm. "I'm Elizabeth Lawrence, owner of this land and proprietor of these powder mills. I want you and your men off my land, else I'll call the High Sheriff." Beneath the cover of her wool kerchief, she could feel the oak butt of her pistol.

"I don't mean to be disrespectful, ma'am, but I got a job to do here. My name's Jarvey." He pulled a piece of yellowed newspaper from inside his coat. "I come from Williamsburg way, lookin' for this woman. She been on the run a good three years, but I don't give up." He eyed Ngozi. "I got the rumor there was a woman livin' up on this river, hidin' out. She's the one, all right."

Elizabeth took the newspaper from him, quickly glancing over the advertisement. *Nigra female, aged approximately 22, missing since fall '71. Called Mary. Reward offered for Nigra's return. River's Walk, Williamsburg.*

Ngozi, wide-eyed with fear, clutched her baby to her bosom and tried to inch her way closer to her mistress.

Elizabeth tossed the rain-spattered paper back at Jarvey. "Can't you read, you jackass? It says she's called Mary. You're looking for a nigra called Mary. Samson's wife is Ngozi."

He lifted his scarred upper lip in a sneer. "These niggers, they all goes by different names, and you know it."

He pointed a crooked finger that had been broken more than once in the past. "I'm tellin' you, that nigger's the one I been lookin' for."

Elizabeth heard Samson groan at her feet. She pointed to several of the workers behind her. "Help Samson up," she ordered. "And then escort these men off my property." She started to turn away.

"We ain't goin' without the niggard," Jarvey hollered.

Ngozi gave a high-pitched shriek, and the baby began to cry again.

Elizabeth whipped around. "I told you," she stated through clenched teeth, "that you had the wrong woman. You are looking for a Mary of Virginia. This is Ngozi, born and raised on this property."

Jarvey's eyes narrowed. "Born on this soil, you say? Then why was the black bitch talkin' that Africa gibberish."

Elizabeth never skipped a beat. "Her grandmother, *half-wit,* taught Ngozi her people's tongue." She tossed him back his riding crop. "Now go. You've taken up enough of my time."

Just as Elizabeth turned away, she heard Jarvey take a step in her direction. Before he had time to react, she spun around. Her wool kerchief fluttered to the ground, as she drew the pistol. There was silence, except for the falling rain, as she cocked the hammer with an ominous click.

She heard her workers behind her suck in their breath. Samson was being hauled to his feet. Someone swore. A child whimpered. Everyone's eyes—including those of the slavers—were on Elizabeth and the flintlock she leveled on Jarvey. "I'll not repeat myself again. Take you and your filth off my property, else I'll kill the three of you and have you buried along the river in an unmarked grave."

Jarvey laughed, but he kept his eye on the pistol. Elizabeth's hand never wavered.

"You wouldn't do that."

She gave him a sweet smile. "Who would ever know?" She swept her free hand in the direction of the mill workers. "They'd never tell, and you know it. Most likely, no one would ever come looking for the likes of you anyway."

"Let's go, Jarvey," one of the slavers intoned. "That bitch is crazy."

"You're right, she is," came a male voice from the crowd. It was O'Brian's voice. He made his way to Elizabeth's side. "So I'd suggest you were on your way, before her finger slips in this rain, and one of you loses your face." He shrugged. "Then, of course, we'd have to kill the other two of you, so there would be no question as to who was right or wrong in the situation."

Elizabeth held the pistol on Jarvey and his men as they walked around the workers and started down the hill. She pointed to several of her workers. "See that these gentlemen find their way off Lawrence Mills property, will you?"

The crowd of workers and their families began to dissipate in the falling rain. O'Brian leaned over and whispered into her ear. "I think you can lower the pistol now," he said, with obvious amusement in his voice.

Elizabeth looked down to see the flintlock still aimed, her knuckles white with tension. Slowly she lowered the weapon. "Don't make fun of me. I was afraid they were going to take her."

"Nah, never happen, not with a woman like you between them."

Elizabeth looked up at O'Brian, but before she could speak, Samson appeared with Ngozi clinging to his arm for support. Someone must have carried the child into the shelter of the cottage.

"I—I got to thank you, Miss Lizbeth, for what you done."

Elizabeth kept her voice low, her words meant for no one but Samson, Ngozi, and O'Brian. "You didn't tell me you were a runaway slave, Ngozi! You should have told me!"

"Ya cain't blame 'er for that one, Mistress. That was my doin'. She wanted to tell ya after you was so nice to her. Honest to God."

Elizabeth glanced at Ngozi's round, dark face. Tears slipped down her cheeks, mingling with the raindrops. The poor woman was obviously petrified. "Well, my guess is that those men won't be back. So I suppose she's safe enough."

"I'll go if you wants me to, Mistress," Ngozi said in her liquidy voice. "I don't want to make no trouble for ya. Ya been too good to me and my chil'."

Elizabeth reached out through the rain and squeezed the woman's hand. "Nonsense. What would I do without Samson? And from the look in that man's eyes, he's not going to let you go anywhere without him." She turned to Samson. "Take your wife in and get her some dry clothes; and you have that head looked at, you understand me, Samson?"

He nodded. The place on his forehead where one of the slavers had struck him was stained with congealed blood. "Yes, ma'am."

Only after Samson and Ngozi walked away did Elizabeth turn to O'Brian. He had come without his hat, so that his golden hair ran with rivulets of water. "Been a day, hasn't it?" she asked.

"That it has." He looked up into the sky. "Damnation, but it's raining hard." He looked back at her. "You're soaked. You'd best get inside, too." He leaned a little closer. "I only wish I could help you get out of those wet things."

Elizabeth couldn't resist a smile. "I don't know about tonight. Maybe I'd best stay in. I imagine Jessop will be by for another Claire discussion. We seem to have them every week as of late."

"Just tell me what ye want, Mistress." He walked away, spreading his arms, grinning in the pouring rain. "Ye know I only live to serve ye."

Elizabeth heard his rich tenor laughter as he cut across the muddy road toward Samson's cottage.

Seventeen

Elizabeth wrote the invoice total down and smiled to herself, only half-hearing what Jessop was saying. Lawrence Mills was actually running in the black this month! Elizabeth had made a profit for the very first time.

"I just wanted you to know that I appreciate your concern for Claire. I'm glad you came and told me about the mark on her neck. I know it must have been hard for you," he said, an emotional catch in his voice. "And I want you to know that I've discussed the matter with Claire, concerning whatever contact she might be having with"—he cleared his throat—"men, and I think she understands our feelings on the matter. O'Brian will not find her wandering about the woods again, I can promise you."

Elizabeth glanced up, giving a perfunctory smile. This really wasn't a good time to chat with Jessop. She had a potential buyer for Lawrence gunpowder arriving momentarily, and she still hadn't come up with a date for delivery. Her gaze strayed back to the figures on her desk.

"Liz, you're not listening to me."

She shuffled through the pile, looking for the sheet of last week's production. *Blast Noah, he said he'd laid it on the desk.* "I'm listening to you."

Jessop came to her desk and laid his palm on the stack

of papers strewn in front of her. "You're not listening to me."

The man was like a mosquito caught in bed netting—annoying as hell. She pushed back her chair with a sigh, giving him her full attention. "I said this wasn't a good time, Jessop. You've barely spoken to me in weeks, and then suddenly you've got to see me immediately."

He touched her shoulder. It was an innocent enough gesture, but her first instinct was to pull away.

"Liz, I didn't really come here to talk about Claire, although I do appreciate your looking out for her. I came because . . ." He glanced away. "I came because I wanted to apologize for my recent behavior. I said things I shouldn't have said, things I didn't mean." He turned his handsome face to look at her.

She hadn't recalled his temples being so gray.

"I guess what I'm trying to say is that I'd like another chance."

Elizabeth nearly groaned out loud. She didn't need this right now. She didn't need Jessop's apologies; she didn't need to think of him or O'Brian or even about herself. These last weeks with O'Brian she'd been caught in a sort of limbo that she wished she could remain in forever. For the first time in her life, she was actually happy. She had her business by day, and by night . . . by night she had companionship, laughter, ecstasy. A woman like herself could have asked for no more.

She looked up, tucking back a stray lock of her dark hair into her linen mobcap. "Jessop, I really can't talk about this now. Johnson is coming in from Penn's Colony. It could be a large order."

He took her hand. "Come and have dinner with me tonight. Alone. I'll have Claire tucked in early."

For some reason his touch made her uncomfortable. Maybe she'd just resigned herself to the fact that she wasn't going to marry Jessop, and she just didn't want to be bothered by him any longer. She withdrew her hand. "All right. I'll see how busy I am."

"You'll cancel."

She rose. "I won't."

He followed her to the doorway. "You will. You'll say you're coming for dinner, and then you'll get so damned wrapped in your numbers that you'll sit here through the dinner hour and end up eating cold bread and cheese alone in your bedchamber. Liz, it's not good for a young woman like yourself to spend so much time alone."

She smiled to herself. She hadn't spent a night alone in more than a month. "Noah," she called through the doorway. "I need those figures on how many barrels we produced last week. I can't find it."

"Coming, Mistress," he called back to her.

Elizabeth leaned back, rubbing her lower back. Maybe Jessop was right. Maybe she was spending too much time in that chair. She looked up at Jessop, who was following her movements like a hound pup. "I'll see. That's all I can promise, now could you go? I really do have work to do, if I'm going to be prepared for Mr. Johnson."

He leaned over, giving her a peck on her cheek. "I'll look for you at nine. No need to dress. All I expect is your lovely face."

Elizabeth watched him go out her office door, and then hollered to Noah as she stepped over the pregnant Lacy sprawled on the floor. "I'm still waiting on those figures, Noah. You'd best get yourself back here, or start looking for another job!"

"Coming!"

She walked to her desk and leaned over it, reaching for her goose quill. If the numbers in her head were correct, she was certain she could deliver Johnson's black powder by the week after next. Now all she had to do was make the sale.

* * *

Jessop never crossed Elizabeth's mind again until eleven that night, when there was a rap on her bedchamber door. Elizabeth was seated in the center of her bed, dressed for bed in a silk nightrail. Papers littered the white counterpane, as she caught up on paying some overdue bills. With Johnson's deposit on his first shipment, she would come out in the black not just for the month, but for the quarter.

"Yes, what is it?" Elizabeth called. She took a bite of the cheese from the plate she balanced on her knee and reached for her pewter wine goblet. These last few days she'd been famished.

The door swung open and one of the downstairs girls appeared. She held up a candle. "Mr. Lawrence sent a boy to check on you, ma'am," Katie announced. "He said you was supposed to come to supper. Mr. Lawrence wanted to be sure you was all right." She peered at her. "You all right?"

Elizabeth chewed the cheese, washing it down with a sip of red wine. Blast it! She'd completely forgotten about Jessop and his supper. She rolled her eyes heavenward. She was so tired that she'd even told O'Brian she wouldn't come to his cottage tonight. All these missed meals and late nights were finally catching up to her. If she didn't have the energy to make love, she certainly didn't have the energy—nor the inclination—to deal with Jessop and his pat apologies.

"Could you please have the boy tell Mr. Lawrence that I apologize for not sending a note. I'm not feeling well tonight. I was just getting ready to blow out the lamp and try to get to sleep early. Have him tell Mister Lawrence to come for breakfast in the morning."

Katie dipped a curtsy and backed out of the room. "Yes, ma'am. Night, ma'am."

Elizabeth took a bite from the bread on her plate. Why hadn't she just told Jessop no? If he was suddenly going to start courting her again, she would have to tell him that she didn't have the time. Now that she had accepted the idea of not marrying Jessop—perhaps of never marrying anyone—she'd grown used to it. The idea became more appealing each day. Why did she have to marry again? She was far enough from her father that he couldn't control her. Without a husband she was free to do as she pleased. The powder mill would support her financially quite well. What else did she need?

A tap on the window glass across the front of the house suddenly caught Elizabeth's attention. That was odd. There were no tree limbs close to that window. She heard it again and froze, her wine cup held in the air. The tapping was now coming in an obvious rhythm.

Someone was tapping a blessed tune on her window!

Elizabeth jumped out of bed, wishing her pistol was at hand instead of down in the office. She set her cup down hard on the sidetable, splashing red wine on the white napkin. Padding barefoot across the chilly floor, she went to the window and threw it open.

The chilling October wind blew through the window in a gust, opening her thin nightrail before she could grasp the corners and pull it around her waist.

"Now that's a comely sight at the end of a long day," O'Brian said, throwing one large foot over the sill.

"What the hell are you doing here?" She took a step back as he climbed through the window. "You scared me half to death," she whispered harshly.

He turned, closing the window behind him. "I could tell how frightened you were, Mistress, by the way you tossed down that wineglass and strode over here. I suppose I should count myself lucky you didn't strike me between the ears with a fire poker."

"If I'd had my pistol, I'd have shot you between the ears."

He grasped her around the waist and turned, lifting her off her feet.

She pushed at his arms. "You can't be here," she said, trying to keep her voice low. "I told you that you could never come here. Someone might hear you."

He kissed her lips and then set her down. He walked to the bed to pick up a cut of yellow cheese. "No, they'll not hear me. You're the one who hollers like a mad-woman when we make love. I make barely a peep." He bit into the soft cheese, then added a corner of bread to his mouth.

Elizabeth knew her cheeks colored. "You said you didn't mind."

He sat down on the corner of the bed, his gaze scanning the paperwork. "I don't mind. In fact, a man likes to know he's pleasing his woman."

His woman . . . O'Brian had never said anything like that before.

"I'm just teasing you, sweetheart," he went on. He looked up from the papers. "Is there more cheese?"

She walked over to the bed, ignoring her nightrail that fell open, presenting him with a narrow view of her naked body. Her hair, still damp from her bath earlier, fell over her shoulders as she leaned over to snatch the plate from his hand. "You're eating my supper."

"I thought you were dining with Master Lawrence tonight." He snatched the last crumb of cheese from the plate.

She ate the last bit of bread. "I didn't." She frowned. "How did you know Jessop wanted me to come to supper?"

"Claire told me."

"Was she down at the mills again?"

"She was, but I sent her home." He took a swallow

of her wine and then put his arms out to her. He, too, had bathed. His hair was still damp, and he smelled of shaving soap. "Come here."

She dropped her hands to her hips. "O'Brian, I meant it when I said you couldn't come here. There are servants sleeping in the house. If someone hears your voice—"

"They'll most likely think it's Master Lawrence come a-visiting, and never say a word." He caught her hand and pulled her to him.

Elizabeth knew she should send O'Brian back out the way he'd come. But now that he was here . . . The room was so cozy with the embers burning in the fireplace, and they had the bottle of wine. The idea of making love in her own bedchamber was appealing . . . the thought of the danger made it tantalizing.

"You can't stay long," she whispered.

He slipped his warm hands inside her nightrail and around her waist. Perched on the edge of the bed, his head was level with her chest.

"Mmmmm," he murmured, taking her puckered nipple into to his mouth to suckle. "Tasty."

She dropped her hands to his shoulders with a sigh. She'd been tired beyond the point of thought only moments ago, but now she was wide-awake. She dropped onto his lap, cradling his head.

"Mary, Mother of God, Lizzy, I can't get enough of you. All day long this is all I think about."

"Sex is all men ever think about," she whispered, arching her back, covering his hand with her own, guiding him as he stroked her breast.

"I've lusted after many a woman many a time before, Liz. But I swear by all that's holy, this is different. You're different."

She threw back her head, laughing huskily. "That's because I'm better than they ever were." She took his cheeks between her palms and kissed him long and hard, her tongue thrusting between his lips. "I please you more than they ever did." She took his hand, guiding it between her already damp thighs. "You please me more than you ever pleased them."

O'Brian gave an animal-like growl, as he flipped her onto her back on the bed in the midst of the papers and climbed on top of her. Elizabeth struggled, pushing his chest. Parchment crumpled beneath her. "Shhhh!" she whispered, laughing. "They'll hear the bed bouncing from downstairs."

He slipped out of his coat and tossed it to the floor. Next came his muslin shirt.

"Your boots, man," she said, running her palms over the crisp blond hair of his chest. "Didn't anyone ever teach you any manners? You don't wear boots in a lady's bed."

He nipped her earlobe with his teeth. "You do if you fear you'll have to make a run for it at any moment."

She laughed, looping her arms around his neck to kiss him. This kiss was softer, gentler. "Take off your boots and lock the door."

As he got up off her, she sat up to gather the paperwork. "And the breeches, too, O'Brian." She tossed a pile of paperwork to the floor, not caring that it would take her an hour to re-sort them. "You won't be needing breeches in my bed."

By the time he locked the door, removed the rest of his clothing, and returned to her four-poster, Elizabeth had slipped out of her silk nightrail and climbed under the counterpane. Despite the small fire in the hearth, she was chilled. Autumn had settled on the Brandywine River.

O'Brian scooted in beside her. "Brrr, you're cold," he muttered.

She molded her body to his. "So warm me."

O'Brian stretched out on his side, and Elizabeth rested

her head in the cradle of his elbow. With a tantalizing slowness, he traced intricate patterns on her bare chest and belly with his fingertip.

Elizabeth let her eyes drift shut. So tonight they would make love slowly, deliberately, savoring each kiss, each caress, as if it were the last. That was something she liked about O'Brian. One night he was so anxious to possess her that, still clothed, he took her on the downstairs floor of his cottage. The next night they might play blindman's bluff chasing each other around the cottage, laughing and tripping over furniture until they fell into his rope bed, still laughing as they made love. And then there were nights like tonight, nights when he would hold her, when he would whisper in her ear, when he would take her desire to the point of madness, before he finally allowed her to climax.

Elizabeth threaded her fingers through O'Brian's damp golden hair, as he kissed the pulse at her throat above where her gold locket hung. Her entire body was alive with sensation, his fingertips leaving a trail of fire behind them.

Elizabeth felt O'Brian lean over her and reach for something on the side table. She kept her eyes closed, lulled by the tingling of her naked body. She heard him drink from the wineglass, pour more from the bottle, and then settle down beside her again.

The first touch of his cold, wet finger made her start. "Oh, that's cold," she whispered.

He was tracing a path across her belly with the wine. She heard him dip his finger again. This time the cold dampness made her shudder.

"I always wanted to be an artist," he whispered.

"Odd art," she answered, hearing the breathlessness in her own voice.

"Odd indeed," he whispered.

O'Brian dipped his finger into the red wine again, and

she felt it puddle between her breasts as he drew in larger circles. The instant he touched one nipple with the chilled wine, it grew hard in response.

"Such a perfect body," he told her softly. "Perfect breasts. Perfect nipples."

Elizabeth lifted her leg to drape it over his, but then remained perfectly still, enjoying his gentle attentions, feeling her anticipation rise with each swirl of his fingertip.

When O'Brian shifted his weight, she lifted her lashes to watch him lean over, to watch his tongue make contact with her damp flesh.

"O'Brian," she sighed, as his hot tongue met with the cold of the wine on her skin. "Oh, O'Brian, you take unfair advantage. You know all the tricks."

"I teach them to you," he whispered. "So that we can share them."

Elizabeth settled back on her pillow, stroking his bare back casually with one hand, as he dipped to touch her belly with his tongue again.

The sensations of his hot tongue mingled with the chill of the wine made her stomach knot and her mind whirl. Her veins coursed with the pleasure of his caress, as she heard herself moan.

O'Brian licked the wine from her belly, working his way upward. Elizabeth held her breath, her skin tingling with anticipation, until his lips met her peaked breast.

Elizabeth fought to keep silent, but it was difficult. She dug her nails into his bare shoulders, arching her back, pressing her hips to his. She could already feel his manhood pressed against her thigh, hot and swollen. She reached down to caress him.

"Lizzy, Lizzy," he whispered in her ear.

Their mouths met. He tasted of heady red wine and passion.

He stroked her silky hair, the curve of her shoulder,

the length of her arm. This wasn't just sex, as Elizabeth had told herself over and over again. It was more.

Tears clouded her eyes as he lowered his head over hers. "What is it, Lizzy?" he asked. He brushed his lips across her cheek. "Tell me."

She almost said it. She almost cried out "I love you." But her practicality won out, and she turned her head. "I'm just happy," she whispered. "That's all." *Of course, she didn't love him. That was foolishness. Hasty words she'd regret later. A woman didn't love a man just because the sex between them was good. A woman like herself didn't love a man like O'Brian.*

O'Brian was brushing his hand over her thighs now, caressing her, teasing her. She opened her legs to him, lifting her hips, encouraging him to touch that place that belonged to no one but him.

The tears in her eyes slipped away as a throbbing, incandescent heat began to spread through her limbs. Elizabeth twisted her hips, meeting his probing fingers. He kissed her again and again, their breath mingling, sharing the taste of the wine he'd drunk.

When O'Brian finally lowered his head over hers, molding his hard muscular form to her own softer one, she drank in his deep green eyes. "Love me," she whispered desperately, half out of her head with want of him. "Love me, O'Brian."

There it was, that word again . . .

A smile played on his lips, as he lowered his mouth to hers in a gentle kiss. He whispered something in reply, but she didn't understand what he said. She moaned with relief as he slipped into her, guided by his hand. Relaxing deeper into the feather tick mattress, she let all conscious thought float from her mind. Again and again she lifted hips to his until she was lost, lost to the sweet fury of the moment.

Elizabeth didn't know how much time had passed. Perhaps hours, perhaps only minutes. Curled at O'Brian's side, she sighed softly, tiny aftershocks of pleasure still rippling through her body. O'Brian lay on his back, his arms flung, his breath falling to a more steady pace.

"Just when I think bed sport can get no better, lass, you prove me wrong," he teased, brushing a kiss against her temple.

She pulled herself into a tighter ball against his warm body, tugging the coverlet over them both. Closing her eyes, drowsy, she contemplated how nice it would be to sleep all night in a bed with O'Brian. She didn't like having to always get up, dress, and return home to sleep alone in this big bed. *At least tonight,* she thought, *he'll be the one to have to climb out of the warm bed and walk home in the dark.*

O'Brian brushed his hand over her bare arm, over her shoulder, his caresses a comfortable aftermath to their lovemaking. His fingers found the gold locket she wore at her neck.

"A gift?" he asked, fingering the gold.

"Mmmhmmm," she murmured, not bothering to open her eyes. "From Paul." She lifted her lashes. "Does it bother you that I wear it?"

He turned the oval locket in his fingers. "I'd not say I'm in the position to be a jealous lover, either of men dead or alive."

She smiled to herself. *He didn't answer the question.*

"To E.T.L. from adoring husband, P.H.L.," he read. "How touching."

She took the locket from his hand and let it fall to her bare chest.

He lay back on the pillow. "Elizabeth T. Lawrence," he mused. "Elizabeth *T* . . . Let me see, what does the T stand for?"

"O'Brian—"

"No, no." He rose up on his elbow to look down at her. "Let me guess. Theresa?"

She laughed, snuggling deeper into the feather tick.

"No, no, not Theresa. Tabitha? No, no, too sweet, too feminine."

"Thanks," she murmured, rolling onto her side, presenting her back to him.

"I've got it! I've got it. Thomasina!"

"No," she answered. "Not Thomasina. The T doesn't stand for a middle name. I never had one. It's Tarrington," she finished sleepily. "Tarrington, my family's name."

"Tarrington?" O'Brian asked, an odd tone in his voice. "Not of Wexford?"

She felt the mattress shift.

"There's a country house in Wexford, but we're from Yorkshire." She rolled over to see him sliding out the bed. *Something was wrong, very wrong.* "O'Brian?"

Eighteen

He snatched his breeches up off the floor and shoved his bare foot through the leg.

"O'Brian, what is it?" She sat up, pulling the counterpane over her breasts. "What's wrong?"

He yanked up his breeches. "Ye never told me you were a Tarrington, Liz," he answered, gritting his teeth.

"What?" She was completely lost. "What are you talking about?"

"Thieving, murdering, futtering Tarringtons, that's what I'm talking about! You're one of them!"

She picked up the pillow his head had rested on moments before and threw it at him. "What the hell are you talking about?" she demanded in a hushed shout.

He thrust his foot into one boot, not bothering with his woolen stocking. "Tarringtons, that's what I'm talking about! Ye took my father's land. Ye took my cousins', and my uncles', and my friends' land, and ye put us out!"

She threw her hands up angrily. "What are you talking about, O'Brian? Took *what* land?"

He grabbed his muslin shirt and tried to turn it right side out. "In Wexford." He ceased the struggle with his shirt to look up her with hatred in his stormy green eyes. "It was where I was brought up."

She was still confused. What was he ranting about? Tarringtons took what land? "I thought you were an Irishman raised in France."

"I was after—after ye took me father's land and burned down our cottage to make yourself that fancy house." She heard an Irish brogue in his angry voice, for the very first time since she'd met him. "That's when my parents sent me to the monastery. When they knew they couldn't feed us all—after me little brother died of starvation that first winter."

Elizabeth remembered the Tarrington Wexford country home. It had been a beautiful house with rich tapestries and long halls, perfect for children's races on rainy days. But she'd been a baby when her father had built it, perhaps not even born yet, for heaven's sake. "Are you telling me that my father took land from your family to build his country house?"

"Charles Elton Tarrington. I'll never forget his name unto my death. We had nowhere to go. No work to be had. No food, no roof over our heads. Me mother separated her children, so the rest of us wouldn't starve, sending us to relatives, hiring out my sisters so they could work for food to feed the others." He reached for his homespun coat. "Me father could find no work. He could no longer feed his family. Do you know what that does to a man?" He wiped his mouth with the back of his hand. "Tarringtons killed me father with the bottle, just as surely as they could with a blade."

Elizabeth sat up on her knees, still clutching the counterpane. His story was so fantastic that she believed him. She believed every word. But why was he blaming her? How could he possibly find her responsible for what her father had done?

Elizabeth looked up at O'Brian. He was searching for something—his other boot. She was trying to understand him. "You say my father took land your family owned. How is that possible? My father was a shrewd business man, not terribly likeable, but I never knew him to be a thief."

"We didn't own the land," he flared sarcastically, "but it was ours just the same. The O'Shays had lived on that land, run their cattle over those hills, and planted their potatoes in those furrows for generations. My father lost the land to taxes, and we became tenants on our soil like many Irishmen. Then the O'Shay land was bought for back taxes by the rich English Tarringtons!"

Elizabeth's dark eyes narrowed. "O'Shays? Who the hell are the O'Shays? Your name is O'Brian!"

O'Brian paled and looked away. His boot dangled from his hand. A long moment of silence stretched into two.

Elizabeth could feel her throat constricting. She climbed off the bed, dragging the counterpane with her. "You're not O'Brian, are you?" she asked softly in disbelief.

He refused to make eye contact with her.

"Son of a bitch," she whispered when he made no reply.

Suddenly she remembered her suspicions the day he'd arrived. There'd been some confusion with his first name. She'd meant to contact her solicitor in Philadelphia, but then he'd turned out to be such a excellent yard foreman, that she'd completely forgotten about it. Because he'd been the answer to her prayers, she'd never questioned him again.

"You lied to me," she accused harshly. Her heart was breaking.

Finally he lifted his gaze to meet hers. "I lied, but my lies didn't hurt anyone. *I* didn't hurt anyone. I didn't take a family's land nor a man's dignity."

Elizabeth chose not to argue with him over what her father had or hadn't done. It was pointless. How could O'Brian possibly think *she* could be responsible for her father's acts? But this, this deception, she'd not let that go. "What happened to the man called O'Brian?" she demanded. "The one I hired. Did you kill him?"

A strange looked passed over his face. What was it? Pain? Bewildered hurt? But then it was gone as quickly as it had come, replaced by a mask of steely anger. "No, I didn't kill him," he responded, his sarcasm thick. "He was my friend. We both ended up on the same boat bound for America by coincidence. He died of poison of the blood, so I took the dead man's name. I did no one any harm."

"But I didn't hire you. I hired him."

"I was a better powder man than Michael, so I didn't cheat you out of anything, if that's what you're worried over, *Mistress!*" he sneered.

Elizabeth couldn't believe that this was the same man who had made love to her so tenderly only half an hour before. There was no tenderness in him now, no understanding, only rage and bitterness.

"You lied to me." She gripped the white counterpane, her knuckles going white. The depth of his deception hit her hard. "You don't even have a wife and children, do you?"

"Michael did."

She reached with one hand and gave him a hard shove in the middle of his broad chest, pushing him back a step. She wanted to hit him. She wanted to call him names. She wanted to scream, and break things. "You mean to tell me that you let me suffer all these weeks thinking I was an adulteress? I laid in that bed," she pointed, "at night and contemplated hell, you bastard!" She was so furious she was close to tears. "All that time I agonized over what I was doing to your wife somewhere across the ocean, and you didn't have a blessed wife to begin with!"

He turned away. "I'd best go before this turns ugly."

"You son of a bitch," she shouted after him, not caring if the entire house heard her. "It's already turned ugly."

He walked over to the window and pushed it open. Elizabeth stood in the chilling wind, the counterpane wrapped tightly around her naked body. She was hurt. She was so angry that she ached inside. And she wasn't just angry with him, she was angry with herself. How had she let him hurt her like this? How could she have let him deceive her? How, in god's name, could she have let herself care so much?

O'Brian stepped out through the open window, and she slammed it behind him, throwing the brass latch. She turned away, refusing to watch him go, and returned to her bed. It wasn't until her head hit the feather pillow that she finally gave in to her tears.

Elizabeth slept little that night, and when she went to the office the following morning, she knew her eyes were still red from crying.

She felt like such a fool. O'Brian had lied to her from the first day he'd set foot on Lawrence land. She'd been deceived by his good looks and his charm. Hell, she'd let him deceive her right into her bed.

So now what was she going to do? She stared at the paperwork stacked high on her desk. She had another appointment today with another potential buyer. After last month's first meeting of the Continental Congress in Philadelphia, emotions were running high. A sense of urgency was spreading across the colonies. The whispers of independence were being heard at every dining table, at every tavern across the untamed land. And if independence came to the colonies, it would not be without war, it would not be without black powder.

Elizabeth's first instinct, of course, was to send O'Brian packing . . . O'Shay, whatever the blast his name was! But the businesswoman in her fought that conclusion. It had taken her a full year to get a yard foreman after the explosion that killed her husband. And no matter what the character of the man, O'Brian was a good yard foreman. He knew the chemical compounds, and he knew the men who worked for him. The workers at Lawrence Mills trusted him, they depended on him. The truth was, they worked for him, not for her. Not until O'Brian had come had the men begun to work as a team to produce the final product.

So where did that leave her? Could she stand to have the man work for her, knowing he was not who he claimed to be? Could she stand to deal with him after being so intimate with him?

When she'd begun the affair, she'd known it would end. She'd been certain that she'd be able to work with O'Brian, even when their passion had cooled. But now that she was faced with the actuality of the situation, she didn't feel quite as confident.

She gazed out the window. Most of the leaves had fallen from the trees to litter the ground in an array of bold browns and yellows. The air smelled of wood smoke and stewed pumpkin. She sighed, reaching for the cup of herbal tea Noah had brought. This whole business with O'Brian had made her ill. Her stomach was in knots; she couldn't eat a thing.

She sipped the tea. The trouble, she knew, was that she'd allowed her emotions to get the better of her with O'Brian. She'd told herself it was just sex she sought from him, but she'd allowed it to become more. Somehow between the sheets she'd allowed herself to become too attached to him. That was her mistake. An independent woman didn't become dependent upon any man for anything.

So, she was resigned to keep O'Brian for the present. She'd let him run her mill and make her profits. But in the meantime, she would contact her solicitor and bid him begin the search for a new yard foreman. Once she obtained a new one, she'd send O'Brian on his deceiving, grudgeful way.

With that settled in her mind, she reached for the ledger Noah had left on her desk. She didn't have time for hurt feelings or regrets. She had work to do.

Less than an hour later the sound of a knock on the door tore Elizabeth from her concentration. "Come in," she called, dipping her quill in the inkwell.

"Elizabeth, dear."

It was Jessop. She didn't turn around.

She'd sent a message early in the morning to his house that she was still ill and couldn't receive him for breakfast. She hadn't been lying. She had been ill to the point of being unable to eat anything but a bit of dry toast and tea in her bedchamber.

"Elizabeth, are you all right?" He walked to the fireplace and stoked the coals. "If you're not well, you ought to be abed, not in this drafty office."

She laid down the quill and turned in the chair, giving Jessop her full attention. He seemed to be honestly concerned for her welfare. Besides, she knew she could use a break. "I'm all right, really, just a touch of a stomach ailment."

He leaned the iron poker against the fireplace and crossed the small room to her. He brushed a wisp of hair off her forehead. "You look pale. Are you certain you wouldn't like to take the afternoon off?"

She spread her hand, indicating her desk. "I can't," she sighed. "I've mountains of paperwork, and I had a mind to work up in the laboratory this afternoon. That sodium nitrate I've been waiting seven months on just arrived from Peru."

He stood behind her and massaged her shoulders. Elizabeth felt so drained that it was easier to let him, than to argue. Actually, his touch felt good. She was so tense.

"Well, I understand how important your work is to you."

She glanced over her shoulder, wondering if this was the same Jessop who only two weeks before had told her that it was inappropriate for a female to own a business. Elizabeth had assumed he specifically meant a profitable business. "You do?"

He went on kneading the muscles across her back and shoulders. "It was wrong of me to try to change you. I understand that now." He came around the chair, dropping one hand, but still resting the other on her shoulder. "Liz, I miss you. I was serious about what I said yesterday. I want you to take back the ring." He'd magically retrieved it from somewhere in his coat. "And I want you to be my wife."

Elizabeth leaned on the desk and dropped her forehead to her hands. Her head was swimming; she was nauseated, and she still had those figures to complete for the potential buyer. Jessop was being so nice to her. He seemed so sincere. But the truth was, she didn't know what she wanted right now. O'Brian had scared her too badly. Their relationship had scared her too badly.

She lifted her head to see Jessop watching her.

"You really don't feel well, do you?" he said gently.

She shook her head.

"Then let's talk about this another time." The ruby ring disappeared as quickly as it had appeared.

"I'd really prefer that," she responded, appreciating his thoughtfulness. When had O'Brian ever been thoughtful like this? "I just need some time to think. We both said some things to each other that maybe we shouldn't have said."

He sliced the air with his palm. "Forgotten, forgiven,

sweet. I just want you back. I want you and me and Claire to be a family, that's all. A happy family."

Elizabeth turned back to the desk, sweeping back the hair that had fallen across her forehead again. The piles of paper spread before her appeared immense. It would take her two days to catch up. "I really have to get back to work," she said without enthusiasm.

"All right. I'll leave you, then." But Jessop didn't leave. He just stood there looking at her. "Liz," he finally asked. "Is there something wrong?"

She could feel the lump rising in her throat. She could feel the tears burning behind her eyelids. Of course, she couldn't tell Jessop about O'Brian. She couldn't tell him how hurt she was, how angry, what a fool she felt. But Jessop was being so nice to her. He seemed honestly concerned. She turned in the chair. "I made a mistake, Jessop."

He went down on his knee, taking her hand in his. "You mean with us? Oh, darling, I've told you, I've completely forgiven you. I know this last year hasn't been easy on you. I know—"

"O'Brian," she said, turning her face away so he couldn't see her tears. "I made a terrible mistake with O'Brian."

His hand wrapped around hers tensed. "What do you mean?"

She took a breath. Jessop would never know. No one would ever know, if Claire or O'Brian never told. "I . . . I should never have hired him. I should have been more thorough in my interview."

"What's the bastard done? If he's touched you, Liz, I vow I'll—"

She laughed a sad laugh. "No. Mr. O'Brian has been nothing but a gentleman." That was at least partially true. "I have no problem with the job he's done for me. Hell, Jessop, he did in one month what I couldn't manage in a year." She pointed to the west. "I've got a magazine out there filled with barrels of excellent black powder right now, thanks to that man."

"But?" Jessop probed.

"But I found out last night that he lied to me." She heard the catch in her voice. *He hurt me,* she thought. *I let him hurt me.* "He deceived me, Jessop," she said, lifting her chin a notch. She wouldn't feel sorry for herself. She wouldn't. "I trusted him and the son of a bitch deceived me."

"How so?"

She turned back to Jessop, refusing to give into emotional weakness. "He's not Michael O'Brian."

"Not O'Brian?"

"O'Brian's dead, died at sea. This is some man who knew O'Brian. He's called O'Shay."

Jessop stood, letting go of her. "I'll go and relieve him of his yard duties this instant."

Elizabeth caught his hand as he passed her. "Wait, Jessop." She took a moment, thinking through her decision before she spoke. "Jessop, I know you want to help me, but I'd like you to stay out of this. It's between O'Brian and me. I hired him. This is my land, my powder mills."

"Well, he certainly can't remain on the property. We don't know who this man is. Heavens, he could have murdered the real O'Brian himself!"

Elizabeth was furious with O'Brian, but she had to be fair. She believed him when he said the real O'Brian had died aboard ship. Whoever the O'Brian she knew was, she knew he was no cold-blooded killer. She may have misjudged him, but not that badly.

Elizabeth rose from her chair, needing to stretch her legs. Lacy, who'd been asleep at her feet, rose, too, but then Elizabeth signaled for her to stay. Elizabeth walked across the room to Jessop. He was dressed tastefully today in a dark burgundy coat and breeches. His graying hair was pulled back neatly in a queue.

"Jessop, I need you to trust me on this. As I said, I got myself into this, I'll get myself out of it. I'm going to find myself a new yard foreman, but until I can find one, I'm going to keep O'Brian on."

"That's out of the question!"

She raised her hand, speaking quietly, but firmly. "It's my decision. And I'll ask that you not mention this to anyone. Our discussion doesn't leave this room. I don't even want to talk to you about it later."

"Elizabeth, you're being—"

She put out her hand to rest it on his forearm. "I'm being nothing but responsible for my own errors in judgment. I was bound to make some mistakes somewhere along the way. Paul made his. You've certainly made your share in the shipping business." She dropped her hand. "Now, I'm confident that O'Brian is no danger to anyone, so for the time being, I'll keep him on. End of discussion."

Jessop started to say something, then didn't. Finally he smiled, reaching out to her. Elizabeth allowed herself to be pulled into his arms and rested her head on his shoulder, her hands at her sides. She was so confused. Jessop was being so nice and O'Brian—O'Brian had been such a bastard about this whole Wexford thing.

"I'll trust you to do the best thing, Liz."

"Thank you."

"But you let me know, if you need me, fair enough?"

She took a step back. "Fair enough."

"So you go back to your work." He gave her a friendly push. "And I'm going to see that Noah gets another log in here, and one of your kitchen girls brings you a fresh cup of tea." He stopped at her office door, his hand on the knob. "Anything else?"

She smiled genuinely. "No. Thank you." But then she called after him. "Wait, yes, there is one other thing."

"Anything, darling."

"Have Noah send for Mr. O'Brian," she said with determination. "I want to speak with him immediately."

O'Brian took the granite steps that led up the hill to Liz's office two at a time, swinging his powerful arms in stride. Noah had said she wanted to see him immediately. Truth was, he was amazed it had taken her this long to send for him. He'd had his few belongings packed since dawn.

O'Brian pushed through the front door, past Noah, not speaking. By now he was certain she had told the clerk the truth of his identity. He'd be surprised if the heartless piece of baggage didn't have the High Sheriff waiting outside to question him on Michael's death, when she was through with him.

O'Brian was so furious he could barely see straight as he strode through the swinging door, headed for the back office. Yes, he was angry with her, but he was even angrier with himself. He felt like an ass. He'd actually cared for her. He'd allowed himself to become emotionally involved with her—something he had sworn he would never do with any woman. Christ, he should have listened to his head to begin with.

O'Brian wondered how he could have fooled himself into thinking he could ever be Elizabeth Lawrence's equal. Elizabeth *Tarrington* Lawrence's equal! And how could he have been foolish enough to have thought he could get away with taking poor Michael's identity? How could he have thought he'd never get caught?

If he hadn't gotten involved with the thankless jade, he'd have done his job, collected his pay, and someday he'd have moved on up the river to start his own powder mill. If it hadn't been for her, no one would ever have been the wiser.

He stopped at her closed door, taking a moment to collect his thoughts. What angered him the most was that when he'd told her what the Tarringtons had done, she'd never blinked. She'd never expressed a breath of sorrow. The cold bitch hadn't cared that his little brother and father lay in a stone grave because of what the Tarringtons had done. She didn't care about the family he loved. She didn't care about him. He'd been a fool to have ever thought she might have.

O'Brian hit his fist on the door, pushing it open.

She swung around in her chair with her head full of silky hair. "Don't you know how to knock?" she demanded in that icy mistress's voice of hers.

He kicked the door shut with the heel of his boot. He crossed his arms over his chest. "What? You weren't expecting me?"

"Lower your voice." She rose, stepping over one of the damned hounds sprawled across the office floor. "I'd like to keep this conversation private, if you don't mind."

He gave a shrug. "Don't see that it matters much at this point."

She narrowed her dark eyes. She really wasn't very pretty when she screwed her face up like that. What had ever made him think that she was so beautiful to begin with?

She cleared her throat, as if she were about to make a grand speech. "I've decided that despite your deceitful ways, you'll remain here at Lawrence Mills."

He raised an eyebrow. "Oh, I will, will I?" He pointed an accusing finger. "That's the way it is with you English Tarringtons. You think you can control other people's lives."

She walked to the window, presenting her back to him as if he didn't even deserve the respect of a face-to-face confrontation. "I'm just going to pretend that the conversation we held last night never took place. I'm going to pretend none of that happened. You'll remain here as Michael O'Brian, and fulfil the duties I contracted you for."

"The hell I will!" he boomed. "I've had enough of you and your ways."

She turned to face him, her arms crossed over her breasts, a smug look on her face. "Then I assume you'll be returning the advance on your salary I gave you that first day you came."

Sweet Mary! He'd forgotten about the money she'd paid him. He'd sent it to Michael's widow and never thought of it again.

Her mouth twitched into a vengeful smile. "No, I don't suppose a man who spends his coin on whores and gaming has the money to repay his employer."

She had him. The conniving witch had him. "Once I find work again, I'll repay you."

She shook her head, obviously enjoying herself. "Not good enough. The way I figure, you owe me four months of work and payment for your passage."

"You didn't pay for my passage!" he flared.

She shook her head. "No, but I paid for O'Brian's, and since you've taken the liberty of stealing the man's good name, I would assume you'd repay his debt."

He shook his finger. "I'll fulfil the six-month contract, but I'll be damned if I stay another day after that."

"So you'll want me to contact the authorities concerning your impersonation?"

He looked down at the sanded floor. His hand ached to slap her. She was so damned egotistical. That was really what burned him. How could he have misjudged her so badly? How could he have ever thought her to be anything but the cold-hearted Englishwoman she was?

O'Brian gave his wool cocked hat a tug, pulling it down over his eyes. She'd won. He'd repay his debt, because that was the kind of man he was, but he'd be damned if he'd act like he was happy about it. "If you've nothing else, *Mistress*," he said sarcastically, "I need to get back to the composition house."

"No. There'll be nothing else. You're dismissed, O'Brian." She turned her back to him to look out the window; and he walked out the door, closing it behind him with a satisfying bang.

As O'Brian passed the office window, he didn't bother to look up to see her watching him go.

And he never saw her tears.

Nineteen

Elizabeth had just risen from her desk to stoke the fire in her office fireplace, when she heard a tap on the window. She turned to see O'Brian's face through the wavy glass. He was signaling to her.

She took her time walking to the window, aggravated, wishing she wasn't. What was wrong with the man that he couldn't come through the front office like everyone else? She didn't want to talk to O'Brian right now. She didn't want to have to deal with him.

The last fortnight had been difficult for Elizabeth, perhaps even more difficult than the first weeks after Paul's death. It was so hard for her to deal with O'Brian on a daily basis, to go about the day-to-day business of running the mills, pretending that none of those nights of passion had ever happened. The worse thing was that no matter how hard she tried, she couldn't stop thinking about him. No matter how she fought it, she found that she missed him. She missed what they had shared.

It wasn't that she was lonely. If only everyone would just leave her alone . . . Claire spent hours in the sitting room playing the spinet, leaving Elizabeth feeling guilty for not spending more time with her.

And Jessop came to visit Elizabeth daily, wooing her with more enthusiasm than she'd ever before seen in the man. He brought flowers, French champagne, Italian chocolates, even treats for her dogs. Last week he interceded on her behalf to have a shipment of coal brought in a week early, so her production wouldn't be delayed. For once he was doing what *she* wanted, not what *he* wanted. He honestly seemed to want to reconcile.

But Elizabeth couldn't bring herself to agree no matter what Jessop said, no matter how he pleaded, or what he offered her. Now he was talking about an extended wedding trip to see her family in England, and then on to France and Italy.

The more Elizabeth thought about marriage, the less convinced she was that that was what she wanted. After the brief fleeting weeks she'd spent as O'Brian's lover, experiencing a happiness she had never known possible, she was afraid to trap herself. She was afraid to limit the possibilities of her life. These last two weeks she'd lain alone in bed at night taking a hard look at herself and what she wanted. The truth was, she was afraid marriage to Jessop would be suffocating compared to the independence she felt right now. She was quickly coming to the conclusion that despite society's pressures, she'd probably be better off to never marry again.

Elizabeth threw the latch on the window and pushed up the frame. She hugged herself for warmth. "What is it, O'Brian? You couldn't come around through the door?"

"I want you to come down to the mills and see something."

"What?" she asked irritably. She just had no patience today.

"I want you to see what we found."

She leaned on the sill, trying not to recall what his lips had felt like on hers. "Found where?"

"I had some of the men cleaning up the old foundation of the stamp mill. You know, what was left after you rebuilt."

"And?"

"Christ, Liz. Will you just come?"

Her gaze met his. He wasn't looking for a fight. He seemed honestly concerned about something. She sighed. "All right. I'll be down there in a minute. Can you wait while I get my cloak?"

"I'll wait for you out here. Hurry up."

She closed the window and grabbed her wool cloak on the way out. Throwing it over her shoulders, she passed Noah seated at his desk, seeming much like a permanent fixture in the room. "I'm going down to the stamp mill with O'Brian. If Claire comes, tell her to start dinner without me." She brushed her hand over her stomach absently. She still wasn't feeling well—all the stress of the last two weeks, she guessed.

Noah nodded as she went by him and out the door, followed by her dogs. O'Brian waited for her outside on the granite steps.

"Must they come along?" he asked irritably as Lacy's mate raced past him, knocking into him as he leapt by.

"They've been cooped up in the office since early this morning. Lacy's carrying pups, she needs the fresh air."

O'Brian walked beside Elizabeth, the blond queue at the back of his neck blowing in the autumn breeze. It was these moments of silence that were really difficult for her. When they weren't talking business, her thoughts strayed.

"So what have you been doing with yourself?" she asked, making conversation. Anything was better than the silence.

He didn't turn his head when he spoke. "Working."

"I mean *besides* working. Been playing the dice at the Sow's Ear?"

"A little."

"How about the redhead? Been playing her?" Elizabeth regretted her words the moment they slipped out.

What O'Brian did in his free time was no concern of hers any longer.

He glanced crosswise at her. "I don't think it's any of your damned business, do you?"

She kicked a pinecone off the step and watched it leap down the hill. "No, I don't guess it is." She chewed on her lower lip. "Maybe you ought to marry the poor girl," she suggested. "I mean, now that you've lost your wife and dear children, you're free to wed."

He frowned as they turned onto the road. "I'm not the type of man to marry, and you full well know it."

"I thought all men were the type. Marriage is a nice arrangement for men. Their wives become their personal servants for a lifetime."

He glanced at her. "I don't want a personal servant."

She lifted the hood on her cloak, chilled by the wind that blew down the road. "I don't think I want marriage either. The closer I get to wedding vows, the less I like the idea."

"Lawrence pressuring you again?"

She nodded. This was the first personal civil conversation she'd held with O'Brian since their falling out. It felt good to have him to talk to again. "He forgives me." She looked at O'Brian to see him arch his eyebrow.

"Oh, he does, does he? For what?"

She knew what he meant. He meant, had she confessed to Jessop about their illicit affair? Of course, she knew he knew better. He was just trying to goad her. She didn't bite. "He forgives me for the names I called him." She opened her arms in a grand gesture. "For my irrational behavior as of late."

"Good of him," he chided sarcastically.

"Exactly what I was thinking."

They walked side by side down the road for a quarter of a mile before he spoke again. "You going to do it?"

"What?"

He swore, tugging on the tail of his queue. "You know what. Marry the jackass."

She shrugged. They were coming up to the stamp mill, where the moist gunpowder mixture was pulverized by a mortar and pestle. "I don't know."

"Well, do what ye like," he paused, "but don't sell yourself short, Lizzy." Then he walked past her. "Over here at the corner of the building. I want you to see what we found."

She followed him around the new stone-and-frame-built stamp mill, surprised by his comment. His words didn't sound like those coming from a man who despised her. She looked up at the building, making herself concentrate.

When she'd been forced to rebuild after the explosion the previous year, she'd changed the shape of the structure, thus leaving portions of the old foundation exposed. She could see where her men had been digging up a portion of the crumbled foundation and filling the hole with clean fill dirt from the woods. She herself had ordered the cleanup only last week.

She stood over the hole, the wind whipping at the hair that fell forward from her hood. "All right." She pointed. "It's a hole." She looked up at O'Brian, who stood across the excavation from her. He was irritating her again. "So?"

He went down on one knee, his face expressing obvious concern. Elizabeth dropped on one knee, pushing aside Lacy's face as the dog tried to nuzzle her hand. "Scat, Lacy. Go on with you," she shooed.

O'Brian waited for the dog to back off. "See it *there?*"

She pushed the hood off her head to get a better look. At first she didn't see anything but a dry dirt hole. She was about to say so, when a bit of paper fluttered above the dirt. She looked up at him. "Why are you showing me a piece of burned paper?"

"I didn't want to disturb it before you saw how we found it."

She reached for the bit of paper. "Found what? You already know what it is?"

"Be careful," he warned. "It's fragile."

Elizabeth dug into the soft dirt mixed with charred ashes with her hand. The ground was cold and dry. Her fingers met with something smooth and hard. She glanced up.

O'Brian nodded. "Bring it out carefully. I dug around it, so it shouldn't be hard."

Cautiously, she pulled the object from the ground. It was a book like the ones used in the office, except the cover was charred and the entire bottom right corner was gone. Bits of ash and burned paper fell to the ground, as she fingered what remained of the hardbound cover. "A ledger?"

"Not exactly a ledger." He took her hand, leading her away from the group of workers that were filling in the hole. "I've a piece here in my pocket that we found loose."

She held the burnt book in her hands, trying to brush the dirt from the cover without causing more damage. Noah had never mentioned he was missing a ledger, and he was the one who had done the books for Paul. Elizabeth looked up at O'Brian, who was watching her carefully. An ominous shiver crept up her spine. Why was he being so cryptic? Just what was inside? "It looks like a Lawrence Mills ledger to me," she said, trying to make light of it. "I've plenty in the office."

"Open it."

Elizabeth looked at the book she held in her hand. Why didn't she want to look inside? Why was O'Brian looking at her that way?

When she didn't open the book, he reached out and opened it for her.

Elizabeth didn't mean to gasp. "Paul's handwriting," she whispered, brushing her fingertips over the faded scrawl. She looked up at her foreman uneasily. "It's my husband's handwriting."

"You're certain?"

She stared at the first page. All she could decipher was a date a year prior to her arrival in the colonies. The edges of the sheet were singed black, the bottom corner missing, but she knew she wasn't mistaken. It was a journal of some sort, and it was Paul's. "Yes, I'm sure."

"That was my guess."

She looked at O'Brian. "How would you know? You said you and the men didn't disturb it."

"I found a piece of a page in the hole. That's how I knew what they'd found."

"Can I see it?"

He reached inside his coat and pulled out a half a sheet of ledger paper, burned on the edges and brown with smoke spots, but still legible in places. It was dated May 18, 1773. Elizabeth had arrived from England by then, but she and Paul had not yet been wed. She'd been residing in New Castle with friends of his, but spending most days at the mills up in the manor house. She strained to read the faded handwriting, picking only a word here and there.

Anxious to be wed . . . the paper said in one place. Further down . . . *I watch them together and wonder* . . . And finally, the most disturbing words, barely readable . . . *terrible suspicions* . . .

Elizabeth looked up at O'Brian, unable to make out any other words or phrases on the page, front or back. "What do you think he was talking about—*suspicions?*"

He studied her face. "I was going to ask you the same thing."

Elizabeth didn't like the tone in his voice. "You're not accusing me again of—"

"I'm not accusing you of anything. But it sounds to me like your husband was aware of something going on here. Something he didn't like."

She held the book to her bosom. Over the initial shock of finding Paul's journal, she realized what the words might sound like to someone who hadn't known her and Paul and Jessop before the explosion. "I barely knew Jessop when Paul and I married. He spent much of his time in his Philadelphia offices then. It wasn't until after Paul was dead that—" She stopped in mid-sentence. "Why am I trying to explain this to you?"

He shrugged his broad shoulders, his tone infuriatingly arrogant. "I don't know, why are you?"

She turned around and started up the road, still clutching the remains of her dead husband's journal.

"I want to see that journal," he called after her with a tone of authority.

"It's mine," she hollered back. "And none of your goddamned business!"

He came running after her. "The hell it isn't. As long as I work for you," he grasped her shoulder, halting her, "I have a duty to know the dangers my men face."

She stared at the ground, fighting the lump in her throat. She didn't know what it was about O'Brian that made her so emotional. She'd never been like this before he came along. "All right, I'll grant you should be concerned with what happened here," she looked up at him, angrily, "but that doesn't give you a right to my husband's personal effects!"

He pointed to the journal she hung onto. "Even if the answers might be there?"

She pushed past him, a tone of dismissal in her voice. "I'll let you know what I find, Mr. O'Brian. See that the work is finished here today. I've fences I want repaired tomorrow."

Elizabeth walked up the riverbank to the road and

turned toward her office, her dogs in pursuit. She held the damaged journal to her breast. As much as she hated to admit it, O'Brian was right. From the words on the salvaged page, it sounded as if Paul had known something was wrong. Perhaps he had even known his life was in jeopardy.

Her jaw set with determination, she started up the steps through the skeletal woods toward her office. In the last few weeks she'd been so caught up with herself—first with her relationship with O'Brian, then with their parting—that she'd not thought much about her deceased husband or his death. The discovery of the journal made her realize that it was important that she find out who killed him. She owed it to Paul, she owed it to her workers, she owed it to herself.

O'Brian sat in the back corner of the public room of the Sow's Ear and lifted a jack of ale to his numb lips. It was said that a man could drown his sorrows in drink. He was beginning to wonder just how many pints it would take. He'd been sitting here nigh on two hours steady tipping the ale, and he still felt as miserable as he had when he'd come in.

O'Brian gave a belch and lifted his jack to a passing bar wench. "Can't a man get a drink in this wallow?"

"Hold your horses, Paddy. I'm movin' just as fast as I can," she shouted, as she went by with a tray laden with an eel pie and a bowl of sweet potatoes.

He rocked back in the battered chair, throwing one boot up on the trestle table. He'd come to the Sow's Ear for a little gaming, maybe a decent fight, a good roll with the redhead afterward, but now that he was here, he didn't feel much like any of it. Fact of the matter was, he hadn't felt much like anything this last fortnight. He worked, he slept, and worked some more. He'd not had a hearty meal nor slept with a woman in more than two weeks, not since he'd found out who Liz was.

She'd ruined both for him. A man just couldn't enjoy life's pleasures with this kind of anger stuck in his craw.

He wiped the back of his hand across his mouth distastefully. So why couldn't he get her out of his head? He knew he'd done the right thing breakin' it off with her. No O'Shay would ever knowingly keep company with a Tarrington. She was guilty by association, plain and simple. He should never have become involved with her to begin with. He knew better.

So why did he miss her? Why was it that every time he saw her—despite the flare of anger he felt—his heart gave a little trip. Christ, he could still smell her in his bed . . . no matter how many times he washed his sheets. He had to have the cleanest sheets on Worker's Hill right now.

O'Brian glanced around the smoke-filled public room. Where the hell was his ale? Maybe he'd switch to whiskey. He wasn't nearly as drunk as he wished he was, and he had to piss again.

He slapped the scarred table. Piss, piss on her! Piss on Mistress Elizabeth Tarrington Lawrence and her egotistical ways.

The day following his discovery of the journal in the foundation of the old stamp mill, she had called him to her office with a list of jobs she wanted done in the next week—a list that would take two weeks to accomplish. Just before she dismissed him, she made an offhand comment about the journal. She said she'd found nothing else questionable in it. She said the pages were damaged, not just by the fire, but by the water the men had used to put it out.

He wondered if she'd lied. She certainly didn't seem to be the murdering type, but how could a man know? It was suspicious. With her husband dead, she'd inherited the mill, the money, and his brother, all rather quickly. Hell, maybe she'd been screwing Jessop since her arrival. It wouldn't be the first time a woman had come to marry one brother, while wishing it was the other. Maybe Paul had caught them.

He dropped his forehead to his hand, resting his elbow on the table. Hell, he didn't know what to think anymore. He'd always been able to trust his judgment, and now suddenly he no longer felt that trust in himself. Mistress Lawrence had put an end to that . . .

O'Brian felt someone kick his leg. He lifted his head, opening his eyes. It was Red.

"Even' luv," she said, swaying her hips. "Ain't seen much of you lately."

"Been working," he grumbled, taking a leather jack of ale from her tray.

She nodded. That was the great thing about tavern wenches and the likes of them. There was no attachment on either side. A man and a woman could enjoy their fun, without getting caught up in nonsense like feelings.

She started to walk away, then turned back. "Say, did that woman find you?"

He drank deeply. "What woman?"

"The sister. Claire, was that her name?"

"What? She was here?"

"Lookin' for you."

"When?"

She shrugged, tugging at the neckline of her bodice to pull it back over her bare shoulder. "Good half-hour, I'd guess."

"Hell," he murmured, getting up. He left his coat and ale there. He figured he might as well pass through the room on the way to the necessity. If Claire was still here, maybe he'd find her. He knew he wasn't the girl's keeper. She was Jessop Lawrence's problem. But he hated to see anyone so fragile in body or mind be harmed.

O'Brian found Claire by the rear doorway, her back pressed to the wall, a drover pressed against her. He was lucky he recognized her at all. Rather than being dressed in her usual ornate gown and cape, she was wearing a man's black cloak; her long blond hair fanned out over her face and shoulders. O'Brian grabbed the drover by the scruff of his coat and dragged him backward. "Touch her again and I'll wrap your whip around your nuts and tug 'til they snap off and roll away," he warned, shoving the man backward.

Either the drover knew O'Brian's reputation, or he hadn't been that interested in Claire to begin with, because he grabbed his whip and made a fast exit through the front hallway.

O'Brian turned to Claire. "What are you doing here, sweetheart? How the hell do you keep getting out of that house of your brother's? It's after midnight."

She smiled seductively, reaching out to caress his cheek. "Evenin', sir," she cooed. "Looking for a friend?"

He caught her hand and lowered it. Her cloak fell open to reveal she was wearing nothing but a white silk nightrobe and matching dressing slippers. He closed the cloak for her, tying it beneath her chin. "Claire, sweetheart, it's me, it's O'Brian."

She stared at him for a moment through a veil of honey blond hair, her eyes unseeing. Then suddenly something appeared to register in her mind. "O'Brian?" she whispered.

"That's right." He pushed back the thick, loose hair that obscured her face. "How about if I take you home and—What the hell?" He took a closer look at her face. Was that a black eye?

He grabbed her hand and led her to the center of the room, where an oil lamp hung. He took her face between his hands and lifted it to the light. Her eye was encircled by a black ring, just beginning to turn green at the edges.

He gripped her shoulders, suddenly sober. "Claire, who hurt you?"

She refused to meet his gaze.

"Did that man, did that drover do this to you?"

She shook her head. "Just met him," she said in her child's voice. "Eye got hurt yesterday."

She was right. The eye did look a day or two old. "So it was last night?" he asked. "Did someone here hurt you last night?"

"Fell. Brother says I shouldn't be so clumsy."

"That doesn't look like a fall to me, Claire. It looks to me like someone hit you."

Claire lifted her gaze, smiling, and thrust her fist out to him. "I have a mousey. Would you like to see my mousey?"

He rolled his eyes. He knew he'd get no more information from her tonight. Once she started on the mouse business, he knew he'd lost her. He pushed her hand down gently, and began to lead her through the crowded room. "I've seen the mouse, sweetheart. Come on with me. I'll get my coat and walk you home." He held her small, warm hand tightly in his. "Hell, I don't belong here anyway."

Twenty

I'm pregnant.

A week later Elizabeth stared, in shock, at her nude reflection in her bedchamber mirror. It had come to her in an epiphany . . . she was pregnant.

She was so scared that her eyes were dry. But her stomach was in knots, her breath short. She could hear her heart pounding, her blood rushing in her ears.

She dropped her shift over her head, over her swelling breasts, over the abdomen that already looked rounded to her when she stood sideways.

Sweet God, how could this have happened?

She laughed aloud. She knew damned well how it happened. She'd spread her legs for her foreman, and he had planted his seed in her.

She reached for her stays, moving in slow motion. She was so stunned, she couldn't think. She hadn't had her flux since she and O'Brian had made love that first time, but her cycle had always been so irregular, so affected by stress, that she hadn't been concerned. No woman in her mother's family had ever gotten pregnant so quickly . . . so efficiently.

She looked up at herself in the full-length mirror again. She was certain beyond a doubt that she was pregnant, she only wondered how she could have gone this long without realizing it. The symptoms had been there for more than a month, she'd just been too naive to see them. She'd been sick to her stomach for weeks, her nausea alternating with periods of being famished. She'd been tired, emotional, and just not felt like herself. Weeks ago her breasts had begun to swell and ache like a thousand tiny pins were pricking them. Now she was getting fat—fat before her very eyes.

Elizabeth fastened the hook and eyes of her stays. *A mother . . . she was going to be a mother.* But she didn't want to be a mother! She didn't want a baby!

She was in shock, but not in such shock that she didn't realize she had to do something and do it quickly. She couldn't give birth to a bastard. She wouldn't do that to an innocent child.

Elizabeth had grown up with a cousin her own age, Millicent, who was born illegitimately, prior to her mother's marriage to Elizabeth's uncle. The little girl was raised knowing she was unwanted, always being treated like a lesser human being because of the circumstances of her birth. She wore cast-off clothes; she dined with the servants. At Christmastide there were no gifts for the bastard girl. At sixteen years old, Millicent committed suicide.

As Elizabeth stepped into her striped petticoat and lifted it to tie the ribbon at her waist, she stared at her own face in the mirror. This was no time for tears or weakness. Suddenly there was a helpless person relying on her. She didn't want a child; she was scared to death of being a mother, of making all the mistakes her own mother and father made. But a baby she was going to have, and she'd be damned if she wasn't going to do the best she could for the wee thing.

Elizabeth reached for the floral cotton gown that lay over the side chair beside the fireplace. She was going to have to act quickly, if no one was to know the truth. Two days, she'd give herself, two days to come up with an acceptable solution to her problem.

She glanced at the case clock over the mantel. "Hell," she muttered, tugging the gown over her head. "O'Brian's waiting for me in the laboratory."

She sat down on the edge of the chair to pull on her stockings and boots. First she'd deal with O'Brian and the new black powder mixture she wanted to try, then she'd worry about the baby.

She leaped out of the chair and started for the door, latching the hooks and eyes of her gown as she went down the hall. "Katie! Where's my cloak?" she shouted down the stairs. "I'll have my tea and biscuits in the office. Katie!"

"Coming, Mistress!" the girl hollered from down below.

Elizabeth heard the commotion of a typical morning in her household as she came down the stairs, still fastening her gown. Her dogs were barking and racing up and down the kitchen hallway waiting for their morning meal. She could hear their nails scraping on the hardwood floor, as they turned and slid around the corner. Two housemaids were arguing in the parlor, and Cook was shouting commands from the winter kitchen.

Elizabeth smiled to herself as she reached the bottom step, smoothing her clothing. Hell, if she could handle Lawrence Mills and all that running it entailed, she could certain handle one tiny baby!

Hours later Elizabeth sat on a stool hunkered over a table, scribbling across a piece of paper. She and O'Brian were in the room above the office that she used to store her records and as a makeshift laboratory.

O'Brian was pacing behind her as she tried to think. The sound of his boots *clip, clip, clopping* was driving her crazy. She wrote down a figure and then scratched it out, glancing up at the vials of pulverized charcoal, sulfur, sodium nitrate, and potassium nitrate. She stared past the vials at the bare, whitewashed wall. After a minute she slapped the quill down on the tabletop. "O'Brian! Will you stop that infernal pacing!"

He stopped behind her stool.

"I was thinking. I like to walk when I think."

"There's no thinking involved here. We exchange the sodium nitrate for the potassium nitrate in approximately the same amount, and it works." She raised her hand to the table where they had created a tiny explosion only minutes before. "We know it works."

He came around her stool to perch on the edge of the table. "Making a little bang on your lab table and producing kegs of good gunpowder are two separate things, Liz. First you need to find the right percentages. That's the easy part, and it will probably take months. Then, if it works, you have to find a place to get large quantities of sodium nitrate."

She rubbed her aching lower back. He was giving her that cocky look of his that made her want to slap him. She wondered how she could ever have found his egotistical manner attractive. The man was entirely too confident, too impressed with his own ability.

"You're being pessimistic, O'Brian—as usual."

"I'm being realistic," he countered.

She stared at a speck on the wall. "You don't think I can do it. You don't think I can figure out the right combination, do you?"

"I think it's going to take time and thought. And right now, you don't have a great deal of time, Mistress. I understand we have more charcoal coming in tomorrow from Penn's Colony. We'll be back on line by noon."

"So soon?" She sipped her cup of tea and nibbled on a blueberry biscuit. Tea and bread seemed to be the only things that calmed her stomach these days. "I was hoping we'd take a few days to regroup. Fences are coming down. Some of the workers' houses need repairs before winter." She ran her fingers through the fringe of her dark bangs in frustration. "If that company store is going to work, it needs to be stocked."

"The store will be better for the workers. They won't have to travel to purchase their flour and bacon. They won't be charged the outrageous interest old man Carney is demanding at his store down the road. When a man is out of coin, he can come and get credit with us, as long as he pays it back when he's paid again."

She held up her hand. "I know, I know. You're right. A company store is needed at Lawrence Mills; it's just that everything is happening so quickly. A store will mean hiring more men to run it, to stock it. Do I offer them and their families housing?" She threw up her hands. "If so, I've got to build more cottages. We're bursting at the seams here, Mr. O'Brian."

He shrugged good-naturedly. "You wanted to be successful, Lizzy. There you have it. Success and a major headache."

She rested her head in her hands, leaning on the table. O'Brian was right. This was what she wanted. She just hadn't thought it would come so quickly. She hadn't realized that even with others to do the physical labor, it took a great deal of work and thought on her part to keep the mills going.

O'Brian dropped his hand on her shoulder. It was probably the first time in a month that he'd touched her. "Liz, are you all right?"

His voice almost sounded tender. For a second, barely a second, Elizabeth considered telling him just what it was that was worrying her. She considering telling him about the baby. It was his, of course. She supposed he had the right to know.

But she couldn't do it. She just could not throw herself at his mercy. He'd been so mean about the Tarringtons.

He blamed her for something her father had done years before!

His words echoed in her head. *Not a marrying man,* he had told her when she suggested he marry the red-head.

Elizabeth knew he wouldn't take responsibility for the child if she told him, his or not. That wasn't the type of man he was.

And even if he wanted to make it right, if he wanted to marry her, she couldn't marry *him.* He was a foreman, for god's sake, nearly a common laborer. Women like herself didn't marry common men.

No, Jessop was the kind of man she needed to marry. Jessop was her solution.

Elizabeth lifted her head. "I'm all right," she said softly, a plan already forming in her head. "Just a touch of a stomach ailment, is all." She thrust her goose quill into its holder and pushed away from the table. "I think maybe I'll check in with Noah and go home for the day."

He folded his arms over his broad chest, still leaning on the table, watching her as she crossed the room. "Is that Mistress Lawrence I hear? She's going to take a few hours off? She's going home before bedtime?"

"Spare me, O'Brian." She turned in the narrow doorway to face him. "I haven't the energy for your shenanigans today."

He lifted an eyebrow mocking her, mocking what they'd shared. "You certain it's illness that takes you from your work, and not dear Jessop? I see him coming day and night, trailing you like a lost pup."

Elizabeth wondered how she could have ever considered the possibility of loving this arrogant bastard. "Actually," her gaze met his, "it is Jessop. He and I'll be confirming our wedding plans this evening." She smiled, wanting to hurt him. Hoping she had. "I have things to do, personal things."

O'Brian opened his palms. "No skin off my back, Mistress. You're the one who's going to marry the ass, not me."

Elizabeth went through the doorway to the narrow, winding steps. "See to your work, Mr. O'Brian." She'd just reached the bottom step when she heard the shatter of glass from above. "Oaf," she muttered. Then she turned the corner into the main office, intent on giving Noah orders. Indeed she did need time to prepare for tonight. She needed time to prepare for the deception of her life.

After careful thought, Elizabeth sent a note to Jessop telling him she needed a break from the mills, and that if he was not offended by her presumptuousness, she'd love to dine with him in his home this evening. The truth was, she couldn't bring herself to follow through with her plan in her own home.

She bathed, washed her hair, and dressed with extra care, wearing one of the gowns that Jessop had purchased for her. It was a ruffled candy confection with billowing sleeves and layers of stiff yellow and orange taffeta. She felt like a daffodil. The waist was too tight, but that just strengthened her determination. She had to do this for the life that grew inside her. She had to do it for Lawrence Mills and what the child—male or female—would inherit someday.

Elizabeth drove herself to Jessop's in a two-wheeled carriage. One of his servants let her in the front door of the dark, ominous house, built of cold gray granite on the side of a hill.

"Evening, Mistress Lawrence," the housekeeper said. "Mr. Lawrence is waiting for you in the parlor." She took Elizabeth's cloak and hat.

Elizabeth took her time removing her gloves, steadying her resolve. She was doing what was right. She knew she was. She had to think about the baby and not about herself. *I'll grow used to him in time, I'll forget about O'Brian and what we shared,* she tried to convince herself as she followed the housekeeper down the dank, gloomy hallway. *Maybe in time I'll even come to love Jessop.*

And maybe hell is cool in the springtime, too.

Elizabeth broke into an exaggerated smile as she walked into the parlor.

"Liz, darling." Jessop put out his arms to her. He was dressed in a ridiculous purple, China silk banyan with a matching turban piled high on his graying head. She'd heard the ensemble was popular in London, but it was all she could do to keep from bursting into laughter. *How in God's name,* she wondered, *am I going to be able to seduce this?*

But she smiled. She came to his outstretched arms, and she made herself kiss him. She thought about the barnyard expansion as his lips touched hers.

"I'm so pleased you came, sweetling. So pleased you took the initiative," he hummed.

Elizabeth heard the housekeeper retreat and the parlor door slide shut. Now she and Jessop were alone. She detached herself from his arms, making an effort of folding her gloves and laying them down with her reticule on a small mahogany side table with cherub legs. The musty smell of the heavy crimson draperies was making her stomach queasy.

"Where's Claire?" she inquired, wishing her sister-in-law were present, wishing *anyone* were, so she wouldn't have to be alone with him. Not yet, at least.

"I sent Sister to bed early." He went to a table already set for their meal, and picked up a nearly empty glass of brandy. "I thought it would be nice to spend some time alone, dear heart."

Good, Elizabeth thought. *He's already been drinking. That will make this easier on both of us.* She smiled at Jessop. "You're right, we do need to spend more time together if . . . if we're going to be wed."

He looked over the rim of the brandy snifter. "Darling . . ."

All these endearments were making her ill. She nodded. "Yes, I . . . I've been thinking about what you said and . . . and I think we should be married. Immediately. I think we should be married immediately," she repeated, trying to sound like she meant it.

He stood there at the table with his glass in his hand, smiling. He looked so pleased with himself. "I'm so happy for us."

Elizabeth felt awkward. She felt so guilty, but not guilty enough to stop the charade. She had her baby to think about now.

She walked across the pale lavender Turkey carpet to Jessop. If she was going to get him into bed, she was going to have to touch him, for god's sake. She put her arms out to him. "I want you to know I'm sorry for the things I said," she lied. "It's just that I've been under so much pressure with the powder mill." She took his glass from his hand, took a sip to fortify herself, and then set it on the table. The warm brandy wine burned a path down her throat to her stomach, strengthening her resolve. What sense was there in waiting through a dinner that would only make her sicker? She had a job to do here. She might as well get it over with. The trick was to make him think he was seducing her.

She rested her hands on his shoulders and made herself look into his blue eyes, wishing they were green. She thrust out her lower lip, hoping to appear seductive. "I don't think we should wait," she whispered huskily. "I don't think I can wait much longer."

"Oh, my love," he murmured, bringing his mouth to hers.

Elizabeth endured the kiss. It was hard not to be repulsed, especially when he thrust his tongue between her lips. He tasted medicinal. But Elizabeth was determined. She had to protect her child.

She pressed her body to his, managing a moan that sounded genuine. She stroked his shoulder.

"Darling, darling," he whispered.

He was touching her now. Elizabeth's stomach was doing flip-flops. She tried not to think about O'Brian as Jessop squeezed her tender breasts, but he kept pushing his way into her mind. No matter what she thought of O'Brian now, she couldn't deny that in bed, the man had been near perfect. His body and hers had fit together like puzzle pieces. He'd been able to anticipate her every need, even before she could. He'd been able to please her as Paul had never been able to, as she knew in her heart that Jessop would never be able to.

Jessop was becoming aroused now, despite the fact that Elizabeth was just standing there. He was slobbering on her, grinding his groin against hers. Through the thin silk of his banyan, she could feel him growing hard against his leg. Feeling O'Brian's arousal had always increased her own. Why was she so disgusted?

"Liz, Liz," Jessop crooned, his eyes squeezed shut. "I can't tell you how long I've thought about this, about you and I . . ."

Then he took her hand and guided it to the silk banyan. "Touch me, please touch me," he moaned.

He was making it easy for her. It would be so easy . . . But she couldn't do it. Maybe tomorrow she could, maybe the next day, when she was feeling better, when she wasn't so nauseated . . .

Elizabeth pulled her hand away from the heat of his engorged flesh beneath the silk. "Jessop—"

He took her hand again, his eyes still shut, his face flushed red with excitement. "Liz, Liz, I hurt so badly. Can't you help me? Can't you just ease my——"

"Jessop." She jerked her hand away, speaking louder this time. She pushed his hands from her and took a step back.

His eyes fluttered open. "Liz?"

She laid her hand flat on her queasy stomach, looking down, wishing the room would stop spinning, wishing she could get a breath of fresh air in the dank, musty room. She couldn't lie like this, not to Jessop, not to Paul's brother. It wasn't right. "Jessop, I have to talk to you."

He seemed flustered for a moment, perhaps a little embarrassed. He reached for his brandy. "Liz, I'm sorry. I apologize for my behavior. It's just that——"

She looked away. She had to say it. She had to get it out before she lost her nerve, that or her last tea and biscuits. "Jessop, listen to me. I . . . I need your help." She looked down at the thick carpet beneath her feet. "I'm pregnant, and I need you to marry me." There. She'd said it.

For a moment Jessop made no response. He took another sip of his brandy and reached for the cut glass decanter on the dinner table. She made herself look at him.

"I see," he said finally, pouring himself a full glass.

"I can't have an illegitimate child, Jessop."

"No. I'd say you can't."

"It would ruin my powder business."

"It would ruin your reputation, my dear." He took another sip of the brandy. "And mine as well. You know how some people are about these things. Such a scandal couldn't help but affect my shipping trade."

"I'm sorry," she said softly. "I didn't mean for it to happen."

"No, I don't suppose you did."

He was being so calm about the whole thing that she almost wished he'd holler at her, say something unkind, break something, anything but just stand there in that stupid purple gown.

"I have to be wed and wed at once," she said. "Else when the baby comes, people will know."

"I see." Jessop pulled out a chair for himself, sat down, and uncovered the soup dish at his place. He reached for his linen napkin and tucked it into the neckline of his banyan. "You're right. The wedding will have to take place at once."

Elizabeth knew she heaved a sigh of relief. "Thank you, Jessop. Thank you so much. I'll make it up to you. I swear I will."

He took a spoonful of the tomato and onion soup and slurped it. "We'll do something quiet. Just you and I and Sister, in Philadelphia, perhaps. We've many friends in Philadelphia we could visit afterwards."

"That would be fine. Whatever you want." She took an embroidered handkerchief from her sleeve and fluttered it in front of her face. She was still slightly nauseated, and the smell of the onions wasn't helping much, but she felt better now that this was resolved, much better. "I could use a day or two away from the mills. I think I'm working too hard."

He took another slurp, wiping his chin with the bottom corner of the napkin. "Yes, a visit in Philadelphia, and then we'll go off Europe before the winter crossing becomes too difficult for you."

"Off to Europe?" For a moment she wasn't certain she heard him correctly. "What do you mean, off to Europe, Jessop? I can't go to Europe. I can't leave my mills."

"You said O'Brian was capable." He took another slurp.

"He is."

"Then he can run the mills in your absence." His bowl

of soup empty, he reached across the table for hers. It didn't matter to Liz, she had no intention of eating anyway. "We'll go to England, France, Italy. I'll do some business, make some contacts. You'll give birth, and we'll return home with no one the wiser."

Elizabeth heard a strange buzzing in her ears. She felt a little weak at her knees. Surely Jessop hadn't meant what she thought he meant. He didn't mean they would leave her baby behind . . . did he?

Twenty-one

"No one's going to take my baby from me," she stated flatly.

Jessop slurped another spoonful of soup, not bothering to look up at her standing beside him. "Surely you didn't think I was going to let the little bastard sleep under my roof." He reached for the pewter saltcellar. "Christ, Liz, I'd be looking at every man who set foot on my property wondering if he was the father, wondering if he was the one you'd soiled yourself with." He sprinkled salt from the tiny spoon over his soup. "We'll put your bastard out, come home, and leave it all behind us."

Elizabeth was suddenly so angry that for a moment she couldn't react. She didn't want a baby. She didn't want the responsibility of a child to raise. But now that she had a baby growing inside her, she'd be damned if anyone was going to take him from her.

Elizabeth brought her fist down on the edge of the table so hard that a champagne glass fell to the floor and shattered. Red soup from Jessop's bowl splashed onto the pristine linen tablecloth. He looked up, startled.

"No one's going to take my baby from me," she repeated.

His eyes narrowed vindictively. "I'd suggest to you that you're not in a position to make that choice."

"I made a mistake, but I'll not punish this child for the rest of his or her life because of my mistake. This child has a right to know who his mother is, to be raised by his mother, to be loved by his mother."

"Please spare me the motherly love speech, Liz." He jerked his napkin from his neckline and threw it over the spilled soup. "Face the truth. You're stuck, and I'm the only one who can get you out of this mess. Obviously the father is not a choice, else you'd not come here begging me as you have."

"Son of a bitch," she whispered. "You haven't even asked me who the father is."

He smiled coldly. "Not interested in knowing. He could be any one of a number of men, considering how freely you wander about."

She stood for a moment, staring at him, her hands on her hips, too angry for tears. "Forget it," she said.

He leaned forward, crossing his legs casually beneath his silk banyan. "Pardon?"

"Wipe that simple look off your face. I said forget it." She snatched up her reticule and gloves. "I'm desperate, but I'm not that desperate," she hollered, heading for the parlor door. She'd not stay here with this man, not for another instant.

"Where do you think you're going?" he barked, following her.

"Home, where I belong."

"That's ridiculous. You can't give birth out of wedlock. These Colonists are freethinking, but they're not *that* freethinking! You'll ruin your business and mine."

She shrugged. "I don't care. I'm not giving my baby away."

He stopped in the middle of the Turkey carpet, folding his arms over his chest. "I can't make you marry me. I can't prevent you from whelping, but I can damned well stop you from ruining me."

She halted in the door. "What are you talking about?" she demanded, not caring if anyone heard her.

"I'll contest the will. I have friends in the courts."

"There aren't going to be English courts here much longer," she countered. "In case you haven't heard, we're going to war."

"I see, so not only have you prostituted yourself, but you've become a traitor, too!"

Elizabeth laughed. "You can't hurt me, Jessop. You can't take away what Paul gave to me." She touched her heart. "He loved me. That was why he wrote that will before we were even wed. He loved me, and he wanted me to be provided for even if something happened to him. He wanted *me* to have Lawrence Mills, not you."

"Odd, isn't it? You having so much to gain from his death."

"What are you inferring? If you want to say something," she jabbed her finger at him, "just come out and say it."

"I wasn't inferring anything."

She turned away, starting down the hall. She had to get of here. The man was making her physically ill. "I'm going home."

"You do that." He followed behind her. "You go home and you think long and hard, you little tart. And when you have, you'll realize you don't have a choice. You want to keep that precious mill of yours, then you'd better be back here in the morning." He caught up to her in the front hall, his purple silk mules slapping on the hardwood floor. "You'd better be here apologizing to me, begging me to take you back."

She looked at him. "That'll be a cold day in hell, Jessop. Mighty cold." Then she opened the door and stepped into the cool night air. She went down the steps, across the drive, headed down the road toward Lawrence Mills. She didn't stop to call for her horse and carriage or even to retrieve her cloak. The walk home would keep her warm, she decided. That and her anger would be enough.

The following morning Elizabeth sat up in her bed, sipping a cup of tea. She was ashamed of herself for what she'd tried to do last night. She had almost prostituted herself to get Jessop to marry her and give her baby a legitimate father.

How could she have ever thought she could marry him? How had she not seen through his debonair act, his aristocratic manners, and handsome smile to his true heart? Jessop was not the man his brother was, not by a furlong. He never had been.

Elizabeth realized now that she had attempted to take all the qualities she had associated with Paul and placed them on Jessop's shoulders after her husband's death. In her mind, she had tried to turn Jessop into Paul. Her marriage with Jessop would never have worked, even without the child she now carried in her womb.

After her conversation with Jessop last night, she realized what a cruel man he was. He might have money, influence, and a circle of important friends, but where was his compassion? Where was his belief in doing what was right? It would have been right for him to have married his brother's widow, to have taken in her child, and forgiven her for her sin. A good man would have done it.

"O'Brian is a good man," she whispered to the empty room. "He would marry me."

So there was her answer. There was plan B. The child was his, obviously—half his—and therefore half his responsibility.

She flung back the covers. She had no time to lose. The baby inside her was growing.

She slipped out of her nightrail and padded barefoot to the fireplace to dress where it was warm. She'd marry

O'Brian and she'd give her child his name, whether it was O'Shay or O'Brian. So what if the man was just a foreman, so what if his family came from Irish cottages? Poor, and of common blood, she knew in her heart that O'Brian was twice the man Jessop would ever hope to be.

Besides, these were the American Colonies. This was the place where the English feudal system fell away and men earned their own wealth, their own respect. Here it would be possible for her and O'Brian to build a family name of their own.

Elizabeth stepped out of her white flannel nightgown and reached for her underclothing. A gown suitable for riding was already laid out. She had plans to ride the Lawrence Mill property lines this morning with O'Brian, and make plans for expansion of their meager pastures. With the company store being built, it only made sense for her to begin raising her own livestock. This winter, when her production slowed down, she intended to have O'Brian and his men build the new fences.

She bit down on her lower lip as she rolled up her wool stocking. Of course, if O'Brian was going to be her husband, it wouldn't really be fitting that he continue his work as her foreman. That would be entirely inappropriate. She tied first one garter ribbon and then the other.

Well, that was a minor detail that could be settled after they were wed, after her child—their child—was safe from the stigma of illegitimate birth.

Elizabeth rode beside O'Brian through the woods, surveying the lay of the land on the east side of her property. The air was cool, but not cold, and the sun shone on their faces. It was a beautiful day for a ride, with a few, bright, lingering leaves still falling softly to their winter bed on the ground.

They'd been riding nearly an hour, staking out where they would run the new cattle pasture. Much of the land was wooded and rocky, but O'Brian seemed confident that he and his men would be able to clear sufficient space for the cattle to roam.

As the minutes ticked by, Elizabeth tried to concentrate on the task at hand, at the same time trying to find an appropriate time to broach the subject of her pregnancy and the necessity of them marrying. It was all she could do to keep from chuckling aloud. Was there such a thing as an appropriate time for such a conversation? What was she going to say? *"Plant the stake there, O'Brian. Oh, and by the way, I'm a good two months pregnant. Care to marry me?"*

Did she simply state the facts and tell him what he had to do? Or did she play up her emotions and tell him how frightened she was, how much she needed him right now, despite their differences?

The businesswoman in Elizabeth told her to stick to the facts. Emotions had no part in a decision like this. He'd gotten her pregnant; he would have to marry her. It was as simple as that.

She sighed. *If only it was . . .*

O'Brian pulled up the reins on his mare and dismounted. "I don't think we'd better go any further than this," he said, pulling a stake and a wooden hammer from his saddlebag. "With you not being certain where the property lines are, we'd best end the pasture here. In the spring we'll bring in a surveyor and find out for certain what's yours and what's Jessop's."

Elizabeth nodded, picking at the hem of her doeskin glove. She felt like such a coward. Why hadn't she said anything yet? Now they would be starting back toward the mills. She'd wanted to tell him when they were alone. She looked up at him, then away. She would just have to do it. Say it.

"O'Brian?"

He was swinging the hammer, pounding the painted stake into the soft humus beneath a locust sapling. "Aye?" He didn't look up.

"O'Brian . . . I've got a problem." She went on faster than before, afraid that if she didn't spit it out, she'd lose her nerve. *"We've* got a problem."

He looked up at her. "What's that?"

She could feel her forehead breaking out in a sweat as she lowered her gaze to stare at her mount's mane. "Oh, hell," she murmured, looking up at him. "O'Brian, I'm pregnant and you have to marry me."

He stood there, stunned. He looked as if she couldn't have surprised him more if she'd slapped him in the face. "What did you say?"

She rolled her eyes heavenward. "What part didn't you understand?" she demanded impatiently. "The part about the fact that I'm going to have a baby, or the part about you having to wed me?"

He swore a French oath so foul that she knew her cheeks colored.

"How did this happen?"

He was obviously not pleased.

"How do you think it happened?" she muttered sarcastically.

He threw down the hammer. It struck an exposed root of the locust tree and bounced off it, startling her horse. He grabbed the horse's bridle, giving it a jerk. The horse steadied.

"You know what I mean!" He came around the side the horse and reached up to grab her arm. Before she realized what was happening, he was pulling her off her sidesaddle. Her booted feet hit the dry, leafy ground.

"I mean how the hell did you get pregnant? You *told* me you couldn't! I asked you before the first time we ever—" He stopped in mid-sentence, then started again.

"I specifically asked you, and you specifically told me I had no reason to worry!"

She threw up her hands. How was it that a man could always turn something into a woman's fault, no matter what it was? Christ's sake, it had taken two of them to create this child! Why was it suddenly *her* fault? "What do you want me to say? I thought I couldn't get pregnant. I was wrong."

He stared at her, his green eyes afire with anger. "Just out of curiosity, what made you think you couldn't get pregnant?"

"A little late to ask now, isn't it?"

"I thought you had some woman's ailment! Christ, Liz, I was trying to be sensitive!" He let go of her arm. "I'm waiting. Amuse me. Tell me why you didn't think you would quicken. Spit into the mouth of a frog and turn around thrice? I understand that works every time!"

She crossed her arms over her chest, impatient with his sarcasm. "Women don't get pregnant in my family for years. They marry in their twenties, and never have a child before their mid-thirties. My mother said it was a curse. She warned me before I married, not to expect a baby for a very long time."

"That's the most ridiculous thing I've ever heard of!" he shouted. "You should have tried spitting into the mouth of a frog." He turned away for a moment, then back to her. "You thought you couldn't get with child because your *mother* was late birthing?" He yanked his cocked hat off his head and ran one hand through his blond hair. "Do you know how stupid that sounds, Liz?"

She looked away, a lump rising in her throat. She could feel tears stinging her eyes. This wasn't how this was supposed to go. She knew he might be angry, but she hadn't expected him to make her feel like this. She did feel stupid. And now she was afraid. Very afraid.

"I don't want a child," he said, lowering his voice an octave.

She stared at the stake only half in the ground. "I don't either, but I've got one." She looked up at him, meeting his angry green eyes with her own angry gaze. "And so do you."

It was his turn to look away. "All these years, all those women, and not a child to my knowledge," he muttered. "How far are you?"

She exhaled. "I don't know for certain. My bleeding hasn't come since you first touched me."

He swore again, this time in Gaelic. "Fine."

"Fine what?"

"Fine. The child is half my responsibility. I'll help support him or her." He pointed at her. "But I won't marry you, Liz. That was never a possibility." He waved his finger. "Never."

"You have to marry me!" she shouted. "I won't have an illegitimate child! I won't lose the mills over this."

"I'm not going to do it. I'll not marry a Tarrington."

Elizabeth brushed past him, stepping up on a fallen tree trunk to climb into her saddle. She didn't know what to say. What could she say? Right now, all she wanted to do was get away from him, before she started to cry. She didn't want him to see how weak she was. She didn't want him to know how much he'd hurt her.

She swung into the saddle, barely seated, and whipped the mare around.

"Come back here!" O'Brian called. "This conversation isn't over."

"It's over," she shouted as she rode away. "It was over before it ever started."

O'Brian struck the nearest tree trunk with the heel of his hand. It hurt, but it made him feel a little better. He cursed under his breath. He cursed Elizabeth, he cursed the Tarrington family, he cursed his mother for ever giving him life.

Behind him he heard Elizabeth's horse cutting through the trees as she made her escape.

He closed his eyes for a moment, lifting his face to the warm sunshine. There. He'd done it. He'd wanted to make her hurt the way he'd hurt when he'd found who she was. Well, he'd done it, quite well, he guessed.

He opened his eyes. "A babe," he murmured. "I'll be damned. I'm going to be a da after all these years of dodging responsibility. Serves me right," he muttered.

Then he smiled perversely. From the sound of the shouting match he and Liz had just had, he knew one thing, the child, boy or girl, was going to have a temper, that was for certain.

He walked over to the stake he'd been driving and picked up the hammer. He swung again and again, as hard as he could, the sound ringing above the treetops. Finally, the stake broke beneath the impact of the hammer and shattered into splinters. He threw the hammer to the ground.

A baby. A child. A child that would grow up to be an adult, of his own flesh and blood. He was scared. He didn't know how to be a father. Not a good one . . .

O'Brian glanced over his shoulder in the direction Liz had just gone. When he had seen the tears in her eyes, he'd wanted to take her in his arms. He'd wanted to hold her, to calm her fears. Despite his anger with her, he had felt a inherent desire to protect the life she carried.

"So now what?" he asked the horse standing by patiently.

The horse made no intelligent response, but it didn't matter. O'Brian already knew what he would do.

He'd marry her, of course. He'd known it the moment she'd told him she carried his child. It was just that she'd been so arrogant about it. So accusing. She hadn't asked him if he *would* marry her. She'd ordered him, just like she ordered him to start up the waterwheel or transport a load of powder into New Castle Town.

She hadn't said she *wanted* to marry him, either. She'd said he *had* to marry her, because she was pregnant. She'd made no indication whatsoever that she cared for him.

Why would she? Who was he fooling to think maybe she missed him, except in between her fancy sheets. That was all they'd ever had between them. He knew it. Maybe he'd just wished for more.

O'Brian picked up the wooden hammer and slowly walked to the horse and dropped it in the saddlebag. He mounted and reined the mare around, starting in the direction Liz had fled.

He'd marry her because he knew it was his duty, because it was the right thing to do. He'd marry Elizabeth Tarrington Lawrence, and he'd fulfil his responsibility as husband and father, because that was what an O'Shay man did.

O'Brian sank his heels into the flanks of the mare and broke into a gallop, ducking tree limbs as he rode through the forest. Him, a married man? Who'd believe it? Then he thought of Michael O'Brian, and he broke into sardonic laughter. This would never have happened if he'd not run into Michael, if he'd not take the man's name and his job. So this was his punishment. His mother had always said a man paid for his sins, not just in purgatory, but on earth as well.

Damned if he wasn't going to pay dearly for his sins now.

Twenty-two

Elizabeth heard O'Brian approach before she saw him. He was coming up fast behind her, crashing through the underbrush, his horse's hooves pounding the ground.

She wished she'd brought her pistol along. A shot over his head would probably send him packing.

"Liz! Liz, wait!"

"Rot in hell!" she shouted over her shoulder. She lifted her reins and urged her mare into a trot. The woods were thick with dying greenbriars, and difficult to navigate. Rocks cropped up everywhere, making the path dangerous. Twice her horse stumbled, but she urged her on. She didn't want to see O'Brian. She didn't want to speak to him. She'd have her baby alone. She'd figure out a way to keep the mills and the baby. She'd do it. She would.

"Liz!" He was closer now. "Slow down. Wait for me!" he called. "Damnation, woman! I want to talk to you."

"I told you the conversation was over!" she shouted as she wiped at her damp eyes with the sleeve of her riding coat. "I don't want to speak to you about it. Not ever again, if I can help it."

He was right behind her now, his horse bearing down on hers. She sank her heels into her mare's sides. "Get up!" she urged.

"You're being childish," he insisted from behind. "You

can't gallop through these woods. You're going to fall off your damned horse and hurt yourself."

"I haven't lost my seat since I was four," she snapped.

His horse had caught up to hers. He rode beside her, ducking low-lying branches.

Elizabeth tightened her grip on her reins, trying to crowd his horse off the old deer path she was following.

"Liz!"

Before Elizabeth could turn her head to retort, she heard a sound, then O'Brian grunt, then a crash. When she glanced sideways, she saw his horse without its rider. O'Brian had apparently been knocked off his mount when he'd failed to maneuver around an old dead oak limb.

She reined in her mare as his mount ran off down the path. "You all right?" she called begrudgingly over her shoulder, as she turned her mare around.

O'Brian was quite the sight. He sat in the middle of the path, minus his hat, looking slightly dazed.

"O'Brian?"

"I think so." He rubbed his forehead. "Damn, that hurt! You ran me off the road. That was stupid, Liz. You could have hurt yourself and the babe."

"*I* didn't get hurt, *you* did." She rode her horse up to him and stopped, looking down at him. "Serves you right for chasing me down."

He sat there looking up at her. "I was trying to catch up to apologize. I shouldn't have reacted the way I did. It was poor judgment, and it was childish."

She made no response but to continue to look down at him.

"Christ, Liz. Ye made me mad, *ordering* me to marry you the way you did."

He was talking in his normal voice to her now. He sounded sincere. She looked out over her horse's neck. "I don't know what to do, O'Brian. I know I got myself into this. I was the one that initiated the relationship. I should have used my head, but I . . ."

He came to his feet and reached out to lay his hand on her knee. "You what?"

She sighed as she turned her head to look at him. "But I wanted you," she admitted. "I wanted you so badly, that I don't think I cared what the dangers were."

"Ah, Lizzy." He reached up and tucked a dark curl beneath her masculine riding hat. "I apologize for my cowardly behavior. I'd not leave you on the drying rack like that. You know me better than that, I would hope." He searched her face for understanding. "I was just angry, that's all."

She nodded. She was tired, tired of the shouting, the fighting. All she wanted was a soft feather tick bed and some peace. "Apology accepted," she said softly, lifting her reins. "I'll go and bring back your horse."

But his grip on her knee tightened. "Wait a minute. I'm not through saying what I have to say."

She didn't want to face him. She didn't want to look into those green eyes of his.

"Liz, look at me."

Slowly she looked down.

He took her gloved hand in his broad one. "Will you marry me?"

She couldn't resist the barest smile. Suddenly he was so serious. "You don't have to do this. You're right. I was a fool. 'Twas my own mistake." She tried to pull her hand from his, but he wouldn't let go of it.

"You're wrong. 'Twas as much my fault as yours. More." He turned her hand in his. "We'll marry for the sake of the child. It's the right thing to do."

She looked into his green eyes. "Oh, O'Brian, I don't want a marriage of convenience. Maybe once that would have been acceptable to me, but not any longer. Maybe

I'd just be better off to leave things as they are. I'll raise the child myself." She paused. "I could do it, you know."

"I know you could. I've got no doubts." He thought for a moment before he responded. "But I want to marry you, Liz. Now, I can't make any promises. We'd have the odds against us, considering our background."

"My family name, my position, yours, Jessop, the mills," she rattled off.

"But listen to me. I can tell you I would give our marriage my best try." He paused. "If you'd be willing to do the same."

She only had to think for a moment. Then she nodded.

"Does that mean yes, Mistress? Will ye be my wife?"

"Whose?" Her mouth was drawn in a thin line, but her eyes were laughing. "Patrick O'Shay's or Michael O'Brian's?"

He brushed his lips over the soft doeskin of her glove. "Paddy's gone, I think. Went over the side of the ship with me dearly departed friend."

"It would make more sense if you keep O'Brian's name. She smiled. "I don't think I could start calling you by another name at this point. As for your *past life,* we can tell everyone your wife and children died of summer fever just after you left home and you only recently received word."

He let go of her hand and took her horse by the bridle, turning the mare back toward the river, and home. He scooped his hat off the ground as they passed it and dusted it on his knee. "So what kind of wedding do you fancy, Mistress?"

"You're going to have to stop calling me that," she chided.

"Fancy wedding with a feast, dancing, and drink?"

"No." She shook her head. What she needed right now was a few quiet days. "No drunken brawls. Please, let's just go somewhere and be married."

He raised an eyebrow, giving her that cocky grin of his. "You mean elope? Wouldn't that be the talk of the Lower Counties? Mistress Lawrence and her hired man! Phew! I can hear them now!"

"I'll go up to the house, pack a change, and meet you at the magazine. I know a little inn at a ferry crossing at Head Of Elk. We could go there."

He spotted his horse grazing up ahead. "You don't want to tell Claire and Jessop?"

She shook her head. She'd tell O'Brian about Jessop. Just not now. "No. Let's just go and do it. I don't want anyone to try and change my mind."

He released her mount's reins and reached for his own. "You mean about you marrying a common man. A yard foreman?"

"I know what kind of man you are, O'Brian. I don't care what anyone thinks, or says for that matter."

He swung into his saddle with a careless ease. "No, I don't guess you do, sweetheart. Not a damned bit. That's what I admire about you."

"The magazine in an hour, then?" She gave a nod, still a little uncertain. "Will you be there, O'Brian?"

He grinned. "Wouldn't miss it for all the black powder in France."

"What do you mean, she's gone?" Jessop demanded angrily.

Claire stood in the twilight shadows of the library doorway. She held her wrap tightly across her shoulders. "She's gone," she said softly. "Samson saw her and Mr. O'Brian ride out at noon."

"Whore!" He swept his hand across the polished cherry sidetable, sending a crystal decanter and several glasses flying. Glass shattered on the floor, and brandy splashed red against the white wall.

Claire held her wool wrap tighter, cringing at the sound.

"Whores! All women are whores! You know that, don't you? Don't you?" he shouted in rage.

Claire was trembling now. "We're all whores," she repeated.

"She spread her legs for that bastard!" he ranted. "She gave that filthy Irish foreman of hers what she refused me!" He paced the carpet. "You know that, don't you?"

A tear trickled down Claire's cheek. "Yes, Brother."

"And not just him, half the men at the mills have had her! The rumors are rampant!" He pointed accusingly at Claire. "She always was a nigger-lover. Now I know why. She likes them in her bed, you know. Two at a time, I hear!"

Claire could only nod, paralyzed by fear.

"Son of a bitch!" Jessop kicked a footstool near the hearth, sending it tumbling dangerously close to the glowing coals. "I knew I should never have let her bring him here. I knew he'd be nothing but trouble." He shook his fist. "But I'm on to them. You know I'm on to them, don't you? Don't you, Sister?"

Claire gave a hiccup. "Yes, Brother. You're on to them."

"You know what that letter I received today from New Castle said, don't you?"

She shook her head.

"It was from an old friend. I have friends everywhere, you know. People who owe me favors. People who watch out for my best interests."

"I know," she echoed, stooping to pick up a broken glass from the floor.

"The letter was to tell me that Liz's Mr. O'Brian had been inquiring into the investigation by the High Sheriff after Paul's death. That futtering potato boy wanted to know if anyone with any black powder experience outside the family had been here after the explosion." Jessop stepped on a bit of broken glass, and it crunched beneath the soft sole of his silk mule. "Do you know what that means, Sister?" He thrust his face into hers. "Do you?"

She was trembling from head to foot now. She shook her head, her curls bouncing violently against her ashen cheeks.

"It means he's putting his beak where it doesn't belong." He stared into her frightened eyes. "He'll have to go, of course. I won't have my departed brother's name soiled. I'll retrieve Liz from her perverted little tryst, and then I'll deal with the bastard." He brought his finger beneath her nose. "One way or another, he'll be gone from here. Gone as if he never existed."

Claire gave a start and her hand slipped, scraping across the jagged glass in her hand. "Ouch," she murmured.

Jessop's face immediately softened. "Oh, Sister, what is it?"

She took a step back, shaking her head. "N-nothing. Nothing, just a little cut."

"Let me see." He held out his hand.

She shook her head. "No . . . no, it's fine really."

"Let me see, Sister," he directed. "I wouldn't want an infection to set in. You know I only want the best for you, sweetheart. For all the women in my care."

"I know that," she whispered.

Jessop took the broken glass from her trembling hand and laid it on the table. Then he opened her curled fingers. A spot of crimson blood stood raised on her index finger. "Oh, Sister," he crooned. "You must be more careful." Then he lifted her bloody finger to his mouth and sucked gently.

* * *

Liz sat across the small trestle table from O'Brian, nibbling on a crust of bread while she waited for the meal they'd ordered. The public room of the Three Horns Tavern at Head Of Elk was quiet so late in the evening. The only other patrons were two drunken redcoats asleep, their heads resting on a table in the far corner of the room.

The small public room was clean, with a blaze of sweet apple wood burning in the stone fireplace. The heavenly scents of roasting pork, cloves, and baked pears drifted in from the kitchen in the rear. The sounds of the host and hostess arguing over a burned crust could be heard faintly in the background.

Elizabeth looked up at O'Brian, who was sipping his ale from a pewter tankard, watching her.

Married, she thought. *I've gone and done it. I've married my yard foreman. And no matter what happens, I won't turn and look back. I won't second guess myself. I'll work with what I have.*

O'Brian smiled. "Christ, sweetheart, you look as if you've seen the gallows."

She glanced down. There was no shiny ring there, but her wedding hand was heavy none the less. "I didn't think I'd marry again," she said.

He grinned. "I didn't think I would either."

His statement made her realize how little she actually knew about this man she now called husband. The man she would call husband, until one of them died. "You've been married before?"

"No. Well, only in my head. To Michael's widow."

She laughed.

"I have, you know."

She leaned across the table. "Have what?"

"Seen the gallows."

She lifted her lashes. Heavens, but he was a handsome man with his angel's blond hair and his sensuous lips. "What do you mean? You saw a man hang?"

"I mean I almost saw them up close, like standing on the scaffold with the crows."

She watched him as he took a long sip from his tankard, draining it. He was serious. "You were almost hanged?"

"Aye." He shrugged. "I tried to blow up a little bridge. The English don't like that, you know, Irish Catholics blowing up Englishmen."

"What happened?"

"I bribed the jailman's daughter." He gave her the same smile, she guessed, he had given the jailman's daughter. "I escaped from prison, found myself enough coin to make it on board a ship bound for the American Colonies, and—"

"Found coin?" she inquired, lifting an eyebrow in challenge. "How is that you *find* coin, and the rest of us work for it?"

He ignored her, going on with his story. "On board the ship was where I met up with poor Michael. God rest his soul." He crossed himself. "Ye know the rest, Mistress."

"I have a feeling there's a lot I don't know." Her gaze searched his. "Maybe I don't need to know."

He reached across the table to take her hand. He turned it in his, smoothing her palm. "You'll see. It'll not be so bad as you think, being married to a man like myself. I'll scrape my boots before I set foot on your fancy carpets, and I swear I'll not belch too loudly in front of your handmaid."

She took the last bit of bread in her hand and tossed it across the table, striking him on the nose with it. She laughed. "I haven't got a handmaid."

"Then who is it that unties your stays and such?"

"I don't know." She looked at him through the veil of her dark lashes. "You now, I suppose."

He held her with his gaze, stroking her hand with his

fingertips. "I was wondering how to broach that subject."

"What subject?"

"Husbandly rights. Or wifely rights, if you prefer."

The sound of his voice made her shiver with pleasure. He wanted her. She could tell by his tone, by his touch. "You mean to tell me you'd sleep with me, knowing I was a Tarrington?"

He looked down at the table where some soldier had carved his name. "Perhaps I was rash in my reaction."

"I'm still a Tarrington," she said softly. "I can't change that. I can't change what my father did."

"I know. And I can't change the fact that I deceived you." He brought her knuckles to his lips and began to kiss them one by one. "So, let's just forget about it. Let's pretend none of it ever happened. Let's pretend I didn't say the things I said."

"For the sake of the baby?" she asked, because she had to know. She had to know if he had married her for her, or for the responsibility of the baby she carried.

"Yes." He looked straight into her eyes. "No. For the sake of you and me, Lizzy."

The warmth of the room, the strong ale, the touch of his lips on her hand were making her dizzy. She wanted to touch him. She wanted to stand naked in the moonlight with him and give whatever she had to give to him.

"Let's go upstairs to our room," she said, watching him by the dim light of the candle that sputtered on their table.

"Tired?" he asked huskily.

She shook her head no.

He smiled. "Good."

They rose, their gazes lingering. He finished the last of her ale and picked her discarded cloak off the bench. Hand in hand they started for the narrow, winding staircase that led to the room they had rented for the night.

Just then the hostess of the Three Horns came through a swinging door from the kitchen, her wooden tray laden with plates of steaming roast pork, diced thyme potatoes, and onion and spinach pie. She was a tall, hefty woman with a head of fiery red hair. "Your meal, sir, madame," she called. "It's hot and ready. I beg you forgive me it took so long. My husband Jacky, he ain't got the sense God gave a turnip when it comes to makin' a pie crust."

O'Brian stopped at the bottom of the staircase and turned back to the hostess. "We've decided we're not hungry, after all." He fished several coins from a leather bag on his belt and dropped them on the tray. "But here's the payment just the same."

Elizabeth watched as the woman's eyes lit up at the sight of the generous payment O'Brian had offered. The redhead looked up at O'Brian, obviously taken with his good looks and charm. "Anything else I can get you, sir, just holler." She batted her eyelashes, flirting shamelessly.

He gave a wave and walked back to Elizabeth, taking her by the arm.

As they went up the steps, Elizabeth glanced at him sideways. "What is it with you and redheads? From toddlers to women so old they're without their teeth? They seem to fancy you, and you them."

He laughed. "I don't know what you're talking about."

"Yes, you do. You're taken with redheads, and you well know it!"

He shrugged good-naturedly. "My ma had a slew of them." He ran his fingers through his own blond hair. "I was the only towhead in the village I grew up in. I just always admired the fire in their souls, I guess."

Elizabeth reached the top step and pushed through the door into the chamber they would share for the night. By the light of several tallow candles in the small room, she could see that the rope bed had already been turned back invitingly. "Just so you're not too taken with their souls," she answered tartly. "Because I'll warn you now, O'Brian. I'll not tolerate infidelity."

He followed her in and kicked the door closed behind him, dropping her cloak on a peg. "You'll not have to worry about that, Lizzy." He brought his hand up between his legs. "I value my prized parts too greatly for that. Were I to dally, I know you'd have them in a jar in your laboratory before I could wink thrice."

She turned to look over her shoulder at him. A sultry smile played on her lips. "So get your breeches off, husband, and show me those prized parts."

He reached down to the tie of his breeches, his gaze never leaving her face. "Yes, Mistress," he teased in a seductive voice. "I'm coming, Mistress."

Twenty-three

Elizabeth looped her arm around the bedpost, as she watched O'Brian slowly disrobe. He was taking his time, tantalizing her, knowing it pleased her to watch him undress for her.

"I've missed you," he said. He held out his work-calloused palms. "I missed the feel of your breasts in my hands. I missed the sight of you all tumble-haired and wanting me." He came to her and brushed his lips against hers in a flirting kiss. "I missed the taste of you, Lizzy."

She sighed, her eyelids drifting shut. There was something about standing fully clothed before a man entirely naked that made her pulse race.

His mouth touched hers again, his lips lingering against hers.

She lowered her hands to his bare shoulders, dropping her head back so that he could kiss the pulse of her throat.

"Lizzy, Lizzy, I laid in me lonely bed, night after night, wanting to come to you. Wanting to tell you I was sorry." He brought his hand down the curve of her spine. "Night after night I wanted to come to your fancy chamber and make love to you, make you mine again."

"But you didn't," she whispered, tracing the line of his arrogant jaw with the tip of her tongue. "You found solace in others, didn't you?" She asked because she had to know.

He grasped her by both arms, and she opened her eyes. "I didn't. I want you to know that since the first time I touched you, Liz, I've touched no other." His passionate green eyes held her spellbound. "I wanted to. I wanted to make myself forget you, forget how special you were to me. But I couldn't do it." He held out his palms. "These hands could touch no other woman." He brushed his mouth with his index finger. "These lips could touch no others but yours."

She smiled, lowering her hands to his shoulders, pressing her clothed body to his hard, naked form. He was a charmer, this husband of hers. "Thank you."

"For what?" He stroked her cheek with his fingers, kissing the tip of her chin.

"I don't know. For saying that. For marrying me. For saving my baby from the shame of having no father's name."

"Ours," he whispered, his deft fingers finding the hooks and eyes of her green floral bodice. "Our baby."

She dropped her head to his shoulder. "I'm afraid," she whispered, heady from his touch. She needed no wine on this wedding night. O'Brian was intoxicating.

"Of what? Nothing will harm you, not as long as I live and breathe."

She shook her head. He pushed the bodice off her shoulders and dropped it to the floor. Next came the stays. "I'm afraid to be a mother. I'm afraid I'll be a poor one. O'Brian, my head is for business, not babies."

Discarding her stays, he kissed the swell of her breasts above the drawstring of her bleached linen shift. His soft, fleeting kisses were punctuated by his words. "You'll . . . be a . . . wonderful . . . mother. You'll . . . see."

"What if I don't love it?" She looked up at him, truly afraid. "Everyone deserves to be loved by their mother."

He kissed her frown. "You think too much, sweet. It

will all come. The love, the caring . . . Don't worry. I'll
be there. We'll get through this."

A lump rose in Elizabeth's throat. *I love him,* she
thought. *I don't know how long this will last, but at this
moment I love him.* She rose up on her toes, kissing him
soundly.

It was too soon yet for such confessions. She was
overwrought with all that had taken place recently. She'd
give herself time to sort out her feelings. She'd give him
time.

*And maybe, just maybe, there would be a point some-
where in the future that he might come to love her.*

She brushed her fingertips over his bare chest, teasing
his hardened nipples, tracing the line of crisp hair that
ran the length of his torso.

"Ah, Lizzy," O'Brian moaned. "You're teas . . ."

Elizabeth could feel her own heart racing, her breathing quickening with desire. It felt so good to be in
O'Brian's arms again. It felt so right.

He pushed her gently onto the bed and went down on
one knee. She laughed, running her fingers through his
unbound hair, reveling in the silky feel between her fingers. "What are you doing?"

He slipped off her flat-heeled shoes, then reached beneath her petticoats for the tie of her stocking. His fingers tickled at first, but then, as he began to unroll the
first wool stocking, brushing his fingertips over her
calves, a heat began to spread from her ankles upward.

Elizabeth leaned back on the rope bed, supporting herself with her hands behind her. He tossed her stocking
over his head and began to massage the ball of her foot,
the arch, each toe.

Elizabeth moaned. She had never thought of legs or
feet as being erogenous, but the feel of his hands on her
anywhere, it seemed, made her tremble.

O'Brian removed the other stocking with the same,

deliberate, tantalizingly slow attention. With both stockings gone, he ran his hand up under her petticoats.

She sighed, leaning back further. The heat of his touch was spreading. Her breasts were tingling. A warmth was building between her thighs. She could feel herself growing moist.

When he ducked his head beneath the two layers of striped petticoats, she laughed at his antics. But then, when his tongue touched her inner thigh that first time, her laughter died away.

She wanted him to get off the floor and come up on the bed with her. She wanted to touch him, to kiss him in the places she knew he liked to be kissed. But she couldn't resist his gentle probing. She couldn't resist the brush of his knowing fingertips, the heat of his tongue.

He knew what she liked. He knew how to make her breathless.

"O'Brian," she groaned. But she didn't stop him.

"Lie back," he whispered. "Let the pleasure take you away from your troubles. You're too tense, sweetheart."

She laughed huskily, lying back on the bed so that her legs dangled over the sides, with him between her knees. She pulled her petticoats up around her waist, shamelessly exposing herself to the cool air. *What did it matter?* she thought, feeling wonderfully wicked. He was her husband now. It was all right to share these pleasures with him.

"That's it," he encouraged, resting his cheek on her thigh. "You're so beautiful," he murmured, stroking the patch of dark hair. "So perfect."

Elizabeth moaned, turning her head this way and that as his fingers explored, as he tasted her. She was burning inside.

She twisted the old quilt on the bed in her fingers, the pleasure of his touch washing over her again and again, taking her higher, closer to the sun. Slowly the sounds of the creaking rope bed, the light of the candle, the smell of the freshly sanded pine floor slipped away. All she was aware of was her own quaking body, and O'Brian's gentle assault.

Elizabeth lifted her hips to the thrust of his fingers. She wanted more than this, she ached to feel his manhood deep inside her, but she couldn't stop this tide of pleasure. It was too late; she was too far gone.

Elizabeth heard herself cry out only a second later. She could smell the scent of her own pleasure in the tiny room. She lifted her hips off the bed to meet his fingers one last, shuddering time. As she lowered her trembling body, she heard O'Brian whisper some soft, sweet nonsense.

She sat up after a moment and looked down at O'Brian. He was smiling. "Come up here," she whispered.

"Tired, darling? Ready to sleep?" he inquired, obviously pleased with himself.

She shook her head. "Still not tired," she murmured seductively. "Now come up here and let's talk about those wifely rights, shall we?"

His laughter was husky and sensual.

As he climbed up onto the bed beside her, she quickly discarded the rest of her clothing and then stretched out on the bed. She could still feel the wetness between her thighs. She was still aware of a gentle throbbing that made her want more.

Elizabeth rolled onto her side, stroking his hard belly as she brought her mouth down on his. He tasted of ale and of lovemaking. She deepened her kiss, exploring the muscles of his broad chest and corded shoulders with her hand, while thrusting her tongue.

She kissed him again and again, taunting him, teasing him, as he had teased her.

He made a move to sit up and pull her down on him,

but she resisted. "Oh, no," she chided, laughing. " 'Tis my turn now, husband."

"Yes, Mistress."

She took his nipple between her teeth and nipped him. "Ouch!"

She laughed again, deep in her throat. "I told you to stop calling me that." She brought her hand along his thigh closer to his manhood, already stiff and throbbing.

"Touch me, Lizzy," he encouraged. "You're making me crazy, woman."

But she only laughed again, drawing a distinct, invisible line with her fingertips around that which demanded her attention most. She was enjoying this power she held over him, just as he had enjoyed her own sweet torture.

"Like this?" she inquired, barely brushing her fingers over the tip of him. "You want me to touch you like this?"

"Yes," he moaned.

Then she drew her hand up his shaft, from the very base to the tip, enjoying the silky hardness in her hand. "And this?"

"Yes . . ."

Then she sat up and lowered her mouth over him, touching the tip of him with the very tip of her tongue, tasting his saltiness. "And like this?" she whispered.

"Ah, yes," he groaned.

"And this?" She took him full in her mouth, stroking the length of his tumescent shaft with her tongue.

"Like that, Lizzy. That's how I want you to touch me. Touch me now, Lizzy . . ."

She pulled her mouth away. "I don't think so," she teased. "I think I'm tired now." She laid her head down on the pillow beside him, looking innocently into his face.

He lifted his eyelids, heavy with passion. "That's not funny," he growled.

She laughed, throwing her leg over him and rising to sit on his lap, his hardness between her thighs. "Perhaps not funny, but fun." She grinned.

O'Brian grabbed her shoulders and pulled her down onto him roughly. He pressed his mouth to hers and kissed her hard, forcing her mouth open, thrusting his tongue between her lips.

Elizabeth groaned, feeling his hard body fit to her own softer frame. She could feel the heat of her own desire building, fanned by his.

O'Brian caught her hips and guided her, using his hand for assistance. Their gazes locked as she lifted and slipped down over him. Her head rocked back in utter, unrestrained pleasure. It felt so good to take him like this. She felt so close to him, looking down into his eyes, watching the passion on his face.

O'Brian lifted his hands to her, and she entwined her fingers with his. Then she began to move, slowly at first, her gaze still fixed on his.

He was calling her, repeating her name over and over again like some magical incantation.

A heavy-limbed aching began to fill her. The rhythm of their lovemaking increased; she lifted herself over him again and again, only to lower herself to meet his thrust. Their breaths mingled. She moved faster, feeling him with each stroke, tightening and then relaxing her inner muscles with concentrated effort.

Sweat beaded on his forehead. She could tell he was close . . .

Elizabeth flattened her own body over his, still holding him deep inside her. Her entire being was consumed by him and the movement of their lovemaking. She couldn't have stopped now if she'd wanted to. Even his pleasure was forgotten, and she stroked faster, stretching to reach that point she was driven toward.

There was a quick surge of pleasure that hit her like

a wall of flames. Elizabeth vaguely heard O'Brian cry out as she was consumed by the fire, by the fire of his might, by the fire of her own ecstasy.

"Liz, Lizzy," she heard him whisper in her ear. She was floating warm and comfortable now, lost in the aftermath.

He rolled her gently onto her side, pulling her into his arms, nuzzling her neck. "I think ye outdid yourself, tonight, Mistress," he teased. "I'll not walk for a week."

She laughed, snuggling closer to him, her eyes closed with contentment. "Give me a few hours of rest, and I'll show you another trick or two."

He lifted up and leaned over her, blowing out the candle on the bed table beside them. "Is that a promise?" He kissed her temple, pulling her close again.

"A promise," she answered, drowsily. "A promise, husband."

Elizabeth slept so deeply that she never heard a sound until the door came crashing in. Disoriented, she reached out in fright to O'Brian, who slept warm beside her.

But O'Brian must have heard the cacophony of splinting wood even before she did, because suddenly he was awake in the bed, calling out in alarm, climbing over her to put himself between whoever was in the doorway and his new wife.

"By god, I've caught you in your sin!" Elizabeth heard a familiar voice in the darkness.

"Don't take another step," O'Brian threatened.

Elizabeth drew up her knees in the bed, covering herself with the clean, warm patchwork quilt. By the dim light of the dying coals in the corner fireplace, she saw O'Brian's silhouette. Beyond him, she could make out two men in the doorway.

"Out of my way," the familiar voice shouted.

Only then, when he stepped into the light of the glowing coals, did Elizabeth put a name to the voice.

"Jessop?" She squinted in the darkness. "Jessop, is that you? What the hell are you doing here?"

O'Brian still stood between them, a chair raised in his hands above his head as a weapon. "Jessop . . . Jesus . . ." he swore.

"Elizabeth, get out of that bed!" Jessop ordered. "Get your shameful self dressed and come with me!"

Slowly, O'Brian lowered the chair. "What is the meaning of this?" he demanded hotly. "Why the hell are you here in my bedchamber, Lawrence?"

Elizabeth now recognized the silhouette of the second man who had broken into the room. It was one of Jessop's hired men from the shipping yard in Wilmington. She didn't know his name, but she definitely recognized him. He was a giant of a man with beefy fists, a crooked nose, and a taste for violence.

"Get up, I said!" Jessop raged at Elizabeth. "Before I have to come to that bed and get you up, you vulgar, little witch!"

Elizabeth almost laughed, except that there was nothing funny about Jessop's raving. He was completely serious, and not a bit drunk.

O'Brian went to the narrow mantel and lit a tallow candle, so that the tiny room was illuminated in yellow light. "You'd better have an explanation to this," he threatened, walking toward Jessop. "Because I'm a grumpy man, when someone wakes me in the middle of the night."

"I'll deal with you later!" Jessop barked, sweeping a walking stick from beneath his black wool cloak. "Just step aside, Irishman!"

O'Brian had never been anything but gentle with Elizabeth, even in his anger, but the look on his face now, scared her. It wasn't that she was afraid for herself, but for Jessop. O'Brian looked angry enough to kill him.

"Don't take another step," O'Brian warned, holding up one hand. Standing nude there in the center of the small room, his muscles flexed, he was a menacing sight.

Jessop stood his ground, but continued to wave his walking stick. "Didn't you hear what I said?" He spoke past O'Brian, still ignoring him. "I said, get your little whoring self up, and out of that bastard's bed!"

Elizabeth never saw O'Brian move until the instant his fist connected with Jessop's mouth. Jessop flew backward under the impact, hitting the door frame before he bounced forward again.

His man jumped to lift him to his feet.

"Speak to her again like that, and you'll get another!" O'Brian drew back his fist.

Suddenly the host of the inn appeared in the doorway, holding a lantern high above his head. He was dressed in a white nightshirt and black boots, a thin man with a nervous squeak to his voice. "God above! What's going on here? I run a decent inn. I told you that, Mr. Lawrence."

Jessop stood there eyeing O'Brian, blood trickling from the corner of his mouth.

By the light of the lantern, Elizabeth saw the glimmer of the barrel of a pistol in the hired man's hand.

"Watch out, O'Brian," she called softly, drawing further back on the edge of the bed. "The man's got a gun."

The innkeeper pushed his way into the room that could barely hold the five of them. "I want to know what's going on here," he demanded in his high-pitched voice. "You . . . you said this man had cuckolded you, Mr. Lawrence. You said you'd come to retrieve your wife."

"His *wife!*" Elizabeth slipped off the far side of the bed and came around, covering herself with the quilt as best she could. That was it. She'd had enough. "His wife! I'm not his wife!" she shouted.

The innkeeper shook his head. "Going to have to call the High Sheriff, I am."

Elizabeth came to stand beside O'Brian. "No need to call the sheriff, sir." She tightened the blanket around her shoulders. "There's obviously been a mistake. I am not this man's wife." She pointed to Jessop, and then more deliberately to O'Brian. "I'm *this* man's wife." Her gaze met Jessop's. "And I've the paper to prove it."

The innkeeper took a step back. "Oh, my . . . well . . ."

O'Brian stared at Jessop in a cocky challenge.

Jessop just stood there, his face pale with shock, his hired man at his side. "There's been a mistake," he murmured.

"No mistake," Elizabeth said meaningfully. She glanced at the innkeeper. "I think we've settled matters here, sir. Thank you for your assistance."

Slowly the nightgowned man backed up through the doorway. "Well . . . well, if it's been settled, I'll just say good night." The innkeeper disappeared down the dark stairway.

"Outside," Elizabeth heard Jessop mutter to his man beside him. "Go on, Jackson. I'll meet you outside in a moment," he ordered, his tone controlled again.

The hulky man glared at O'Brian, but tucked his pistol beneath his cloak and left the room behind the innkeeper.

For a moment there was an ominous, dead silence, as Elizabeth stood beside O'Brian, the two of them naked, with Jessop staring at them in obvious disgust.

Jessop curled his upper lip. "You married him?"

She crossed her arms, not caring that the quilt slipped to bare the curve of her shoulders. "Yesterday."

"That was a stupid thing to do, Elizabeth. It won't fix things, you know."

She took a half-step closer to O'Brian. "Oh, I think it will." She smiled. "I think we're going to be very happy together. We're very much alike, you know. Together I think we can make my mill very successful." She knew she was taunting him, but she couldn't help herself. Jessop had hurt her deeply. He had pretended to be her friend, to care for her, to love her even, when it had all been a lie.

"I think you'd better go now," O'Brian said, businesslike. "My *wife* and I would like to go back to bed."

"I understand." Jessop nodded cordially. "She being with child, she needs her rest."

O'Brian glanced at Elizabeth, as of to ask, He knew?, but then looked back at Jessop, dropping his arm protectively over Elizabeth's shoulder. "I take responsibility for what's mine, Lawrence. You'd best be on your way now."

Jessop lifted his brows, his forehead wrinkling quizzically. "She told you the little bastard was *yours,* did she?" He laughed. "The minx, she told me it was *mine.*" He backed out of the room. "My sincerest apologies to you both for interrupting. I'll see you back on the Brandywine." He tipped his cocked hat and then he was gone, closing the door behind him.

Elizabeth stood there for a moment, her gaze on the closed door. She could feel O'Brian standing beside her, watching her.

"It's not true," she said softly. "I never told him the baby was his."

He gripped her shoulders forcing her to turn and look at him. The quilt slipped into a puddle of cotton at her feet. "How did he know about the babe?" he questioned, obviously trying to keep his temper in check.

She lifted her gaze to meet his. He deserved an explanation. She knew that. "I told him."

"You told him the child was his?"

She frowned. "No. I told him I was pregnant." She made herself go on. If this marriage of theirs was to work, she had to be honest with him. "I asked him to marry me."

His rich tenor voice hung in the chilly early morning air. "So I was second best?"

"No. Yes . . . No, it wasn't like that." She reached up to stroke his cheek.

He made no response; his face didn't soften.

"No," she exhaled, her hand still touching his face. She didn't understand herself why she'd done what she'd done. How could she explain to O'Brian? "You weren't second best," she said firmly. "Believe me when I say that. It's just that I was scared. I didn't know what to do. You and I were fighting, and he'd asked me to marry him again. It made sense at the time."

"So why didn't you marry him? Why'd you come to me, Lizzy?" His voice was so stark, so strained.

"Because I couldn't go through with it. Because I realized what kind of man he was. Because I already knew what kind of man you were."

After a moment, he took her hand from his face with his own hand. "Let's go back to bed, wife. There'll be time to sort this all out later."

A lump rose in Elizabeth's throat. He sounded so suspicious. She climbed into bed.

God, how could Jessop have done that to her? How could he have inferred that she had ever slept with him?

Because he hated her and he hated O'Brian. Now she knew it. Now she was forewarned.

Twenty-four

Elizabeth stood at the window of her office, staring out through the frosty glass. It had snowed last night, leaving a blanket of soft white to cover the rolling hills of the Lawrence land.

Winter had been late in coming, but it had definitely settled in. Last week, the first of February, the Brandy-wine River had frozen, so her black powder production had come to a halt. It would be several weeks, Elizabeth guessed, until the warmer winds of March would come through and melt the ice.

She rubbed the small of her back, hoping to ease the ache that was becoming all too familiar. It was just as well that the river had frozen over. She needed the break. It would take her a good month to catch up on all the paper work piled on her desk and Noah's. Then she needed to start planning for springtime. O'Brian wanted six more men when the mills went back on line. She needed to do the hiring and make preparations for the families the new men would bring with them.

Elizabeth heard one of Lacy's puppies growling and looked down to see two spotted pups fighting over a knotted kitchen towel she'd given them to play with. She smiled. Her office was overrun with dogs and puppies, so overrun that she knew she needed to make arrange-ments to get rid of some of the pups. Maybe she'd take them to Worker's Hill and give them away there. Then she'd be able to see Lacy's offspring racing about the mills come spring.

Elizabeth turned back to the window. She was fidgety today. She didn't feel like dealing with boring paperwork. She didn't have the energy this late in the afternoon to go up to the laboratory and work for a while. She drew a line with her warm fingertip on the cold window glass. The snow looked inviting.

Maybe she'd go for a walk in the snow, she decided. She needed some exercise. With the arrival of winter and her pregnancy, she hadn't been getting out enough.

She pulled her cloak off the peg and reached for the wool mittens she'd left drying on a stool. Lacy rose when she spotted her mistress dressing to go out.

"No, you stay here, girl," she ordered, throwing the heavy, green wool cloak over her shoulders. "I'm not going to chase your pups through the snow today." She put out her hand. "Stay."

The dog slid to the floor and several puppies ran to their mother to nuzzle her teats.

God help me, that'll be me in a few months, Elizabeth thought depressingly. She ran her hand over her growing abdomen. She was getting so fat so fast. Thank goodness she'd acted the minute she'd realized she was pregnant. She'd not have been able to hide this belly for long. Even under her heavy petticoats, she knew people were beginning to notice, though neither she nor O'Brian had announced her condition to anyone.

She passed Noah on his stool. "Going for a walk. Back after a while. Let the dogs out if you hear them whining, will you? I just don't want them following me down to the yard."

"Yes, ma'am."

She stepped out into the cold air and squinted in the sunlight reflecting off the snowbanks. She took a deep breath. The cold air was sharp in her lungs, but invigorating.

She started down the steps, taking care on the patches of ice. Maybe she'd walk over to where the company store was being built on Worker's Hill. O'Brian might be there.

O'Brian.

She sighed. Why was it that nothing ever turned out the way a person thought it was going to? She kicked at a snowdrift at the bottom of the granite steps that led to the main road.

Her marriage to O'Brian was definitely not going as well as she'd hoped it would. She had told herself that the difference in their upbringing was of no consequence. She told herself that class made no difference. She thought herself beyond that narrow thinking. But the problem wasn't how she looked at him, or treated him, but the difference in how they thought the world ought to be.

O'Brian refused to take his responsibility as master of Lawrence Mills seriously. He still acted like a yard foreman. He didn't order the serving girls in the household as he should. The man went down to the kitchen in the morning and fried his own eggs, for heaven's sake! He refused to have decent clothing made, despite Elizabeth's insistence that she had plenty of money for such necessities.

And worse was that the relationship between them hadn't really changed. Elizabeth didn't feel married, the way she had when Paul was alive. She couldn't complain about sex, it was wonderful with O'Brian. But he didn't treat her like she was his wife. In many ways they were still mistress and hired man. He still fought with her, only not just over the mill, but over ridiculous things, like wearing the old boots he had come to the colonies with, and going to church service on Sunday. Then there was his refusal to hire a manservant to shave him and prepare his clothing each day. O'Brian wouldn't take money from her either. Instead he went down to the Sow's Ear and gambled with the commoners for pocket change.

Elizabeth walked past the silent stone buildings perched on the edge of the river; the refinery, the composition house, the stamp mill, the grain mill, and the glazing house. It looked so strange to see them closed down, without the buzz of activity she'd grown used to. There was an eerie silence to the river as well. The familiar rush of water was absent, making the mills seem more dead than alive.

Elizabeth chuckled to herself. Was it pregnancy that had made her so dismal? She turned up Worker's Hill, taking her time, enjoying her walk. She liked walking here among the people who worked for her. She liked to smell their winter stews cooking. She liked to see their winter clothes hung still and frozen on clotheslines to dry. She liked to hear the laughter of their rosy-cheeked children.

Several men and women spoke to her as she passed their cottages. Up ahead she could hear the sound of hammers driving nails, and she knew the men were at work on the company store.

In the distance, nestled in the snow-laden pine woods, she saw the skeletal framework of the roof line. O'Brian was doing a good job overseeing the construction of the building. It was going up fast. As she approached, she heard men's laughter. Then she saw a snowball fly.

She chuckled, glad to see her men having a little fun. She had hoped that building the company store would give them a chance to rest a little, while still earning their usual pay. She ducked as a snowball flew dangerously close to the end of her nose.

"Watch it!" she shouted good-naturedly. She pushed back the hood on her cloak to let the sunshine fall on her face. Her breath formed frosty clouds over her head.

Two snowballs flew from behind the cover of a work

wagon. The assault was returned by several men who ducked behind a pile of kiln-dried wood, and the air was filled with hurling snowballs.

Suddenly something that sounded much like an Indian war cry filled the air, and a man came charging from behind the cover of the wagon, firing snowballs he held cradled in the other arm.

Elizabeth stopped in the snow. She didn't have to guess who the snow-throwing Indian was. She knew. She'd heard the same war whoop only a few nights before in her bedchamber.

O'Brian charged the open area between the woodpile and the wagon, his comrade, Samson, only a step behind. Men appeared from everywhere, pelting Samson and O'Brian with an arsenal of hard snowballs.

The men were laughing and slapping each other on the backs. Some stomped and slapped their clothing, trying to get the snow from beneath their collars and inside their boots.

Elizabeth crossed her arms over her chest, frowning. "O'Brian?"

He came to her laughing, his face red from the cold air and the sting of a well-placed snowball. "Liz."

"Walk with me?" she asked, trying to keep her tone civil.

He was beating the snow off his chest, still laughing with the others. "Get back up on that roof," he told the men. "Samson."

"Mr. O'Brian?"

He pointed. "See to those supports. Make sure those men don't take a shortcut. I don't want anyone hurt. I'm going to take a little walk with the mistress. I'll be back."

Samson gave a salute and went back to shaking the snow off his wool cap.

Elizabeth gritted her teeth. She hated it when he called her *mistress*, especially in front of the men. But he just said it in jest, she knew that. To complain only aggravated the problem.

They walked side by side through the snow down the hill. "You ought to put up your hood," he said, bringing his hands together to get the snow off his leather gloves. "The temperature's been dropping all afternoon."

She ignored him.

They walked past a large rock jutting from the ground. "Want to sit? You could rest."

She set her jaw, gritting her teeth. "I don't need my hood. I'm not cold. I don't want to rest. I'm not tired." She crossed her hands over her chest. "By the king's cod, O'Brian. I'm pregnant. I'm not an invalid, and I'm not stupid. I'm just pregnant!"

She shouted the last words so loudly that a woman cleaning a rabbit on her front stoop looked up. Elizabeth walked faster.

"Saints in hell, you got a bee in your shift today? You were sour at breakfast, too."

She rolled her eyes. "I can't believe you were up there throwing snowballs with those men. How are they ever going to learn their place with you, when you insist on behaving like one of them?"

He picked up a handful of snow and threw it at her. "What? You don't enjoy a good snowball fight?"

She put up her mittened hand to deflect the snow. She refused to be drawn into his playfulness. "You know what I'm talking about. We've talked about this time and time again."

He looked ahead. "No. You talked. I listened."

She stopped. They were back on the main road again and they were alone. She dropped a hand to her hip. "And what do you mean by that?"

"I mean you're beginning to sound like a fishwife, woman. Ye berate me day and night about duties, appearances, and such, and I have to tell you I've had my fill."

She looked down at the snow. "You're my husband now. You own these mills."

"You own the mills. I just work here."

She looked up him. The last few weeks his face seemed to be hardening. He didn't laugh as easily. He didn't grin at her the way he had those days in September, when she could have spent day and night in his arms.

"Whatever I have is yours," she chanted, repeating what she'd said a hundred times since they'd wed. "You're master here at Lawrence Mills. What was mine is now yours by English law. You don't even have to work now, O'Brian. We can hire a new foreman."

"Your first husband worked."

"The mills weren't making any money. He couldn't afford a foreman."

He swept his snowy cocked hat off his head and beat it on his knee. "And what would I do all day if I didn't work, Mistress?" He raised an eyebrow. "Play the futtering spinet?"

She turned away. "You needn't be crude."

He sighed, and then after a moment spoke. "I'm sorry, Liz. I'm trying." He ran his fingers through his hair, pushing it back over the crown of his head. "Don't you see, the men are confused. First I was the foreman, and now I'm the mistress's husband. We were just beginning to work so well together. I can't suddenly become the fancy man of the manor house. I want them to trust me. I want them to see us as a team. I want them to take pride in what we produce here."

She caught his hand in hers. She was beginning to feel like the fishwife he accused her of being. And that wasn't what she wanted. It wasn't what she intended. But she had this land, the money, and she wanted to share it with O'Brian. She wanted to give him what he'd never had before. Maybe she wanted to make up for what her father had done to him and his family in Ireland. But she also wanted him to take the responsibility of being the master along with the benefits.

"I'm sorry, too," she murmured, twisting his hand in hers. She was no good at this, this building a marriage. She didn't know how to act. She didn't know what to say. She could just imagine what a disaster her attempt at motherhood would be. "I don't know what's wrong with me. It's not you. It's just that I don't feel like myself." She groaned. "I'm getting so fat so fast. I thought I'd have a little time to get used to the idea before I started to look like I was going to have a baby."

"You're not fat."

She glanced sideways at him. "Would you tell me if I was?"

He grinned. "I wouldn't care." Then he reached out and dropped his arm over her shoulder, the way a husband would. "You're being too hard on yourself. We knew this was going to take some time, Liz. It wasn't going to happen overnight." He chuckled, brushing his lips against her hair. "Pity we couldn't spend all our time in bed."

She laughed with him, staring out at the beauty of the frozen river that stretched before them. "Pity," she repeated. "There are no disagreements there."

He gave her a quick hug and then let go of her. "Why don't you go on up to the house? I'll come shortly. We'll have a light supper, I'll order someone to take away the dishes . . . and then I'll let you beat me at a hand of cards."

"Let me? Ha!" Then she smiled slyly. "All right, but only if you can promise we can go to bed early."

He winked. "You, madame, have a deal."

Elizabeth stood there alongside the road, watching her husband until his broad shoulders disappeared. Then she turned back toward her office and the big house, suddenly melancholy. *Why,* she wondered, *did she feel like she was hurtling through a dark tunnel. And when was she going to crash?*

"Miss Lizbeth! Miss Lizbeth!" Elizabeth heard as she saw Samson streak by her office window. She jumped up and ran, nearly colliding with him in the front office. *There was no explosion,* she told herself. *I never heard an explosion, so it can't be that.* "Samson, what is it?"

He was breathing hard and sweating profusely. He'd obviously run a good distance. "Mr. . . ." he panted. "Mr. O'Brian! He's hurt, ma'am. You gotta come."

Elizabeth beat Samson to the outside office door. "Where is he?" she demanded as she raced down the steps. She had no trouble running, despite the size of her growing abdomen.

"Down to the magazine, Mistress." He pointed left, over the treetops. "He was knocked clean out."

Elizabeth ran faster. "What happened? Tell me what happened, Samson. How'd he get hurt?"

Samson shook his head. "Careful on the ice, Mistress." He grabbed her hand, helping her down the last flight of granite steps to the road below. "I don't know 'xactly what happened. One of the boys came and fetched me."

"Just tell me what you know," she snapped impatiently.

Samson nodded his head. "He got hit by a runaway wagon full a new barrels, Mistress."

"He what?" She was getting out of breath now, but she kept running. Suddenly O'Brian seemed accident-prone. Last week when he'd been helping put the company store up, a rafter he'd been inspecting had come loose and swung down. It hadn't hit him, but if it had, it would have killed him. Now this . . .

"How could he have gotten hit by a runaway wagon? That's ridiculous."

They were coming around the bend in the river now. The new magazine where they stored their powder stood in the distance. "I don't know, Mistress. All I know is the boys say he got hit by a wagon parked up that old road on the side of the hill." He pointed to the hill to the left of the main road.

"What was a wagon doing parked up there? No one is supposed to be using that road."

Samson shrugged. "Don't know."

Elizabeth spotted a group of men squatting in a circle around someone prostrate. She recognized the old home-spun coat O'Brian insisted upon wearing, despite the number of new coats she'd bought him. An overturned wagon lay on its side on the far side of the road, missing one wheel. The snowy ground was littered with splintered wood and broken barrels.

"O'Brian?" Elizabeth lifted her skirts, taking the last few steps to him. The men backed off to give her room.

O'Brian lay on his back, his forearm thrown over his forehead so that his face was obscured. "How badly is he hurt?" she demanded, dropping to her knees in the snow.

"Don't know, ma'am. Can't find nothing broken. He just ain't woke up," said Johnny Bennett.

Elizabeth carefully picked up her husband's hand and lowered it to his side.

O'Brian stirred, wrinkling his face in the glare of the sunlight off the snow.

"O'Brian?"

His eyelids flickered.

She leaned closer, bring her face to his. "O'Brian," she said softly, knowing her voice trembled. "O'Brian, it's Liz. Are . . . are you all right? Can you hear me?"

Slowly he opened his eyes. Elizabeth gave a labored sigh of relief. Her heart was pounding, and she was completely out of breath. "O'Brian?"

He blinked, trying to focus. "Well, isn't that a pretty face for a man to wake up to."

She rolled her eyes. "So is that what you're doing here? Sleeping on the job? And here these men thought you'd been knocked unconscious."

He grinned. "Ye always were a clever piece." He took her hand and sat up. He rubbed his hand over the back of his head. "Guess I hit pretty hard when I jumped out of the way."

She peered into his face. "Just sit a minute and get your bearings. Anything else hurt besides that thick head of yours?"

He blinked. "My ankle." He moved his legs gingerly, wincing when he turned his left ankle.

She looked down at his booted foot. "I suppose I don't have to ask you which one?"

"Suppose not." He reached out for Samson, and his friend helped him to his feet.

Elizabeth dropped her hand to her hips. "You want Samson to help you up to the house?"

"Hell, no." He glanced around. "Damnation, that's a whole wagonful of barrels spread across this road." He limped forward a couple of steps and picked up a splintered barrel stave. "I hate to lose all these barrels after the cooper worked so hard on them."

Elizabeth frowned. "The cooper can make more barrels. What I want to know, is how that wagon got up on that road, and more importantly, how it came *down* the road without a horse pulling it." She and O'Brian, Samson, and Johnny stood looking up at the old woods road. The other men were beginning to pick up the shattered pieces of the barrels. Someone was attempting to turn the wagon upright.

O'Brian shook his head. "I don't know. I came down here just like I do most afternoons. I wanted to get a count on how many barrels of powder we had left. Johnson was asking me what we still had to sell."

"And the wagon just appeared out of nowhere?" Elizabeth asked, still not convinced. "You didn't see anything?"

O'Brian dropped his hand on her shoulder for support. "Johnny, Samson. You help these men get this picked up. I want a new wheel on that wagon today."

The two men nodded and walked away, leaving Elizabeth and O'Brian to their privacy.

O'Brian looked at Elizabeth. "Where's your cloak? It's freezing out here."

She put her hand to her shoulders. She hadn't realized she'd forgotten her cloak until he'd mentioned it. In the excitement, she hadn't been cold. "Must have left it in the office."

He frowned, shrugging off his homespun coat to drop it over her shoulders. She snuggled inside the warmth of the heavy coat. It smelled like fresh wood shavings, and him.

"So you didn't see anything?" she asked as they started back up the road toward the house.

"I heard the wagon come rolling down the hill. I barely had time to get out the way, but—"

"But?" She stopped. "What did you see?"

"I'm not sure."

She studied his serious green eyes. "Tell me."

He started walking again. "Claire, Liz. I thought I saw Claire . . ."

Twenty-five

Elizabeth stood on the steps outside her office door, breathing in the warm, sweet smell of the lilacs. Spring had come to the Brandywine, the river was running freely again, and her abdomen was continuing to grow.

She ran her hand over her belly. It was only April. By her calculations, the baby couldn't possibly be here before late June. How could she be so big already? she wondered dismally. At the rate her girth was increasing, she'd not be able to walk in another month.

But she would walk. She would walk, and she would inspect the mills that were now up and running at full production. And she'd keep up her end of the operation. She'd finish her paperwork for the incoming orders, even if it meant early mornings and late nights.

O'Brian was already complaining that her work days were too long. Of course, he was up before dawn, and often didn't return home to fall into bed until well after dark. When she tried to compare herself to him, he grew furious. He said she wasn't taking care of herself properly. He accused her of not holding up her responsibility to their child. Only last night he'd come home at midnight to find her waiting up for him in her nightrobe. They'd gotten into an argument over her lack of appetite. He said she needed to eat more. She told him he had only to look at her to see she was eating far too much. She punctuated her statement by breaking a Chinese vase full of daffodils on the wall behind him. This morning he'd left their bedchamber at dawn without speaking to her.

Elizabeth gave a sigh. The only good thing that seemed to be coming out of this marriage was that Jessop had apparently decided to let her go on with her life. His threats had apparently been empty and only spoken out of anger. She saw him rarely, and when she did, he was remote, but cordial. He was apparently very busy with his shipping business. She had heard through Claire that if war came, he intended to profit from it by shipping for the English army.

Elizabeth pressed both hands to her lower back to ease her aching bones. The baby had shifted, so that she now found it difficult to breathe. At least he or she seemed to be healthy. The child's constant rolling and kicking was evidence enough for her. Claire said her mother had always said an active child would be a bright, happy, healthy child.

Elizabeth prayed it was so. She didn't know if she could deal with a baby who was deformed in mind or body. What if she had a child with a mental illness like Claire?

Poor Claire . . . Jessop had forbade her to see Elizabeth; he said she was a poor influence, so they were forced to visit in secret. Claire came often to Lawrence Mills, and Elizabeth encouraged her to do so. O'Brian seemed to be able to bring her from the depths of her depression, when Elizabeth couldn't. And despite the fact that Claire's mind seemed to be slipping, she still delighted in eluding her brother.

Elizabeth looked out over the sloping hill through the lush tree line to the road below. The road was quiet now, because it was early morning, but soon it would be alive with activity. The mills would hum with the sound of steady work. She smiled. This was what she had dreamed of. This was what made her happy. She liked the challenge of the black powder industry. She liked the fact that she had been able to accomplish on the Brandywine what others—men—had not.

Elizabeth was just turning to head into the office, when she spotted Samson coming through the woods up the hill. It struck her as odd that he hadn't taken the path, so she waited for him.

"Samson?"

He tugged his straw hat off his head and held it to his chest. His face was grim. "Mistress."

"What is it, Samson?" She studied his dark, suntanned face. "What's wrong?"

His dropped his gaze to the ground to study his bare feet. "I done somethin' bad, Mistress. Terrible bad."

Elizabeth's brow furrowed. "What is it, Samson?"

When he looked up at her, there were tears in his eyes. "I kilt a man this mornin', Miss Lizbeth."

Elizabeth felt her heart jump in her chest, but she remained calm. Samson was no killer. There had to be an explanation. "By accident? You mean there was an accident?"

He shook his head. "No, Mistress. I done it straight on purpose. I whacked him on the head with a log o' wood."

Elizabeth brought her hand to cover her mouth. She didn't want to overreact. Samson was obviously scared, and he'd come to her for help. She wouldn't fail him. "Samson, tell me who the man was."

He looked her straight in the eyes. "It was that slaver come to get my Ngozi again. I think he was called Jarvey. I come up from where I was washin' in the river, and there he was in my house." He brushed at the tears that ran down his cheeks. "He was tryin' to carry her and my baby out. He said he was takin' them out dead or 'live, it didn't matter to him. He said he'd get his coin either way."

It broke Elizabeth's heart to see this giant of a man, all muscle and brawn, crying like he was. "So you killed him?"

"He pult a knife on me." He turned to show her a deep gash in his arm. "Then he pult it on my baby, and said he'd cut 'er up and use 'er for bait on the river." He sniffed, wiping his nose with the back of one massive, black hand. "He said the carp liked nigger-baby bait. That's when I kilt 'im. Only took one whack."

Elizabeth ran her hand over her neat chignon. "All right, Samson. Have you told anyone else about this?"

He shook his head. "I'm sorry Miss Lizbeth. I'll take my punishment. Just don't let 'em take my Ngozi and my Dorcas."

Elizabeth reached out to run her hand down along Samson's bare arm, wanting to comfort him. He was even more muscular than O'Brian. "I want you to go find Mr. O'Brian, and I want the two of you to meet me at your cottage. Go straight there, do you understand me?"

He nodded, his eyes still filled with tears. "I'm sorry I brought this on you, Miss Lizbeth. I didn't mean it. Honest. You been too good to me and my Ngozi for this."

"Just go find Mr. O'Brian. Do it now."

Samson turned and went back through the woods the way he'd come. Elizabeth stood there for a moment and watched him, feeling as if she would cry herself. But she wouldn't. Her tears would be of no help to Samson and his family. The hard fact of the matter was that they wouldn't help the dead man, either.

Elizabeth called Lacy, and the dog and her mate came running from the woods where they'd been chasing a rabbit. Feeling the weight of the child she carried, she went down the granite steps that led to the road below, wondering how in sweet god's name she was going to make this one right.

Elizabeth had just stepped into Ngozi and Samson's cottage, when he and O'Brian arrived. Ngozi stood on the far side of the neat, meticulously clean, single-room house, clutching her daughter to her bosom. In the center of the swept pine floor, lay the man called Jarvey. He was face down, his head turned to the side, his gray eyes staring and sightless. Across the back of his greasy head was an obvious indentation. The weapon, a piece of hickory firewood, lay just where Elizabeth guessed Samson had dropped it.

Elizabeth took a deep breath. She waited for O'Brian to speak.

"Well, hell," he murmured, going to stand over the body. "You sure did kill him, didn't you, Samson, old friend?"

Samson stood near the closed door. Elizabeth could hear Ngozi crying softly.

"Yup. I kilt him, Mr. O'Brian. I checked for breath. Ain't none."

O'Brian crossed his arms over his chest. He stood directly over the body across from Elizabeth. "What do you think?"

"What do you mean, what do I think? I think the man is definitely dead."

He frowned, impatiently. "What do you want to *do*, Liz?"

She lifted a hand. "I suppose I'll have to send for the High Sheriff." She looked behind her to Samson. "You'll have to go with him, but I'll go, too. I'll explain what happened. It was self-defense, Samson. You can't be prosecuted for self-defense."

O'Brian groaned. "Oh, please, Liz . . ."

She looked at him. "What? Samson killed him. There has to be a report. Someone's got to come for the body."

"And you don't think there'll be retribution for what he did?"

She spread her hands. Why did he take everything she said so personally these days? "You can't convict a man for self-defense."

"Not a white man. Not a rich man." He indicated Samson. "But Samson here is poor, and he's African. He'll get no fair trial." He pointed to Jarvey. "Mr. Jarvey here was an upstanding citizen of the King's Crown. He was returning lost and stolen property." He hooked his thumb at Ngozi and the child. "Samson won't have a chance, Liz. He'll be hanged, probably without a trial."

Elizabeth looked at the dead man sprawled on the floor. Then she looked back at O'Brian. "So what are you saying?"

O'Brian shrugged. "He came in at dawn. No one saw him come or go. His horse is already gone, got spooked and ran downriver."

"So?" She knew where he was leading. She'd considered the very same, but hadn't had the guts to say it.

"So, if Mr. Jarvey here, were to take a swim, say in a fast-moving river . . ." He shrugged. "Who knows what could happen? Might hit his head on the rocks." He shook his head, feigning pity. "Men drown in that river all the time."

Elizabeth glanced at Samson, who had come to stand beside her. "Would you do that?" she asked. "I couldn't help you." She looked directly at O'Brian. "Mr. O'Brian couldn't help you, because then we'd be contributing to the crime."

Samson stared at her with his earnest face. "I'll do what you say, Miss Lizbeth. I'll go to the High Sheriff, if you want, or I'll get rid of 'im."

Elizabeth looked across the body to O'Brian. He was watching her.

"It's up to you, Lizzy."

She thought for a moment, then turned to go. "What's up to me? I don't know anything. I haven't seen anything. I'm just out for my walk with my dogs. Care to walk with me, husband?" She looked over her shoulder at O'Brian. He was smiling. His smile was for her, and it made her heart flutter. Despite their differences, there were times when she truly did care for the man.

O'Brian walked around Jarvey's dead body, took her arm, and escorted her out of the tiny cottage. Elizabeth heard the door close behind them. The dogs ran to meet them, and jumped and barked as the two started down Worker's Hill.

"I'm proud of you, Lizzy," O'Brian said after a moment. "I know that was hard for you. You have this idea of what the perfect world is and how it should be. The thing is, you need to realize, it's not the same for everyone."

Her hand was warm in his. These days she felt like she lumbered more than she walked, but beside O'Brian, her feet were light. "My conscience is clear. It was self-defense." She looked at him. "He was only defending his family. I'd do the same for you."

He laughed, his rich tenor voice ringing in the green, leafy treetops over their heads. "Ah, Lizzy. You're as brave they come." He kissed her temple. "And just as sweet . . ."

Elizabeth sat at the desk in the bedchamber she shared with O'Brian, making a list of guests she intended to invite to a party she was giving. She didn't care much for entertaining, but she realized that a good business-woman sometimes did things she'd rather not. Her black powder customers expected her to invite them to her home, and they expected her to feed and entertain them.

She decided she'd not act as a hostess often, but when she did, it would be a party to remember. She had already hired musicians and started the menu. Now the guests had to be invited.

Elizabeth sipped a glass of wine mixed with fruit juice, and stared idly as she thought. For a while, she'd been uncomfortable in this room. When she and O'Brian married, he insisted on sleeping in a different bedchamber from the one she had shared with Paul. She'd accused him of being ridiculous. That first night in the big house, she'd gone to bed in her own room thinking he would give in and join her. Instead, he'd entered her bedchamber and carried her out, half-naked, laughing and fighting him.

O'Brian said she was welcome to sleep in the room when he was gone on business. With her confinement time drawing closer, he was going to New Castle and to Philadelphia to make sales and buy supplies for her. But when he was home, when the master was home, he said they would sleep together in this chamber. He said he refused to wrestle with the ghosts of husbands past.

She smiled, her gaze moving from the pair of scuffed boots by the bedside to a pair of discarded breeches thrown over a chair. There was evidence of O'Brian everywhere; a hat, a book he'd been reading, a pile of crumpled papers with his scrawled handwriting. She could even smell his shaving soap. She had always kept her own chamber neat, but for some reason she didn't mind his untidiness. Somehow his discarded clothing was evidence of his willingness to stand by her. It was evidence of his willingness to try and make their marriage work.

She turned back to her list, scribbling a name. She glanced at the case clock on the mantel. Claire had said she was coming for supper. Jessop was having guests and had relented, saying she could come for a visit. Claire was very excited about coming, and had asked several times if O'Brian would be there. Elizabeth had made him promise he would shorten his work day and join them for supper on the upstairs balcony.

Elizabeth heard the sound of the spinet in the parlor downstairs, and realized Claire must have arrived early. Elizabeth supposed she ought to get up and get dressed. She'd come from the wheel mill so hot and grimy, that she'd had the housemaids draw her a bath. It had been delightful to soak in the copper tub in the late afternoon shadows of her bedchamber. Now she was sitting in her dressing gown with her hair still damp on her shoulders. She was tempted to join Claire in her dressing gown. The thought of not having to redress was appealing. Her clothes were beginning to grow tight and uncomfortable, and it seemed these days that she was always overly warm.

But Elizabeth was determined not to allow her pregnancy to get in the way of her day-to-day activities. There was no reason why she couldn't have a child and still run the mills. And she'd not give anyone reason to think otherwise.

She was just rising from her chair when she heard a whine and a scratch at the door. When Elizabeth swung it open, Lacy dragged herself on her belly through the doorway. Elizabeth crouched down, stroking her dog's head. "Lacy, what's wrong, girl?" Her mate came padding down the hallway, swaying slightly. "Freckles?"

The dog slumped in the doorway beside his mate.

Elizabeth lifted Lacy's head to peer into the hound's eyes. They were glassy and dilated. There was a fine line of froth around her closed mouth. "Lacy?"

The dog whined weakly and laid her head on Elizabeth's knee.

Elizabeth jumped up and stepped over the dogs, hollering down the hallway. "Katie! Katie, come here," she shouted above the sound of the spinet. When the girl didn't respond immediately, she shouted again.

Claire must have stopping playing, because all Elizabeth could hear now was the sound of Katie's footsteps. "Ma'am?"

"Katie, come here." She waved to the young girl who was running down the hall toward her. "Do you know what's wrong with the dogs?"

She came to a halt to stare at the two spotted hounds lying in the doorway. "Don't know, Mistress." She looked up at her. "Are they sick?"

Elizabeth looked down at the two dogs lying unnaturally on the floor. Even from where she stood, she could see that their breathing was becoming shallow and more rapid. She knelt beside the dogs, running her hand over their backs. Both were trembling, their legs shaking. "Yes, they're sick," she snapped. "I think they're dying." She looked up. "I'm sorry, Katie. I didn't mean to be short with you. Would you run and fetch me some cool water in a bowl?"

Just then O'Brian came down the hallway in his stocking feet, carrying his boots. He passed Katie going in the opposite direction. "What's going on?" he called.

Elizabeth rose, pointing to the dogs. "Lacy and Freckles. They're sick. I don't know what's wrong."

He dropped his boots on the plank floor and knelt. He lifted the muzzle of first one dog, then the other. He laid Lacy's head gently back on the floor. "Looks like they've been poisoned, Liz."

"What?" She stared at O'Brian. "Why would someone poison my dogs?" She stood with her arms hanging helplessly at her sides, trying not to cry. For heaven's sake, they were just dogs. But they were *her* dogs, and she loved them. "Why would someone want to hurt an animal?"

Katie came running back down the hallway carrying a pottery bowl, water sloshing over the sides. Elizabeth took the bowl and went down on her knees. "Here you go, girl, here Lacy," she said. "How about a drink, girl?"

But the dog wouldn't lift her head.

Elizabeth tried Freckles. He whined, but he didn't try to drink, and he didn't open his eyes.

Elizabeth dipped the edge of her dressing robe in the cold water and wiped both dogs' muzzles.

O'Brian put his hand on her shoulder and knelt beside her. "I'm afraid there's nothing you can do, sweetheart," he said gently. "They'll not live much longer."

She looked at him. "How did this happen? It doesn't make any sense."

"Did you feed them today?" He took her hand and helped her to her feet.

"Yes. The same as I do every morning. I fed the pups, too. Those that came."

"The first thing to do, then, is to check the pups."

"You mean some of the scraps I gave them from the kitchen might have been bad?"

He toyed with a damp curl at her shoulder. "No. That's no tainted meat. These dogs were poisoned. I once saw a man die the same way."

Elizabeth looked to Katie, who stood there, her hands twisted in her muslin apron. "Go outside and call the pups in the garden. See if any of them look ill. Then go to Worker's Hill. Samson had one of the pups; so does Jeremiah. I think both of their dogs ate here this morning."

Katie nodded her head. "Yes, Mistress. I'll do it right away, Mistress."

Elizabeth shook her finger. "And don't dally, Katie. I'm waiting on you."

"Yes, Mistress." She bobbed a curtsy and went running down the hall.

Elizabeth looked back at O'Brian. "You're certain there's nothing I can do for them?"

He shook his head. " 'Fraid not."

"Then I want to go down to the kitchen. Maybe some-one fed them something down there."

O'Brian slapped his shirt, covered with coal dust. "Let me change and get a pair of shoes on, and I'll come down with you."

But Elizabeth was already headed down the hallway in her dressing gown, her loose hair flying over her shoulders, her bare foot padding on the polished floor. "Meet you downstairs," she called over her shoulder.

Elizabeth hurried down the front staircase, passing the parlor on her way to the summer kitchen. As she went by she saw Claire seated before the spinet, her hands poised to play. She was just staring at the keyboard, mak-ing no indication that she saw Elizabeth as she went by.

Elizabeth went down the hallway, through the back door, through the breezeway, and into the kitchen. Cook met her at the doorway with a flurry of her hands. It wasn't often that Elizabeth came to the kitchen in her dressing gown.

"Did you feed my dogs?"

" 'Scuse me, Mistress?" Cook stared.

"I said, did you or someone feed my dogs? I know they're always sniffing around the kitchen."

Cook shook her head. "I tell them girls, don't be feedin' those dogs in my kitchen." She raised her palms heavenward. "But you know these shiftless, young things. They does what they want most of the time."

Elizabeth frowned, walking around the worktable, looking into the stew pot over the fireplace. She even opened the beehive oven and peered inside. She saw nothing unusual. There were no scraps on the floor.

She went through the kitchen and out the back door to the kitchen herb garden. There beside the well was the water bowl she always left for the dogs. And beside it, an empty pie pan . . .

Elizabeth snatched up the pie pan and lifted it to the

fading afternoon sunlight. There were a few scraps of crust and bits of meat still in the pan. She sniffed it, but nothing smelled odd. She carried the plate back into the kitchen.

"Where did this come from?" she demanded.

Cook and two kitchen maids turned to stare at their mistress.

"Not my pie," Cook proclaimed, glancing at the dish. "I don't mix pork with potatoes."

The girls shook their heads, their eyes wide with fear. "We don't make anything but what Cook tells us to," one offered bravely.

O'Brian came striding into the kitchen. He had changed into a clean shirt and breeches and a pair of scuffed, but clean boots. He'd dampened his hair and pulled it back neatly in a queue with one of her black hair ribbons.

"You find it?" he asked.

She offered him the pie plate as evidence. "I found this out by the dogs' water dish. No one here seems to know where it came from. Cook says it didn't come out of her kitchen. She doesn't make this kind of pie."

O'Brian stood there staring at the plate, thinking for a moment. Then he took the pie plate from her and took her hand, leading her out of the kitchen into the breezeway that led to the house. He halted in the breezeway. "Would it be wrong of me to ask Claire if she knows anything about this?"

Elizabeth ran her hand over her protruding stomach, so easily recognizable in the thin dressing gown. "Claire? Don't be ridiculous. She loved my dogs. You were the only one who didn't like them."

"I didn't poison your dogs, Liz."

"I know you didn't. I'm just saying, it doesn't make sense. Claire would never hurt anything or anyone."

"She's crazy," he said, lowering his voice. "We both know that."

"She's crazy, yes, but she's harmless."

He grimaced. "I think I'll ask her just the same."

"She's in the parlor playing the spinet. She came for supper."

He started down the breezeway carrying the pie pan. "I know, I saw her when I came down the stairs."

Elizabeth and O'Brian entered the parlor together. Claire was still sitting at the spinet in silence.

"Claire," O'Brian said.

Elizabeth hung back in the doorway, deciding to let him handle her.

Claire turned, her pretty blond curls bouncing. Her face lit up at the sight of O'Brian. "Elizabeth said you were coming. I waited for you. We're going to have supper together, aren't we?"

"Yes, we are. Up on the balcony, your favorite place." He spoke to her gently, as if she were a child. "We'll eat shortly, but I want to ask you a question, Claire." He showed her the pie plate. "Do you know where this came from?"

She looked at the pie plate, then back at him. She tightened her lips, shaking her head no.

"Now think," O'Brian said. "You don't recognize it? I need to know because Liz's dogs are sick, and they might have eaten this pie."

Claire stared at him with her big blue eyes. "I can't make pie," she said softly. Then she lifted her closed hand. "Mousey makes pie. Sometimes Mousey brings pie for supper, but dogs like pie, too, so Mousey gives dogs pie." She smiled her prettiest smile. "You want to see my mousey, Mr. O'Brian?"

Elizabeth covered her mouth with her hand, as O'Brian turned to look at his wife. Their gazes met. They both understood what Claire was saying. She had brought the pie for supper, then given it to the dogs instead.

She was saying she had nearly poisoned them all . . .

Late that night Elizabeth lay beside O'Brian in their bed. She couldn't sleep. She just lay there in the darkness, staring up at the ceiling. She couldn't believe her dogs were dead. She loved those dogs.

O'Brian was quiet beside her, but she knew from his breathing that he wasn't asleep either.

Both dogs had died, and O'Brian had buried them at the edge of the garden near a bed of asters. They'd sent Claire home without supper. Then Elizabeth and O'Brian had had a terrible argument concerning what to do.

O'Brian insisted it was time to have a talk with Jessop. After the runaway wagon incident, he'd agreed not to say anything, because he had no proof of her involvement. He wasn't even certain he'd seen Claire near the wagon that day. But now O'Brian was afraid that she was becoming dangerous. Elizabeth agreed that they would have to be more careful with her, but she feared that if they told Jessop, he might have her committed to a home for the insane. Elizabeth didn't want that to happen. Claire was too delicate to survive such a place. Elizabeth knew she herself would rather be dead than go to a place like that, and knew Claire would feel the same way, even if she couldn't express it.

Elizabeth rolled onto her side. She just couldn't get comfortable anymore. No matter which way she turned, she couldn't sleep.

"I don't mean to be cruel, Liz," O'Brian said out of the darkness.

She rolled onto her back. "I know you don't."

"It's not that I want to see Claire punished. It's my concern for you and for the child."

"Our child. And she could have poisoned you, too," Elizabeth countered. "You've forgotten that she was the one you saw the day you were almost hit by that wagon."

"I don't think there's a connection."

Elizabeth sighed. "No. I don't either. I just think she's sick, O'Brian. Two days ago Katie caught her teetering on the rail of the balcony, stark naked except for her gloves and bonnet. She was drinking lemonade and spitting the seeds on the gardener below."

He laughed.

She sank her elbow into his side. "It's not funny."

"I know." He chuckled, rolling onto his side to face her. He stretched his hand over her abdomen. "It's sad. But I have to admit I would have liked to have seen such a sight."

Elizabeth sighed. His touch felt good. She was amazed to find that her pregnancy had not diminished either her sexual drive or his. He honestly didn't seem to care that she was getting fat and slow. He said he found her shape rather appealing. She thought he lied.

His hand brushed over her breast, and she smiled in the darkness.

"I'm sorry about your hounds," he said, raising up on his elbow to touch his tongue to her pert nipple.

"You hated them. You said they were annoying pests."

"I'm still sorry."

She let her eyes drift shut as he closed his mouth over her breast. "So show me how sorry you are," she whispered with a chuckle. "Make it up to me . . ."

Twenty-six

O'Brian sat on a chair in front of the window, his heel propped on the edge of the bed. He had just bathed and was wearing a pair of burgundy breeches. The rest of the trappings Elizabeth had chosen for him to wear were laid out on their bed. He turned the glass of whiskey in his hand, watching the amber liquid splash up the sides. He wasn't in the mood for this, not tonight.

Elizabeth stood in front of the full-length mirror, dressed in a pale green organza gown, fastening her emerald earbobs. "You're not dressed yet," she called over her shoulder.

He sipped the whiskey. "That's because I don't want to get dressed."

"You'll have to hurry. The guests are arriving."

"I don't want to go down there."

She sighed. "I thought we discussed this. I need you to be there to answer questions concerning our powder production. You know more about it than I do these days."

He groaned, wondering why in hell he'd ever agreed to this party in the first place. He wasn't comfortable in social situations, not unless they were in places like the Sow's Ear. He lifted his other foot to prop it on the bed. "Face the truth—I have. I don't fit in, Lizzy. I'm not one of them. Never will be."

"Nonsense. You don't have to be one of them. You're the master of Lawrence Mills."

His gaze returned to the whiskey in his hand. It had been a long day. He'd shoveled coal all morning, and then he'd had to deal with a drunken worker and a problem with the grinding wheel in the wheel mill. He was tired to the bone. He didn't have the patience for this tonight. "No," he said, just a little agitated. "You're the master of Lawrence Mills. I'm just the foreman."

Elizabeth whipped around. She was a sight to behold with her apple green gown, dark hair, and pale skin. It was a pity she was frowning. She frowned a lot at him these days.

"Please, let's not start this tonight. I've got to go downstairs and appear to be enjoying myself."

He shook his head, reached for the whiskey bottle on the sidetable, and poured himself another dose. "That's not the way to go through life, Lizzy, acting one way when you feel another."

She lowered her hands to her hips. Even in her state of late pregnancy, O'Brian still thought she was the most beautiful woman he'd ever laid eyes on. It was too bad she wouldn't just stand there and look pretty for him, instead of giving him the berating he knew was coming.

"I'm not going to be drawn into this conversation," she said, taking on her mistress's tone with him. "You agreed to host this evening with me, and you're going to do it." She took a step toward him and snatched the glass from his hand. "And would you go easy on the drink? I want you sober." She set it on the table.

O'Brian had a comment on the tip of his tongue, but he kept his mouth shut. He could get mean when he drank. He got up from the chair and went to the bed to pick up his shirt.

"I'm going down," she said from the doorway.

He nodded, not trusting himself to speak. The further

along she got in her pregnancy, the crosser she became. She wasn't just demanding of him, either, but everyone who worked for her. He pitied poor Noah, having to deal with her all day long. At least O'Brian could hide in the powder yards.

He perched on the edge of the bed to roll up his clocked stockings. It seemed as if Elizabeth was trying to prove something these days, he just didn't know what. And he didn't know how much longer he could take it.

The thing was, O'Brian felt like he was trying his damnedest to do what she wanted him to do. The mills were running as smoothly as they ever had. And he was trying to be the husband she wanted. He was trying to read what she thought he ought to read. He was trying to cultivate a taste for her finer foods. He was trying to wear the lacy breeches and coats she bought for him. But he was doing a piss-poor job of pleasing her. He knew he was.

O'Brian wondered now why he'd married her. Certainly there was the child. But a woman with the money she had now, with the reputation she was building, she could have bought herself a husband easily enough. She hadn't needed him, no matter what she thought at the time, not really.

He really didn't know why he'd married her. Out of a sense of duty, he guessed. But he knew there was more to it than that. He knew that somewhere in the back of his mind, he'd thought Elizabeth might come to care for him, really care for him. He'd been a fool. All he was doing was making her miserable.

He pulled the smooth linen shirt over his head and reached for the ruffled stock that went with it. No matter what his reasoning had been at the time, the fact of the matter was that he *had* married Elizabeth. And he wasn't a quitter. He had agreed to try and work this thing out with her, at least for the sake of the child. He guessed he'd just have to try a little harder.

O'Brian finished dressing, drained his glass of whiskey, and headed for the bedchamber door. He could already hear music coming from the downstairs parlor and the vibration of laughter. From the sound of the party, Elizabeth was making out fine on her own. He figured, for her sake, he'd just try to stay out of everyone's way and try not to make an ass of himself.

Downstairs, O'Brian wandered from room to room, a glass of whiskey in his hand. He greeted men he recognized, laughed with them, pretended to be enjoying himself. He sampled the feast Elizabeth had worked hard to plan, and listened to the musicians in the parlor. He avoided Elizabeth, but he watched her.

There were younger women in the rooms, some perhaps more comely by the day's standards, certainly more slender, but they paled beside his Liz. Despite the late stage of her pregnancy, and the hint of tired, dark circles beneath her eyes, she was the most beautiful woman at Lawrence Mills tonight. There was something about the way she carried herself, the way she glided from group to group, that was a sight to watch. She had a way of taking command, yet making every man wonder what it would be like to lie with her.

O'Brian knew he should feel privileged that she had chosen him to marry her. Who would have believed it back in Ireland, a Tarrington woman wedding an O'Shay? But tonight the whole idea depressed him. He felt inadequate here in a place where she seemed to belong.

O'Brian leaned against a doorjamb. He needed another drink. Actually he didn't need the drink, but he wanted it. He was beginning to feel rowdy. Too bad he wasn't at the Sow's Ear, he might have been able to wrestle up a good fight.

* * *

Elizabeth stood between two gentlemen, smiling and nodding, pretending to listen, agreeing at all the right times. But she wasn't paying attention to them or their boring conversation. She was watching O'Brian.

She knew he was avoiding her. She didn't blame him. She knew she'd been hard on him tonight in their bedchamber. She didn't know why she acted the way she did with him. It was just that her head was so full of thoughts these days, that there were times when she thought it might burst. There were the mills, Paul's death that was still unexplained, and what about Claire and her illness?

Elizabeth ran her hand over her abdomen that seemed to be growing by the minute. The closer her time came to deliver, the more frightened she became. She was so unprepared for motherhood, that fear clouded her every waking moment.

She knew she needed to take a step back and look at what she wanted from O'Brian, what she wanted to give, but she just couldn't think about it now. She just couldn't deal with him. After the baby was born, then she'd have time to think. There would be time then to admit to herself how she felt about him, maybe even admit it to him.

O'Brian wandered out of sight and Elizabeth tried to concentrate on the conversation at hand. The two men beside her were talking politics and discussing the crazy Virginians. She forced a smile. Her shoes were tight on her feet, and she couldn't catch her breath in this blasted gown. But Jessop would be here tonight; he'd said he'd come by. And she wanted to look good. She wanted to look successful. She wanted him to see that she and O'Brian were happy together.

Elizabeth heard the sound of shattering glass, and she glanced in the direction of the parlor across the hall. She wondered if it was a drunken guest who'd just smashed a tray of crystal wine glasses, or one of her kitchen girls. Then she heard more glass break and the sound of splintering wood. The musicians, who were playing a country dance, seemed to lose their beat for a moment or two and then picked it up again.

There was definitely something going on in the front parlor . . .

Elizabeth lifted her skirts, smiling graciously. "Would you excuse me, gentlemen?"

They bowed as she slipped between them and across the hall. There was a crowd beginning to gather in the parlor doorway, both men and women, all talking at once and staring into the room.

"Excuse me . . . Pardon . . ." Elizabeth smiled and pushed her way past her guests.

There was another shattering of glass just before Elizabeth slipped around the corner and spotted two men rolling across a sidetable, locked arm in arm in a fistfight.

Elizabeth swore beneath her breath. She knew that burgundy coat immediately. Her face grew hot with embarrassment, and she crossed the room toward her husband and the guest he was fighting with.

"O'Brian," she said through gritted teeth. "Please! Gentlemen, I want you to stop this brawling at once."

But neither man heard her. She still didn't know which guest it was that was fighting with O'Brian. She stepped over the man's periwig on the floor. "Mr. O'Brian!" she shouted.

The musicians had lost interest in their song; their instruments were now squeaking and belching off-key notes, adding to the din of the room.

O'Brian and the guest rolled off the table and hit the floor hard. O'Brian slammed his fist in the man's chin, throwing his head back. Both men were shouting and exchanging curses.

For once Elizabeth didn't know what to do. Did she physically break up the fight? Did she ask some of her gentleman guests to risk injury to break it up? Or did she just let the two fight it out, as if this was the public room of the Sow's Ear?

What really made Liz angry, as she stood there in debate, was that her guests, now crowding into the parlor, were obviously enjoying the brawl! Suddenly these proper, genteel ladies and gentlemen were hooting and hollering, laughing, and clinking glasses. Men were demonstrating to each other how straight their own fists flew, and the ladies were giggling behind fluttering, painted fans.

Elizabeth had half a mind to turn around and walk out of the house. She'd leave O'Brian and the man to fight it out. She'd leave her guests, who were obviously enjoying the fight more than they had the food and drink and music. Elizabeth didn't know where she'd go, or what she'd do, but at least she would be out of this mess.

She look down at the two men still fighting. She finally thought she recognized O'Brian's opponent. His name was Donally, Charles Donally. The man was a drunkard and a horse's ass, but he was one of her best coal suppliers. He was one of the few men she dealt with in the business that never failed to proposition her. Even after she'd married and grown heavy with O'Brian's child, good old Charlie never failed to offer her the service of his cod.

Elizabeth ran a hand through her curly bangs. O'Brian and Charlie staggered to their feet. Then Charlie hit O'Brian in the center of his chest, and O'Brian went flying backward into the arms of a bearded fiddler. If Elizabeth didn't break up the fight soon, she'd be replacing every glass in the house, every stick of furniture in the room, and half a dozen musical instruments.

By chance, Elizabeth caught sight of a monstrous bowl hidden discreetly behind a serving table. The beaten tin container was filled with ice and ice water, and used to chill the glasses before serving drinks in them. With a twinkle in her eye, she snatched up the heavy bowl of sloshing ice water. She ignored the buzz of her guests.

"Damn you, O'Brian," she muttered as she crossed the room. "Damn you for embarrassing me like this. See if this doesn't cool you off!"

O'Brian and Charlie had just tumbled to the floor again, knocking over a Chinese vase filled with fresh wildflowers. The expensive vase shattered as it slid across the cold hearth and hit the brick fireplace.

Elizabeth lifted the heavy bowl and threw the contents as hard as she could on both men.

The guests burst into laughter. O'Brian and Charlie came up off the floor spitting and sputtering in confusion.

"Now that I have your attention, gentlemen," she said, her sarcasm thick. "I'd ask you to spare my room further damage." She looked at O'Brian straight in the eye. "Might I have a word with you, sir?"

O'Brian's queue had come undone. The sleeve of his coat was torn and hanging. His lower lip was bloody, and he was so soaked with water that he was puddling at her feet.

"By all means, wife," he answered as sweet as honey.

The guests parted to let them through. Elizabeth walked to the entrance doorway, her chin held high, and stepped outside onto the old round grindstone that served as the stoop. O'Brian came out and closed the door behind him.

For a moment Elizabeth was so angry, she couldn't bring herself to speak. She wasn't just angry, she was mortally embarrassed. And worse, she was hurt, hurt that he would do this to her.

Elizabeth took a deep breath. The air was warm and humid, but not overly warm. The yard smelled of fresh flowers and newly turned soil. Candles glowed along the walkway, and insects buzzed over them.

"Well?" she finally said. She would have rested her hands on her waist, but she had no waist left.

He looked at her with a glimmer of anger. "He started it."

"God's teeth, O'Brian! You sound like a schoolboy!"

He looked away. "I'll not stand to hear derogatory remarks about my family's heritage."

Elizabeth groaned. "You know Charlie is a drunk and a fool. You've said so yourself. Why do you care what he thinks?" There was a catch in her voice. "Why don't you care what *I* think?"

He scuffed his boot on the stone step. "We should have known this wouldn't work. I should have known."

She threw up her hands. "Oh, so it's that now, is it?"

He brushed his damp, silky blond hair off his forehead. "I don't fit into your life like you want me to, Liz. I never will." He looked at her, his green eyes intense. "It's time we both faced the truth. I think that's what I was trying to tell you earlier. I'll never be what you want me to be."

He looked so sad that she wanted to take him into her arms. She wanted to be understanding, even tender. "I don't know what you're talking about," she answered flatly, trying to remain as unemotional as possible.

"You damn well know you do. We were fools to think we'd ever be compatible. We're like two bulls in the pasture locking horns."

"It's not as bad as you think. I've been to many a party where the entertainment was the host or hostess. Sometimes it's a brawl, occasionally it's public fornication," she added in an attempt to lighten the conversation. It didn't seem to work. She sighed, looking out over the candlelit garden. "So you made a mistake."

"You're damned straight I did," he answered without looking at her. Then he turned to go.

"Where are you going?"

"Upstairs through the back. I think I've had enough party for one night, don't you?" When she didn't answer, he went on cordially. "Please say good night to my guests for me, will you?"

Suddenly her anger was gone. His tone scared her. "Will you wait up for me? I'd imagine everyone will be going home soon."

He stopped on the step, dropping his hand to the rail. He didn't turn to face her. "I think it would be best for both of us if I move . . . if I move into another bed-chamber."

Elizabeth wanted to protest. She didn't want to sleep alone. She didn't want to sleep without him. But he was being so matter-of-fact, that he made her mad. If he didn't want to sleep with her anymore, who was she to foist herself upon him?

"Fine," she said.

He stood there another moment saying nothing, his broad back to her, then he walked off into the dark around the back of the house.

Elizabeth stood there for a long time, staring out into the darkness, fighting her tears. She hated feeling like this. She hated feeling as if he had betrayed her. But she didn't cry. Instead, she put on her best smile and went back into the house to see to her guests.

Twenty-seven

Elizabeth leaned over the rail to watch the water wheel lift the churning water high into the air, and then throw it downward with its mighty force. No matter how often she came here to watch the wheel turn, she still found the might of the water overwhelming.

She tucked a stray curl beneath her mobcap. She felt like that water pouring over the wheel sometimes. She felt out of control, as if the world around her was choosing her fate and forcing her on a path she didn't want to follow.

It had been more than two weeks since the party, and still O'Brian refused to return to her bed. Elizabeth had tried everything. She had screamed and shouted. She'd attempted to make him feel guilty. She even tried sweet-talking him, but to no avail, He seemed convinced, for some reason beyond her understanding, that the marriage wasn't going to work.

Elizabeth knew things had been less than perfect. She regretted things she'd said, things she'd done these last months. But she hadn't realized he was so unhappy. She hadn't known how unhappy she had made him. Maybe he was right, she mused dismally. Maybe they weren't meant for each other. Maybe there were just too many differences between them.

But the closer the time came for her to deliver this baby, the more frightened she became. She was afraid to bring the child into the world without him. She was afraid she couldn't do it. It wasn't that she was a coward. She didn't fear the physical pain of birth as much as she feared having the complete responsibility of another person. She was afraid that she would be a bad mother. She was afraid that she wouldn't love the boy or girl child that rolled and kicked inside her with such enthusiasm. She was afraid that she couldn't do it without O'Brian. But, of course, she didn't know how to tell him. She didn't know how to tell him she needed him, because she'd spent a lifetime working toward not needing anyone, not depending on anyone.

Elizabeth heard O'Brian's voice behind her above the roar of the waterwheel, as he gave an order to one of the men. Self-consciously, she smoothed her hair. Despite their personal problems, at least they'd been able to carry on a civil relationship when it came to the business. That they still shared, even if they no longer shared a bed. O'Brian seemed to be more than willing to spend time with her, as long as it concerned the powder mills.

O'Brian leaned over the rail beside her and stared down at the churning water. "I got two loads of supplies in for the company store this morning. Flour, sugar, some spices."

She nodded. She really missed him at night. She was finding it hard to sleep alone, to not feel so forlorn in the big bed. "I think we should go ahead and start opening up," she said in her best business tone of voice. "I know the store isn't fully stocked, but if it's a service, we should be offering it."

It was his turn to nod. "I'll get right on it. The storeroom in the back still needs shelves, but I'll have them done this week. That new man you hired, Perkins, is excellent with his hands and a length of timber."

She voiced a sound of agreement, and then there was

silence between them. O'Brian acted as if he wanted to say something else, but he didn't.

She turned her head to look at him. He was startlingly handsome this morning, in his tight homespun breeches and simple muslin shirt rolled up to the elbows so that a person could see the thick corded muscles of his forearms. His face had grown suntanned, his hair lighter from the sun. But Elizabeth saw a concern, maybe even a sadness in his face. The way he looked at her made her feel as if somehow she'd failed him.

She glanced down at the water again. "Is there something else, O'Brian?" She tried hard not to sound like the mistress of the mills, but his wife instead.

He folded his hands, obviously in thought. "Do you know anything about the other man who was killed?" He looked at her. "The same night as Paul."

She tried to think. Those first days after the explosion were such a blur in her mind. And that was before she knew much about the mills. That was before she'd come to know the men and women who worked here. She shook her head slowly. "I honestly can't tell you. I feel bad, but I don't even know what his name was. I'd have to look it up. I do know he had no family."

"Was he killed in the actual explosion? I mean, saints in hell, Liz, it was the middle of the night. It's odd enough Paul was down here, but one of his men, too?" He leaned on the rail again. "Maybe he had something to do with the explosion. Maybe he was even responsible."

"That wouldn't explain the accidents," she countered.

"No. Maybe not. But we need to look into every corner. We need to consider every possibility. It's the only way we're going to find out what really happened here."

She shrugged. "I can look into the records. I'd suggest asking some of the workers. Johnny or Samson could probably tell you something about the man who died."

"I suppose they could. I was just trying to keep my

thoughts to myself. If any of the men knew that we suspect Paul might have been murdered, they might panic. It's funny what fear can do to a man. Men start to suspect the men who work beside them. Soon they begin to accuse. It wouldn't be good for the mills, or the safety of the workers."

"Mr. O'Brian! Mr. O'Brian!"

They turned to see one of the men shouting to O'Brian. "I can't hear you over the sound of the wheel," he hollered, pointing. He glanced at Liz. "I'll be right back. Let me go see what Joe wants."

Elizabeth nodded and turned to watch him walk away. She leaned against the rail with her hands behind her back and relaxed a little, letting her head tip back. The cool spray of the water off the wheel felt good in the heat of the afternoon.

Elizabeth didn't know what happened next, but suddenly there was a splintering of wood and she was tumbling backward, falling . . . falling . . .

Time slowed until it barely moved. It was as if she was dreaming, yet she knew she wasn't. Elizabeth heard herself scream; she heard the roar of the water in her ears. She was still falling, tumbling, her petticoats tangling in her arms, covering her face.

There was an instant of stark, paralyzing fear just before she hit the water, and then her mind exploded with the force of the frigid water she hit. She went under, caught in the power of the churning water that came pouring over the wheel. Her mouth filled with water, so did her ears, her thoughts. The water was trying to push her down, push her under. It was trying to kill her and her baby.

Elizabeth struggled to find the surface, to fill her aching lungs with air. She fought with her arms and legs, moving frantically, trying to swim in the water that was rushing in every direction. But which way was up? Her heavy skirts were pulling her, tangling around her arms and legs, binding her so that she would sink.

For a moment Elizabeth ceased to struggle. She stopped kicking her legs and waving her arms wildly. The rush of the water pushed her down to a place where she didn't have to struggle . . .

She was going to drown, she knew that with the last bit of reason she possessed. The initial shock of the freezing water was now numbing. She wasn't cold anymore. She wasn't even particularly frightened. She opened her eyes to see the white froth of the water and the cloud of her dark petticoats in front of her face.

But she didn't want to die. She couldn't. Not when she carried this baby, O'Brian's baby . . .

Where was O'Brian? The panic rose in her aching chest again. She was growing light-headed . . .

O'Brian? She could hear his voice in her head, calling her. She wanted him. She wasn't ready to leave him. She wasn't ready to give up . . .

With every bit of strength Elizabeth had left, she began to struggle. She knew which way was up now. The main force of the water was coming down on her head. That was the way she had to swim, into the greatest might of the water, because down, down where she didn't have to fight it, was death.

The first time Elizabeth lifted her head above the water, she gasped for air. But she had barely drawn in a single breath, before she was dragged down again by her wet petticoats and the rush of the water.

Now Elizabeth was mad. This wasn't how she was going to die. She had too many things left to do. She had too many things she knew she had to tell O'Brian. She'd been a coward. She'd known for some time now what she had to tell him, what she had to make him understand.

She had to tell him she loved him.

Elizabeth fought again; slowly, agonizingly, she pulled herself to the surface. A single breath of sweet air, and she went down again. She wanted to cry out in desperate frustration, but she could make no sound under the bubbling water.

Then she felt it . . .

O'Brian's arms wrapped around her. She knew it was him! She knew his touch as well as her own.

O'Brian grasped her around her middle that had grown so big and ugly, and he lifted her upward. She didn't have to struggle. He fought for her.

Elizabeth wrapped her arms around his neck and sucked in great breaths of air.

"Liz? Liz?" He was calling her name again and again. "Sweet Mary, Mother of God, can you hear me, sweetheart?"

She couldn't answer him yet. She was still coughing and choking, shivering so hard that her teeth were chattering. She didn't have enough breath to speak, but she managed to nod. She managed to smile.

Here, closer to the rocky shore, away from the rush of water pouring off the water wheel, he treaded water, somehow managing to keep her afloat as well. He pressed his mouth to her temple in a kiss, and she closed her eyes. She was safe now. Her baby was safe. O'Brian was here.

O'Brian carried her in his strong arms out of the water and up the slippery bank. Elizabeth knew she should make him put her down. She could certainly walk herself; she was no invalid. But she was tired, so tired and cold, and he was so warm. It was so easy to lie in his arms and let him carry her.

She heard a flurry of activity, the sound of men's voices, even the barks of Lacy's pups. But she was too exhausted to lift her head, too tired to care what the men thought of the master carrying the mistress, both soaking wet, down the road.

O'Brian took her home. The maids ran to come to his aid, but he sent them for tea for her. He told them he would take care of the mistress himself.

Elizabeth soon found herself in her bedchamber; he put her down lightly on the edge of a chair. He stripped off her wet clothing, and dried her hair and body with a thick Turkish towel he must have found in the linen press.

She was hesitant to let O'Brian see her nude body, so deformed from the child. In the last weeks since they'd shared a chamber, she'd grown so much larger and more awkward. But she didn't have the strength to fight him, and when he pulled her wet shift over her head, he didn't seem to mind her ugliness. O'Brian slipped a warm cotton sleeping gown over her head, and lifted her into his arms to lay her gently in the bed they had shared.

He pulled a light counterpane over her, and she snuggled into the pillow. What a sin to nap in midday, she thought to herself. But maybe she'd take just a little rest, and then she'd dress and go to the office.

She felt him slip his hand over hers. She smiled sleepily. She wanted to open her eyes, she wanted to see his face, but she couldn't. She was so tired that she couldn't think. "Don't go," she whispered, ". . . Want to talk to you . . . want to tell you—"

"Shhhh," he hushed, stroking her hand with his warm one. "Don't talk. Rest now. You can tell me later."

She shook her head, rolling it back and forth on the embroidered pillow. "Want to tell you now," she protested weakly. It was as if the water had taken from her every stone of strength she possessed. "It's . . . it's important, O'Brian . . . Paddy."

He smoothed the wet hair on her forehead and leaned to kiss her. "Go to sleep, Liz."

"Don't go," she whispered.

"I won't," he said, sitting back down beside her again. "I'll sit here until you fall asleep."

She made herself open her eyes so that she could see his face. She'd been so afraid under that water that she'd never see him again. "No, I mean *don't go.*" She brushed the smooth sheet on his side of the bed. "Lie with me now. Sleep here tonight."

He looked away, and a lump rose in her throat. He didn't want her. He didn't want her so ugly and swollen. He was disgusted; she knew he was. What had he said such a long time ago? He wasn't a marrying man? She knew now that it was true. He wasn't a marrying man. He wasn't the type to deal with fat pregnant women and their wild mood swings. He liked his women slender and unencumbered by screaming infants.

She took her hand from his. She would have cried, but she was too exhausted to cry. She was too confused by her own revelation that she loved him, and by his obvious disgust with her.

"I think it's better if I remain in my own room," he said quietly.

She didn't say anything. What was there to say? She wouldn't tell him that she loved him, of course. Not now. Not now, because it was too late. He didn't love her. He never would.

She rolled awkwardly onto her side, her back to him. For a long time she lay there half-asleep, but unable to sleep. Finally she heard the bed creak. She felt the mattress lighten as he stood. The bedchamber door opened and closed, as tears slipped down her cheeks.

O'Brian finished his day's work, checked on Elizabeth, who was still sleeping, and then went down to the Sow's Ear. The public room full of smoke, the sound of laughter and rolling dice, and the smell of men and their ale, seemed to be the only place he could think these days.

He ordered tea, because he didn't feel much like strong drink. The serving wench teased him about the tea, but she brought it anyway. And when he'd finished that cup, she brought a second one. He was in a pensive mood, so he kept to himself in the corner of the public room near the fireplace.

The accident today had come too close to tragedy, and he blamed himself. Last summer when he'd come to Lawrence Mills, he'd promised Elizabeth he'd find out what had happened to her husband. Now the man was nearly two years in the grave, and still O'Brian had no answers.

That wasn't the only way he'd failed her. He'd said he would make a try at their marriage. He'd said he would make it work. Well, he was doing a piss-poor job of it, wasn't he? The fight he'd gotten into at her party was just proof he'd put his foot in a doorway he didn't belong in. He knew he was hurting her. That's why he wouldn't move back into her bedchamber, as she had asked.

He sipped his strong, hot tea. She hadn't known what she was saying. She probably hadn't meant it. She was so exhausted, that she didn't know what she wanted. Neither did he for that matter, and hell, he hadn't taken a tumble from that height into the river.

It was a miracle that she was alive. O'Brian knew that. It was a miracle she hadn't eaten the pie Claire had brought them, and it was a miracle she hadn't drowned. He had to find out who the killer at Lawrence Mills was, because he was afraid he was running out of miracles.

O'Brian had gone back down to the wheel mill after he'd put Liz to bed, and he'd taken a look at the railing that had broken. He couldn't tell for certain, but it looked as if someone had weakened the wood by loosening the nails that held the rail.

O'Brian brought his fist down hard on the center of the table. He felt like he was hurtling through the blackness of a stormy night, not knowing where he was going or why. He felt like something terrible was going to happen, but he didn't know what, and he didn't know how to stop it. He didn't care for himself, his life didn't really matter. No one would care if he was gone. But Liz did matter, Liz and the baby she carried in her womb.

O'Brian found himself staring at the hard-packed dirt floor. Then he suddenly realized that there were a pair of dusty feet on the floor in front him. He looked up to see the red-haired barmaid. "Red." He offered her a smile. She'd been a good tumble. And she was a sweet girl.

"Even' to you, Paddy," she said, not her usual cheerful self. "Ain't seen you in months. Heard you was in a few times to play the di, but I must've missed ye."

He took a sip of his tea. "So what have you been up to, Red? Duke told me you gave up servin' here."

She swished her soiled petticoat. "Been sick. Couldn't carry trays for spillin' my insides out the back door."

Theirs had been solely a physical relationship. Neither party had been particularly attached to the other, but O'Brian cared if the girl was ill. "Something serious?"

A thick tear slipped from her eye, then another.

O'Brian grasped her freckled hand and pulled her down on the bench across the table from him. "What is it? You know ye can tell me. If it's the clap ye got, I know an old woman—"

"No." She shook her head. "Worse than that, Paddy." She looked up at him, her eyes red from her tears. "I got one on the hearth."

He squinted in the semidarkness of the public room. "What?"

Now she was sobbing. "One on the hearth, in the oven. I'm gonna have a babe-eee," she wailed.

O'Brian rolled his eyes. He wasn't certain he could deal with another pregnant woman, not right now. Then a terrible thought struck him. "It's not mine, is it?"

She waved her hand. Her tears had now turned to hiccups. "Nah, I ain't but a few months, but I'm sick as a dog that eats grass, and I'm afraid my pap and ma are gonna realize I was servin' something at the Sow's Ear besidin' ale." She sucked in a great breath, as if she were going to burst into tears again.

He would have laughed at the words she'd chosen, but of course, he couldn't. Red was obviously in dire trouble. He took her hand and patted it to calm her. "There, there, don't start crying again. I can't help you if you're going to cry.

She sniffed, wiping her runny nose on her clean sleeve. "You're going to help me? But nothing can help me but a fast husband, and you already got yourself a fancy wife." She shook her head. "I got to marry fast. My sister, she got big with a baby, and my pap and ma put her right on the street. We never saw Chastity agin."

"Who's the father? Do you know?"

She nodded, looking down at the battered trestle tabletop. "His name was Gene, the bastard. He was an officer, he was. Said he'd marry me. 'Cept then I found out he had a wife and a brood of chicks up Penn's Colony way. He cain't marry me."

O'Brian thought hard for a moment, then spoke. "If I find you a husband—a decent man—would you take him?"

"Won't no decent man marry me carryin' another man's guppy."

"You'd be surprised." He pointed his finger. "But I'm warning you, I find you a man, he marries you, there'll be no sneaking behind his back. There'll be no other men, Red."

She threw up her hands. "I swear by all that's holy I'll be chaste. Just find me a man, Paddy, so's I don't have to tell my pap what I done."

O'Brian pushed back his mug of tea and rose. "You leave it to me, Red." He smiled. If only his other troubles were so easily solved. He knew a man that ran a flour mill not two miles down the river. He was a widower with two children, and was just saying yesterday that he needed a young, healthy wife. "Check back here tomorrow night. I won't be able to come, because I've got to make a trip to Philadelphia, but I'll send someone with a message. I'll find you a husband."

She leaped up from the table and threw her arms around him planting a teary kiss on his lips. "Thank ye, Paddy. I won't forget ye, I swear I won't. And . . ." she jumped up and down, "I'll name my first boy child after you, I swear I will!"

He started for the door, ready to head back to the mills. He had some inquiries to make concerning the man who'd died with Paul Lawrence. "You best name him after your new husband," he advised with a wink.

Twenty-eight

It was half past one in the morning when O'Brian crept into the house. He peeked into Elizabeth's room to see that she was sleeping soundly with one of Lacy's pups on the end of her bed. By the light of the moon that poured in through the open window, he could see her face on the pillow. She was so beautiful with her rosy lips and dark hair splashed across the white linen bedding.

He felt his heart trip as his gaze fell to her abdomen. She thought she was ugly and fat. She thought he no longer found her attractive. The truth was, he liked her full breasts, and he liked the thought that his child grew safely inside her. That was why he had to find out who the killer was, so that Lawrence Mills would be safe for his child, even if he couldn't be here with him or her.

O'Brian looked at Elizabeth's face one last time. He longed to climb into bed beside her. They didn't have to make love. He would have been content just to hold her. But he couldn't, of course.

He closed Elizabeth's bedchamber door and walked down the long hall to the sparsely furnished bedchamber he now slept in alone.

O'Brian stripped off his clothes, leaving them in a careless pile on the polished hardwood floor. He climbed into bed and tucked his hands behind his head. He'd talked to Thomas at the flour mill, and Thomas had said he'd be willing to marry Red and take her unborn child, sight unseen. He said he was partial to redheads.

O'Brian rolled over onto his side. He found it hard to sleep without Liz; he'd gotten so used to her warm, soft body curled against his. Tomorrow he had to go to Philadelphia. He'd be gone three days, but maybe when he got back, he and Liz could talk. Maybe if, just for once, he could get her to express what she was feeling, maybe the two of them could find a way to right this marriage that was going so wrong.

He closed his eyes and drifted off into a dreamless sleep.

The sound of the bedchamber door swinging open and hitting the wall with a bang woke O'Brian suddenly the following morning.

"O'Brian, you son of a bitch!" he heard Elizabeth shout before he had his eyes open.

"Liz?" He sat up in bed to see her charging toward him, already fully dressed for the day. She scooped a book up off the nearest table and threw it at him, striking him in the arm before it bounced onto the floor.

"You liar!" she shouted, obviously not caring if the entire household heard her. A half-grown pup bounded in the door after her.

He slid his legs over the side of the bed, rubbing his eyes. "What are you talking about?"

She picked up a ruler from the same table and threw it at him. It flew through the air end over end, and the only reason it didn't hit him square in the middle of the forehead was because he had the sense to duck.

"Liz!" He put up his hand to deflect the next object she hurled at him. "That's enough. Now calm down long enough to tell me what the hell you're hollering about now!"

She folded her arms over her chest, resting them on her belly. "You," she accused. "You promised when we wed that you'd be true to me, but I should have known better. I knew you were a philanderer before we wed. What must have been wrong with my brain that I didn't think you'd be just as popular with the ladies *after* we were married as *before!*"

He narrowed his eyes, trying to figure out what in sweet Jesus's name she was babbling about. "Liz—"

"You said you were just going down there to play cards," she went on in a tirade. "You said you hadn't seen her in months! Then there you are in the middle of that public room, plain as a preacher's wife, kissing that red-haired whore!"

"How did you know I was at the Sow's Ear last night?" He reached for his breeches. Somehow it was easier for a man to deal with an angry woman when he had his breeches on.

"What does it matter how I knew! Half the men at these mills go down there to waste their hard-earned coin on gambling, drink, and women! You think no one gossips here? Good god, O'Brian, I know what's said at the Continental Congress each day before they break for dinner!"

He gave a low whistle as he stood up, pulling his wrinkled homespun breeches over his hips. Damned if she wasn't hot this time! "Look, Liz. Red kissed me. You ask your sources. They saw nothing else, because nothing else happened. We left separately. I never saw her again after I walked out of the tavern a little after eight."

"Oh, she kissed *you,* did she? I asked you to stay with me, and you chose to march yourself down to that filthy pigsty and kiss that little tart." There was a quiver in her voice. "You could have slept with me last night, but you chose to be with her instead."

He was trying not to lose his patience. "You're mixing everything up, Liz, and you're getting it all wrong." He stuffed his hands into the sleeves of his plain muslin shirt and tugged it over his head. "I went down to the Sow's Ear to have a cup of tea—"

"Tea!" She laughed.

"I went down to have a cup of tea, because I needed to think. I talked to some of the men about Joey Marble, the man who was killed with your husband. I also checked the rail at the wheel mill, and found out that it had been tampered with. I was trying to get everything straight in my head, trying to figure how it all went together; Claire, the accidents, Paul's diary that referred to a woman—"

She rested one hand on her hip, impatiently. "Where does the redhead and the kiss come in, that's what *I* want to know."

"Red was at the tavern." He sat down on the edge of the bed and rolled on his stockings. "She was crying."

"Poor girl."

"She's pregnant." Before Elizabeth could speak, he put his hand up. "And no, it's not mine. I told you, I've never touched a woman since the first time I laid with you."

She just stood there looking at him, tapping her foot. It was obvious she didn't believe him. He went on anyway. "She was scared, and she asked me for advice. I offered to help her out."

"What? You going to take a second wife?"

Now he was mad. He'd had enough of her suspicions and her sharp tongue. If she didn't trust him, what was the point in the marriage? He wasn't going to spend his whole life defending himself. He wouldn't live that way, not for Elizabeth, not for anyone.

"I found her a husband, if you must know," he said sharply, pulling on his second boot. "Now, if you'll excuse me."

"Where are you going?"

"Philadelphia. Remember? We have to have that new grinding wheel."

"Send Johnny Bennett for it."

He reached for his hat. If he didn't get out of here, he was going to say something ugly. "I'd rather go myself. I think we could use a couple of days apart, to get our heads straight." He brushed past her.

She whipped around. "A few days! How about a few months? No, no, a few years might be better, like forty or fifty!" she shouted.

He stopped in the doorway, but he didn't turn around. He could feel his heart pounding in his chest. "Just speak your piece, Liz. What are you saying?"

"I'm saying maybe it would be better if you went." Her tone changed. Before her voice had been filled with emotion. Suddenly she was cool and reserved. "I think that after the baby is born, you should just go. I'll pay you for the work you've done here."

"I don't want your money," he said under his breath. *She's sending me off,* he thought numbly. "Maybe I should just go now," he intoned, afraid to turn around, afraid she'd see the moisture in the corners of his eyes.

"What?"

He shrugged. "It might be best."

"You're not even going to wait to see your baby?" Her voice cracked.

He knew he was hurting her, but he didn't care. He wanted to hurt her like she was hurting him. "Why not? I was never certain the child was mine in the first place."

He knew his words must have shocked her, because he heard her breathe in sharply, and for once she had no retort.

He walked out the door and turned down the hallway, his boots pounding on the polished plank floor. Somehow he managed to go down the front steps, and ignore her sobs.

* * *

"Where have you been, Sister?" Jessop stood in the stable, plucking off his butter-soft leather riding gloves.

The groom took the reins from his master and left the barn discreetly, leading the gelding.

Claire's lower lip trembled. "Walking, Brother."

He glanced at her. He was in a foul mood. His groom was brother to one of the men who worked at Lawrence Mills. The groom had had supper last night with his brother, and overheard a conversation between O'Brian, foreman turned master, and the brother. O'Brian had gone too far now. Jessop knew he had to do something and do it immediately. How else would he save Claire?

He glanced at his sister and her pretty bobbing blond curls. "Walking?" he sneered, raising his upper lip at the corner. "Walking where? Have you been down there with those men again, you little tart?"

She winced. "No, Brother."

He slapped his gloves in the palm of his hand. "Then where?"

She looked down at the clean straw, her painted yellow fan clutched in her hand. "I went to Liz's, but I didn't stay long, honest I didn't," she said quickly.

"You little bitch!" he shouted, throwing his gloves at her.

She lowered her head, so that the gloves struck the brim of her straw hat and glanced off.

"I told you you were not to go there without my permission! Didn't I?" When she didn't answer right away, he took a step toward her. "Didn't I, Sister?"

She nodded, her entire body trembling. "Yes. Yes, you said I couldn't go, but yesterday she fell in the water, and I was afraid she was hurt."

He scowled. "Yes, yes, I heard all about that. Now you listen to me. I have to go somewhere. I hate to leave you here, but you need to stay in the house. I'll tell Martha to spend the night with you, so you won't be frightened."

She thrust out her lower lip. "I don't want Martha to stay with me. I want to go to Liz's." As she spoke, she kept her head lowered. "She's going to have a baby, and I want to be there. I want to see the baby boy."

"You'll sleep in your own room. You'll not go over there, not *once* while I'm gone! Do you understand me?"

He was thinking now, devising a plan in his head. He'd rid himself of Liz, the baby, and the foreman all at once. Then Sister would be safe. No one would ever know the truth then. There was an Indian in Dover who would do it for the right price, he was told. He'd go to Dover and find him. Tonight.

When Claire didn't answer, he grabbed her arm, squeezing it. "I said, do you understand what I'm telling you? You're not to go near that house, while I'm gone. No matter what happens."

Claire shook her head stubbornly, still not looking up. "I'm going to see the boy baby. I am."

"Shut up, Claire, before I shut you up."

"I'm going to hold him," she went on in a small, wistful voice as she rocked her empty arms. "I didn't get to hold the other—"

Jessop drew back his bare hand and slapped her hard across the face. He hated to do it. He hated to hurt poor Sister, but she had to learn to keep her mouth shut. She had to know what could be said, and what couldn't be.

His hand made a loud sound as it met with her cheek, and when he drew back, he could see his palm print on her pale face.

Claire lifted her own gloved hand to touch the place where it must have stung. She lifted her head to look him directly in the eyes. "You were a bad man to do that," she said softly. "You were bad to do all those things."

He looked around to make certain no one could hear his sister's ramblings. "Hush, Claire. Do you want to spend time in your bedchamber?"

But for once he couldn't bully her. She shook her head, looking very much like a bewitched little girl. "You are very bad. I know that now. And I'm going to get you. I'm going to make it so you never hurt anybody again." She opened her palm just a little, looking into it. "He's never going to hurt you again, mousey."

Jessop stood there glaring at Claire for a minute. She was now babbling something to her invisible pet, as if he wasn't even there. Jessop had half a mind to take her with him to Dover. If she was with him, he knew she'd stay out of trouble. But something told him it would be better if she stayed. What if the Indian bungled the job?

Jessop leaned over and picked up his gloves from the barn floor. "I'll be going shortly. I suggest you return to your bedchamber, and take some time to think about how naughty you've been. I'll have Martha bring you a light supper."

Jessop headed for the house, and Claire followed him. Sister was difficult to deal with sometimes, but she always did the right thing. She was always obedient, and that was why he would always protect her from the evil world around them.

O'Brian sat back in the wagon, with the brim of his straw hat pulled over his eyes to shield them from the sun. Samson held the reins, driving north, having the sense to keep quiet and give his master time to think.

O'Brian felt so bad that he was sick to his stomach. He shouldn't have left Liz like that. He should have gone back and told her he was sorry. Even if the marriage wasn't going to work, he shouldn't have said those things. He didn't know what had gotten into him. He didn't know why he'd been so cruel.

But instead of going back and saying he was sorry, he was headed for Philadelphia to have a grindstone made. Work, it was always the answer. It was always his escape. Ironically, it was the same way with Liz. He was sure she was sitting at her desk this very moment, tackling a pile of paperwork. He laughed without humor. They were cut from the same cloth, weren't they?

After more than two hours of silence on the bumpy road, Samson finally cleared his raspy throat and spoke. "You and the mistress have a big one?" he asked, keeping his eyes on the road.

O'Brian tipped up the brim of his hat so that he could see Samson. He'd been so lost in his thoughts, he'd almost forgotten his friend was there. "What?"

"A big fight? One of the kitchen girls said you and the mistress was screamin' your lungs out this mornin'."

O'Brian leaned back on the rough plank seat again. "I guess everyone for a mile around heard us."

Samson gave a long whistle. "Me and Ngozi, we had a few of 'em those first months we was wed. It was differ'nt you know—just visitin' when I liked, and bein' *married* to 'er."

O'Brian scowled beneath the brim of his battered straw hat. "No, this isn't just newlywed quarrels. It's not going to work, between me and the mistress, Samson. I think I'm going to be moving on."

Samson pulled up on the reins, bringing the two mules to a sudden stop in the center of the road. "What?"

O'Brian sat up again. "What are you doing? Let's go." He threw out his hand. "It's going to take a full day to get to Philadelphia as it is."

"What am *I* doin'?" Samson bellowed. "What are *you* doin'?"

O'Brian stared at the man who had become his friend. Samson never had a whole lot to say, and he'd certainly never raised his voice to O'Brian before. "I don't know what you mean."

"Hell, if you don't, man! I'm talkin' about you and the mistress. Don't tell me yer just gonna walk off, her gettin' ready to have your baby!"

"You don't understand," O'Brian groaned. "It would be better for Liz and the child. Our marriage isn't going to work. It would have never worked. We're just too different. The worlds we came from are too different."

Samson gave a snort. "Different! You and the mistress is as alike as two peas in a pod! I ain't never seen a man and a woman that fit together better. The both of you is just too stubborn to admit it." He looked away as if in disgust. "I don't which one of yous is worse. I truly don't."

O'Brian sat there on the edge of the wagon seat for a moment, staring out over the mules' heads at the rutted dirt road in front of them. "I can't live with her, Samson," he finally said. "I can't go on making her so unhappy." He shook his head, losing focus. "But I can't imagine life without her, either."

Samson picked up the broad leather reins and gave them a snap. The mules moved on, pulling the creaking wagon behind them. "My mama, she always said love was a thing so close to hate, that one could cut ya in half as easy as the other." He shook his head. "It's a terrible thing, master, lovin' your wife."

O'Brian looked at him in puzzlement. "What did you say?"

"I said, it's a terrible thing, a man lovin' his wife. Terrible responsibility on a man's shoulders."

Was that it? O'Brian wondered. Do I love her? Is that what I've been running from all these months? Is that why I've been so hard on her, on myself? Because I loved her, but I didn't want to?

Samson stared at O'Brian and then turned away impatiently. "Don't tell me you ain't tole her!"

"You don't understand. That's not the kind of person she is. She doesn't talk about feelings. Hell, I sometimes wonder if she's got any at all."

Samson smiled sadly. "Everyone want to be loved, O'Brian. Me. Miss Lizbeth." He looked at his friend. "Even you."

"There's so much bad between us now, Samson. It doesn't matter anymore. I did things I shouldn't have done. I said things I never should have said. She couldn't forgive me." He shook his head adamantly. "She doesn't love me. She loves the mill. She loves that damned river. She loved her dogs, but not me."

Samson glanced sideways. "So you just gonna walk away? You ain't gonna fight for her? And you think you're such a big man." He shook his head slowly. "It's a shame."

O'Brian threw up his hands. "What's the point? She told me to get out. She practically admitted the baby wasn't mine."

"Then I guess yer gonna have to decide just how much you love her. When you love someone, ya got to forgive 'em." He paused and then looked up at O'Brian. "You care if the chil' is yours or not?"

O'Brian thought for a minute. "No," he answered honestly. "I don't think I do. That's why we never really talked about it. I guess inside I wanted her so badly, that it didn't matter why she married me, only that she did."

"Tell me something," Samson said. "If you could have anything right now, what would it be? Pot a' gold? A ship full of riches? A title other folks got to bow to?"

O'Brian chuckled, knowing what he was getting at. "I guess if I could have anything right now, I'd have Liz."

He put out his arms as if he was holding her. "Here. Now."

Samson shrugged. "Seems to me, then, that you got to tell her ya love 'er. Ya loved 'er all along. Even if she throws it in your face, and tells you to take your white ass off her land, at least you tol' the truth. Ya tol' her what was in your heart. You tried."

O'Brian thought for a long time about what Samson said. In his mind he ran through all the bad things that had passed between them; all the things they said to each other, all the things they did. But he also remembered the good times. He remembered her husky laughter, her smiles. He remembered how she made him feel inside, when she looked up at him with those dark eyes of hers.

They must have gone three or four miles before O'Brian spoke again. "You're right," he said finally. "You're right, friend. I wouldn't be much of a man, if I walked off not telling her the truth. Even if there's no hope. Even if she never cared for me to begin with, I need to tell her. If not for her sake, then my own."

"Ya want me to turn these ol' mules around, Master?"

"No." He pointed ahead down the road. "We'll go into Philadelphia, and we'll get her that grinding stone, the best one we can find or have made." He laughed. "It will be my peace offering, or my farewell gift, depending on how she takes what I have to say."

Samson chuckled and O'Brian joined in. Suddenly that black storm he was catapulting through seemed to calm. Somewhere ahead he thought he saw a ray of sunshine.

Twenty-nine

It was late afternoon, and Elizabeth and Claire were walking along the river. Claire picked wildflowers on the grassy bank, while Elizabeth watched the water rush over the rocks.

Elizabeth rubbed her abdomen with a slow circular pattern. She'd woken up this morning with a dull ache in her lower back and random contractions. Her fall the previous day must have brought her labor on prematurely. But then she'd talked to Katie, who had related what her betrothed had seen in the Sow's Ear, and for a time Elizabeth forgot her uncomfortableness.

That was when she'd gone to O'Brian's room, looking for a fight. She felt so betrayed by him. But it wasn't the redhead. She believed him when he said he'd not dallied with her. That was just an excuse.

What she was really upset about was the fact that she had asked him to stay with her yesterday, to sleep with her last night, and he'd refused her. She knew then that O'Brian didn't feel the same way she did about him. It was just her tough luck that it had taken her all this time to realize that she loved him, and now he was gone.

She sighed, watching Claire stoop to pluck a daisy. It was all spilt milk now. She couldn't dwell on it, what had passed between her and O'Brian. She couldn't think about it.

She stopped in mid-step, surprised by the intensity of

a contraction. Up until now they had been erratic, and nothing more than uncomfortable.

She glanced up at Claire, who had run ahead. She supposed they shouldn't have walked so far from the house knowing she was in labor, but she'd needed to get away from the mills. She'd needed a little peace.

Claire turned around. "You all right?" she called, one hand filled with flowers.

Elizabeth took a deep breath and exhaled slowly. Already another contraction was coming. She hadn't expected her labor to speed up so quickly. She had thought it would be hours, days maybe, before the baby came. Now suddenly she was a little frightened.

She took two steps toward Claire, and had to stop again as the wave of tightening came over her. She grimaced. "I think we need to go back, Claire," she said, trying to remain calm so as not to frighten her.

Claire came running. She was a picture of loveliness in her striped yellow petticoats and yellow and white straw bonnet. "What's the matter?"

Elizabeth breathed deeply and waited for the contraction to pass before she spoke. "The baby, Claire," she said as brightly as she could manage. "I think he or she is about to make his entrance into the world."

Claire dropped the flowers and grabbed Elizabeth's arm. "The baby! You have to lie down!"

Elizabeth blinked, trying to keep her head clear. "I haven't much experience with this, but I think you're right." She glanced over her shoulder. It was a long way back to the her house at the mills, perhaps two miles.

Claire stared at the path they'd followed. "It's too far," she said. "Isn't it?"

"I don't know. I can try and walk, but you may have to go for help." She grimaced as another contraction washed over her. "I think this baby is in a hurry all of a sudden."

"No. No. You'd better come to my house!" Claire took her arm, tugging. "It's not far."

Elizabeth stood where she was. She wouldn't go to Jessop's house. She wouldn't let her baby be born in his presence. "No. Really. I think I just want to go home."

"Brother's not there," Claire said, as if she could read Elizabeth's mind. "He went to Dover. He won't be back tonight or the next night."

Elizabeth stood there rubbing her swollen middle for a moment, trying to think. Claire was right. It did make more sense to go up to her house than to try to make it all the way home. Once they reached Jessop's, one of the servants could go back to Lawrence Mills to get help. Ngozi had promised to help her with the delivery when the time came.

"All right," Elizabeth finally said. "You're right, Claire." She was surprised by how sensibly her sister-in-law was behaving. It was almost as if she were her old self again. "I'll go with you to your house, but then you have to promise me you'll send for Ngozi."

Claire took Elizabeth's arm, and they turned back. The house was less than a quarter of mile. It took a long time to get there, because Elizabeth had to stop for each contraction. By the time they reached the front door, she was covered in perspiration and panting from the exertion.

Claire pushed through the front door into the dark hallway. "Martha! Martha!" she shouted. "Help me!"

The housekeeper came hustling down the hallway. "Miss Claire! You're supposed to be in your room. What are you—" She stopped in the hallway to stare at Elizabeth.

"Liz is going to have her baby," Claire said. "You have to help me get her upstairs. She can use my bedchamber."

Martha scowled. "The master won't like this much," she hissed. "He don't want that trash in this house."

Elizabeth hung on to the staircase rail. "It's all right," she told Claire, panting. "Just send for a wagon from Lawrence Mills."

Claire swung around to face Martha. "It isn't all right," she shouted like an angry child. "Martha works for *me,* not just my brother. I'm the mistress here, and she'll do what I tell her and she'll be quiet about it! Won't you?" she demanded.

Martha bobbed her head. "Yes, Mistress."

Claire pointed. "Now. You help me get Liz upstairs."

Slowly Elizabeth climbed the stairs with the women, one on each side of her. Elizabeth could barely think now through the pain, through the intense concentration it took to remain in control. Nothing mattered right now, but this baby and bringing it safely into the world.

When the women stripped her down to her shift and helped her into the bed, she barely put up a fight. She realized she wasn't going to make it back to Lawrence Mills to have the baby. This baby was coming too fast now.

Elizabeth concentrated on breathing because that made the contractions come and go easier. Claire wiped her forehead with a cold cloth and then offered her a cup of sweet tea.

Elizabeth shook her head. She was beyond words. Her mind and her body were now controlled by the baby. "Water," she managed. "Cold water."

"Drink it," Claire insisted. "It will help the pain."

Elizabeth was so thirsty and so tired that she drank several mouthfuls, and then fell back onto the pillow. After only a few minutes, the room began to grow smaller, sounds softer. Even the pain seemed to ease. It was if someone had placed a blanket of fog over her, numbing her feelings, her thoughts, her own words.

Now Elizabeth was barely aware of the bustling in the room, as Martha and Claire prepared for the birth of the baby. Claire gave her more tea and she drank it, enjoying the release from the pain, from thinking.

Elizabeth lost all track of time. She heard a case clock chime somewhere, but for some reason she couldn't count the chimes, so she didn't know what time it was.

Somewhere in the back of her mind, she recalled women whispering tales of the agony of childbirth. This didn't seem so bad to her; there was pain, but it was by no means unbearable. It actually seemed more like hard work. Perhaps it was whatever Claire had given her in the tea that made her feel that way.

Now she was just floating, floating with the contractions that were growing harder and closer together. She twisted her hands in the sheets, pulling hard to fight the pain. Her baby would be here any moment. She knew it as if by instinct.

Three days later at midmorning, O'Brian and Samson rode down the center of a back street in Philadelphia. With the new grindstone loaded in the wagon, they were headed home to Lawrence Mills. Now that they had picked up the grindstone, O'Brian was anxious to get moving. He wanted to get back to Liz. He needed to settle with her. No matter what was going to happen, he felt like he needed to know.

Samson had just urged the mules around a corner near a fish market, when O'Brian heard him speak in his native tongue. As long as O'Brian had known Samson, he'd never heard him speak anything but the King's English.

"What is it, Samson?"

Samson pulled up hard on the reins, and the wagon creaked to a halt. He looked stricken.

O'Brian touched his friend's arm lightly. "Samson?"

"A ghostie," the man muttered, honestly seeming to be afraid.

"What?" O'Brian turned his attention to the man behind the fish booth, wrapping a large trout in a bit of brown paper.

"Ghostie," Samson repeated. "There."

O'Brian glanced at the fish man, then back at Samson. "You been in the sun too long, friend?"

Samson continued to stare wide-eyed. "He's a ghost, I swear he is." Samson pointed a trembling finger. "That there's the ghost of Joey Marble."

There was something about the name that sent an alarm off inside O'Brian's head. Joey Marble, Joey Marble . . . "Christ," he whispered. "You mean the man that died in the fire with Paul Lawrence?"

Samson could only nod and stare.

"You absolutely certain?"

He nodded again.

O'Brian swung out of the wagon. "Saint's in hell, Samson! That's no ghost! That's a man of flesh and blood! And damned if he hasn't got some explaining to do!"

O'Brian hurried across the street, cutting in front of the mules. He'd barely reached the far side when the fish man looked up, spotted Samson, and took off, tossing his packaged fish into the air.

"Samson!" O'Brian shouted over his shoulder. "Get off that blessed wagon! Don't let him get away!"

The fish man, who had to be Joey by the way he was running, ducked down a narrow alley between wooden shacks. O'Brian followed him down the alley at a dead run. It stank of rotten fish; rats scattered in every direction, trying to escape from the human being.

"I just want to speak to you!" O'Brian shouted. "Joey! Wait!"

But the man kept running. He turned a sharp corner and his wide-brimmed hat flew off his head. O'Brian crushed the hat with one step of his foot, as he turned the corner behind Joey.

In his hurry to get away, the man was running toward the water instead of the city. O'Brian panted, forcing himself to run harder, faster. Joey was a tall, wiry man with long legs made for running, but O'Brian was slowly gaining on him.

Joey burst from the alley and crossed a narrow, muddy street. Rotten vegetables floated by in a puddle of water. A woman herding some goats gave a shout of protest and swung her staff, when Joey burst through the middle of her livestock, scattering them, with O'Brian right behind him.

Joey leaped into a wagon filled with open barrels of salted eels and jumped off the far side. Not wanting to give up a second, O'Brian climbed over the wagon after him. "I just want to talk to you!" O'Brian shouted, panting. "I'm not going to hurt you!"

O'Brian didn't know what part Joey had played in the explosion at the mills, but there was one thing he knew for certain, the man knew something, . Why else would he be trying so hard to get away?

Suddenly the docks loomed up ahead. The street was growing more congested with wagons pulled by horses and men. There were women buying fish, barking dogs, and ragged children darting in and out of the stands where the fishermen sold their catch.

Out of nowhere, Samson appeared up ahead. O'Brian heaved a silent sigh of relief. He didn't want to have to chase this man into the water. Samson put out his broad hands. Joey tried to duck and run, but despite Samson's size, he was also swift. He caught Joey by the scruff of his torn muslin shirt and lifted him off the ground.

"You ain't no ghost," Samson accused. "You're Joey, ain't you?"

O'Brian came to a halt, panting heavily. He leaned on his thighs to catch his breath. "I don't . . . know . . .

what you're . . . running from," he said. "I . . . just want to . . . talk to you."

Joey shook his head frantically. "I ain't said a word! Tell Mr. Lawrence, I ain't. I just come back, because I couldn't take the long winter up Massachusetts way. The cold was too hard on my bones!"

O'Brian eyed Samson, then looked back at Joey. Samson slowly lowered the fish man to his feet, but he didn't let go of him, for fear he'd take off again.

"My name's O'Brian. I'm the foreman at Lawrence Mills." He saw no reason to mention his relationship to Liz. Hell, he didn't know that there was a relationship left to mention. "You're supposed to be dead."

Joey swallowed hard. It was obvious he was scared.

"Look," O'Brian said impatiently. "Either you talk to me, and you answer my questions, or I'm going to beat them out of you." He raised his hands. "It's that simple."

Joey looked at Samson as if to question the validity of O'Brian's statement.

"You better talk to the man, 'cause he ain't one to be put off. At this point you best be worried about him and not Mr. Jessop," Samson warned.

Joey looked back at O'Brian, his eyes wide with fear. "Mr. Lawrence said he'd kill me, if I talked."

"Let's get out of the street," O'Brian said, indicating a nearby building with a nod of his head. "Into that tavern." He grabbed Joey's arm, and he and Samson escorted the man across the street, trying not to look too conspicuous. "We're going to get to the bottom of this," O'Brian threatened in a frighteningly even tone, "or you, Joey, are going to be feeding the fish in the Philadelphia harbor."

Elizabeth leaned over the new pine cradle beside her bed, and laid her sleeping daughter down. The infant made a cooing sound as she snuggled into the soft cotton blanket.

Elizabeth smiled a smile only a mother could understand. She had been so afraid to have this child. She had feared she wouldn't love her. But O'Brian had been right. He'd been completely right, and she'd been completely wrong. All those months she'd agonized over this. Because of her own fears, she'd made everyone around her miserable, and without reason. The moment she brought her daughter to her breast, the love had come, just as O'Brian had said it would. Her love for her daughter had washed over her like an ocean wave.

Now, three days later, Elizabeth couldn't remember what her life had been like before little Morgan had arrived. She wondered how she could ever have felt like a whole person, with this tiny piece missing from her heart.

Elizabeth tucked the blanket over the baby's back and sat down on the edge of the bed to watch her. These last three days had been the best of her life, and yet the worst.

She fought the lump that rose in her throat. She wanted O'Brian so badly right now, that she ached for him. But, of course, she knew he wouldn't come. He was in Philadelphia getting the new grindstone with Samson. It would serve her right if he never came back, after the way she had treated him. For all she knew, Samson might be headed home alone right now. If O'Brian had any sense at all, he would continue north and never look back.

A tear slipped down Elizabeth's cheek, and she wiped it away. Despite the late hour, she'd sent Katie to fetch her some supper, and she didn't want the girl to see her mistress crying.

Elizabeth pulled a handkerchief from her sleeve and dabbed her eyes. If it weren't for the fact that Morgan was only three days old, Elizabeth would have packed up the baby and gone to Philadelphia herself to look for O'Brian. She needed to tell him that she was sorry. She needed to tell him that she loved him. Even if he hated her, she needed him to know before he went.

And she needed to tell him about the other baby . . .

Elizabeth rose and walked to the open window. She could hear the gentle pitter-patter of rain, as it struck the glass window. Her tears slid down her cheeks like the rain on the glass.

Much of it seemed like a dream. Morgan's whole birth was still fuzzy in her mind. She remembered walking along the river. Then she remembered going to Jessop's with Claire. The rest was hazy. She remembered the pain, the contractions, the pushing, but even that seemed to have happened to someone else and not herself.

But what she remembered distinctly was the cry of one baby, then, only minutes later, another. She was almost positive there had been two babies . . . at least, there were in her dream.

After the birth, when Elizabeth held Morgan in her arms, she'd asked Claire about the other baby. Had it died? She didn't even know what sex the child was.

But Claire had gotten a strange look on her face, and said there was no other baby. Then she gave Elizabeth more tea to ease her sore muscles and help her rest. The sour housekeeper had laughed later, when Elizabeth had asked about the other baby. She said that women often hallucinated when giving birth. She said she'd once dreamed she had a sheep rather than a son. Looking back now, she said, she wished she'd had the sheep.

So Elizabeth had stayed with Claire a full day, nursing the baby, drinking the tea that Martha and Claire insisted was good for her. But after a while, Elizabeth realized she didn't like the way the tea—or whatever was in it—

made her feel. Even pain would have been preferable to the numbness. So she refused to drink it.

And when Ngozi came to visit Elizabeth, she insisted that Ngozi send a wagon back for her immediately. If no one would come for her, she threatened, by god, she'd walk home with the baby. Once she stopped drinking the medicinal tea, she felt much stronger anyway.

So Ngozi and Johnny came back to Jessop's for her last night. Elizabeth didn't tell anyone else about the other baby, because she didn't want to seem foolish. She didn't want to appear to be the paranoid new mother. She assumed that it had all been a dream, and that the dream would fade in her mind. But in the last twenty-four hours, it hadn't. In fact, it had gotten stronger. Now she thought she could hear the other baby crying in her head. And the more hours that passed, the longer she held Morgan, the more she missed the little baby in her mind.

A woman's scream rent the air and Elizabeth whirled around, the hair standing up on the back of her neck. She raced for her bedchamber door, and flung it open.

"Katie?" What Elizabeth saw made her stomach lurch.

Katie was lying on the hall floor on her back, her throat cut and bloody, her eyes staring lifelessly at the ceiling. Around her, spread across the floor in a puddle of dark blood, were the cups and bowls from the supper tray she'd been bringing to her mistress. There was no one else in sight in the hallway, but, of course, Elizabeth knew someone was there.

She stepped back into her room and threw the bolt on the door, her heart pounding. She had no weapon. Her pistol was in the office. She could scream for help, but that would only endanger any servant who came to her!

Elizabeth grabbed her sleeping infant from the cradle and whirled around to see the doorknob turning. How would she escape? How would she save her sweet Morgan?

Then she saw the open window.

Thirty

First the door handle jiggled a little, then it rattled angrily.

Morgan whimpered as Elizabeth tucked the infant, in her blanket, beneath her arm, and made a dash for the window.

Something banged hard against the bedchamber door . . . someone . . . and Elizabeth heard the sound of splintering wood. Panic tightened in her chest, until she could barely breathe. She threw the window open and started to climb out. She had no idea which way she was going once she was on the roof, but anything was better than standing here and being slaughtered like Katie had been slaughtered.

Elizabeth was just getting over the sill, when the door broke open. As she dropped onto the kitchen roof below and slammed the window shut, she caught a glimpse of a red man in buckskins.

An Indian? Why would an Indian be chasing her? If he was a thief, why didn't he take what he wanted and go?

Baby Morgan began to wail as Elizabeth raced barefoot, in her dressing gown, along the slippery slate roof. It was raining harder now, soaking her and the baby. She heard the rumble of thunder, and a breath later she saw lightning streak the sky, filling the air with eerie light.

Behind her she heard the window open, but she didn't

take the time to look back. Elizabeth reached the edge of the roof. There was nowhere to go from here, but down onto the kitchen's lean-to roof. She stood there for a moment, her bare toes curled on the warm, wet slate. She jiggled Morgan to comfort her.

Elizabeth could hardly see for the pouring rain. Morgan was wiggling in her arms and crying out in protest of her wet blanket. It was a good eight- to ten-foot drop to the lean-to roof below, and there was no way for her to lower herself and still hold tightly to Morgan.

She glanced behind her. The Indian was running along the roof behind her now, his moccasins padding on the wet slate. By the glow of the lightning in the darkness, she saw the glint of a long-bladed knife he held in his hand, and she imagined a smear of Katie's blood on it.

With a cry of fright, Elizabeth leaped off the roof. She hit the cedar-shingled roof below hard, and rolled with Morgan still in her arms.

"Liz!"

She heard a voice coming from somewhere on the ground.

O'Brian. Sweet Jesus, it was O'Brian. He'd come for her. He wouldn't let this madman murder her or her baby! Why hadn't she known that all along?

"O'Brian!" she shrieked. "Up here on the kitchen roof!" She pushed herself up off the cedar shingles and ran toward the edge. She knew the baby was still unhurt in her arms, because the little girl was now screaming and flailing her tiny fists wildly.

"Liz!"

"Here!" Then she saw him on the ground below.

Samson stood holding a lantern high over his head. Both were soaked from the rain.

"What the hell are you doing on the roof?"

"He's chasing me!" she screamed.

"Who?"

"I don't know! Take her," she hollered, nearly hysterical. "Take Morgan. Don't let him kill her! Take her, O'Brian!"

O'Brian had the good sense to realize he had to act instantly. He threw up his hands, and Elizabeth leaned over the roof to drop Morgan into her father's arms.

She felt as if her heart was wrenched from her chest, when she let her baby fall. But she knew O'Brian would catch her. She knew that even if this mad Indian murdered her, Morgan would be safe with her dada always.

Just as Elizabeth let go of her baby, she felt a hand grip her shoulder. She screamed, whipped around, and pounded the man with her fists.

"Liz!" O'Brian cried out.

Ignoring the knife she knew could kill her, Elizabeth screamed and fought her attacker wildly. She dug at his eyes with her fingernails, she slashed at his throat. The Indian was so much stronger than she was, but she had so much to live for. She slipped and fell on the wet slate. She realized the man stank of whiskey and uncured hides, as he fell with her, miraculously close to the roof's edge.

Through the pouring rain, by the glow of the lightning that arced overhead, she saw the Indian scrambling to get to his feet. With a smirk of satisfaction, she brought her leg back beneath her wet dressing gown, and kicked the man as hard as she could. He let out a bellow of surprise, as he went sliding over the wet roof to the ground below.

By the time Elizabeth crawled to the edge of the roof, the Indian had bounced to his feet, still holding the deadly knife.

Everything happened so quickly then. O'Brian was still standing there, holding the baby. Samson threw himself, unarmed, at Elizabeth's attacker.

She saw the look of surprise on Samson's face, as the Indian sank the blade into his chest.

Elizabeth screamed, and Samson fell back into the muddy grass. All she could think of was that O'Brian and her baby were next. Before she could get off the roof they would both be dead, and then she'd have no reason to live.

But before Elizabeth could turn around to drop off the edge of the roof, she saw a streak of light below and heard the boom of a flintlock. O'Brian had been armed! And he shot the Indian at point-blank range.

The Indian flew back under the impact of the musket ball that hit him in the center of the chest. He was dead before his black braids hit the ground and splashed in a puddle.

Elizabeth gripped the edge of the roof, hung over, and let herself drop. Water and mud splashed up on her bare legs, as she hit the soft ground. She dropped to her knees beside Samson, and lifted the man's head. Raindrops ran off his face. By the light of the lantern that rested on the ground beside him, she saw him smiling up at her.

"Samson?" she whispered.

He took her hand and sat up, holding the oozing wound that had come very close to his heart. He flexed his shoulder. "I be all right, Mistress. It just knocked the wind outta me." He grinned. "My Ngozi, she'll fix me right up with a hot cup a' brew and a good, healing poultice."

By now other men and women from the house were beginning to gather. The men came out in nothing but breeches, carrying old muskets and pistols. The women, in their nightclothes, shrieked at the sight of the dead Indian, and all began to talk at once. Someone must have heard the shot from Worker's Hill, because Elizabeth could hear a commotion as men took the shortcut to the house through the woods.

Elizabeth rose slowly, her gaze turning to O'Brian. He was just standing there, rain running in rivulets down his face, staring at the tiny bundle he cradled in his arms.

Morgan had quieted and was now cooing softly.

Elizabeth walked slowly toward them, emotion bubbling up inside her. *Give me another chance,* she prayed. *Please. Because I want you, O'Brian. I love you and I need you.*

Elizabeth stood beside him and looked down at the perfect little girl that seemed to be their most common ground now. "And look at you, Mr. O'Brian," she teased, "grinning like the brewer's horse." Then she saw that there were tears, and not rainwater in his eyes.

He wiped at his face with the back of one hand. "She's a beauty, isn't she, Liz?"

"I thought so," she answered, looking down at their daughter. "But I may be a little prejudiced."

He ran his hand over her perfectly shaped, little head. "She's a redhead, isn't she? Just like me brothers and sisters."

Elizabeth was grinning now. "Pay back, I guess, for all the things I said about red-haired women."

"Ah, Liz," he put out his arm and pulled her tight against him, kissing her wet lips with his. "We have to talk," he said, drawing her toward the house. "I have to tell you something."

She grabbed his sleeve. "The Indian killed Katie, and I don't know why."

"I think I do. We'll talk about it inside."

A lump rose in her throat as she thought of the other baby, the baby in her dream. "I have to tell you something, too," she whispered. Then she pressed her cheek to his shoulder. "I have to tell you a lot of things."

"Let's get her in out of the rain." He paused. "What's her name? I don't even know her name. When was she born?"

"Morgan. Morgan O'Brian. And she's three days old tonight."

"Ah, god's teeth, I'm sorry, Liz." He kissed her again, and the two ducked through the sheet of water pouring off the roof, and slipped inside the warm, dry kitchen.

A short time later Elizabeth and O'Brian met in the downstairs parlor. Both of them had changed into dry clothing. She was wearing sturdy petticoats, a plain bodice with a kerchief thrown over her shoulders, and her boots. He wore his typical homespun breeches and rough weave muslin shirt.

Elizabeth had nursed the baby and tucked her in. Katie's body had been taken to Worker's Hill by her betrothed, to be properly prepared for burial. Despite Elizabeth's insistence that Samson and Ngozi go home and tend to his wound, Ngozi was watching over Morgan, while Samson was guarding the bedchamber.

O'Brian closed the parlor door firmly, so that their conversation would remain private. He put out his arms to her, and she came.

"I'm so sorry," she murmured, pressing her face into the warm hollow of his shoulder. "I've been so foolish all these months. I was so afraid to have the baby. I was so afraid to love you."

He swept the hair from her cheek and kissed her soundly on the mouth. "I've got my own sorries to offer. I've been so pigheaded that I couldn't see the snout on the end of my face." He tipped his nose with a finger. "But Samson set me straight." He looked down for a moment, then back up at her, his green eyes filled with emotion. "All this time, I didn't see it, or chose to ignore it. I love you, Liz. I've loved you since that first day I came to Lawrence Mills."

"When you punched me?" she teased.

They laughed together.

"How could we have wasted all this time being so bullheaded?" she asked him. "If only I'd reached out to you when I was afraid, instead of pushing you away." She smoothed his unshaven cheek with her palm. "But I do love you," she whispered.

He pulled her against him, smoothing her hair. "I'm still never going to be the man you want me to be, Liz. Ye have to understand that."

She looked up into his face. "I didn't want to change you." She looked away. "Yes. Maybe I did. But it was foolish. I don't want a man like Jessop. I know he reads the right literature, he wears the right tailor's clothes, he has all the right friends." She made a face. "But that was why I didn't want to marry him."

O'Brian's face suddenly darkened.

"What?" she asked, still holding onto him, still unwilling to let go. There was so much to say, so much to share. She knew it would take time. But she knew she could do it. They could do it.

"That's what we have to talk about, Liz. I think I know why that Indian was here. He was trying to kill you and me both. And I think I know who sent him."

She put up her hand. "No, wait. I don't want to hear all this. Not yet." She took his hand in hers. "I have to tell you something. Now, I know you're not going to want to believe me, but you have to."

O'Brian listened without interrupting, as she related the strange tale of Morgan's birth. He asked several questions, but then only nodded and let her go on. Finally she was done, and she just stood there looking into those brilliant green eyes of his, praying he would believe her.

"That's pretty farfetched, Liz," he said finally.

"I know," she whispered, a tremble in her voice. "I'm not asking you to believe in what I *think* I saw, or what I *thought* I remembered." She took his hand and brought it to her left breast, so that he could feel her heart pounding. "I want you to believe me, because of what I feel inside." She fought her tears. "I have to know. If the baby died, all right. At least I'll know."

He stared into her eyes for a moment. "You think Claire could have done this? You really think the housekeeper would be in on it?"

She splayed her hands. "I don't know. It doesn't make sense, but I'm telling you, our baby is missing, and dead or alive, and I have to find him. I have to know the truth."

"The best place to start, then, is with Claire."

Elizabeth clasped his hands. "You'll do it? You'll help me try to find out what happened?"

"If Claire did keep the baby, it would have to be at the house." He frowned. "But Jessop would have to know about it, too. You can't hide a baby."

She shook her head. "Jessop's still not back from Dover yet."

"No," he mused. "I don't guess he would be."

"What?"

He waved his hand. "I'll tell you about it later. One crisis at a time. Let's go." He held out his hand.

"Now? We'll go now?"

"Yes, now. Ngozi can stay with Morgan until we return." He took her hand and led her toward the door. "Can you ride? It would be faster."

"Yes, I can ride!" She pushed ahead of him, beating him to the parlor door. "We'll saddle the horses ourselves."

The thunder and lightning storm had passed over by the time Elizabeth and O'Brian reached Jessop's house, but a light, drizzling rain still fell.

The two dismounted and went to the front door.

O'Brian tried the doorknob and, when it wouldn't turn, he beat on the door with his fist. It seemed as if only seconds had passed before the door swung open and they were met by a sleepy-eyed Claire. She was dressed in a thin, white nightgown with white bows at the neckline and elbows. She looked like an angel.

O'Brian pushed his way in through the door, with Elizabeth following. "Where's the baby, Claire?"

She stared at him, wide-eyed. "What?"

"The baby. Liz had two babies here that night, but she only went home with one."

Claire shook her head adamantly. "One baby. One baby for Liz."

He glanced down the dark hallway. "Where's the housekeeper? I want to speak with her. Now!"

Claire thrust out her lip. "She went away. I gave her money, and I told her to find new employment. I didn't like her. I never liked her."

O'Brian glanced at Liz. Both seemed to recognize that something wasn't right here.

O'Brian turned his gaze back to Claire. "Look at me," he demanded. "Claire, look at my face."

Slowly she turned to him. Tiny tears ran down her pale cheeks.

"Claire, I've been your friend since I came here."

She nodded. "You've been my friend. You were nice to me. You never hurt me or said mean things."

"That's right. And when people are friends, they don't lie to each other. Now just tell me what happened to the other baby. Did the housekeeper take the baby? Because, if she did, we have to know. We want our baby back, Claire."

"One baby for Liz," Claire whispered in a singsong voice. "One baby for Claire."

Elizabeth covered her mouth with her hand to keep from crying out. She knew she had to let O'Brian handle this. He was the only one who could deal with Claire. He was the only one who could make this right.

O'Brian offered his hand. "Take me to the baby, Claire. Let me see Claire's baby."

Suddenly her face lit up. "You want to see my baby? Oh, he's a beautiful baby boy."

A sob rose in Elizabeth's throat, but she controlled herself. She feared the baby's life might depend on her and O'Brian's next reactions.

Claire curled her finger. "Shhhh, you have to be very quiet, when the baby sleeps." She picked up the lamp she'd carried to the door and left on a table. "Have to tiptoe."

So Elizabeth and O'Brian followed Claire down the hallway, down another narrower hallway, toward the kitchen where Liz had never gone. Behind a staircase was a small doorway.

Elizabeth brought her finger to her lips. "Shhh."

Then she opened the door and led them down the steep stairwell to the cellar. They walked through the dark stone chambers toward a glowing light in the distance.

It was all Elizabeth could do to keep from pushing past Claire and running ahead. But O'Brian grabbed her hand and held it in his, giving her a squeeze. *Take care,* he warned with the squeeze.

So Elizabeth followed Claire into the last chamber, where light glowed from a lamp left lit. On the far side of the wall, Elizabeth spotted a very old cradle, and in the cradle was a bundle wrapped in a blanket.

Elizabeth halted where she stood. The baby wasn't moving. Was her son dead? Had he been dead all along, and Claire hadn't known it?

Claire smiled. "Do you want to hold him?"

Elizabeth couldn't do it. She couldn't take the step forward toward the silent cradle.

O'Brian let go of her hand and walked toward Claire. "Yes, I'd love to hold him," he said in his brightest voice.

Claire set down her lamp and reached into the cradle.
Tears ran down Elizabeth's cheeks, as Claire handed
the still bundle to O'Brian. Elizabeth held her breath as
he pulled back the snowy white blanket, and she saw a
glimpse of bright red hair.

"Is he—" Elizabeth couldn't say it.

O'Brian touched the baby and lifted his head with a
smile.

Elizabeth gave a strangled cry, as she ran the short distance between them. "Thank you, thank you, God," she
whispered. And then she looked down at the baby in
O'Brian's arms. It was a boy with plump cheeks, and his
tiny chest was rising and falling with each breath. He was
just sleeping, her little lost baby was just sleeping.

O'Brian gently placed his son in Elizabeth's arms, and
then he looked at Claire, who was smiling like a proud
mother. "You have a very beautiful baby, Claire," he said.

She nodded. "He eats a lot."

Elizabeth looked up. "You fed him?"

"Of course. You have to feed babies. Goats' milk,
that's what Martha said she gave her babies when her
titties dried up. That was what I gave him. And he ate,
and he ate, and he ate."

Suddenly Elizabeth was afraid for the old housekeeper.
Had Claire done something terrible to her to shut her
up? Even if she hated the woman for conspiring with
Claire to steal her baby, she didn't want the woman mur-
dered. "Claire," Elizabeth said as gently as possible.
"Can you tell me where Martha is?"

"I told you. She left with a pocketful of money. She
said I couldn't keep the baby, but I told her that if she
didn't shut up, I would make Jessop shut her up good.
So she said she would go, if I gave her money." She
nodded. "She was afraid of him, you know. She just
didn't know how to get away with no money." She smiled

innocently. "Now she has money, because I took a whole bunch out of Jessop's strong box."

Elizabeth would have laughed, if it weren't for the seriousness of Claire's illness.

Suddenly there were footsteps in the cellar. O'Brian had just tightened his hand around Elizabeth's arm, when Jessop appeared in the archway of the room they stood in. He was dressed in a silk banyan and his hair was mussed, as if he'd been asleep.

"What's going on here?" he demanded.

"I thought you were in Dover, so no one would suspect you when we were killed in our sleep," O'Brian intoned angrily.

Elizabeth looked at O'Brian, wondering what in god's name he was talking about. Could Jessop have possibly sent the Indian to murder them?

Jessop frowned. "I don't know what the hell you're talking about. I came home because I was concerned for Sister." He snapped his fingers. "Sister. Come here at once, and tell me what's going on here." He glanced around the small chamber, where empty wine bottles sat in baskets lined along the walls. "Where did that baby come from?"

Claire broke into a smile. "That's my boy baby, Brother. Remember? He died. But now he came back. You want to hold him?"

Elizabeth tightened her grip on the sleeping child in her arms. She could feel O'Brian tensing beside her.

Jessop suddenly had a strange look on his face. "What are you babbling about? Go to your room, Sister. Go now," he bellowed.

But Claire shook her head. "You took my baby from me once, but you can't have him again. You said I was bad to have the baby in my tummy, and you let that lady hurt me and make the baby come out dead. You said it was God's punishment for my evil lusts. But this baby didn't come out dead."

"That's enough!" Jessop shouted, his face growing beet red.

Claire thrust out her lower lip in a pretty pout. "You've been bad a long time. Since I was a little girl. You said it was my fault. You said I *made* you touch me. You said I made you hurt me like that with your ugly *thing.*"

"Sweet Mother of God," O'Brian swore beneath his breath.

Elizabeth could only stand there and stare in horror. Was Claire saying what she thought she was saying? Was she talking about incest?

Jessop looked at O'Brian and Elizabeth, lifting a hand weakly. "She doesn't know what she's saying, you know. She's very ill." He tapped his temple. "My poor, poor, dear sister is very ill."

"Don't say that!" Claire shrieked, startling them all. "Don't say I'm ill. Don't say I'm mad! *You're* mad! You're the one who's mad! You killed my baby. You killed our brother, when he found out what we were doing! He never hurt me like you did, but you made that Joey Marble help you blow him up! Then you tried to make me hurt Liz and O'Brian, so they wouldn't know." Her blue eyes narrowed. "I hate you for that. For all of it. You hear me! I lied every night when I told you I loved you. I lied!"

"No." Jessop shook his head, twisting his hands in the silk of his banyan. "You don't understand, Sister. I did it, because I love you. I did it, because I wanted to protect you. To protect you from the evil of the world."

"Sounds like *you* were the evil in the world," O'Brian said with disgust. "Not only did you kill your own brother to cover your perversion, but then you tried to kill Liz and me, when we got too close to the truth."

Tears ran down Jessop's cheeks. Suddenly he looked

older than his years, with his thin face and prematurely graying hair. He was so pathetic. "I'm sorry, Sister," he kept saying over and over again. "I'm so sorry, sweetheart. I loved you. I swear I always did. Forgive me. Forgive me, please."

"No. I don't forgive you," Claire said. "I told you I would pay you back for all the ways you hurt me."

Elizabeth saw her move her hand from the filmy folds of her white nightgown, and she saw the glimmer of the flintlock pistol's barrel, but it was all over in a fraction of a second. It was over before anyone could react.

O'Brian threw himself at Claire, knocking her over, but not before she pulled the trigger and shot Jessop through the forehead.

Elizabeth screamed, pulling her baby to her chest.

O'Brian pulled the discharged pistol from Claire's hand, although to what end, Elizabeth didn't know. Claire only had one shot, and she used it well.

O'Brian got up off the floor and walked over to Jessop's body. His eyes were still open, but lifeless and unseeing. O'Brian reached down and pushed his eyelids closed. Then he came to Liz. "You all right, sweetheart? How about the little one?"

"We're fine," she said numbly. "I just can't believe—" She lowered her head. "I mean I know things like this happen in families, but not Jessop, not Claire."

"It's not her fault," he said quietly. "Apparently it had been going on for a long time."

They both turned to look at Claire, sitting on her bottom on the dusty floor. She was looking intently into her cupped hand, seemingly unaware of what had just transpired.

"It's no wonder she is the way she is," Elizabeth mused, her heart wrenching for poor Claire. "So much has happened to her. She's seen such terrible things."

O'Brian ran his fingers through the damp blond hair

that had fallen over his forehead. "I need to send some-one for the High Sheriff."

Elizabeth looked at Claire. "What are they going to do with her?"

"Probably nothing, if we testify for her. I'd say it was self-defense, wouldn't you? He was killing her mind one day at a time. The bastard got what he deserved."

"What are we going to do with her then? She's my responsibility."

He shrugged. "Why not just let her live here? We can get someone to stay with her and watch her. Maybe Ngozi and Samson. My guess is, she's harmless enough now. What was making her sick is gone. Who knows, over time, she might even improve."

They looked up to see Claire rising. She brushed the dirt off the back of her white nightgown, as she came toward them. "I can't keep the baby, can I?" she asked sadly.

O'Brian shook his head no. "I'm afraid not, Claire, because, you see, he's really ours, mine and Liz's."

Claire hung her head, her blond curls brushing her cheeks. "I knew that. I was just pretending." Then she looked up, her face brightening. She raised her cupped hand. "But I can keep mousey, can't I?"

"Yes, you can keep mousey."

Then Claire walked past them, around Jessop's dead body, as if he was nothing but a speck of dust on the dirt floor. She disappeared in the darkness of the cellar, singing softly to herself.

O'Brian faced Elizabeth and wrapped his arms around her, looking down at the baby and then up at her. "What's say you and I go home and give this marriage thing an-other whirl?"

She smiled through the sadness of all that had hap-pened, thinking what a pity it was that two people had to go to hell and back to realize how much they loved each other.

Elizabeth pressed her lips to his. "What say we do."

He dropped his arm over her shoulder and led her out of the chamber, the baby still sound asleep in her arms. "Aye, Mistress."

She sank her elbow into his side, as their laughter mingled. "Really, O'Brian, you've got to stop calling me that . . ."

Epilogue

20 Years Later
Summer 1795
Lawrence Mills

Elizabeth stood on an empty powder keg and reached for another succulent peach. She eased it into the cloth bag she wore over her shoulder, as a spotted hound went flying by, nearly knocking her off the keg.

Elizabeth heard the sound of her youngest daughter's laughter, and she smiled. The years had been better to her than she'd ever dreamed. When war had come to the land—as she had predicted it would—she and O'Brian made the difficult choice to side with the colonists. Over the course of the fighting, they provided what black powder they could to the rebel army, given their limited resources once the ports were closed. At one point General Washington even sent soldiers to the Brandywine to defend the black powder source. Now, years later, with independence still fresh in the air, Lawrence Mills was running at a steady profit and competing with the bigger French powder mill upstream. Through the years there had been explosions, but never of the magnitude of the one that killed her first husband.

That turned her mind to husband number two. She reached for another peach, her smile turning mischievous. Life had not been easy with O'Brian all these years. They fought nearly as much as they had *before* they were wed, and still about the same things. The older Elizabeth got, the more she realized you can't change a person. You love him or her for who they are, and you accept the faults with all the goodness. So her scandalous marriage had never been placid, but as her dear husband reminded her often, she need never fear growing bored with him.

Elizabeth stretched to reach another peach and, when her fingertips didn't meet with the soft, sweet fruit, she hiked up her striped cotton petticoat and climbed into the tree. As she dropped another peach into her bag, steadying herself on the rough branch, she heard her daughter, Meagan, come running through the orchard, laughing and screaming like a wild Indian. "Help me, Mama! Help me! It's the dada beast!"

Elizabeth heard the sound of loud, human growling and snarling, as her five-year-old daughter raced by.

Meagan turned around the peach tree her mother balanced in, and put her hands to her ears with a squeal. "Aunty Claire says for you to hurry up and get ready for supper. She says Morgan and her new husband will be here—"

There was more growling as O'Brian appeared through the trees.

Meagan gave another high-pitched squeal. "And there's a letter come from William and Mary College from Patrick." She darted off. "Don't tell him which way I went, Mama!"

Then her daughter lifted her skirts above her knees and dashed off through the trees.

Elizabeth dropped another peach into the bag. How truly fortunate she was. She and O'Brian had five living children between the ages of five and twenty. And her dear sister-in-law, Claire, had pitched in all these years taking over the household so that Elizabeth could concentrate on the business. After the tragic death of Jessop, Claire had improved significantly. She never became the woman she had been in her younger years, keeping her childlike innocence, but she grew well enough to function in the world again.

Elizabeth heard a growl, and something shook the tree. She glanced down to see O'Brian looking up at her with two thin wooden slats for fangs protruding from his mouth. He was dressed in an old pair of homespun breeches and simple muslin shirt with his hair pulled back in a queue. He looked more like one of the servants than the master of the house, but Elizabeth had given up dressing him years ago.

She laughed at the grimace he made.

"Have you seen my supper?" he growled. "I'm looking for my supper. Small red-haired girl child." He held his hand up off the ground. "Yea high."

"Sorry, beast." She picked another peach. "I think your supper outsmarted you this time."

He pulled the slats from his mouth and tossed them on the ground. "Good, because my blasted fangs were killing me." He looked up into the tree again. "What are you doing up there? You're going to fall and break your neck, woman. What is it you're always telling me? We've got servants to do these tasks."

In response, she tossed a too soft peach at him, hitting him in the forearm.

He grabbed her ankle and she laughed, trying to shake him off. "Don't, you're going to knock me out of the tree!"

"Stop fighting me, or you're going to knock yourself out of the tree."

She threw another peach at him, hitting him on the shoulder this time.

"Now look what you've done to me!" He wiped at

the sticky yellow fruit smeared on his shirt. "I'll have to change for supper!"

Elizabeth peered down at him in his working man's garb, lifting one feathery eyebrow. "You don't think Claire was going to let you come to supper looking like *that,* do you?"

With a growl, he grabbed both of her legs just below her knees and started to pull her out of the tree.

Elizabeth gave a shriek, trying to hold onto one of the gnarled branches, but, of course, her strength was nothing in comparison to his. He pulled her out of the tree as she laughed and flailed her arms, beating him on the back.

"How dare you strike your master," he grumbled in his beast's voice. He turned her so that she was facing him, her feet still well off the ground.

"Let me go, beast! You're smashing the peaches in my bag!"

"A kiss," he growled. "A kiss is the price the maiden pays for her release."

So Elizabeth leaned and gave him a chaste peck on the cheek.

"A kiss!" he snarled, louder. "A true kiss is the only thing that can change this beast into a mere man again."

Feigning surrender, she wrapped her arms around his neck and pressed her lips to his in a deliberate, tantalizing kiss.

O'Brian slowly let her ease downward, until her feet met the ground. He groaned as she slipped her tongue between his lips, deepening the kiss. "Ye taste like peaches," he said when they parted for a breath.

She slipped her hand between them to the bag that still hung on her shoulder. "That's because I've been picking peaches." She showed him one soft, ripe peach. Then, on a mischievous impulse, she took the fruit and smashed it into his chest just below his Adam's apple.

"Liz! That's sticky!" he protested.

She laughed as he grabbed the peach from her hand and smashed into her chest, just above the neckline of her bodice.

"Oh, yuck!" she groaned. "I'll have to have a bath before I can go to supper now!"

"Nah, I can take care of this problem." Then he lowered his head and took his warm wet tongue and began to lick the sweet juice that ran between her breasts.

Elizabeth threw back her head, giving a sigh of pleasure. It amazed her that after all these years—graying hair and all—she was still so attracted to O'Brian. He could still make her heart pound and her veins course hot with passion.

"O'Brian," she giggled. "It's practically broad daylight."

"Evening," he muttered, tugging at her bodice, so that he could slip his hand into her gown. "Almost evening."

She draped her hands over his shoulders, unable to resist the feel of his hot tongue on her breasts. "O'Brian," she groaned. "Meggy will come back."

But he ignored her protests as he did those delicious things with his tongue that he knew she liked. As he kissed her, he stroked her back, her buttocks, sending shivers of delight through her entire body.

Before Liz knew what was happening, they had settled on the ground, locked in an embrace.

O'Brian had discarded her peach bag and his shirt. They rolled in the soft rotten peaches that had fallen on the ground, laughing, kissing, licking the sweet juice from each other's skin.

"Hey there, Mistress. I've got a little something to show you," he teased in a husky voice.

"And what might that be?"

He took her hand, his green eyes locked with hers,

and slowly lowered her hand to the straining bulge of his breeches.

"Oh," Elizabeth whispered, wide-eyed and innocent-like. "Is that for me, Mr. Foreman?"

He winked. "Open the package and see, sweet."

And then the two burst into laughter, rolling in the soft orchard grass, the last of the day's sunlight shining down on their contented faces.

About the Author

Colleen Faulkner lives with her family in Southern Delaware. She is the author of fourteen Zebra historical romances, including CAPTIVE, FOREVER HIS, FLAMES OF LOVE, SWEET DECEPTION and SAVAGE SURRENDER. Colleen has also had short stories published in Zebra's Halloween anthology, SPELL-BOUND KISSES, and Zebra's Christmas anthology, A CHRISTMAS CARESS. Her newest novella, MAN OF MY DREAMS, will be published in Zebra's June Bride Collection, TO HAVE AND TO HOLD, which will be available in bookstores in May 1995. Colleen is currently working on her next Zebra historical romance, DES-TINED TO BE MINE, which will be published in February 1996. Colleen loves hearing from her readers and you may write to her c/o Zebra Books. Please include a self-addressed stamped envelope if you wish a response.

Please turn the page for
an exciting sneak preview of
Colleen Faulkner's
newest historical romance
DESTINED TO BE MINE
to be published by Zebra Books in
February 1996

Prologue

Tsitsho of the Bear Clan of the Mohawk crouched low behind an inkberry bush at the edge of the hard wood forest, his hand resting on the hilt of his war hatchet. Cautiously he surveyed his surroundings. He heard the call of a whippoorwill, and the sound of swaying tree limbs. He smelled the scent of a scurrying squirrel, and of the white men in the cabin in the midst of the clearing.

He watched the smoke rise from the stone chimney and knew that it was soft pine they burned. Somewhere a hen clucked.

Tsitsho guessed a family lived inside the cabin. Outside he saw evidence of a woman and children; clothing hanging to dry on a rope strung between two trees, a leather ball left abandoned near the stone steps of the single room cabin. A family, yes, that was good. It was what he'd been looking for.

Suddenly the cabin door swung open and a bearded man stepped out into the morning sunshine. He wore boots, white cloth men's leggings, his chest bare. He leaned the musket he carried against the hewn wall behind him and stretched, raising his arms over his head.

Tsitsho felt his heart pounding beneath his breast. Out

of habit, he touched the mark on his left cheek as he eyed the white man.

This was what he had come for. This was why he had walked hundreds of miles. This was what he had risked his life for time and time again. This was why he had killed his brother.

Tsitsho was no coward, so he rose, stepping out of the shadows of the morning forest.

Immediately the man in the beard gave a cry of alarm, reaching for his musket.

"Yahten!" Tsitsho called, raising his hands. "Do not shoot." The English words tasted strange on his tongue. "I mean you no harm."

The white man aimed the musket, staring at Tsitsho's colorfully tattooed chest, evident beneath the sleeveless, quilled leather vest. Tsitsho watched the white man as he took in his appearance; his loincloth and beaded moccasins, his hair shaved in a scalplock, the mark on his face. Tsitsho knew the man was judging him. He knew the white man feared him and he knew that he was justified in that fear.

"What do you want, you scurvy redskin?"

Tsitsho shook his head, his blue-eyed gaze meeting the white man's. "No. I am no Mohawk. I am English. A captive." He was surprised by how quickly the English words came back to him. How many years had it been since he'd heard or spoken them? Six? Seven?

The man took a step closer, squinting in the bright morning sun. "God above," he swore. "You've got blue eyes. Who are you?"

Tsitsho let his broad hands fall to his sides. By his calculation he was only eighteen years old and yet at this moment he felt as if he'd lived five score years . . . ten. Painful memories flashed through his head; the Mohawk attack on his English family, his mother's screams, the torture, the slow acceptance. He felt the weight of his stillborn son in his arms and he remembered the acrid stench of his wife's funeral pyre.

Slowly Tsitsho lifted his gaze. "My name is Duncan. Duncan Roderick, the Earl of Cleaves."

One

Taking her sister's hand, Jillian slipped out the glass paned double doors into the peaceful sanctuary of the overgrown garden. "Gemini!" she swore. "There's as much confusion in that house as at a Gypsy fair."

"We're supposed to be supervising the unpacking of the silver plate," Beatrice protested weakly, glancing over her shoulder as she was led away. The sound of a splitting wooden crate, crashing silver, and the shrill voice of their mother could be heard through the open windows. "We shouldn't disobey. Mother will be frightfully angry."

Jillian's laughter rose, filling the hot, humid air as she led her sister over the flagstones that drew them deeper into the sadly unkempt garden. "Can you believe we're finally in London?" she declared. "I was beginning to fear Father was going to keep us hidden in the country until kingdom come!"

The Hollingsworths had just arrived in the city from their country home in Sussex. A full year had passed since King Charles II had been restored to his throne and finally Jillian's father had agreed it was safe to bring his family to London to their home on the Strand that had not been occupied, except by caretakers, in two and a half decades. After the years between the death of Cromwell and the return of the Stuarts of semi-anarchy, Lord Hollingsworth, a Royalist, had insisted upon keeping his family in the country until he was certain the government was stable again. The Hollingsworths had returned for the fall season of parties and suppers, to visit relatives, and to see the eldest daughter, Beatrice, finally wed.

Jillian dragged her sister down the flagstone path ducking beneath low-lying branches and vines grown wild with years of neglect. The garden was filled with the heady sweet scent of blooming flowers and the humming, chirping sounds of insect song. "Father said the new gardener had the Chinese goldfish delivered this morning. Don't you want to see them?" Jillian arched one brow, her freckled face beaming with excitement.

"No, no I really do believe it's best we follow Mother's bidding. I—"

"Oh, stop your bellow-weathering, Bea. It's time you started making your own decisions. In a few short months you'll be a married woman yourself, with your own properties and a husband to order about!"

Beatrice blushed, covering her mouth with her delicate palm. "I can't believe it, Jillian. After all these years, he's really coming for me. I'm going to be a countess!"

The two sisters walked to the stone fish pool and sat down on the water's edge. Jillian peered into the fresh blue-green water in search of the exotic fish. "Fiddle! They must be hiding." She dipped her fingers into the cool, inviting water. "I knew he'd come for you. Father said he was waiting for his call to the judicial courts before he returned to England for you. Now that he's been declared the true heir of his father's estates and his title has been returned to him, he's finally in a position to wed you properly. God's teeth, Bea. You wouldn't want to marry a penniless Colonial, would you?"

Beatrice studied her younger sister's face. "It's true enough I'm anxious to be out from under my parents' feet and a woman of my own right. Heaven help me, I'm nearly twenty-eight, but what if what cousin Elizabeth says is true? What if he is a he-devil with a forked tail?" She lowered her voice superstitiously as if mere mention of the beast could conjure him up. "What if he is scarred so horribly that he truly must wear a mask?"

Jillian pulled a thick strand of her own bright red hair off her shoulder and tucked it into her mouth thoughtfully. "Gossip! It spreads like summer fire in the meadow! A man in a mask, indeed!" She touched her sister's arm lightly. "Father met him at Whitehall Palace only a week ago. You don't think the man could have hidden a forked tail in his breeches, do you?"

"Elizabeth said all of London is calling him the Colonial Devil," Beatrice whispered, her hazel eyes still wide with fright. "They say he has the eyes of glowing coals and the hair of a wretched ghoul."

Jillian dragged her hand through the fish pond, watching the water part and the lily pads sway. "We'll meet him tomorrow and see for ourselves, then won't we?" But when she saw the frightened look on her sister's face, she reached out to take her smaller hand in hers. "Ignore such prattle. Elizabeth is a liar; everyone knows it. She's just green with jealousy because you're marrying an earl and she's marrying an earl's son. Heaven's Saints, by the time Toddy Burke inherits, Elizabeth will be toothless and bald."

Despite Beatrice's fears, she couldn't resist a chuckle. "Oh, Jillian. I don't know what I'll do without you when I must go to America with my husband. I'll miss you terribly!"

On impulse, Jillian slipped off her kidskin slippers and began to roll down her hose. "Nonsense, once Jacob and I are wed, we'll come, too. There's nothing for us here.

We'll live in a parsonage within riding distance." She
spun around, lifting her apple green taffeta petticoat up
above her calves. "I always wanted to see the American
Colonies with their red savages anyway."

"Jillian! Father said he would hear no more of the
parson's son." She looked this way and that, fearing
someone might be eavesdropping in the deserted garden.

Jillian lowered her feet into the cold water and gave
a sigh of delight. "I'll have Jacob, I will, and Father
won't stop me. We'll elope if we have to."

Beatrice wrapped her arms around her own waist in
fear. "Don't say, that, please don't say that, Jilly. Promise
me you won't do anything foolish. Promise me you won't
ruin our family name by marrying a man below your
station."

"I'll promise no such thing. I always told you that
when I married, it would be for love." She lowered her
feet deeper into the water, leaning over to peer into the
stone pond. "Where the blast are those goldfish? Father
paid nearly ten pound for the lot of them. For that sum,
I vow, you would think they'd be big enough to see!"

Beatrice giggled. "Jillian, you'll be in that pond in a
moment. Put your slippers on. Someone will see you and
tell Father!"

Jillian gave a wave of her hand dismissing the thought.
"It feels wonderful." She lifted her long mane of red
curly hair off her prickly hot neck. "Want to try?"

Beatrice shook her head.

"It's so cool, I just might climb all the way in and
take a swim." She leaned over, still searching for the
fish. "I warrant you I'd find the little buggers then!"

Beatrice giggled. "You wouldn't!"

Jillian threw a mischievous glance over her shoulder
in sister's direction. She was standing on the shallow side
of the pond, her abundant taffeta skirting pulled up
around her knees. "Was that a dare I heard?"

Beatrice broke into nervous laughter. "No. No it wasn't. It wasn't a dare!"

"Sounded like a dare to me . . ." Jillian sang, already beginning to unfasten the pearl buttons that ran the front length of her gown. "You should know better. You know I can't resist a dare . . ."

Beatrice jumped up from the stone wall, throwing her hands into the air. "Jillian! Please. I was only teasing! Have you lost what little sense you ever had? Someone will see you!"

"Who, pray tell?" Unfastening the last of the tiny buttons, she pulled the gown over her head. "Every maid and footman are busy hauling crates," she insisted through the stiff folds of the gown as she struggled to pull it over her head. "Mother, Father, and the sisters are all occupied with unpacking. I'll just take a quick dip and no one will be the wiser." Finally her head appeared through the abundant skirting of the gown. "Catch!"

Beatrice gave a little squeal as she dove to keep the hem of the new gown out of the fishpond. "You've really gone too far this time, Jilly," she hissed at her sister who had begun to wade into the deeper water. "You know what Father said. He said he'd send you back to Aunt Prudence in the country if you didn't act like the lady you were born to be."

"He won't send me back because he's trying to keep Jacob and I apart. Not that it will do any good, because Jacob is coming for me." She unhooked her busk and tossed it through the air, discarding it along with her gown.

Jillian heard her sister give another little squeak as she lowered herself into the pond. "There's one! I see one of the goldfish!" she cried, laughing. "Oh, Bea. You should come in, too. They're so beautiful."

Jillian turned her back to her sister, pushing her wet linen smock aside where it floated in the cool, clean water. Twice she tried to catch one of the fat, bright goldfish the size of her palm, but both times they managed to slip through her fingers. She was just about to turn and head back for the pool's edge when she heard her sister give a strangled cry of fright.

"Bea? Bea, what—"

Jillian knew her jaw must have dropped as she spun around, and for a moment she felt her heart flutter beneath her breast. "God above," she blasphemed.

There in the overgrown garden standing not six paces from the fishpond was a giant of a man . . . a man with a purple veil covering the left side of his face . . . a man of threatening masculinity.

Beatrice stumbled backward a step, the gown and busk bundled in her arms.

"It's all right," Jillian assured her sister as she waded quickly toward the pool's edge. In her rush, she made no attempt to cover her nearly naked form, draped in the wet, transparent linen of her smock. For though her sister was nearly six years her senior, Jillian had always felt it was her responsibility to look after Bea, ever since they were children in their nursery.

"Can . . . can I help you, my Lord?" Jillian managed, knowing full well this must be her sister's betrothed. Who else would be wearing a scarf to cover his face? *So the tales were true,* she thought, wondering impulsively if she should be looking for his forked tail.

But the man did not smile like the devil. Or perhaps he did, for Jillian's great grandmother had always said Satan would not come to her with a forked tail breathing fire and shouting obscenities, but as a handsome man with a come *hither* smile, and words as sweet as clover honey.

Instinctively Jillian put herself between the stranger and Beatrice. Beatrice was now making little mewing sounds, too frightened even to move. Surely she, too, realized who this man was.

"Well," Jillian demanded of the gentleman, for he surely was a gentleman by his dress. "Why are you here in this private garden? You've scared her half to death!"

His lazy smile made her forget the purple scarf that obscured one side of his face. He was robed fashionably in a rich burgundy doublet and wide-legged breeches with a short brown periwig and a plumed cavalier's hat dyed the same shade of red. Around his waist was strapped a fine sword. What she could see of his face was suntanned and ruggedly handsome. Earl or not, here was no milk-sop dandy of the King's court, this man of her sister's. His unobstructed eye was the color of the morning sky, so piercing that he seemed to see through Jillian to her very soul.

"I must ask your business, here, my lord," she repeated, her voice true and clear. "Because you're trespassing."

He swept off his hat and bowed as if they were the Queen's maids of honour, keeping eye-contact with her. "The baron is expecting me, madame. I am Lord Duncan Roderick, Earl of Cleaves, your servant." He raised an eyebrow, his voice mocking her as he returned his hat to his head. "And might you, by my good fortune, be Beatrice Hollingsworth?"

Bea, standing behind Jillian, sucked in a strangled breath.

Jillian shivered in her wet shift, not because of a chill, but because the earl looked at her with an expression she'd never known. He frightened her, yet intrigued her at the same time, and for a moment she forgot that he was her sister's intended. For the briefest second she contemplated what it would be like to be this man's bride.

Suddenly she crossed her arms over her breasts, trying to cover her unclothed form. "No, no, my lord I'm not," she snapped tartly. "A sister." She didn't know what made her answer so rudely, perhaps because she did find him attractive, even with his obvious deformity. She frowned, angry that her sister's betrothed would be so ill-mannered, angry because she knew this man was not a good match for Beatrice. The poor girl had to be out of her wit with fear. *How could Father have betrothed her dear Bea to such a brute of a man?*

Jillian made eye-contact with the earl once more. "Now if you'll excuse us, my lord," she murmured, beginning to back up, still positioned between him and her sister. She reached behind her back to take Beatrice's trembling hand and then turned and ran, pulling her sister behind her.

Duncan stood there on the flagstone path of the overgrown garden a full minute, chuckling to himself. What good luck to find a half naked woman in Hollingsworth's garden, what poor luck she wasn't his intended wife. He was instantly attracted to the chit with her flaming red hair, nutmeg eyes, and rosy breasts. Now a woman like that—she wouldn't be so difficult to bed and get with his heir.

Duncan sighed. He knew he might as well get on with the call. He'd been too long in putting it off already. He had promised Lord Hollingsworth last week that he would come by and meet the daughter he'd been betrothed to since he was a boy. It was time he had a wife and his duty to his dead father kept him to the promise. Besides, Hollingsworth owed the Rodericks a considerable sum of money. This marriage would settle that riff and Duncan would have one less financial matter to deal with.

Duncan followed the path the two women had fled by, through the garden, through open glass door, into a sunny dining parlor. Boxes and crates were stacked everywhere with footman and maids running in circles. Duncan stood there in the doorway a moment, undetected, then cleared his throat.

A young girl looked up from where she leaned into a wooden crate and gave a frightened squeal.

"Your master," Duncan ordered, well used to such reactions and bored by them. "Tell him the Earl of Cleaves has arrived."

The young girl backed her way out of the parlor, bumping into a portrait as she made her way out the door. "Yes, m'lord," she cried, trying to upright the painting of someone's sour-faced grandfather. "Right away, m'lord."

Not a minute later Lord Hollingsworth and his wife came hustling into the disorganized parlor.

"Your lordship, let me offer my apologies for not being about to greet you at the door!" Hollingsworth bowed. "I hadn't been informed you arrived. Such a chore organizing a place that's not been occupied in twenty-five years and dealing with a household of females with vapors. You understand?"

Duncan bowed gracefully and nodded, trying to be polite. "I understand entirely, sir."

Lady Hollingsworth tapped her husband's arm with a painted fan.

"Goodness, my apologies again." Lord Hollingsworth took a lace handkerchief from his ruffled sleeve and wiped his wide forehead, beaded with perspiration. "My wife, sir, Lady Hollingsworth. Lord Roderick, the Earl of Cleaves, my dearest."

Lady Hollingsworth, a plump woman with sleek hair dyed the color of eggplant curtsied. "Your servant, my Lord. What a pleasure it is to finally meet you," she bubbled.

Duncan bowed again, this time with irritation. He was convinced that if only the English would give up this absurd notion of introducing and being introduced, they'd gain a full score of years to their lifetime. "Your servant, madame."

She rose, red-faced, clasping her hands so that her breasts rose above her pink silk decolletage. "Would you care for a refreshment, my Lord?"

"No, no thank you. I'm expected elsewhere shortly."

"Surely you're staying for supper?" She nudged her husband.

Hollingsworth gave a start, flustered. "Indeed, indeed, sir, you would honor us with your presence."

"The kitchen is a mess, but I've just hired the most wonderful cook," her ladyship prattled. "He's just arrived from France. There'll be fresh goose with the most exquisite raspberry jelly."

Duncan lifted his hand wishing he were anywhere but here. Even an Iroquois red ant hill was beginning to look inviting. "I assure you I cannot stay."

The Hollingsworths then lapsed into a weighty silence standing there in the dining-parlor a rolled tapestry separating them from Duncan. They were obviously trying not to stare at the purple veil he wore, but were doing a poor job of it.

Finally Duncan, completely losing his patience, spoke up. "I've come but to meet your daughter and sign the necessary agreement. I haven't much time."

Lady Hollingsworth raised her hands to her purple hair. "Heavens, yes. My apologies, your lordship, for my ill manners." Then she spun on feet surely too small for her ample frame and fled the parlor.

This time Duncan made no attempt at polite conversation with Hollingsworth. Instead, he crossed the room where three works of art rested along the wall, having just been removed from their crates. He studied first one painting, then the next with great concentration. Reaching the third, he crossed his arms over his chest with a sigh of approval. "Ah, a Botticelli."

"A collector, are you, your lordship?" Hollingsworth was wiping his damp brow again, obviously relieved to have something to speak of.

"No. Only an admirer."

The sound of feminine footsteps in the hallway immediately caught Duncan's intention. His betrothed was approaching. Finally he would have a look at his dear lady-wife-to-be.

But Duncan took his time in turning to greet her, giving himself a moment to fantasize. He couldn't help but wonder what she would look like. Would she be short and plump like her mother? Or would she be like her young sister? Would she have hair the color of autumn leaves and a rich, deep, sensual voice? Would she be a cold fish a man had to drink himself half silly to bed, or would she have a body he would crave to touch?

Duncan frowned. With the luck he carried, he guessed she'd have yellow bucked teeth and a hairy wart growing from her chin. He turned to greet her.

She had neither.

But just the same, Duncan was immediately disappointed. His betrothed was none other than the cowering woman in the garden. She was small with tawny hair and a pert mouth. She reminded him of his mother . . .

"Your lordship, this is my daughter, Beatrice Mary."

The woman dipped low into a subservient curtsy, obviously frightened out of her wits.

Duncan bowed, a bad taste in his mouth. Now that he had gotten a closer look at her, he suddenly felt ill. "Your servant, madame."

"Yours, Sir," she responded her voice barely above a whisper.

Duncan watched her as she lifted her small, trembling hand to brush her neckline.

This wasn't going to work, damn it.

Duncan knew he was expected to marry this Hollingsworth. It was his duty. The Rodericks and the Hollingsworths had betrothed their children as infants before the war. Duncan owed this to his deceased father. It was the right thing to do . . . and yet how could he marry a woman who looked so much like his bitch mother?

Immediately the thought of the redhead in the garden flashed through his head, replacing hazy images of his *dear lady mother,* Constance. Duncan recalled the silhouette of the redhead's rounded breasts pressing against the wet linen of her smock. He had been able to see the pale brown of her areolas through the transparent undergarment. Her pink nipples had taunted him, teased him . . .

Duncan looked up at Hollingsworth, scowling with displeasure. "You have other daughters?" He did not look at Beatrice again, though he could hear her hyperventilating.

"Yes . . . yes, I do," Hollingsworth's voice trembled. "Beatrice is the . . . the eldest."

"I want to see them."

Hollingsworth looked up with rounded eyes, his mouth gaping open to show a recent abscess. "My . . . my lord?"

Duncan raised his hand beneath the purple veil and wiped his mouth. "Humor me," he stated flatly. "I want to see her sisters." *If I must marry a Hollingsworth,* he reasoned, *why not the best of the lot?* "Now."

SURRENDER TO THE SPLENDOR OF THE ROMANCES OF F. ROSANNE BITTNER!

CARESS	(3791, $5.99/$6.99)
COMANCHE SUNSET	(3568, $4.99/$5.99)
HEARTS SURRENDER	(2945, $4.50/$5.50)
LAWLESS LOVE	(3877, $4.50/$5.50)
PRAIRIE EMBRACE	(3160, $4.50/$5.50)
RAPTURE'S GOLD	(3879, $4.50/$5.50)
SHAMELESS	(4056, $5.99/$6.99)

DISCOVER DEANA JAMES!

CAPTIVE ANGEL (2524, $4.50/$5.50)
Abandoned, penniless, and suddenly responsible for the biggest tobacco plantation in Colleton County, distraught Caroline Gillard had no time to dissolve into tears. By day the willowy redhead labored to exhaustion beside her slaves . . . but each night left her restless with longing for her wayward husband. She'd make the sea captain regret his betrayal until he begged her to take him back!

MASQUE OF SAPPHIRE (2885, $4.50/$5.50)
Judith Talbot-Harrow left England with a heavy heart. She was going to America to join a father she despised and a sister she distrusted. She was certainly in no mood to put up with the insulting actions of the arrogant Yankee privateer who boarded her ship, ransacked her things, then "apologized" with an indecent, brazen kiss! She vowed that someday he'd pay dearly for the liberties he had taken and the desires he had awakened.

SPEAK ONLY LOVE (3439, $4.95/$5.95)
Long ago, the shock of her mother's death had robbed Vivian Marleigh of the power of speech. Now she was being forced to marry a bitter man with brandy on his breath. But she could not say what was in her heart. It was up to the viscount to spark the fires that would melt her icy reserve.

WILD TEXAS HEART (3205, $4.95/$5.95)
Fan Breckenridge was terrified when the stranger found her near-naked and shivering beneath the Texas stars. Unable to remember who she was or what had happened, all she had in the world was the deed to a patch of land that might yield oil . . . and the fierce loving of this wildcatter who called himself Irons.